Clare's
New
Leaf

Also by Robert L. Haught:

Here's Clare

Now, I'm No Expert

The POTUS Chronicles

Clare's
New
Leaf

ROBERT L. HAUGHT

This is a work of fiction. The characters, incidents and dialogues are products of the author's imagination and are not to be construed as real and any resemblance to actual persons, living or dead, is entirely coincidental.

Design and pre-press by Lighthouse24

ISBN-13: 978-1532860317
ISBN-10: 1532860315

Clare's New Leaf

1

CLARE FELT THE SUN'S RAYS on her back blending with the warmth of the sand beneath her to soothe and create a perfect moment of relaxation. She had untied her halter top to allow an even tan. If Henry were there he would be encouraging her to expose her entire body. But her Southern girl modesty wouldn't permit such a bold move, even though she was in a remote location – a secluded spot at Trunk Bay, one of the world's ten top beaches. Henry had discovered it on a previous trip to the U.S. Virgin Islands. It was his suggestion that they take a trip to the Caribbean and spend a week on St. John. He didn't have to twist her arm.

With two-thirds of the island protected as a national park, preserving its natural beauty, St. John is less touristy than its overdeveloped neighbors. But in the Cruz Bay area on the western coast are a number of shops, bars, restaurants and some classy resorts. There are no high-rise hotels or other tall buildings on St. John, so Henry had reserved a beachfront suite at the Westin resort. On this fifth day of their visit Henry was at the Westin attending a business seminar. He dropped off Clare with a promise to return and whisk her away for a nice dinner. While he was participating in discussions about corporate inversions and offshore bank accounts, Clare Sullivan de Lune was happily allowing her cares of the past year to melt away.

She needed this escape from reality after enduring a tumultuous time in California during which she became a widow and experienced a dramatic change in her life. The bright spot was her chance meeting with Henry Jackson, who became her new love interest while helping raise funds for a major political campaign. Fortunately both of them were wealthy enough to enjoy fine food and wine as well as travel to exotic destinations while planning a new destiny together.

St. John has no airport and is accessible only by water. They had flown from New York to St. Thomas, then caught a Red Hook ferry for a 15-minute ride to the Cruz Bay dock and took a cab to their hotel. After a casual dinner they retired early. The following day they rented a car and did some exploring on the 19-square-mile island. They began with a late morning walk through Wharfside Village, dropping in at a number of the galleries and shops along the way before lunch at Café Roma. After an afternoon by the hotel's palm-lined pool they enjoyed an evening back in town at the Beach Bar.

Another day they checked out the shopping at Mongoose Junction, where the stores offered a variety of handmade items. On Hart Bay in the Chocolate Hole area they saw several attractive villas on the hillsides, making notes for a possible rental on a return trip to St. John. On the day before Clare's beach outing, they ventured a drive to the north side of the island to see the ruins of the Annaberg Sugar Plantation. On the way they passed some hiking trails in the the national park and regretted they had not brought appropriate footwear. But they took advantage of a self-guided tour through the remaining structures of a 1780 factory producing sugar and rum. They enjoyed some spectacular mountain and bay views from this historic spot, which is a popular site for "destination weddings." During another evening taking in the St. John night life at the High Tide Bar and Seafood Grill in Cruz Bay, Clare and Henry talked about what more they could see of this marvelous Caribbean paradise.

But for now, Clare's only plan was to enjoy this beautiful beach and let her mind wander. While reviewing the twists and turns life had handed her since she left home following graduation to see the world, Clare admitted to herself that she had been lucky to have had some very rewarding and satisfying experiences. She had recounted some of those in her campaign biography, *Clearly I See*, but she had left one chapter, her home life in Georgia, relatively blank.

That was a story she preferred not to be made public, particularly the ending. But here, on this lonely beach, she allowed her private thoughts to take her back to her days growing up on a pecan plantation in Georgia. She had fond memories of that simple time of her life. As the firstborn child of Pat and Betty Sullivan, she had all the material treasures any teenage girl could want. Yet she somehow felt trapped in a dull and unsatisfying existence and she yearned to escape. Her younger sister, Rebecca Jean, was quite content to do the bidding of their parents and chart a future of marriage, children and a peaceful life in the Georgia countryside. Because of that, she was convinced that her mother favored her kid sister. "She was the apple of her eye," she told herself. "And I was the worm." For the moment, despite the bitterness of her departure from home and family, Clare felt a longing to see her folks again. The warmth of the sun and the sand engulfed her and that feeling began to slip away.

Just as she was about to give in to her drowsiness, she heard an unfamiliar voice saying, "Hello-o, gorgeous." She looked up, taking care not to raise her naked upper body, and saw a strange man standing over her. In her half-conscious state, Clare's first thought was, "Is he real or a nightmare about a creature that had risen from the sea." Underwater goggles were pushed up on his forehead, his black trunks were dripping wet and he held a pair of moss-colored swimming fins at his side. He wore a slimy smile which sent a chill through her frame as he stood staring down at her. She struggled to shake off a frighteningly helpless feeling.

"Who are you?" she shouted impulsively. "What are you doing here?" As she gained her full senses she realized these questions were quite foolish. He was nobody she knew and he obviously had been swimming in the waters of the bay. But he replied anyway.

"I'm somebody who would like to get to know you," he said with a wicked grin.

His leer triggered a wave of revulsion and, glaring at him angrily, she screamed, "Get away from me! Now!"

"Oh, I don't think so," he said, as he dropped to his knees by her side. Suddenly she was frozen with fear as she saw the lustful desire in his eyes, his pleasure at finding a beautiful, half-nude woman all alone in a desolate area of the beach.

Clare screamed again and stiffened as she saw this man bend toward her face. She pressed her body down, turned her head and closed her eyes, bracing for his clammy touch. Luckily, that didn't occur. She heard the man emit a loud grunt and looked back to see him plunging face forward into the gritty sand, the result of a powerful kick in the behind administered by a tall, athletic figure. With a vast feeling of relief she recognized Henry, who was raising his foot to thwart the stranger's attempts to rise.

"Oh, Henry," Clare said, quickly retying her swim suit top. "I'm so glad to see you. And you were just in time."

As Henry stopped to help her to her feet, the once-fearsome pervert from the deep scrambled to his feet and ran away as fast as he could, leaving his fins, along with his unfulfilled desires, behind.

"Have you had enough sun and excitement for the day?" Henry asked.

"I certainly have," she said. "Please take me away."

On the ride back to the hotel, Henry asked about the unpleasant experience on the beach, which Clare wanted to put out of her mind.

"Why didn't you give him a sample of your martial arts training?"

"Well, yes, I could have put his face in the sand like you did, but that would have required giving him a Luna- type peep show," she said, recalling the first time Henry met her stepdaughter, who was pulling a T-shirt over her braless chest at the time.

3

"And you didn't have your protective team with you," he said, referring to the Smith & Wesson pistol she had carried as a California state senator.

"No, nor any other concealed weapon," she replied sarcastically. "Can we change the subject? How was your seminar?"

"Okay. And I had a surprise. One of my classmates at Harvard was in the group. Phil Sterling. I hadn't seen or heard from him in years."

"And he remembered you, of course?"

"Well, we were pretty close friends back in those days. In fact, I probably spent more time with him than anyone else. We did a lot of partying together."

"I'll bet. What's he doing now?"

"He's been quite successful as a real estate developer – at least to hear him tell it."

"Sounds like a braggart."

"I wouldn't be that harsh. But he is a strong believer in self-promotion."

"Is he married?"

"Yes. His wife's name is Barbara. They live in North Carolina."

"Oh. Is she a southerner?"

"I don't know that. But we'll meet her this evening. I invited them to join us for dinner."

Clare didn't quite know how to react to that unexpected announcement but decided to contain her impulsive negative feelings.

Henry had made reservations at ZoZo's, an upscale restaurant in the Caneel Bay resort. By coincidence it was located amid the ruins of another 18th century sugar mill. They were to rendezvous with the other couple in the hotel lobby and share a taxi.

Clare tried to find out more about these strangers she was about to meet but Henry had little to tell her except, "You'll like Phil. He's very friendly."

She spotted him immediately when they entered the lobby. He was the pudgy guy wearing yellow slacks and a gaudy shirt carrying on an animated conversation with an older gentleman while their wives sat together on a resort-style couch. He broke away when he saw Henry and Clare arrive.

"Henry, my old Harvard buddy," he said in a voice much too loud for the room. "And this must be your lovely wife."

Clare froze as Phil approached her with open arms, flashy rings sparkling on both chubby hands. She quickly extended her right hand, candidate style, and blocked his move with a handshake. Turning to the short blonde in a stylish gown, her ears, neck and fingers dazzling with diamonds, she introduced herself.

"I'm Clare. Barbara?"

"That's me," said the other woman with a syrupy drawl. "Philip calls me 'Barbie'", she giggled. ("I'll just bet he does," Clare thought.) "I'm happy to meet you."

"Shall we go?" said Henry. "I called for a cab and I see one waiting."

Phil got in the back seat with the two wives and Henry sat in front for the jostling ride from Cruz Bay to Caneel Bay. The water glistened with light as the sun began to set.

A smartly dressed host ushered the foursome to their table, which was in the outdoor area of the circular dining room. It offered a stunning view of the bay and on the horizon the flickering lights of St. Thomas could be seen.

Clare was seated directly across from Phil and she became uncomfortably aware of his stare which remained fixed on her throughout most of the evening.

ZoZo's, probably the island's most expensive place to dine, featured a menu of northern Italian cuisine prepared by a culinary team headed by a chef whose recipes were influenced by his own Italian family as well as the local fish and produce grown in the Caribbean.

A round of drinks helped stimulate some small talk among the uneasy diners. Phil delivered a much-too-long toast to the reunion of two long-ago friends. Henry skillfully steered the conversation toward the menu selections.

Phil ordered a steak, after loudly demanding to be assured it had been aged for 28 days as the menu promised. Barbara had a watermelon salad and fresh pappardelle, requesting the gluten-free substitution. Clare chose the restaurant's specialty, osso buco, and Henry decided on roasted mahi mahi.

"I'll defer to the winery owner for dinner wines," Phil graciously declared. Henry selected a 2005 Paolo Scavino Cannubi Barolo and a 2011 Kistler Chardonnay from California's Sonoma coast.

Although it was difficult to get a word in with Phil's incessant banter, Clare managed to ascertain that Barbara was a native of North Carolina and that she had been married to Phil for thirteen years. Nobody asked about Clare's background and neither she nor Henry volunteered that she had run a strong campaign for governor of the most populous state.

Phil made himself the center of attention through dinner, recalling his and Henry's times at Harvard – which Henry seemed to enjoy – and bragging about his career in real estate. Clare was grateful when the waiter took orders for dessert. She and Barbara settled on tiramisu and the men had ricotta cheese cake.

Henry maneuvered Phil into the front seat for the taxi ride back to the hotel. The four exchanged brief courtesies and headed for their rooms with

Phil raving about what a good time they had and suggesting, "Let's do this again tomorrow evening."

On the way to their room Clare sent Henry a silent plea: "Oh, please, no!"

The next morning over coffee Clare brought up the subject of Henry's newfound buddy.

"About your friend Phil," she said. "Did you know him in Harvard Business School?"

"No," said Henry. "He's just a Harvard graduate. He wanted to get out and make some money."

"And I gather he met his goal."

"I think he's done pretty well."

"Well, if it's all the same to you, I had just as soon not spend this evening with them."

"Okay."

"In fact, I think I'm ready to go back to the states."

"Any particular reason?"

"I've had a wonderful time here on St. John but I've been thinking a lot about the family I abandoned and I've got a feeling that I'd like to see them."

"A little guilt feeling maybe?"

"Maybe. But would that be all right with you?"

"If that's what you want to do, sure. And if your mother says it's all right."

"I'll check with her, of course."

And she thought to herself: "If we get out of here now, I'll never see Phil Sterling again."

2

ON THE FLIGHT BACK from St. Thomas, Clare thought a lot about her decision that this was a time to reunite with her family in Georgia.

She had left on a bitter note. After her mother's constant nagging about settling down in Georgia, marrying a nice southern boy and raising a family, when she took the Rhodes scholarship she and her mother had a very angry showdown in which Clare cursed her mother and her father, also in anger, raised his hand and almost slapped her.

She had broken off contact after that and did not call or write while she was abroad. When she returned to the states she had given brief thought to stopping in Georgia en route to California, but the memories were still too dark. So she had moved on with her life.

She had kept up with her younger sister by eavesdropping on her Facebook page. Rebecca Jean had done as her mother wanted. After college she returned home, met a suitable husband and at 28 was a mother.

When they landed in Atlanta Clare got her courage up and called home.

"Momma, it's Clare," she said. Betty Sullivan was overjoyed.

"Judy Clare? Is that you? Oh, baby, I can't believe it's you. How are you? I know you must feel awful after all you've been through the last few weeks."

"I'm okay, Momma. Really. I'm so glad you're still speaking to me."

"What do you mean? I'm so glad to talk to you after all these years."

"I know. And I'm sorry. I really am sorry. About everything. About the way I left home and never returned. It was awful the way I left and I want you to know I'm so sorry."

"It's all right, baby. That was so long ago. Your daddy and I have long since put that sad day out of our minds. He's sorry for how he acted. It was an impulsive thing out of love for me. But that's all behind us. You know your sister got married and had a baby?"

"Why, yes, I heard through one of my high school classmates," Clare lied. "A little girl, right?"

"Yes, and she is the sweetest little thing. I wish you could see her."

"Well, that's why I'm calling, Momma. I'm at the Atlanta airport – just got here after a little getaway trip. I wondered if I'd be welcome to come for a visit."

"Why, gracious sakes, of course. Oh, that would be wonderful. You say you're in Atlanta? When can you be here?"

"Well, we can rent a car and be there in the morning."

"Excuse me, did you say we?"

"Yes, Momma. My new friend Henry is with me. I'd like for you and Daddy to meet him."

"Well, I should say so. This is exciting news. I can hardly wait to tell Pat when he comes in. You said friend? So you haven't remarried since Gary was killed. I'm sorry we never got to meet him.

"I am, too, Momma. But you'll like Henry."

"I don't suppose he's from the South?"

"No, Momma. He's from the state of Washington. His family has a winery there. He's president of the company and he was my finance manager for the governor's race."

"I'm so sorry you lost, honey. But in a way I'm not. That would have been such a worrisome job. I hate to think of all the pressure."

"Well, it just wasn't meant to be. And with the loss of my home in the mudslide I'm at a point where I really need to take stock and start to build a new life. I want to begin by reuniting with my family."

"Oh, I can't tell you how much it means to hear you say that."

"I'll call you from the road tomorrow to give you an idea when we'll be there. Oh, I almost forgot to ask – you're still at the home place, I hope?"

"Oh, yes. Your daddy wouldn't think of living anywhere else."

"I can't wait to see you – all of you, Clare said, sobbing.

"It will be wonderful to have you back home."

3

ONCE THEY GOT beyond the web of Hartsfield-Jackson Atlanta International Airport the drive down I-75 was smooth. After passing the turnoff for Macon traffic was lighter and Clare began to remember some scenes of rural Georgia. Once they left the interstate and headed toward pecan country there was little to see but blue sky over various shades of brown and green.

After almost three hours on the road Henry inquired, "Are we getting close?"

"I think so," Clare said. "You need to realize it's been a very long time since I was in this part of the world."

"You did say you knew how to get to where we're going."

"Oh, yes. Don't worry."

Just to make sure, Clare called her mother as promised and received assurance they were on the right road. Cell phone reception was not too reliable so the conversation was brief. Clare was pleased to hear the excitement in her mother's voice.

Close to half an hour later, as pecan groves began to come into sight, Clare said, "slow down." Henry did so and awaited further instruction. "Turn right at the next intersection."

The gravel road led into the woods and became curvier. Once they had gone about a mile they rounded a curve and saw a sign: "Sullivan Pecan Farm." Viewing the vast acreage with a white two-story house peeking through the trees, Henry said, "That sign could easily have said 'plantation'." Clare replied, "But that would be too pretentious."

As the road narrowed into a well-worn drive and they approached what some might call the mansion, Clare said quietly, "That was my childhood home."

"Not bad," Henry observed, taking in the entrance distinguished by four tall white columns. Gray steps led up to a porch that ran the full width of the house which was partially obscured by some old shrubbery and a huge snowball bush. A giant maple tree and some smaller dogwoods stood on the front lawn.

Henry was taken by a pair of trees with large shiny leaves that dominated the scene. "What are these?" he asked, pointing.

"Magnolias," Clare said. "They grow throughout the South."

"Where are the 'sweet magnolia blossoms' that Al Jolson sang about?" Henry inquired.

"They are beautiful, but you'll have to wait for warmer weather to see – and smell – those."

Flanking the double door were wide windows with open shutters on both stories. Pointing to an upstairs front window, Clare said, "That was my parents' bedroom. Mine and my sister's are on the back."

As they pulled up and parked, Clare reached for Henry's hand and squeezed it. "I hope I'm doing the right thing," she said. "Everything will be just fine," he reassured her.

They walked slowly toward the house and as they started up the steps, the front door swung open and a smiling Betty Sullivan appeared. She turned and shouted, "She's here!" and stepped out to greet them.

Henry allowed Clare to precede him onto the porch, where she ran into her mother's arms, tears streaming down her face.

The reunion was a highly emotional moment for both women. They hugged, then stood back to look at each other, then hugged again.

"Oh, baby, I'm so happy you came back," Betty Sullivan said, sobbing.

"I'm really glad to be here," said Clare. "And I want you to meet Henry. Momma, this is Henry Jackson."

"Judy Clare – I mean, Clare told me about you on the phone," Betty said in a sweet Southern drawl, her blue eyes sparkling.

"It's my pleasure, Mrs. Sullivan," Henry said, grasping her hand.

"Please call me Betty." Standing between them with one arm around each of the visitors, she said, "Welcome to our place. Please come in."

The first face Clare saw when she entered the family living room was that of her father. Pat Sullivan was graying at the temples and lines framed his weathered face, but the warmth of his smile brought back memories of happier days on the farm.

They embraced each other and Pat said softly, "Welcome home, child." She teared up, held him close and said, "Oh, Daddy. Thank you, thank you for saying that."

Pat's gaze turned to Henry and the two men met with a firm handshake. "I'm Henry Jackson. I'm so glad to meet Clare's parents. You raised a fine woman."

"We think so," Pat said.

Betty came to stand with her husband. They both kept their eyes on Clare, trying to make themselves believe this sophisticated woman of the world was the same young girl who left them behind all those years ago.

"Let me look at you, dear," Betty said. "We've read about you in the papers and seen you on TV, but that's not the same as you being here … right here with us."

Clare smiled broadly, dabbing at her tears, and looked past them at two figures coming through the archway of the dining room — her little sister all grown up and a curly-haired little girl of her own.

"So you've decided to come back," said the stern-faced woman in a brown pants suit.

"Yes, Rebecca Jean … for a short visit. It's good to see you." She bent to say hello to the niece she'd just met. "And what is your name?"

"Elizabeth Ann," said the girl's mother before she could reply.

"That's a sweet name," Clare said.

Smiling proudly, Betty said, "She and Harry named her for me and his mother."

Clare was not accustomed to having this kind of conversation and could only stammer, "How nice." To her sister she said, "I look forward to meeting your husband."

"You're not married, I take it," said Rebecca Jean, staring at Clare's ring finger.

Straining to keep her composure, Clare replied, "No. This is my very special companion, Henry Jackson."

Pat spoke up. "Betty tells me you were a lot of help to her in her campaign, Henry. Are you from California?"

"Not until this past year. I was born and raised in the state of Washington."

"What kind of business are you in, if you don't mind my asking?"

"My family has a winery — Mt. Jackson Vineyards, founded by my grandfather."

"Henry's third generation," Clare said. "He's the president."

"Well," Henry said quickly. "I've taken a leave of absence and my brother has taken over that role."

"Harry is a very successful pharmacist," Betty said. "You'll get to meet him tonight when we all get together here for dinner."

Clare, startled, said, "Oh, that's too much trouble. You don't have to do that. I just wanted to come by and see you all again."

"Not another word, dear. This is a special occasion. We need to have a celebration."

Pat moved toward the door, saying, "I'll help you bring in your luggage."

"You'll be staying with us, of course," said Betty.

Clare and Henry both protested, trying to be polite. "We don't want to impose …"

"Nonsense. We've got plenty of room. There's just the two of us here now," Betty said, nodding to Rebecca Jean.

"That's very kind of you," said Henry. "But we called ahead and made arrangements at the Pecan Country Inn."

"We'd better go now," Clare said. "What time should we come for dinner?"

"You shouldn't rush off. You just got here," Betty said.

"Momma, they've probably got things to do," Rebecca Jean interrupted.

"Well, all right. Why don't you come around six and we'll visit a while and eat around seven," Betty said.

"That sounds wonderful," said Clare, giving her mother another hug.

Betty and Pat followed them onto the porch and waved as they got into the car and departed. Both were relieved that they had managed to avoid the awkward situation of an unmarried couple sleeping under the same roof as her parents.

"That was quick thinking, Mr. Jackson," Clare said.

"I saw a sign on the highway," Henry said. "I took a chance on the place still being in business."

"Let's see if we can find it."

They drove through a small town named Shellville and found the Pecan Country Inn on the other side. There was a vacancy, which wasn't too surprising, since there was only one car in the parking lot.

Opening her suitcase, Clare said, "I'm glad I brought one nice dress, along with the beachwear." She shook it out and laid it on the bed, smoothing out the wrinkles.

"I think the reunion got off to a good start," Henry said.

"With Momma and Daddy, anyway," Clare said. "My sister really gave me the cold shoulder."

"What's her problem?"

"Oh, I think she resents me going off and doing some exciting things while she stayed home and did what our mother wanted."

"I'm sure she'll come around."

"I hope so."

Going back through town they stopped at a house that had a sign for flowers on the fence. Clare and the owner managed to put together an arrangement suitable for a centerpiece, which she presented to her mother upon their return to the farm.

"Why, thank you, dear," Betty said. "This is a beautiful bouquet."

"I'm sorry I can't contribute anything for dinner," Clare said, as they walked toward the kitchen. Pat invited Henry into the sitting room and they left the two women talking about cooking.

"I think there'll be plenty. I've got a roast in the oven and we'll have mashed potatoes, corn, green beans, fried green tomatoes and hot rolls."

"That sounds wonderful!"

"And pecan pie for dessert, of course."

"Oh, that's my favorite. Henry's, too."

"So you've known him for how long?"

"Almost two years."

"Are y'all planning to get married?"

"Maybe someday. But we haven't made any plans."

A frown came over Betty's face as she stirred the creamed corn.

"Times have changed, mother," Clare said.

"I know. But I haven't."

Rebecca Jean poked her head in the kitchen and Clare was glad to see her.

"Harry called and said he was going to be held up at the store but he'll get here as soon as he can."

"He's a dear boy," Betty said.

"Where's Elizabeth Ann?" Clare asked.

"With her granddaddy, of course. He really loves my little girl."

Clare said to Betty, "Are you sure there's not anything I can do?"

"Thank you, but I can take care of everything."

"Well, if not, would you mind if I took a look at my old room?"

"Of course not. Rebecca Jean, take her up and show her what we've done to it. And you all can get reacquainted."

"All right, mother," came the reply, and without another word the two sisters headed for the stairway.

Clare swallowed and broke the silence. "Becky, I really am glad to see you. I've missed you."

"Oh, have you?" her sister snapped. "I'll bet you haven't given one thought to me or any of us while you were traipsing around Europe and then settling in a place clear across the country to build your career. You've been too busy mingling with the rich and famous to think about your family back home."

Clare decided not to respond. She knew her sister needed to vent.

As they reached the top of the stairs, visions of Clare's onetime bedroom flashed through her mind. Back then, her bed was covered with a quilt her mother had made. Almost a dozen colorful pillows she had fluffed up on the bed during the day found homes on the floor at night. Dolls she had collected through the years rested on shelves along with other coveted childhood souvenirs.

When Rebecca Jean opened the door a totally different scene met her eyes. Instead of her full-size bed, there was a daybed with a green plaid cover and two orange pillows. On one wall was a sewing machine and a table laden with bolts of cloth of varying patterns. Beside a rocking chair was a basket with knitting needles. What once was a girl's bedroom now was her mother's sewing room.

"You didn't expect us to leave your room undisturbed after you left us, did you?" her sister jibed sarcastically.

"No," Clare said quietly. "Thank you, anyway, for bringing me up."

When they came down and started to check out the dining room, Clare overheard some scraps of conversation between her father and Henry.

"This past year has been hard on pecan growers," Pat said. "We had a lot of rain during the summer and that resulted in an excessive number of cases of pecan scab disease, which reduced the quality and size of the nuts."

"So you had a short pecan crop," said Henry.

"Yes and that means prices will be going up for consumers."

"That's too bad. Changing the subject, I believe Clare said her family generally supported the Democratic party but that you didn't vote for Jimmy Carter."

Pat snorted. "He was a terrible peanut farmer and an even worse president. In fact, the only good president we've had in recent years was Ronald Reagan."

"You and my father would get along very well," laughed Henry.

Seeing the table all set and smelling the tempting aromas coming from the kitchen, Clare guessed correctly that it was about time to sit down for dinner.

There was one empty chair at the long dining room table. Rebecca Jean's husband was still detained at the Bradley Drug Store. Betty gestured to the others to go ahead and sit and when they got settled Pat said quietly: "Let us pray."

After the blessing, Betty added a word of thanks for the occasion – Clare's homecoming.

Everyone enjoyed the old-fashioned "country supper" and there was more talk about the food than the visitors.

Harry Bradley arrived almost midway through the meal and politely offered his apologies for being late. Clare was struck by his appearance – tall and slender, prematurely bald and wearing horn-rimmed glasses with thick lenses. She also was startled to see that he was accompanied by an attractive young woman who seemed to know all the family members. Harry introduced her to Clare and Henry as Honey Belle Wagoner, his store manager.

"Honey was good enough to give me a ride," he explained.

"Well, y'all pull up chairs," said Betty. "You can eat with us, can't you Honey?"

"I would be much obliged to, Mrs. Sullivan. Thank ya," she said. Clare noticed that she spent most of the time in conversation with Harry.

Betty's pecan pie drew compliments around the table. Clare obligingly asked for the recipe.

Harry and Rebecca Jean excused themselves soon after everyone returned to the living room. "It's past Elizabeth Ann's bedtime," she explained. There were no parting words between her and Clare. Harry and Henry did shake hands with a quick, "Nice meeting you." Honey Belle batted her eyelashes and smiled. "I'll be leavin' too," she said.

Pat and Henry resumed their couch conversation while Clare joined her mother in the kitchen and persuaded her to permit an extra hand in drying dishes.

When they moved to where the men were sitting, Clare remained standing and signaled Henry it was time to go. He rose, shook hands with Pat, and said, "I've certainly enjoyed meeting Clare's parents. Perhaps we ought to be calling it an evening."

"Oh, do you have to go so soon," said Betty with a pained look on her face. "We just barely got started on catching up."

"I'm so sorry, Momma," Clare said. "I really am happy we had this time together."

"So am I. So happy." Betty said, wiping a tear with her apron. Pat nodded in agreement.

15

"Thank you so much for the delicious dinner," Clare said, moving toward the door. "It has really been good to see all of you."

"What are your plans for tomorrow?" Betty asked.

"We're going to start working our way up the coast," Clare said. "I told Henry that when I was growing up here I really never saw too much of the South and I'd like to do that."

"Oh," Betty said, with a tone of disappointment, "I really do wish we could have a longer visit. Are you going to stay in this part of the country?"

"I'm not sure," Clare replied. "I still have a lot to sort out after my California experiences. But at the moment I don't have any desire to go back to the West Coast. I'll keep in touch, I promise. And maybe we can get together again — much sooner than before."

"I do hope so, dear," Betty said, giving Clare a hug.

Pat stepped forward and put an arm around his daughter, saying to both of them, "You'll always be welcome to our home."

Fighting tears, Clare took Henry's arm and went down the steps, turning to wave as they headed toward the drive. Clare paused on the way to reach down and pick up a fallen magnolia leaf. She looked at it thoughtfully as she twisted the stem one way and then the other.

"It's funny," she said, almost to herself. "Somehow I feel as if I'm turning over a new leaf."

She slipped the leaf into her handbag and with another wistful look back, she and Henry got into the car and slowly drove away. She kept her eyes focused on the old homestead until it was out of sight.

4

THEY AROSE EARLY, had a quick, light breakfast at the inn and headed for I-75. The distance from pecan country to the main highway seemed considerably shorter than when they found their way to Clare's former home.

Clare was quiet until they were well along their route. Then all she said was, "I think the homecoming was a good decision." Henry reached over and squeezed her hand.

The cell phone signal jolted her out of her contemplative mood. "It's Luna," she told Henry, who remembered quite well Clare's stepdaughter, who was her campaign manager.

Luna was not big on preliminaries. Her voice came roaring over the speaker. "Where the hell are you?" she demanded. "The last I knew you were traveling across Canada on a train."

Clare decided to ease into telling the young woman who had never heard of chow-chow that they were in the South.

"Well, we spent a few days in New York and then flew to St. John," she said.

"In Newfoundland? Why would you want to go there?" Luna replied.

"No, no. We went to St. John in the Virgin Islands. It's a beautiful island and we had a nice time relaxing there. But then we decided to come back to the states."

Luna had calmed down a bit. "I wondered where your travels had taken you."

"You're not going to believe what we did next," Clare said.

"So tell me."

"We went to see my folks in Georgia."

"You're right. That is hard to believe. Did your old man greet you with a bullwhip?"

"Nothing like that. My mother and daddy were both very happy that I came home."

"That homecoming must have been a barrel of laughs," Luna said cynically.

"It was fine. My younger sister still carries a chip on her shoulder because I left home to see the world and she stayed, got married and started a family. She has the sweetest little girl."

"I think I'm going to be ill. And did the workers come in from the field and strum their banjos by the moonlight?"

"Luna! Don't talk about my family that way! Besides, times have changed since *Gone With the Wind*."

"So you've gone back to your roots in the South?"

"For a visit. We'll let you know where our travels take us. And how are you? And how are things going with your advertising and public relations business?"

"Fine. Just got a new account. It's a diaper service company that uses drones to pick up and deliver."

"How interesting."

"We developed a campaign for them and came up with a new name for them: The Stinky Stork: 'delivers a new bundle of joy and whisks the stinkies away'" Luna said with pride.

"Very clever," Clare said.

"My boss liked it."

"Oh, and how is the incomparable Gene McQueen?"

"Wild and crazy as ever," said Luna. "But very successful."

"It's great to talk to you," Clare said. "Thanks for calling."

"Luna hasn't changed much, has she?" Henry said.

"No. And I'm glad."

The miles ticked off rapidly as they made their way to Macon, the closest city of any size. By the time they arrived at the city limits it was still too early for lunch and Clare said she'd like to take a drive around town to recall old memories of places she had visited in her youth. Since it was Henry's first trip he didn't mind learning more about the city whose tourism slogan was "Song and Soul of the South."

"I remember coming here for the Cherry Blossom Festival," Clare said. "It's a 10-day event held in March each year since 1982 and it's a gorgeous sight with more than 300,000 Yoshino cherry trees in bloom."

"That's hard to believe," Henry said.

They decided to concentrate on the cultural history of Macon and save the ancient Indian grounds and historic Fort Hawkins for another visit. With a map from the downtown visitors center as their guide, they got a taste of the role that music has played in Macon's development.

Passing the lifesize bronze statue of Otis Redding in Gateway Park, Clare said, "Macon is the home of musicians ranging from rock and roll pioneer Little Richard to country music singer Jason Aldean." She gave Henry some directions and said, "I know we shouldn't spend too much time here, but there's a place you've really got to see."

As the car turned into the historic Vineville district, Clare said to Henry, "We're going to 'The Big House', which now is the Allman Brothers Band Museum."

"Hey, that's great!" Henry said. "I was too young to know the band in its earlier years, before two of the brothers were killed in motorcycle accidents. I was in high school when the band was reformed in the late '80s."

"I've only seen the house from the street," Clare said. "It didn't become a museum until 2009."

At that point they arrived at the wrought iron gates with the band's iconic mushroom logo and they began the tour, which took them through the three-story Grand Tudor house which the Allmans acquired in the early '70s. They left almost two hours later, not quite believing they had been in the bedrooms of these legendary Southern rock musicians as well as their Casbah Lounge with its drug paraphernalia and the infamous seven-head shower.

They were way past ready for lunch so, on a recommendation, they went to the Grits Café and enjoyed Vidalia onion soup and sandwiches with chocolate caramel bread pudding for dessert.

Their hunger satisfied, Henry and Clare left Macon on I-16 heading for Savannah, about 2 ½ hours east.

5

CLARE FELL INTO her contemplative mood again. After a long period of silence Henry asked, "Is anything wrong?" She replied, "No. I'm just feeling a bit melancholy."

He resumed his concentration on the road. But a little while later he began to snicker. That was out of character for Henry. So Clare asked, "Are you laughing at me?"

"Of course not," he said. "What you said about being melancholy somehow reminded me of a line from a nightclub comic I saw in Vegas years ago."

"Well, please tell me what was so funny," Clare said.

"Oh, it wasn't all that funny," he said.

"Come on, now. You've aroused my curiosity. You've got to tell me."

"Okay. He was firing off jokes about his girlfriend and he said: 'I call her my melancholy baby. She's got a head like a melon and a face like a collie,'" Henry said, snickering.

Clare didn't laugh. "I don't see what's so funny about making fun of the woman you love," she said.

Henry gave her a pat and said, "Well, I certainly wouldn't make fun of you."

"See that you don't."

It was getting to be near dusk by the time Clare and Henry reached the outskirts of Georgia's oldest city. The emerging lights of the homes and buildings signaled the day's close and the night's beginning, but like so much of life in the South the change was gradual and natural.

As they entered the historic district they began to pass the many homes, churches and other structures that survived both the American Revolutionary War and the Civil War.

"Look, there's the Low House," Clare said excitedly

"Where?" Henry said.

"There," she said, pointing.

"That one? It doesn't look any lower than others around it."

"No, silly. It's the former home of Andrew Low, the father of Juliette Gordon Low. She was the founder of the Girl Scouts. The first time I saw Savannah was a Girl Scout trip. We came on the bus."

"I hope you didn't have to camp out in a tent."

"I don't remember too much about it, but I know we didn't do that."

Henry skillfully maneuvered the car through the streets leading to the Savannah River and arrived at the East Bay Inn as darkness made its final descent.

This charming boutique hotel, distinguished by its tall windows and wrought iron façade, traces its history to the 1700's but the present building dates to 1852 and over the years it has housed offices for cotton merchants, a bakery and a drug company.

One of the inn's amenities is a complimentary wine reception in the lobby. Henry caught a glance at a label and decided the wine was acceptable enough for a prelude to the evening. The cheese that accompanied it helped take the edge off their hunger as they browsed the selection of menus for places to dine.

"If you are up for a walk, I'm intrigued by 'The Old Pink House'," Henry said. "It's not far from here."

"I'm game if you are," she said.

The scent of gardenia blossoms filled the air as they strolled hand in hand through the cobblestone streets. The Pink House was not hard to find because of the distinctive shade of stucco which covered old brick. It occupies a prominent spot on Reynolds Square, one of 22 that define the limits of the historic district.

Henry and Clare enjoyed a memorable dining experience, sampling some outstanding Southern cuisine, including crispy scored flounder with apricot shallot sauce and braised pork shank with pineapple glaze.

After dinner they meandered back to River Street, where Henry called attention to the full moon. "This reminds me of the time in California when our romance began," he said.

"On the balcony of my Santa Barbara villa," Clare said.

"It also makes me think of 'Moon River', one of the biggest hits of Johnny Mercer. He was a native of Savannah, you know."

"I didn't know that," she said.

Watching the moonlight on the bay, they exchanged a kiss and called an end to a romantic evening in a setting of enduring Southern charm.

For breakfast they enjoyed the expanded continental buffet in the inn's café before setting forth to see more of Savannah's favorite sights. High on Clare's list was the locale of John Berendt's *Midnight in the Garden of Good and Evil* — popularly known in Savannah simply as "the book." Henry, a Johnny Mercer buff, wanted to walk where the great songwriter had walked. They were able to do both with a visit to the Mercer Williams House. It was too far to walk so they took the trolley, which allowed them to have a quick tour of Savannah's favorite attractions.

The mansion at Monterey Square where the movie of Berendt's book was filmed was designed for General Hugh W. Mercer, Johnny's great grandfather. Construction began in 1860 and was completed after the Civil War. Like many homes throughout the city it was neglected over the years. In 1969 it was restored by a dedicated preservationist, Jim Williams, a key figure in the "non-fiction novel."

Within walking distance was Johnny Mercer's birthplace on Gwinnett Street, as well as Forsyth Park, where he saw bands playing there regularly. The beautiful park also is known for its large fountain, surrounded by benches where people were lounging and enjoying the scenery.

They took a taxi back to their hotel and walked over to the Cotton Exchange restaurant for lunch, where they savored crab chowder soup and shrimp and grits.

When the waitress came to ask "how is everything" her eyes suddenly became saucers as she stared at Clare. "I know who you are!" she said excitedly. (Not likely, but possible, Clare thought.) "I've seen you on TV." (Again possible, but not probable.) "I love all your songs." (Huh-uh.) "May I call you Reba?"

"I'm highly flattered," Clare said. "But I'm not who you think I am." She didn't bother to tell the disappointed waitress that Reba McIntyre also was a favorite of hers.

After a bit of shopping they checked out and loaded up to leave. That's when Henry discovered the car wouldn't start.

He called the rental agency and after an uncomfortable wait a driver with a new BMW arrived and a tow truck took the prior vehicle to the shop. They were only slightly delayed in departing for their next stop, Myrtle Beach, S. C.

They rode in silence for several miles. Then both began to speak at once.

"You know, Clare ..."

"You know, Henry ..."

"Go ahead," Henry insisted.

"I was just thinking. I love to travel, and you do, too. I really have enjoyed the trips you've planned since the election and its aftermath. We've been to some wonderful places. And I do appreciate so much your willingness to indulge me in my desire to go home to Georgia and reunite with my folks."

"I was happy to do that. I did enjoy meeting your mother and father," Henry said.

"Travel is about all we've been doing for the past few months," she said. "We're still wandering sort of aimlessly. I wonder if we ought to start thinking about beginning a new life somewhere."

"That's funny ... well, not funny, but coincidental," Henry said. "Because those same thoughts have been running through my mind."

"Really?"

"Yes. I've felt for some time that I wasted quite a bit of what could have been my most productive years. I know I broadened my education by going to school and seeing a good bit of the world. But I didn't put it to very good use."

"I beg to differ. I think you put your experience to very good use in raising money for my campaign and giving me some good advice," Clare said.

"I'm glad you think so. That has been the only real job I've had since coming back to the states."

"What about the winery?"

"That was mostly just a nice office with my name and title on the door. Pop continued to make all the major decisions."

Henry paused, then said. "I guess I'm getting a little itchy to try something in the business world."

Clare let Henry's musings sink in and meld with her thoughts.

"I guess what got me started on this was listening to Phil talking so enthusiastically about what he's doing in his career," he said.

Clare restrained herself from offering an opinion, in consideration of Henry's apparent fond feelings toward this man she found to be so offensive.

"Do you have any idea what kind of business you'd like to get into?" she asked.

"No, not really. I don't think I'd be very happy working for someone else. So it would have to be something where I would be in charge."

"You could always buy another winery and go into competition with Mt. Jackson Vineyards," Clare said with a chuckle.

"No, I don't think so."

"You know, Henry – as I started to say a while ago – I've had sort of a yearning to do something, too. Maybe take up sculpture again, or something else in the arts."

23

"That sounds good. It would be a shame not to pursue your talents," Henry said.

"The other thing is – since reuniting with my family I'd sort of like to stay on the east coast. If they had a health problem I'd want to be able to go home right away."

"Well, I'm very glad we've had this meeting of the minds. Let's talk some more as we go along."

The drive on I-95 and U.S. 378 was uneventful and Henry and Clare got to Myrtle Beach and the resort area known as the Grand Strand by sundown. They checked into a hotel overlooking the boardwalk and on a recommendation from the desk clerk went to an ocean view seafood restaurant near a pier.

It was a pleasant, relaxing evening – the kind Clare welcomed after the stress of the past few days. From their table by the long window they watched the waves lapping against the shore, and presently a small ship came into view and docked.

While Henry ordered after dinner drinks, Clare excused herself to go to the ladies room. On the way back to the table she noticed through the window a crowd of people moving past, having disembarked from the ship. One particular individual wearing a familiar wine-colored sport coat caught her eye. He could have been a double for Phil Sterling! Or could it really be him?

He was walking alone, his hands in his pockets, and he wore a glum expression on his face. The more she watched the more convinced she was that it was Henry's friend they saw their last night in St. John. Her curiosity was about to get the best of her.

Resuming her journey to the dining room Clare passed a cocktail waitress and stopped to ask, "What's that boat out there?"

"You mean the 'Royal Flush'? Why, that's a casino. Offshore gambling is legal in South Carolina and it's quite popular."

"Thank you," Clare said, and thought to herself: "How interesting." She decided not to say anything to Henry because of the incredibility of the sighting.

They spent the following day getting to know Myrtle Beach and enjoying the daytime beauty of the 60-mile-long Grand Strand. At the visitors center an enthusiastic booster of the expansive oceanside resort loaded them down with brochures and maps as she ticked off the features that draw 14 million visitors each year: 60 miles of wide, sandy beaches; freshwater, ocean and deep sea fishing; More than 100 golf courses; outlet malls and a variety of other shopping opportunities; live entertainment theaters; and over 1,900 restaurants.

"A friend of ours suggested we have lunch at Murrells Inlet," Henry said.

"Oh, yes. You must go there," the woman said, drawing the route on a map.

As they were standing up to leave, the overly helpful guide said, "If you're going to the beach I should mention that we have a thong bikini ban. Any swimwear revealing any portion of the buttocks is not permitted anywhere in public in Myrtle Beach. Violators may be arrested, jailed, fined and have their photographs posted on police websites."

"So much for wearing your Speedo," Clare said to Henry with a wink.

They had a laugh about that as they headed down the U.S.17 bypass to their lunchtime destination, a historic fishing village on the southern end of the Grand Strand. Their restaurant of choice, Capt. Dave's Dockside Seafood, is known for casual fine dining. Clare had shrimp and grits and Henry the signature dish, Pan Crusted Grouper, and they weren't disappointed. After the meal they took a stroll on the Marshwalk, a wooden walkway running behind the row of restaurants and offering scenic views of the inlet.

Before returning to the main part of the city they stopped briefly at Huntington Beach State Park. Clare had a strong desire to tour the nearby Brookgreen Gardens, which she had heard so much about. But they decided that to have time enough to enjoy the gardens properly would require a return trip.

Rather than check out the beaches to see, as Henry jokingly suggested, if the thong ban was being enforced, they opted to go back to the hotel and spend some time at the pool before going out for the evening.

The Alabama Theater, one of half a dozen bigtime entertainment venues in North Myrtle Beach, originated with the country music group of the same name. It opened in 1993 and continues to produce nightly shows incorporating many musical genres. Clare was intrigued with the production called *ONE: The New Show* offering an evening of music, dancing and comedy featuring country, gospel, Broadway, pop and rock performances. She couldn't resist singing along with the melodies of a number of Broadway musicals.

"I have had so much fun today," she told Henry, and she meant it, although at various times during the day she had flashes of the previous evening when she saw through the restaurant window Henry's Harvard classmate, Phil Sterling, getting off a gambling boat. She was torn between telling Henry about the incident or sparing his feelings by remaining silent. She reasoned that they would have no further connection with the man and his flighty wife so why say anything?

Continuing their journey north on Highway 17, as they were leaving Myrtle Beach Clare saw a road sign for Calabash, which was just across the border in North Carolina. She was excited.

25

"Henry, can we stop in Calabash?" she said.

"I suppose so. Why?"

She told him about her conversation at the Hollywood fundraising party with her director friend Zacharias Bacharach about a movie he had been shooting in this small town. The film, titled *Goodnight, Mrs. Calabash*, was based on a supposedly true incident involving Jimmy Durante. The famed entertainer was traveling cross-country in the 1940s and stopped at a restaurant there.. He enjoyed the food and the service so much that as he started to leave he paused at the door, turned to the owner, and said, "Goodnight, Mrs. Calabash." That became his signoff line at his performances.

Clare wanted to go to the site of the legend but they discovered that three restaurants laid claim to that title. There also were varying stories about the identity of "Mrs. Calabash." While having coffee in one of the places they did learn, and there was no doubt, that Calabash is widely known for a distinctive style of preparing fish and other seafood: dipping it in a special batter and cooking it in a deep fat fryer for two minutes.

It was too early for lunch but they made a note to come back and try "Calabash seafood" sometime. As they were finishing their coffee Phil got a text message on his phone. He read it to Clare:

"It's from Phil … Phil Sterling. He says: 'Exciting business opportunity for you. Let's talk.' And he gave his phone number. Wonder what that could be about?"

Clare studied his face and then reluctantly said, "Well, you won't know unless you talk to him."

6

CELL PHONE RECEPTION wasn't good inside the restaurant so they went to the car and Henry placed the call. Phil answered immediately and he and Henry talked at length ... or rather, Phil talked and Henry listened and took notes. Clare picked up on one bit Henry repeated.

"You're in Wilmington, you say?"

She remembered from looking at their map that Wilmington, N.C. was the next large city on their way north. In her mind she knew what was coming next.

Henry was energized. He was all smiles. He hadn't been that excited since the night he and Clare played "20 questions" in the double deck lounge on the balcony of her villa.

"You remember we were talking about doing something besides travel ... and I said I'd like to get back into the business world? This may be my chance!"

"What did Phil say?"

"Well, you know he has built a career as a successful real estate developer ..."

"Yes, he talked about that a lot when we had dinner in St. John," Clare said.

"He's on to a deal that he says will double the size of his operation in Wilmington. Oh, I forgot to mention ... that's where he and Barbara live."

"So?"

"He wants me to become his business partner!"

"Really? And what would that involve?"

"Naturally I would have to 'buy in', so to speak."

"Naturally. How much?"

"He said we could get into that after we discuss the proposition. He wants to get together – the four of us – after we get to Wilmington."

"Phil certainly is a fast mover."

"Yes, he is. Always has been. What do you think?"

"I can tell you're really turned on by his offer. But I guess I'm habitually skeptical about something that sounds too good to be true. It's your decision, but I would want to know a lot more about it than he has told you."

"I want this decision to be ours, not just mine, because it will affect both of our lives. I would at least like to meet with him and get some more of the details. Besides, it will be fun to have another evening with Phil and Barbara."

("Yeah, right," she thought.) "I'm glad to hear you say you're thinking of us as a couple," Clare said. "What's the plan?"

"He asked me to call him after we got checked in to a hotel. He recommended the Hilton. It's on the river and has a great view, he says," Henry said.

"According to the map, we're only about an hour away from Wilmington," Clare said. "But if we're talking about dinner, we can take a longer route and see some more of this area."

"Okay."

"We can take Highway 211 over to Southport. Looking at the triple-A book, it sounds like an interesting seaport village. Why don't we do that?"

"Sounds good to me. The other alternative is to go on in to Wilmington and do a little exploring before contacting Phil and making plans for this evening."

"If that's what you'd rather do, okay. I'm good with that."

They proceeded on U.S. 17 for about 45 miles until they reached the Brunswick County suburbs of Wilmington. A large billboard caught their attention. Featuring a photo of an attractive model, it glorified "Sterling Homes – Fine Living You Can Afford". They passed three large housing developments: Brunswick Forest on the right, Magnolia Greens and Waterford on the left.

They continued on U.S. 76 into Wilmington, crossing the bridge over Cape Fear River, from which they could see the USS North Carolina, the most highly decorated American battleship of World War II, now a museum ship and memorial docked on the riverfront. The nine-story Hilton Wilmington Riverside also stood out in the brilliant sunshine that welcomed them to this historic port city.

With two conventions in progress, the 272-room hotel was almost fully booked, but there was a suite available and Henry took it. When they saw how spacious it was – not to mention the outstanding view – they were glad.

"I'm not going to call Phil right away," Henry said. "We need to have some time to get the feel of the city."

"From what I've seen so far, I like it," Clare said. "But it's a nice day to take a little walk around."

"That's what I was thinking. Let's see if we can get a map in the lobby."

The hotel concierge was most generous in providing the visitors with a map, city guide and multiple brochures. It was getting close to noon and since they had had only a light breakfast they were getting hungry. When Henry mentioned lunch, they were directed to the Cotton Exchange right across Front Street.

They were charmed by the old historic brick building which housed a variety of shops and restaurants. Clare scanned the guide's descriptions of eating places and quickly settled on The Basics because it promised "authentic Southern food." She was assured of her choice when she learned later the chef had come from Athens, Ga., to open the restaurant.

The menu offered several tempting choices. Clare decided on Brunswick Stew and Henry had a pulled pork barbecue sandwich. He was intrigued by the dessert menu's listing of Coca-Cola cake and he was not disappointed – once the waiter finally delivered it. There's something to be said for an unhurried lunch, but they didn't have all afternoon to get acquainted with Wilmington.

A stroll along the waterfront appealed to them so they crossed over to Water Street and continued south admiring the river views and the old homes and other buildings that gave this portion of Wilmington a charming historic character. They passed a variety of eating places with tempting menus in the windows, including Le Catalan French Café Wine Bar and Elijah's Seafood Restaurant. Henry took note of the Port City Java coffeehouses, Wilmington's answer to Starbucks.

Heading back north on Third Street Clare and Henry passed Latimer House, an Italianate Victorian style home built in 1852 by a prosperous businessman, and St. James Episcopal Church, established in 1729, the oldest church in the city.

Crossing Market Street, a major thoroughfare, they approached the city hall and the county courthouse and just beyond them Thalian Hall. Clare had been eager to see this distinctive Wilmingon landmark dating to the early years of the 19th century. She had read in a brochure about its development in the middle 1800's as a rare combination of city hall and theatre. It expanded tremendously during the Civil War. Following Lincoln's assassination John Ford of Ford's Theatre in Washington leased Thalian Hall. In the years that followed it was the venue for appearances by touring stars such as Buffalo Bill Cody, John Phillip Sousa, Lillian Russell and Oscar Wilde. Because of her interest in the arts, Clare was pleased to note a series of fundraising campaigns had begun in 1974, following a fire, for restoration of the theatre. Today, she read, it provides a wide variety of entertainment through local and traveling productions.

During a quick tour, Clare and Henry were impressed with the splendor of the Main Stage, the scene of live theater for more than 150 years. Clare felt a thrill just to be standing in the exquisite auditorium. They learned that Thalian Hall (its name comes from Thalia, the Greek muse of comedy), with its Grand Ballroom which seats 682, features not only stage productions but serves as an art film house through the Cinematique series. A smaller studio theater is the focus of a program for school students.

The theater experience stirred memories of Clare's appearances in some amateur theatrical productions and her brief career as a cruise ship entertainer. She had a spring in her step as she hummed some show tunes on their way back to the hotel.

Not surprisingly, Phil Sterling had left several phone messages and Henry wasted no time returning his calls.

Their conversation was relatively brief:

"Hi, Phil. This is Henry.

"Yes, well, we just got back to the room. We went out to get a bite to eat and decided to take a look around.

"Dinner? Yes, of course. Where shall we meet you?

"Here? Okay. You have our room number. We'll look for you around seven."

Henry had a puzzled look as he hung up the phone. "He wants to eat here. He says Ruth's Chris Steak House is his favorite restaurant."

"That is a bit surprising, but I know the food is excellent."

"The evening should prove to be interesting."

"Could be."

And so it was.

7

HENRY AND CLARE HAD RELAXED with a cocktail from the minibar supplies while awaiting the arrival of the Sterlings. The knock on their door came at precisely seven o'clock.

When she first saw Phil, Clare could hardly believe it was the same obnoxious character she met in St. John. Rather than loud slacks and a sport jacket, he was attired in a custom-tailored gray suit with a pale blue tie, such as a successful businessman might wear. His manner was also different – cordial but not ebullient. He appeared to have lost a little weight. She couldn't help but notice that he seemed to look as if he had aged – the worry lines in his face were much deeper and the wide-mouthed grin of the vacationing tourist was replaced by a nervous smile.

He greeted Clare with a gentle handshake and a "Good evening, Clare. It's so nice to see you again. You remember my wife, Barbara?"

"Of course. How are you?"

Mrs. Sterling looked every bit the part of an executive's wife, clad in a fashionable cocktail dress complemented by sparkling jewelry.

"Delighted to be with you and to welcome you to our city," she said.

"Why, thank you. We really like what we saw when we took a walk around this area earlier."

"Well, this is the waterfront," Barbara said apologetically. "Wilmington has some much nicer areas to see."

Henry was his usual charming self. "Shall we be on our way?" he said to the group.

The restaurant hostess extended an effusive greeting to Phil and he returned it, calling her by name. She showed them to their table, which was in a choice window location offering a perfect panorama of nighttime Wilmington.

Unlike the experience at Zo Zo's on the island, Phil did not dominate the conversation by bragging on himself and his real estate business. Instead he played the role of a welcoming host, pointing out some interesting features of the port city

"Wilmington is an old city, isn't it?" Henry asked.

"Over three centuries," Phil replied. "It dates to the 1720s when English colonists began settling the area. Because of its importance as a major port, Wilmington played a key role in the Revolutionary War, the Civil War and World War II. Over 200 ships were built here during that war."

"One of the first sights we saw coming into Wilmington was the U.S.S. North Carolina," Clare said.

"Yes. She actually was built at the New York Naval Shipyard. She was the first American battleship to enter service in World War II and she became the most highly decorated battleship of the war. As a memorial and museum, she's a leading tourist attraction."

"How long have you and Barbara been here?" Henry inquired.

"We came in the late 1980s," Phil said. "I saw Wilmington as an area with great promise, and I turned out to be right. It experienced a phenomenal growth in the 1990s, at one point ranking as the second fastest growing city in the country, behind Las Vegas."

"That's impressive," said Henry. "And from what I've seen it appears to continue doing well economically."

"That's exactly right, Henry, and that's why Wilmington offers tremendous opportunities for two smart people like you and Clare. That's especially true for my business, real estate. Since 2000 we've had a population growth of almost 19 percent. More people moving here means a need for more places to live, of course."

"You mentioned an exciting business opportunity," Henry said.

"And I'm dying to tell you about it. But it appears the food is on the way. So for now let's enjoy our meal."

As they were finishing dessert, Barbara picked up on the earlier conversation about the Wilmington area.

"We just love living here," she said. "I might sound like I work for the chamber of commerce, but I just can't say enough good things about Wilmington. Like most Southern cities, it's quite charmin' but it also has a style all its own. Our colorful history has been preserved quite well. We've got cobblestone streets and history museums, gorgeous gardens and wonderful restaurants, art galleries and theaters featuring top productions. There are churches of all denominations, including First Presbyterian, where President Woodrow Wilson's father was pastor.

"But I'll bet you didn't know we have a movie production studio and a thriving film-making business. In addition to the water sports activities you can see right here on Cape Fear River, we've got three marvelous beaches within half an hour's drive. Oh, and so much more. I just can't wait to show you around."

"Maybe later in the week," Phil said, anticipating Henry would be interested in his offer of a partnership in Sterling Homes.

Over coffee, Phil got around to talking about the business opportunity that was behind the offer. It centered on a pending proposal to construct a new bridge over the river to replace the existing span which had been in place since 1969 and was carrying increased amounts of traffic.

"The bridge is part of a 9.5-mile project from Wilmington to Brunswick County that will cost more than $1 billion."

"Excuse me, Phil, but how is that going to affect your business?"

"I'm getting to that. The North Carolina Department of Transportation has not finalized a plan for the location of the so-called Cape Fear Cross. Many studies have been made. The department announced last year that it has selected 12 alternate routes for further study.

"There has been a lot of speculation about which route will be the one chosen for the construction. Some organized opposition has developed against certain routes that would run very close to existing residential development. But wherever the road is finally located will undoubtedly mean a boom in real estate and commercial building in the near future."

Phil leaned in closer and lowered his voice. "Sterling Homes has a chance to get in on the ground floor. How is that possible?" Smiling broadly, he said proudly: "I know the final location of the project!"

Henry and Clare reacted with astonishment. "But that's a secret, isn't it?" said Clare. "How do you know?" said Henry.

"I have a good contact with the Department of Transportation. He told me the final route already has been chosen, but officials are going through the motions of studying 12 routes to buy time and try to allay opposition. But in return for past and future favors, this source has confided in me about the area where the bridge and road project will be built."

Clare, studying the bright looks on the faces of both Phil and Henry, strived to avoid an appearance of the skepticism she felt.

"Now here's my plan for Sterling Homes. Much of the land that will be taken by this construction is open space and unoccupied. Other parts are potential possibilities for acquisition. I have put in motion an operation to quietly buy up parcels of property along the route which naturally will become quite valuable when the project is finished. To acquire enough to gain a distinct advantage over our competitors will require a considerable amount of capital, of course. And that's where your opportunity lies, Henry. If you foresee the possibilities that I do – for vast housing projects, manufacturing plant locations and shopping malls – we can both make a sizeable fortune. If you believe, as I do, that an investment of funds at this stage will reap enormous rewards, then you'll join me as a partner in my firm and we can move ahead on one of the most exciting ventures I've ever been involved in."

Henry leaned back and let out his breath. "All I have to say is wow!"

Clare rose and announced, "What I have to say is, please excuse me while I visit the ladies room."

Joining her, Barbara said, "What do you think?"

"I don't know what to think. It seems too good to be true."

"But Phil is absolutely positive his source is giving him good information."

"But if not, he and Henry would be risking the loss of a great amount of money."

"Phil would tell you that he wouldn't have got to where he is without taking some risks."

"I suppose Henry might say the same."

On their return to the table – a path of some distance – the women discussed their names – particularly how Southern ladies traditionally bore two first names.

"I'm Barbara Lee – after the general, of course. What's your other name?"

Clare related the story of how she was called Judy – her first name – for the early part of her life, until she decided she'd rather go by Clare.

"And what's your family name?" she asked.

"Worth. Barbara Lee Worth."

"That's my daddy's bank!" Clare exclaimed.

"It's my daddy's banking business," Barbara said, smiling.

"Well, what do you know," Clare said. "I never dreamed I would meet the daughter of one of the South's leading bankers."

"Well, I don't talk about it much. I'm proud, naturally, but it's a little embarrassing."

"If you don't mind my asking, how did your parents feel about you not marrying a man from the Old South?"

"Momma wasn't too bothered about it, but that's definitely what Daddy preferred. And he really hated to see me leave Raleigh, where all the family is located."

"But Phil saw the possibilities offered by Wilmington and you settled here."

"Yes. And what he saw turned out to be right. Life can take some interesting turns, can't it?"

"That has certainly been my experience."

The men were heavily engaged in serious talk when their wives rejoined them.

"We're just talking about plans for tomorrow," Phil said. "Henry thinks he needs a little more convincing, so I offered to drive him around the area and show him some of Sterling Homes' work and also to look at the area where the new road will be built. I'm going to pick him up about 9:30 a.m. and we'll be gone most of the day."

"Well, if that's the case," said Barbara, "I'll take Clare on a tour of Wilmington and the suburbs, and we might just do some shopping."

"We'll definitely go shopping. I'm going to need to expand my wardrobe considerably if we stay here very long."

"How about if I come by for you around 10?" Barbara asked. "That's a more civil time to get started, don't you think?"

"That will be fine," Clare said.

With that, the foursome ended a somewhat different and most eventful evening.

8

CLARE WAS IN THE SHOWER when Henry left to join Phil for a day of touring Wilmington and surrounding areas. She had a granola bar and coffee and was waiting in the lobby when Barbara arrived for their shopping date.

Seating in a red Porsche was snug but Clare did enjoy the feel of a luxury automobile. As Barbara pulled away from the Hilton she said, "We don't really have any upscale shopping centers in Wilmington. There are few nice dress shops. But I'll show you what's here."

"I think we pretty much saw what's downtown on our walk yesterday," Clare said.

From 3rd Street Barbara turned onto Castle, a tree-lined street dotted with storefronts.

"This isn't the normal way out of downtown, but I wanted to show you the antique district," Barbara said, and pointing, "There's also Vintage Values, one of many upscale consignment shops here – that is, if you tire of trying to find clothing that suits you in the retail outlets."

They also passed, on the left, the Cape Fear Playhouse – "a popular little theater" – the home of Big Dawg Productions. After a few blocks Barbara cut over to Dawson and merged onto Oleander Drive, which took them to Independence Mall.

"This is the only enclosed shopping center in Wilmington," she said. "There are four department stores: Sears, J.C. Penney, Dillards and Belk. I'm a bit partial to Belk, since it was founded by a North Carolina family in a suburb of Charlotte."

"I don't believe there are any Belk stores in California," Clare commented.

"Well, then let me introduce you," said Barbara as she turned into the mall parking lot. They spent the better part of an hour in Belk and Dillards and Clare found a few things – enough to start a new wardrobe.

From there they proceeded for about a mile. Barbara then turned onto College Avenue, explaining, "I'm taking a little detour, but I want to show you the beautiful campus of the University of North Carolina at Wilmington." She talked briefly about the university and its educational and cultural features.

"They have a marvelous theater where you can see art films and special high-definition screenings of a variety of productions," she said.

Returning to Oleander they headed toward Wrightsville Beach, on the way passing near Airlie Gardens, a 67-acre park featuring huge live oaks – one ancient tree dating to 1545 – and gardens growing a variety of flowers and shrubs. "You'll have to visit Airlie sometime," Barbara said. "It's open the year round."

Crossing the Intercoastal Waterway, she told Clare: "We're having lunch at one of my favorite spots, the Oceanic Restaurant. Phil doesn't like it. He prefers fancier places to eat. But I love it, and I think you'll enjoy it, too."

Situated right on the beach, the Oceanic stands three stories overlooking the Atlantic Ocean. It is attached to the historic Crystal Pier, rebuilt after being battered by a spate of hurricanes over the years and reopened in 2013.

They took a table on the second floor which offered a sweeping view of the mighty ocean and they could almost hear the sound of the waves rolling onto the shore. It faintly reminded Clare of the beach at Villa de Lune, but she quickly turned her thoughts away from the memory of her beautiful home's mudslide demise.

"This menu looks very tempting," she said. "Do you have any recommendations?"

"If I had nothing but the hush puppies I would be happy," Barbara said. "But you can't go wrong with the fried seafood platter."

"I'm not sure I want that much," said Clare. "I think I'll try the crab cakes."

"Oh, they're great!" Barbara said.

Wine didn't seem appropriate for this kind of meal so they each had a glass of draft beer.

During lunch the two women chatted more about life in Wilmington and Clare ventured a few inquiries about Phil and his business – after all, he was at that very time trying to persuade Henry to relocate to the area.

Barbara ordered more hush puppies and another round of beer.

"What's the story about you and Henry?" Barbara boldly inquired.

Clare related how they met and grew close during the campaign and even closer in the tragic aftermath.

"Are y'all going to get married?" Barbara probed.

"We've been so busy with other things we really haven't talked about it. We love each other and there's nobody else – now – for either of us. So we'll wait and see."

"Well, he looks like a keeper to me. Don't let him get away."

"Barbara, if I may ask, what made you decide to marry Phil?"

"I didn't think I would. But he was a BMOC, primarily because of his performance on the football team. He was good in bed. And he made me laugh. Add to that – he's very persuasive, as you'll see."

"So you think he'll convince Henry to become his business partner?"

"I'd say there's a pretty good chance of that."

Barbara insisted on getting the check. "Thank you," Clare said. "You made a good choice for lunch."

They drove back to the point where they turned off for the beach and continued on Eastwood Road past a tasteful sign reading "Landfall", which Clare commented on.

"Landfall is what they call a limited-access residential community. It's over 2,000 acres and adjoins the Intracoastal Waterway. It's one of the older developments in the area and has some of the finest homes. It's where we live."

Taking a moment to recover from that surprising announcement, Clare said, "That surprises me. I thought your home would be in one of the Sterling property developments."

"We bought there when we first came to Wilmington and before Phil got his business going," Barbara said. "He was strongly attracted because of the golf course, tennis courts and other facilities for those who have an active lifestyle. Besides that, Phil believes that it's not wise to live where the builder is too accessible to the buyers."

"From what I can see it's a beautiful setting."

"I'd love to show you our house. And I think we've got time."

She waved at the guard as they passed through the gates and after a couple of turns and a few graceful curves they reached the Sterlings' street. At the end of a long tree-lined drive stood their two-story gray brick with a charcoal roof. Twin bay windows framed the double-wide front door. As they made their entrance Clare could not restrain her awe.

"You said you bought this place when you first came to Wilmington and before Phil got his business going? How ..."

Barbara obviously knew what Clare was thinking. "We used some of my family money for the down payment. I also loaned Phil the startup capital he needed. But we had an understanding that he could not be dependent on that source for future financial needs. And he has worked hard to stand by that agreement. Would you like some tea?"

"Why, yes, thank you," Clare said as she looked from one room to another on the way to the kitchen — one that rivaled hers in the villa. They sat in a sunny breakfast alcove and had their tea with some homemade cookies.

"I would give you a house tour," said Barbara, "but perhaps our time today would be better spent doing some more shopping." Clare agreed.

Next stop was the nearby Mayfaire Town Center, which Barbara described as "more upscale." Clare could tell from the names of the shops. Besides a Belk department store, Mayfaire had a Talbots, Chico's, Ann Taylor, New York & Company, J. Crew and a number of exclusive boutiques. Clare took a look around at one that Barbara had suggested and came away with some scarves and a handbag. She was very much impressed with Mayfaire.

Barbara took Market Street back downtown. On the way they passed a complex of buildings identified collectively as Ivy Cottage. "This is a combination of consignment and antique shops. They have an outstanding collection of furniture, furnishings, art, jewelry — you name it. No clothing, but just about everything else. It's a fun place to shop whether you buy anything or not."

"I look forward to doing some exploring here sometime," Clare said.

In the downtown area, Barbara pointed out the Bellamy Mansion Museum and some other historic houses. "I believe you said you had seen Thalian Hall on your walk. Another theater you might want to check out is the Red Barn Studio Theater. It's an intimate 50-seat theater founded by actress Linda Lavin. There's another little theater being formed, which doesn't have a name yet. A friend of mine is providing some of the backing."

As they neared the hotel, Clare said, "Barbara, I want to thank you for a wonderful day — the city tour, the shopping, the lunch, tea in your beautiful home. And I also enjoyed getting to know you better."

"It was my pleasure, Clare. And I hope I'll be seeing more of you in the months to come."

Clare smiled and said, "We'll see."

9

CLARE WAS SURPRISED to find Henry waiting in the room after Barbara dropped her off.

"Hi! I thought you and Phil would still be out looking at and talking about real estate," she said.

"Haven't been back long. We had a good day. How about you? Looks as if you did a little shopping."

"Well, it's a start. Barbara and I really did have a good time together seeing Wilmington. We made a full circle and went all the way to Wrightsville Beach."

"You didn't go in the water, I trust?"

"No, but we had a delightful lunch at this place right on the beach. Well, tell me quick. Did you decide to join up with Phil in his bold venture?"

"I'd rather tell you about it over dinner," Henry said. "Let's try that French café we saw on our walk."

They both had done quite a bit of walking during the day so they opted for a taxicab for the short ride to Le Catalan French Café and Wine Bar on South Water Street. Housed in a small building with clapboard siding, cream-colored with white accents, Le Catalan had an unobstructed view of the river. A large striped awning extended to cover some of the outdoor seating on an expansive deck.

"This would be a perfect spot to watch the sunset over the river, in warmer weather," Clare said.

They were ahead of the normal dinner crowd so there was no wait to be seated. While Henry studied the menu Clare marveled at the unashamedly French décor. Wine cork artistry was on prominent display – corks used for edging at the ceiling, swirl designs on the walls, and even a "plant" with cork branches on the bar.

Henry put down the menu, looked around and exclaimed, "This takes me back to Paris!"

A French-speaking waitress took their order. Both wanted to try the cream of tomato and basil soup. Henry chose a shrimp and orzo gratin and Clare the mushroom feuillete. For variety they had wines by the glass so they could enjoy tastings from the extensive wine list.

Clare noted that Henry was in an especially good mood. She sensed an excited feeling about his day with Phil. He was eager to tell her about his Wilmington experience as well as the personally guided tours of Sterling Homes. Phil had proudly showed off his two major developments. One was a moderately-priced collection of homes beyond a well-landscaped entrance marked "Rainbow's End." The other was a more compact section with larger lots and more expensive dwellings. It was named "Hanover Village" and it contained a small commercial area where residents could buy food, drugs and other necessities. From Henry's enthusiastic descriptions Clare could tell he was impressed with what his former classmate had been able to do in a city the size of Wilmington.

"I admit I had some doubts about Phil – how much of his pitch was exaggerated. I had to see for myself. And today I did. And after witnessing the results of his imagination and planning in real form, I come away with a good feeling about his new project. I'm inclined to accept his offer and join forces with him to make it happen. But I want to know what you think, Clare."

"You apparently got to know Phil much better by spending the day with him. I also learned a few things about him from his wife. They may not have any bearing on your decision, but I find them interesting nevertheless."

"Such things as …"

"Well, to put it bluntly, he married a banker's daughter. Not just any banker, either. Her father is the founder of Worth Banks, one of the largest banking chains in the South. To Phil's credit – or perhaps I should say because of Barbara's sound thinking – he got to be successful without too much dependence on his wife's money. And believe me, they are a wealthy couple. They have a showplace of a home in an exclusive residential area called Landfall."

"Yes, he made a passing reference to that."

"Barbara used her family money for the down payment. Phil was transitioning from being a real estate salesman with unexceptional earnings to beginning a career as a developer. She also loaned him the starter capital he needed with the understanding that these were exceptions not to be repeated."

"And has that worked out all right?"

"She says it has. So, as I say, this is just some interesting background I wanted to share."

"But it would appear that it didn't shape his character development."

41

"Thanks to Barbara he had to make it on his own."

"And that he did," Henry said, signaling an end to that line of conversation.

"In this case, Henry, it's your money and I have no right or reason to tell you how to spend it."

"I know you have some reservations."

"True, but this is something that appeals to you. You've said you'd like to get back into the business world. And if you don't become Phil's partner you'll never know what you might have missed."

"How do you feel about living here?"

"It's not L.A., or even Santa Barbara," Clare said. "But Wilmington has a lot to offer. I like being near the water, of course. The area is subject to hurricanes, but I don't think there's any place that's safe from natural disasters of one kind or another. The city is beautiful, it has a rich history. There are artistic and cultural attractions which appeal to me. I believe I would enjoy living here. Plus, I'm back in the South and closer to my family. And that's a good feeling."

"Then I guess we might start giving some thought to where we might live," Henry added.

"Do you have any ideas?"

"Phil is very high on Landfall. I told him I didn't want to buy anything this soon and he understood. He said he happened to learn about a rental property near where they live. It's a good-sized house with a gourmet kitchen, beautiful yard and a pool. The couple who owns it wanted to spend a year abroad so they are renting it furnished. It sounds like something we might at least want to take a look at."

"Of course. Why not?"

Henry saw the waitress approaching with their dessert – Le Catalan's famous chocolate mousse.

They were also having espresso. But Henry was inspired to suggest a glass of champagne as well. Clare agreed.

"After all, this is an occasion for celebration – let's toast the beginning of a new phase in our lives together."

10

CLARE AND HENRY SPENT the next couple of weeks getting settled in their new surroundings. They looked at the rental property in Landfall that Phil had suggested and found it to be satisfactory as a temporary residence. It was a three-bedroom, three-and-a-half-bath with curved staircase to the second floor, fireplaces in the living room and family room, a spacious kitchen with granite countertops, dining room with plantation shutters, lots of windows and French doors, and a courtyard with small pool and spa. The bedrooms and living areas were tastefully furnished, although Clare quickly saw possibilities for some extra decorative touches that would help to personalize their new living quarters.

As Phil said, it was close by – only four blocks from their house – and on a much smaller lot, but nicely landscaped. Henry was able to get a six-month lease with option to extend.

Clare needed her own transportation so she bought a dark blue Lexus luxury sedan. (Henry's substantial investment in Sterling Homes entitled him to a company car.) She wasted no time revisiting some of the stores Barbara had shown her and began stocking the empty closets. Also, she couldn't resist checking out Ivy Cottage, where she picked up some sconces and a pair of unusual candlesticks.

Henry spent long days with Phil learning the ropes of the real estate development business. On an occasion when the two men were away overnight for a meeting in Charlotte, Barbara invited Clare to see a play at the Red Barn Studio Theatre. Founded in 2007 by actress Linda Lavin, then a Wilmington resident, and her husband, Steve Bakunas, it was the venue for quality productions of dramas and comedies by contemporary American playwrights, some of them starring Lavin. After the couple relocated to New York, where the Tony Award winner resumed her professional career, they signed a three-year lease with the Thalian Association in 2013 for use of the Red Barn rent free. On this evening they were joined by Nancy Galloway, a friend of Barbara's who was involved in organizing a new community theater outside of downtown.

During intermission, Clare expressed an interest in the undertaking and asked so many questions Nancy took note and observed: "You sound as if you might have a background in the theater." Clare mentioned her experience as a cruise ship entertainer, playing it down. "That hardly qualifies as a background in the theater. It does hold a fascination for me. And living in L.A. I did become acquainted with some producers and directors."

"That must have been exciting," said Barbara.

"One director in particular," Clare said. "Zacharias Bacharach."

"Really! I met him at a reception while he was in Brunswick County filming a movie about Calabash," Nancy said. "I understand he's going to be back here soon shooting a TV series."

"Wilmington has been the site of a number of those," Barbara said. "*Dawson's Creek* is one of the best known. There also was *One Tree Hill* and *Sleepy Hollow* – and the list of feature films produced in Wilmington or nearby counties is as long as my arm."

"Most people are unaware that Wilmington has a large film industry," Nancy said. "It began back in the mid-1980s when Frank Capra, Jr. and Dino DeLaurentis came seeking a location for Steven King's *Firestarter*. They found it at the Orton Plantation mansion south of the city, and along with that a large warehouse they converted into a movie studio. Today we have EUE/Screen Gems with ten sound stages. It's the largest lot east of California."

"You certainly have a lot to be proud of – and that's not a pun!"

"Please excuse us for doing so much boasting," Barbara said.

They all laughed and as the lights were dimming went back to their seats.

11

ON THE FIRST SUNDAY following their move, Clare felt a twinge of conscience. "I need to call home. I promised my mother I'd let her know if we settled anywhere."

"Good idea," said Henry. "And I'd better check in with my family. He took his cell phone to the family room and Clare dialed up the Sullivan pecan farm.

"Hi, Momma. It's me."

"Judy ... Clare, how are you? Where are you?"

"That's why I'm calling ... to let you know that we're in Wilmington, North Carolina. And we're going to be here for awhile."

"Wilmington." Betty Sullivan pondered, then said. "I don't think I know anybody there. But North Carolina's just two states away, so that's not too bad. You can come to see us more often."

"That's right. But not right away. Henry has gone into partnership with a successful real estate developer here and there's a lot to be done adjusting to a new job and for me a new place to live."

"Yes, I guess so."

"Well, how are you and daddy ... and Becky?"

"We're all getting along about as usual. I'm a little worried about your sister."

"Why is that?"

"I don't know. She just doesn't seem to be herself. Something's bothering her, but I can't figure out what. And she doesn't say anything."

"Maybe she's just not feeling well, and she'll get better."

"I hope so. And your Aunt Dora ..."

"What about her?"

"She's really doing poorly. She's in that nursing home, you know, and they take pretty good care of her. But she's getting up in years, and I don't know how long she'll be with us."

"Now, don't you worry, Momma. Whatever will be will be."

"I know. But she's my only sister and we've shared a lot together."

45

"Well, you probably need to be getting ready for church. Please take care of yourself. Say hello to Daddy for me. I'll call you again sometime soon."

"Please do. I'll love to hear from you. I'm so glad you're back close to us."

As she went to join Henry, Clare overheard part of his conversation with his father.

"Yeah, Pop. I think I'm going to enjoy this real estate venture. Maybe I can put some of my many years of learning to good use. Most of all I can apply some of the lessons you taught me about business. Clare just walked in. I'll let her say hello."

Clare took the phone and said, "Hi, Pop. How's everything going?"

The familiar growl was pleasing to her ears.

"Life's just not the same without seeing you often, my dear. But Jean and I are getting along just fine. And Drew is really showing signs of progress."

"So Henry's young brother is adjusting well to being president of Mt. Jackson Vineyards?"

"Yes, and that takes a load off of me. Henry told me you had been to see your folks in Georgia. That's a good thing. I'm a strong believer in family ties."

"I was a little apprehensive about how the reunion would go, but I'm very glad I did it. It's really good talking to you, Pop. Take care of yourself."

"I will. Got to stay in shape for our next pickleball match."

Henry said his goodbyes and they sat down for a cup of coffee. Clare wanted to feel him out about his new partnership."

"I think we're off to a good start," he said. "There's an awful lot about real estate that I didn't know, but Phil is spending quite a bit of time breaking me in. I'm glad he didn't have me doing anything this weekend so we could spend some time together."

"So am I."

Say, how would you feel about going for a Sunday drive?"

"I'd like that. Got any ideas?"

"I remember when we were heading to Wilmington from South Carolina you mentioned a place called Southport. I think it's less than an hour's drive. We could go down there and look around and maybe have lunch."

"I'm for it," said Clare. "Let me change and get some things together. I want to take my camera."

Before long they were in Brunswick County cruising down Highway 133 in Henry's Chrysler sedan.

They stopped at the visitor's center to pick up some brochures and learned from a helpful guide that Southport, located at the mouth of the Cape Fear

River, dates to 1792. With its age-old oak trees, coastal cottages and historic buildings it retains the charm of a quaint fishing village. "Movie makers have been drawn to our town for its waterfront views and downtown locales," the guide said, "and a number of movies and TV series have been filmed here. You might have seen one of the fairly recent movies, *Safe Haven*."

Clare remembered Barbara's friend, Nancy, mentioning Southport as part of the Wilmington-area movie industry.

They drove down several streets in the residential areas and the downtown section, passing the Old Brunswick County Jail and other historic landmarks. Then they turned down Howe Street, found a parking place and took the Riverside Walk. It begins at the City Pier, jutting out into the waters of the river, and the adjacent Waterfront Park. Hand in hand, Clare and Henry walked along Bay Street, pausing to read the wooden signs identifying points of historical interest as well as native plant species. Henry sat on a bench while Clare snapped pictures of waterfront scenes, the "Old Baldy" lighthouse and the Southport Marina along Cottage Creek.

They noted several casual restaurants in the Yacht Basin offering fresh seafood and it was noon already. The brochures had mentioned the Provision Company and they liked the looks of it, except for the waiting line extending out the door – a testimonial to its popularity. They decided to go back to Moore Street and peek in some of the stores. In one of the antique shops Clare bought a mantle clock which she thought would go well in their new place of residence. She also picked up a couple of Southport "pickle forks" that local craftsmen had fashioned by bending back the two outside tines.

Returning to Yacht Basin Street a little later, they had only a short wait at the Provision Company, where they ordered from a chalkboard menu. Henry had a house special: ½ pound of steamed shrimp with crab cake and cucumber salad. Clare's choice was a cup of seafood chowder and conch fritters. Both drank beer in the bottle. They left telling each other they definitely would make a return visit to Southport.

12

MIDWAY IN THE FOLLOWING WEEK, Barbara surprised Clare with a special invitation.

"There's a dance at the country club Saturday night and Phil and I want you and Henry to go with us."

"Oh! But we're not members."

"That's all right. You'll be our guests."

"Well, that's really nice of you. Are you sure?"

"Sure as sugarcane makes syrup."

"Golly. I'll have to go shopping. I don't have anything to wear to a fancy dress ball."

"Don't worry. It's not formal. A cocktail dress will do just fine. And Henry doesn't need a tux. Just a business suit."

Barbara suggested they come to the Sterlings' house and all go together.

When she saw Henry that evening he said Phil hadn't mentioned the double date to him.

"I guess I'm not surprised," Clare mumbled.

For their first social outing Clare thought she should at least wear a long skirt and at a Mayfaire shop she found a sequined black top to set it off.

Phil was a gracious host, welcoming them to their home – Henry for the first time – and offered cocktails. Clare took a glass of Prosecco from a tray. Henry wanted to test Phil's bartending skills.

"Let's see if you're as good at mixing martinis as you are at selling houses," he said.

Phil served up a perfect martini and Henry complimented him as they went to join their wives.

"How do you like living in Landfall so far?" Phil asked Clare.

"It's very nice," she said. "And Barbara has been a lot of help in getting adjusted to a new place."

Henry added: "We really appreciate your telling us about this house, completely furnished, being available for rent."

"A fortunate circumstance," said Phil.

It was only a short distance to the Country Club of Landfall, a low-lying classic structure overlooking a 27-hole Jack Nicklaus Signature golf course. It is one of two clubhouses, the other being at an 18-hole course designed by another golfing great, Pete Dye. Approaching the circular drive Clare admired the large round bed of floral and green plantings and behind it a large gabled roof with a fan window sitting on white columns.

Upon entering the club and taking in its grandeur and the gaiety of the gathering crowd, Clare recalled many special evenings from her former life in the Los Angeles area. Smartly dressed servers greeted the foursome with trays of champagne in crystal flutes. A reception was in progress, with hors d'ouevres being passed.

Phil exchanged greetings with a number of acquaintances, selectively introducing various ones to Henry and Clare, who were warmly welcomed. It was their first taste of high society in Wilmington and Clare enjoyed it immensely. Although the setting was similar the circumstances were much different from the fundraising receptions she and Henry had attended when she was running for governor. She could relax and bask in the sheer pleasure of the occasion.

Presently they moved into the grand ballroom, where tables had been arranged around three sides with a large dance floor in the middle. Clare was impressed with the six Swarovski crystal chandeliers sparkling overhead.

After the orchestra had played its opening numbers and more and more couples took to the floor, Henry extended a gentlemanly bid and Clare took his hand for a foxtrot and remained for a waltz. During the second dance, their hosts came near and Phil gestured to change partners.

Clare was not accustomed to dancing with anyone but Henry but she goodnaturedly allowed Phil to take her into his embrace, a bit too close for her comfort. She was relieved to see he was a smooth dancer and she was hardly aware that he had maneuvered her to the outer perimeter of couples.

"I want to tell you something, Clare," he said, to her surprise. "You are a very attractive woman."

Her guard went up immediately but she decided to see what followed his provocative declaration. She refrained from saying, "thank you." The one-sided conversation grew even more intense.

"I'm partial to redheads," Phil said. Clare's impulse was to stomp the floor and scream, "my hair is auburn, you idiot!" Instead she countered with, "But you married a blonde."

"Yes, I know," he replied. "There were reasons."

Clare knew that the primary reason began with a big dollar mark. She was on the verge of suggesting they return to the table when he modified his Valentino guise.

"Let me ask you something," Phil said, naturally arousing her curiosity. "Our TV spokesperson, Darlene Shields, is pregnant and will need to relinquish her position very soon. I have not been successful in finding a suitable replacement and I wonder if I might interest you in the job."

"Me?" Clare replied with a breath of excitement. "Why me?"

"I'm aware that you are quite comfortable being in the public eye. You even had a TV show in California."

"I'm surprised you knew that, but yes, I did. It was called, *Here's Clare* and that title became my campaign slogan in my race for governor."

"You're certainly qualified by experience and from being around you I think you have the ideal personality and appearance to take the message of Sterling Homes to the public. It wouldn't take too much of your time and I really would like to have you as a member of our organization."

"Well, you really caught me off guard, Phil. I admit I'm somewhat intrigued. But I'll have to give your offer some thought."

"Please do. But don't take too long. Darlene has cut her last set of TV spots and we don't want to lose momentum on our sales. And Clare ..."

"Yes?"

"Thank you for the dance."

Phil was just full of surprises, even displaying some manners. They returned to the table, Clare in a slight daze.

Waiters expertly choreographed the serving of an exquisite dinner prepared by the club's excellent kitchen. Unfortunately Clare found it difficult to concentrate on the various courses thinking about the possibility of doing something besides shop for herself and the house and engage in mundane social activities.

She could hardly wait till they got home to tell Henry and get his reaction.

13

"THE DINNER DANCE AT THE CLUB was really quite enjoyable," Clare said, as they walked in the door.

"Even dancing with Phil?" said Henry, with a slight edge in his voice.

"Actually that was one of the most interesting parts of the evening," she said.

That definitely was not the answer Henry had expected.

Clasping her hands behind his neck, she said teasingly, "He propositioned me."

"What!" Henry exclaimed.

"No, it's not what you're thinking. He made me a proposition – a job offer."

"What kind of offer?"

When Clare outlined Phil's invitation for her to become the TV spokesperson for Sterling Homes, Henry showed interest. He could sense her excitement over the prospect and offered no objection.

"I think you would be good at it – of course, you'd be good at anything you tried."

"Now, now. I really do think I'd be a good fit."

"Well," Henry said, "you might be interested in knowing that Phil also has made me a proposition."

"Oh? Tell me about it."

"In addition to Sterling Homes, there's also a Sterling Properties. Phil set it up to focus on commercial building enterprises. He wants me to take over that part of his operation while he continues to concentrate on the residential side."

"That seems only fair, considering the size of your investment, Clare said. "What about his plan for acquisition of sites for both residential and commercial building along the route of the new bypass?"

"He created a holding company for that. He doesn't want to have his name associated with it because that would tip off his competitors."

"Sounds like a lot of sneaky goings-on," Clare said, then wished she hadn't.

"Don't worry," Henry said. "I'm keeping my eyes and ears open."

Clare had difficulty going to sleep, thinking about Phil's proposition, and when she did she dreamed about starting a new career as the Sterling Homes TV spokesperson. She had a flashback of the day she and Henry were coming into Wilmington and saw the billboard with the attractive woman. In her dream, the face was hers!

She did wait for Phil to call for an answer, which he did Sunday morning.

"I believe I would like to give the job a try," she told him.

"You will love it," he said, "and you'll be doing me a great service."

He asked if she could come to the advertising agency for a routine interview and some camera test shots, adding, "Barbara can bring you."

She thanked him and a short while later she had a call from Barbara. They agreed to leave in an hour. "And today I'll take you to lunch," Clare said.

The ad agency was located in Hanover Square, a commercial section of Hanover Townhomes, Phil's newest development, where he also had his office. The owner, Lee Lyons, came out to greet them and gushed, "I am so thrilled to meet you, Ms. de Lune."

"Please, call me Clare."

"Very well, Clare. You and Mrs. Sterling please come with me to my office and we'll get started."

As they took seats, Lyons said, "we'll dispense with the usual interview. I found out all I need to know about you from the Internet and from what Mr. Sterling told me."

"We have been running ads with varying frequency on the Wilmington stations and those within a 50-mile radius," he said. "We alternate between two or three ads a month so viewers don't get tired of seeing the same one too often. Although I'm sure they wouldn't get tired of seeing you, Ms. ... err, Clare."

Clare, blushing, said, "How long are these ads?"

"Most of them are 60-seconds but some are 90, and occasionally we do a 120 – for instance, if we're running a special promotion."

"That sounds like a pretty ambitious schedule, if you don't mind my saying so," Clare said.

"It's what Mr. Sterling wants and it has proven to be very successful," Lyons responded. "I know it sounds like a lot of work, but we have an experienced professional team producing the ads and therefore the effort has become rather routine."

"How much time would I be giving to the effort?" Clare asked.

"No more than one or two days a month. We normally shoot them here in our studio, but sometimes – for example, to promote an open-house weekend, we go on location. That's about the only time an extra day is required."

"Do you mind if I see your studio?"

"Not at all. Please come with me."

Barbara said, "I'm glad you asked. I've never seen their operation."

Clare naturally compared the agency's facilities and equipment with that of the station in California where she had done her *Here's Clare* show. She was quite impressed.

"You've obviously invested quite a bit of money in this phase of your agency's work," she said.

"Mr. Sterling has been quite generous with his support," Lyons said proudly.

Walking back to his office, Clare brazenly inquired, "Well, Lee, am I hired?"

"You most certainly are, Clare." They all laughed. "I'll need you to sign an employment contract and some other forms."

"How soon will you need me to start?"

"I believe Mr. Sterling told you that Darlene Shields, who has been our spokesperson for the past four years, is taking a maternity leave."

"Yes, he said she had done her final shoot."

"So as not to have a gap in our schedule for airing, if at all possible we'd like to set up a time next week for you to come in."

"I'm ready to get started," Clare said.

"Our writers have already prepared the copy and you may take that with you today. It will be good if you can set aside a full day for the shooting. We do a run-through for each ad – most of which will involve shots of you from different angles, intermingled with frames of text and maybe some animation. These preliminary sessions are essential also for timing."

"This is all beginning to come back to me," Clare said, with some excitement in her voice. "Oh, one other question. What about wardrobe?"

"Normally nothing that you wouldn't already have in your closet will be required. If there are any special needs, someone from the agency will go shopping with you – and make the purchase, of course."

That ended the meeting on a merry note and Clare and Barbara headed off for lunch.

Clare said she'd like to try a place on Market Street she had seen during one of her visits to Ivy Cottage, Hieronymus Seafood Restaurant and Oyster

Bar. "I've eaten there but it was a long time ago," Barbara said. "I would love to go back."

They were slightly ahead of the normal lunch crowd so they had good seating. Barbara called attention to the fresh catch specials posted around the dining room. "For dinner you can have your fish prepared one of six styles – Herb grilled, blackened, Greek, nut crusted, lemon caper and Carolina," she added.

"It appears the lunch menu limits it to fried, blackened or grilled," Clare said. "But that's all right. Everything looks good."

When the waiter brought water and cheesy, buttery biscuits, Clare decided to celebrate her new role as the Sterling Homes spokesperson with a Hieronymus Bloody Mary. Barbara said, "I remember they make a delicious strawberry daiquiri using berries grown in North Carolina. I'm having one of those."

"What's the story on this place, if you know?" Clare asked.

"It began as a family restaurant back in the '80s, I believe, by brothers who were commercial fishermen," Barbara said. "Through the years they have offered fresh seafood, fresh local vegetables and good service."

"It can't get any better than that," said Clare.

When their cocktails came they were ready to order. Both had She Crab soup, a house specialty. Barbara chose a Southern favorite, shrimp and grits, and Clare had grilled scallops.

They chit-chatted over their meal about Wilmington, the Saturday night dance at the club and the prospects for getting a new little theater organized. When that type of conversation began to lag, Clare boldly brought up the subject of children. She volunteered that she and her late husband had been too occupied with other pursuits to start a family. She awaited a response from Barbara and she said quietly, "Phil and I weren't able to have children."

"Oh, I'm so sorry," Clare said.

"It's probably just as well, considering the way our lives have turned out. But I'm sure my parents, especially Daddy, regretted not having grandchildren to spoil."

"I guess we're just not supposed to get everything we want out of life," Clare said.

14

CLARE'S FIRST TAPING OF ADS for Sterling Homes went well, thanks to the time she had spent in preparation for the session. She received compliments from both the producer and the camera crew for the professionalism she exhibited. The shooting was all done inside the agency studio except for one shot "on location" – in one of the nearby Hanover townhouses.

The scene was in the kitchen. The camera zoomed in on Clare drying her hands on a dish towel. Looking straight into the lens (her audience) she said, "What's your favorite room in the house? Mine is the kitchen. Maybe it's because I enjoy cooking. But even if I didn't, I do spend a lot of time here."

She walked to the side which contained the refrigerator and the range and oven and continued: "For that reason I want my time in the kitchen to be a pleasant experience. I want everything – the sink, the stove, the fridge – to work just right. All the time.

"And if it's a Sterling home, you can be sure they will. These homes feature appliances that are top quality – like everything else in the house." A quick video tour followed.

Back in the studio, she closed with, "Remember our motto: fine living at affordable prices."

That ad gave Clare an idea that she wanted to mention to Phil.

Barbara kept her posted on plans for the new little theater. The organizing group had made a fortunate discovery: a successful director with a background of stage and studio experience in New York had moved to the Wilmington area and she had enthusiastically joined in the effort. Her name was Gloria Levine and she and her husband, financier Benjamin Handelman, had relocated to the area a little over a year ago.

Handelman, who was retired, wanted to go to a warmer climate. An avid golfer, he also wanted to be accessible to a course that suited his preferences. They settled on Brunswick Forest, a well-planned development on U.S. Highway 17 west of Wilmington, and had a home built to their specifications on the relatively new Cape Fear National golf course.

As interest in the new theater grew, Gloria invited Barbara, Clare and Nancy Galloway for a visit, with lunch following. Clare hadn't seen Nancy since the Red Barn Studio Theater evening.

It was a bright sunshiny day and the views from the bridge crossing into Brunswick County were exceptionally scenic.

As they turned into the entrance of Brunswick Forest, Barbara remarked, "I can't let Phil know I came here."

"Why is that?" Nancy asked.

"He hates this development. The truth is, he resents missing out on the opportunity to be in on it. He tried to buy some of the land when plans were being made around 10 years ago, but all 4,500 acres were owned by Lord Baltimore Properties, established by the founders of the Amoco gasoline business."

"I think my husband said it's the largest and fastest growing community in the coastal South," Nancy said.

"That's the claim. They say they now have over 1,300 property owners in a dozen neighborhoods," Barbara said. She pointed to the professional and business "villages" on the right and beyond that the Visitors' Center.

"What's this large building?" Clare asked.

"It's the Fitness Center and it's one of the amenities the developers are most proud of. It has five tennis courts, indoor and outdoor pools and a large workout area with the latest exercise equipment," said Barbara.

Nancy spoke up. "It's a good thing Phil isn't listening, You're making a pretty good sales presentation."

"No, I'm just giving you some information. It will help you see why Gloria Levine and her husband decided to live here instead of in the city of Wilmington. It's not a retirement community but it has a lot of the same features."

"We must be getting close to their home," Clare said. "I see some golf carts on the horizon."

In just a few blocks Barbara turned into a beautifully landscaped yard fronting a large brick and stone dwelling with a three-car garage. Gloria Levine met the group at the entrance and extended a gracious welcome.

"Come in, sisters," she said.

To say she had a commanding presence would be like describing the USS North Carolina as a big ship. Her broad smile and outgoing personality exuded warm hospitality.

Clothes-conscious Clare took note of her attire – black slacks with a colorful blouse that accented her bronze skin and dark brown hair. Her eyes

56

took in the appearance but were drawn to an object silhouetted in the sun-filled area with the coffered ceiling. It was a grand piano, and not just an ordinary instrument. It was white with gold trim. Clare couldn't remember having seen another one like it.

"Come in, come in, and sit down," Gloria said, pointing to a long white sectional sofa that curved around one corner of the spacious living room. She offered mimosas as her guests were admiring the tasteful décor, saying, "I'm so glad we have this opportunity to get to know one another. I'm very excited about this new theater venture."

"We can't tell you how happy we are to have you as one of the organizers," Barbara said. Each of the three visitors gave a brief narrative about their lives and what brought them to the Wilmington area.

"Now we want to know more about you, Gloria," Nancy said.

"I was born and raised in Atlanta," she said, and volunteered that she had encountered discrimination early in life. "Being both African American and Jewish, I was a double target," she said with a hearty laugh. "I had a talent for the piano so after high school I went to the Juilliard School and studied hard — hard enough to achieve my goal of becoming a concert pianist. I also took some drama courses that whetted my interest in the theater."

Clare burst out suddenly. "I can't hold back any longer. Ever since we walked in the door I have been admiring that marvelous grand piano. Now that I know your background, I just have to ask: do you still play?"

"Oh, heavens yes," Gloria said. "I practice some every day. Is now a good time?"

Everyone joined in a Clare led a chorus of approval.

Gloria sat at the white bench, composed herself and launched into Bach's "Brandenburg Concerto No. 1." After about a minute of enthralling her audience, she found a good place to pause and took a bow. "Now, for a change of pace ..." she said.

With the first three notes, Clare shouted, "Oh, no!"

A startled Gloria stopped abruptly and looked questioningly at Clare. The other women stared at her in disbelief.

Clare, blushing, rushed over to Gloria to apologize. Taking Clare's hand, Gloria said, "What's wrong, dear?" "I am so sorry," she said. That was terribly rude of me and it had nothing to do with your playing."

She then explained how she had come to acquire an embarrassing name when Clare Sullivan became the bride of noted racing enthusiast Gary de Lune. "You can imagine going through several years of your life being introduced as

"Clare de Lune." She then told how she changed to Clare Sullivan de Lune as a candidate for governor.

Gloria, laughing, said, "That's a good story. I'll remember to tell my husband Ben."

"I guess he's on the golf course," Barbara said.

"Oh, yes. He can't seem to get enough of it."

"Do you play golf?" Nancy asked.

"No, but I joined the Brunswick Forest Pickleball Club. Have any of you played pickleball?"

"Once," said Clare, "in Washington state, where the game originated."

"I didn't know that. Hmmm," Gloria said. "Well, do allow me to play something light. How about some Gershwin?"

With that she filled the room with the strains of "I've Got Rhythm." Clare nodded back and forth to the tune and at the bridge she stood up and belted out the lyrics. She also mixed in a few dance steps.

Gloria led the applause and complimented Clare on her performance. "Where did you learn to sing and dance like that?"

Clare gave the group the short version of how she was a cruise ship entertainer during a portion of her early life and still loved music.

"Well, you've still got that style, girl. Is anyone hungry? I want to take you to our little country club. It's small, compared to some of the others around, but it's nice."

A short drive later Clare saw what Gloria meant. The clubhouse at Cape Fear National was a miniature version of the Landfall Country Club, even to a gabled roof above the entrance. Double doors opened to a bright, airy dining room with an open fireplace and a towering rock chimney. Tall windows created the illusion of bringing the natural outdoor setting inside, even in the dead of winter. Outside was a covered patio with panoramic views of the ninth hole. A private dining room was equally elegant, but had a more subdued décor. Naturally, the clubhouse contained a cozy bar and lounge for golfers and guests.

The Forest restaurant menu offered an appetizing variety of soups and salads along with selections ranging from burgers and wraps to chef's seafood specialties.

The group continued discussing plans for the new theater over lunch. In one of her drives around the area, Gloria had discovered an old abandoned church building in the rural suburb of Gourleyville. She was excited about the possibilities of acquiring it and transforming it into a 100-seat theater.

"It sounds wonderful," said Nancy. "I just wonder if some people might feel a little uncomfortable in that setting watching a play that might have some four-letter words?"

"Could be," Gloria said. "But in the first place I don't contemplate having much of that kind of fare. I tend to favor classic drama mixed with Neil Simon and musicals."

Clare chimed in, "And also, the Grand Ole Opry in Nashville formerly was housed in the Ryman Auditorium, which had been a church tabernacle."

"I remember my daddy referring to it as the 'Mother Church of Country Music'," Barbara said.

"When we finish here I want to give you a little tour so you can see for yourselves," Gloria said.

On the way Clare drew her out about her career as a director in New York. She learned that Gloria's experience included both theater and TV. Her most recent stint before retiring was directing a soap opera, *The Last and the Lonely*, which had won some Daytime Emmy awards.

Grass and weeds had grown up around the deserted church in Gourleyville, but the women could envision a facility where theatrical productions could be presented. It was easily accessible by public roads and had a large parking area. They tried to peek in the windows but the stained glass blocked their view.

Gloria said she had a contact and would find out if the building was for sale and what the price might be. That led to some discussion about finances. Gloria said her husband, Benjamin had agreed to head up a fund drive. Clare volunteered that she and Henry would be willing to make a donation.

They all complimented Gloria on her "find" and thanked her for the tour and lunch.

Clare had a lot to tell Henry.

15

CLARE COULD TELL Henry wasn't fully tuned in when she related the events of her day with Barbara, Nancy and the remarkable Gloria Levine. When she got to the part about the old church being considered for the new theater and the organizing group's need for finances, she thought, "if that doesn't get his attention, nothing will."

"Henry, what's wrong?" she asked. "Something's bothering you. What is it?"

"Nothing, I suppose. It's just that … I guess I'm not accustomed to being a partner with someone."

"So Phil is being difficult to work with?"

"Not that exactly. He simply doesn't seem to have his mind fully on the job. He spends an awful lot of time on the phone. Maybe that's natural. But he and I really don't communicate that much."

"Do you think it's just a phase?"

"I don't know. It's almost as if he has another life outside of his business and Barbara."

"You don't suppose he's having an affair, do you?"

"I have no reason to suspect anything like that. There was something that happened in Charlotte that didn't seem quite right."

"That meeting with bankers you attended?"

"Yes. One of the local guys invited a few of us to go to the races."

Clare instantly had a vivid recollection of times she went with Gary to the Charlotte Speedway.

"What happened?"

"Phil kept disappearing. He would be gone for a half hour or so, watch part of a race and then leave again."

"And I take it he wasn't going for hot dogs and beer?"

"If he did he didn't bring any back. I didn't think it was any of my business to ask him what he was doing, but I really was curious."

Knowing what she did about Phil's gambling habit, Clare figured out his absences right away. He was down doing some underground betting. Again she decided not to say anything to Henry about what she had observed.

"When it got to be late, I caught a ride back to the hotel with our local host," Henry said. "I don't know when Phil got in. He didn't look very well the next morning but I assumed he just had a bad hangover."

"Maybe so. At any rate, I'm glad you shared your concerns with me."

"You're a good listener. That's one of the many things I like about you."

"Would you like to tell me some more?" Clare teased.

"I'd rather show you," he said, as he took her in his arms and kissed her.

The next morning, after showing Henry off to work, Clare planned her day. She had scheduled herself to attend a sculpture exhibit opening at 10 a.m. but after that she was free. She made a spur-of-the-moment decision to pay a surprise drop-in at the main office of Sterling Homes.

It was her first visit so she introduced herself to the receptionist, who very efficiently said, "I'll let Mr. Jackson know you're here."

"I'm not here to see Henry," Clare said. "I'd like to have a few words with his partner if that's possible."

"Oh," the receptionist replied. "Mr. Sterling has some people in his office now, but they should be leaving shortly. I'm sure he will be pleased to see you. May I get you some coffee?"

"No, thank you," Clare declined and took a seat, taking note of the certificates on the walls attesting to the success of Sterling Homes.

About ten minutes later Phil Sterling emerged, following three men wearing dark suits and grim expressions. One carried a black suitcase. They exited without a word.

"Clare! What a surprise!" he said. "I'm delighted to see you. Does Henry know you're here?"

"Actually I'm here to see you, if you have a minute," Clare said and added, with a glance at the receptionist, "I know I should have made an appointment ..."

"No, not at all. Come in."

As they entered Phil's large office, he asked, "What brings you by?"

"It's about the TV ads," she said.

"Hey, I've been meaning to call you and tell you what a great job you're doing," he said.

"Thank you. I'm enjoying it. But I just wanted to offer a suggestion that I think might make them a little more effective."

"Of course. I'm all ears."

"We're promoting Sterling Homes and I think we could capitalize on your name. Sterling ... Quality."

"Say, I like the sound of that."

"This is just an idea. But how about an ad that begins with me saying: 'When you're looking at model homes, how many times have you been turned off by sights like this: nails popping through wallboard, paint with streaks, molding pieced together carelessly, shower tile installed improperly.' We would need visuals for those examples, naturally. Then I'd move on to glorifying our homes with such remarks as: "You won't find anything like that in Sterling Homes because they are homes of good quality – Sterling Quality." The scriptwriters can do a much better job than I've just done. But what do you think of the idea?"

"I like it very much," Phil exclaimed. "It brings a new, fresh approach to our advertising. I'm surprised nobody has thought of it before. I'll pass this along to the ad agency people."

"I don't think it will be too difficult to get shots of shoddy quality to use in the ad."

"No, I'm sure we can get those in some houses we've acquired for resale and haven't been remodeled yet." He stood, shook her hand and began escorting her toward the door. "Thank you so much, Clare. It's great having you on our team."

The phone rang as she started to leave and she slowed her departure long enough to hear Phil say nervously, "Yes, you made yourself perfectly clear. I know what I have to do, and I will do it. Just give me a little more time and …" The other party apparently hung up.

Clare found Henry waiting in the outer office. He gave her a smile and a hug.

"What are you doing, checking up on me?"

"Well, I did wonder if you guys ever did any work or just spent your time in two-martini lunches," she said. The receptionist blushed.

"Speaking of that, may I take you to lunch – minus the martinis, that is?"

"If you have time, that would be wonderful."

They dined at a small café a short walk away and she related the purpose of her visit and the conversation with Phil. She didn't mention the phone call she overheard.

As they were about to go their separate ways after lunch, Clare took Henry's hand and said softly, "You know, after last night and this mid-day rendezvous, it almost seems like we're dating."

Henry smiled and squeezed her hand.

"I like it," she said.

"So do I."

16

BEN HANDELMAN RAN an aggressive fundraising effort for the new theater which brought in enough money to acquire the site his wife, Gloria Levine, had found, and also sufficient funds to convert the old church in Gourleyville, N.C. into what the planners had named the Tri-County Playhouse. They counted on drawing both performers and financial supporters from counties encircling the location.

The Wilmington metropolitan statistical area, comprising New Hanover and Pender counties, is the second fastest growing metro area in North Carolina. In Wilmington, on the campuses of UNCW and Cape Fear Community College, were rich sources of talent. Pender, north of Wilmington, and Brunswick County, stretching all the way south to the outskirts of Myrtle Beach, S.C., offered potential for non-performing but essential roles for those trained in carpentry (for building sets), electricity (lighting) and sound (audio engineering).

The planning group knew they faced a number of obstacles to establishing a new theater company, the primary one being determining there was a need for one. They set forth their rationale in a mission statement which essentially said that while the city of Wilmington had some outstanding facilities, similar offerings were unavailable to the many new residents streaming into the greater metropolitan area.

They were fortunate to have the services of an experienced New York director, Gloria, and her husband, a former financier. The support of Barbara and Phil Sterling also was valuable not only from a financial standpoint but because of their wide range of contacts throughout the three-county area.

Nancy Galloway's husband, Stu, was a lawyer and he volunteered his services for drawing up bylaws for the new theater company, registering as a business and other legal matters. The board of directors consisted of Barbara Sterling as president (she was well known in the cultural circles of the city); Gloria Levine, vice president; Nancy Galloway, secretary; and Ben Handelman, treasurer. Clare applied her knowledge of publicity and promotion to the enterprise. From her campaign she understood the value of having someone on board who was skillful in using the various forms of social media. She discovered the right person in Crystal Bailey, a UNCW student interning with Sterling's ad agency who was eager to get involved with the new venture.

With many of the key bases covered, Gloria concentrated on developing ideas for theatrical productions. She focused on the inaugural effort, which would go a long way toward establishing the Tri-County Playhouse as an entertainment venue that attracted a large number of subscribers.

Her background as a concert pianist led her to favor a musical production, but perhaps that might be too ambitious an undertaking to get the project off the ground. That could come later in the season. She also realized there were a number of limitations that guided her decision. So she set down some parameters: a relatively small cast, a simple set, a play that would be fairly easy to stage, a story that would have broad appeal.

Among the stack of scripts she had acquired for consideration was one by a playwright friend of hers in Manhattan. The play was titled *Good Wives* and it was based on a book written by Louisa May Alcott, who later incorporated it into her classic growing-up novel, *Little Women*. The central characters are the four March sisters, who have grown up, married and begun careers and, in some cases, families.

Since the story was a period piece, set in the post-Civil War years, costuming presented a bit of a challenge. But it so happened that one of the Tri-County Playhouse volunteers was a talented seamstress who could make the women's clothing. Also some of the local antique stores and consignment shops had some items for both sexes in their inventories.

After reading the script, Clare decided she would like to try out for the part of Mrs. March, mother of the girls, who called her Marmee. It was not as large a role as those of the younger women, but an important one because of Marmee's interaction with the rest of the family. She found a place in Wilmington to take some acting lessons and they did a lot to build her confidence. Clare learned later that she had some competition from a woman named Victoria Potts who had acquired some experience as an amateur performer prior to coming to the Wilmington area. So in this latest chapter of her life, Clare found herself becoming a candidate again.

17

THE PLAY, and the opportunity to do some real acting, rapidly took full control of Clare's thoughts and actions. She got a copy of *Little Women* and not only read it but studied the plot and the various characters like a class assignment. At home she carried the script from room to room, reading Marmee's lines over and over. She kept it by her bedside and following a goodnight kiss for Henry it was the last thing she saw before going to sleep.

So concentrated was she on the forthcoming tryouts that she had to ask Henry to repeat what he had just told her upon his arrival home from work.

"I said there's a national convention of real estate professionals in New Orleans this weekend and Phil wants us to attend with him and Barbara."

Clare froze. How could she tell him she couldn't go anywhere. She was too busy preparing to launch her acting career.

"I don't know if I can get away, sweetheart. Gloria Levine has scheduled the tryouts for *Good Wives* and I really want to land a part in this first production of the Tri-County Playhouse," she said.

"When?"

"The play?"

"No, the tryouts."

"Two weeks from this coming Friday."

"Well, then, there shouldn't be any problem. Surely you can take time out for a weekend in New Orleans. It will be fun. You've been there, haven't you?"

"Just a whirlwind visit years ago."

"You haven't been there with me. I know that," he said. "And I guarantee you'll have a good time."

"I can't think of what I've got to wear …"

"Talk to Barbara. Maybe the two of you will need to go shopping again."

Clare excused herself to check on a casserole in the oven, her mind racing with thoughts of the complications brought about by this surprise development.

After dinner she called Barbara, who was full of the excitement that Henry had tried to convey. The two of them arranged to go to the Mayfaire shopping center and pick out some suitable attire for the brief getaway.

Clare was beginning to work up some enthusiasm for the trip but she was still uptight about the play tryouts. Henry noticed and encouraged her to talk about it.

"This is something that's very important to you, isn't it?"

"It really is. As you know, I've been at loose ends since ending my career in California. You have your work to occupy your time. I need something, too. I don't know whether theater is it or not but I'd sure like to find out."

"You know I'll support you in any way I can," Henry said.

She told him about the woman she had to beat to win the role of Marmee. "She has some experience in the theater. The only stage where I have performed was on a cruise ship."

"You're wrong. You were on one of the biggest stages in the country when you ran for governor of California. And as for experience – remember what that no-good congressman said about you …"

"Jack Bull? Yes, he really let me have it with his charges about my lack of experience in government."

"But you answered those charges and gave it right back to him. You can do the same thing here. I know you can."

"Thank you for your confidence," she said, giving him a hug.

18

NEW ORLEANS WAS still arousing from sleep when the foursome arrived at mid-afternoon and checked in at the Hotel Monteleone. The city would come alive later on after the sultry heat gave way to the coolness of dark and sounds of jazz and blues would fill the air and visitors would begin to fill the well-known streets of the French Quarter – Bourbon, Rampart, Chartres, Royal – and Jackson Square.

During the check-in Clare observed Phil Sterling across the lobby. He was in an animated conversation with three men in dark suits. They had their backs turned so she couldn't tell if they were the same ones she saw leaving his office that day she dropped in.

"Let's check out the room," said Henry, interrupting her concentration.

"Sure."

The Monteleone is one of the oldest and grandest of hotels in what is known as America's most European city. It dates to 1886 when Antonio Monteleone, owner of a Sicilian shoe factory who had immigrated to the United States, purchased a 64-room hotel on Royal Street. It has grown in size and stature to a luxury establishment with 570 guestrooms, an award-winning restaurant and the famous Carousel Bar and Lounge. Their room was spacious with elegant décor and a view of the Mississippi River.

The plan was to meet the Sterlings in the bar for cocktails and go dine in one of the city's many outstanding restaurants. But there was time enough for a stroll, as they were wont to do. So Henry and Clare quickly unpacked and went sightseeing.

They didn't have to go far to sample the flavor of New Orleans. The streets are lined with antique shops, art galleries, boutiques and restaurants. Just down the street from the hotel is Brennan's, famous for its breakfast but also an exquisite place to dine in the evening. As they made their way through the historic Vieux Carre, they admired the iron grillwork everywhere, the balconies overflowing with greenery, and the French and Spanish influences in the architecture. They saw no signs of Hurricane Katrina, which wrought disastrous flooding in many parts of the area.

As they drew closer to Jackson Square, visitors were taking tours in horse-drawn carriages with drivers in white hats and crowds were gathering around street musicians playing trumpets, clarinets, banjos and other instruments producing a melange of melodious notes in a prelude to nightfall when the sounds of the legendary Quarter resonated from block to block into the wee hours of the morning.

Henry bought some beignets and cafe au lait at Café Du Monde and he and Clare found a bench where they could enjoy both the snack and an inspiring view of the St. Louis Cathedral. Then it was time to return to the hotel. They went up a block to take a different route back via notorious Bourbon Street. Hours later they would be walking in the street with other nocturnal celebrants.

Before entering the hotel they took a moment to look at the sweep of the mighty Mississippi, busy with cruise and cargo ships as well as paddle-wheelers carrying giggling children and their parents. Along the shoreline they saw from their vantage point the Audubon Zoo and Aquarium, the D-Day Museum and a huge building Clare did not recognize. "That's Harrah's Casino," Henry explained.

After dressing for dinner they headed down to the fabled revolving bar with its colorful carousel canopy which the hotel history boasts "has been spinning" since 1949. They found Barbara seated in a crescent-shaped stationary bar area which had been added during an expansion of the lounge. She was sipping a Sazerac, a traditional New Orleans drink, and enjoying the music of a jazz quartette.

"Phil asked me to tell you he might be running a little late," she said. "He said he had a meeting with someone."

They sat and ordered their own refreshment – for Henry the bar's signature cocktail, a Vieux Carre, named for the original designation of the French Quarter, and for Clare a French 007, created by a Carousel bartender. Barbara had worked up an appetite so they chose a couple of selections from the "bar bites" menu.

As would be expected, conversation centered on the new theater venture. Clare expressed her uncertainty about getting the part in the play that she wanted and received assurances from her husband and best friend that she would get her wish.

The hour grew later and Barbara was visibly annoyed that Phil had not shown up. She did remark, however, that "by now I should have gotten used to waiting for him." She grumbled that it seemed like he was always having to meet with someone. Clare thought to herself: "It's no mystery where he is. Harrah's casino is just a short walk from here."

After a while longer, Barbara declared, "I'm getting hungry. Phil didn't say anything about dinner reservations, so let's just eat in the hotel restaurant. I'll tell the waiter to let Phil know where we are."

The Criollo Restaurant, adjacent to the Carousel bar, was already nearing capacity. Open a little over two years, it attracts not only hotel guests but locals with its creative cuisine and décor, inspired by the Monteleone's literary heritage. William Faulkner, Tennessee Williams, Eudora Welty and Truman Capote are among the familiar names on the hotel's roster.

Criollo is the Spanish word for Creole and the style is reflected in the dinner menu, which features such appetizing selections as Barbeque Shrimp and Boudin, Crawfish Bisque and Baked Stuffed Creole Redfish.

The group had barely got seated and ordered drinks before Phil Sterling made his appearance. He swept in, all smiles, and extended lusty greetings to everyone. "I hope you don't mind that we didn't wait for you any longer, Philip," Barbara said. "No, no, no," he said. "I apologize for being late, but I have some really good news." ("He must have done well at the gambling tables," Clare thought to herself.)

Phil continued: "There are some financiers from Chicago at this meeting scouting out possibilities for investment. I've just spent over an hour with them promoting our Wilmington project and I think I have them sold."

Clare couldn't resist asking if they were the men he was talking to in the hotel lobby.

"I did speak to them, yes," he said. "Waiter, bring me a Tanqueray martini, very dry, with a twist."

"Were they the same ones I saw coming out of your office the day I dropped by to see you?" she pressed on boldly. Henry nudged her with his elbow.

"Let me think. That could be. I had sent out some feelers and they made an unannounced visit to see the area," Phil stammered.

Henry spoke up. "You didn't tell me anything about that, Phil."

"I guess you were out of the office at the time and I just forgot to mention it later," he said.

Picking up the menu Phil abruptly changed the subject. "Hey, we don't need to be talking business. Let's get some food."

That ended the discussion for the moment. But Clare's suspicions about Phil being a compulsive gambler deepened even more.

Henry was quiet — quieter than usual — the rest of the evening.

19

THE NEXT DAY the men went to their meeting and Clare and Barbara went shopping. They spent most of their time exploring antique shops, the majority of which they found on Royal Street. At the French Antique Shop, Clare was attracted to a 19th century bronze Boulliotte lamp suitable for a bed side table. It was discounted to $1,200. But she passed up the bargain because there was only one and she needed two. They admired a display of Cartier jewelry at M. S. Rau Antiques, an elegant shop with crystal chandeliers – a French Quarter landmark for over 100 years. Keil's Antiques, established in 1899, also had some tempting jewelry offerings as well as a wide selection of objets d'art. Ida Manheim Antiques, a third generation gallery, featured museum quality furniture, tall case clocks and an impressive collection of 19th century oil paintings.

The shoppers were somewhat limited in their purchases because they were flying commercial. Of course, their husbands could afford to pay for shipping if necessary. But Barbara had long ago furnished her home quite well and Clare wasn't looking for anything special. She did acquire a two-bottle English tantalus that fit well in her tote bag.

Before they knew it the morning had flown by and they stopped in a café for a bowl of gumbo. Over lunch Clare commented on Phil's mood at dinner. "He was quite excited about his conversation with the Chicago financiers," she said.

"Yes," said Barbara. "I'm glad to see him cheerful for a change."

"I'm sure real estate, at the level where he is, can be a very high pressure occupation."

"That's true. But he really thrives on it. How about Henry?"

"I think he's liking it so far. He'd probably like more of a challenge. But maybe that will come later."

They talked a little about the new theater project. Clare told Barbara how much she would like to break into acting with the first production.

"I brought the script with me on this trip and I'm learning Marmee's lines so I can be ready for the tryouts," she said.

The women spent the afternoon at the pool and spa on the roof, enjoying panoramic views of the city.

Phil had made reservations at NOLA, the second of three restaurants opened by Chef Emeril Lagasse in New Orleans. It is a casual eatery featuring rustic Louisiana cooking in an open-action kitchen, with a chef's food bar a signature wood-fired brick oven.

Phil had his usual martini, the wives chose NOLA's special version of the Cosmopolitan and Henry selected a Moscow Mule served in a copper mug. The mouthwatering menu offered a variety of seafood dishes, grilled steaks and pork and hickory-roasted duck with sides that included smoked cheddar grits and bourbon mashed sweet potatoes. The diners finished off their meals with Elvis' Peanut Butter Pudding, Strawberry Shortcake Profiterole and other tasty desserts.

Dinner conversation was light. Phil was still on a roll. He and Henry exchanged some observations about the day's convention sessions and speakers. Barbara and Clare enjoyed people-watching. They couldn't believe what some of the women were wearing – or almost wearing.

It was only a short walk to the spot where the Preservation Hall Jazz Band has been playing almost every night since 1961. They were able to find seating for the 10 p.m. performance, which ended their day on an upbeat note.

On the following day, while the men were in the convention's closing sessions, Clare and Barbara rode a streetcar on the St. Charles Avenue Line (the Desire Street line quit running in 1948) and took a walking tour of the opulent Garden District. They reveled in the beauty of the antebellum mansions and gorgeous gardens, in bloom 12 months of the year. They also visited the Lafayette Cemetery, an above-ground cemetery.

They joined their husbands for lunch at Mr. B's Bistro, across the street from the Monteleone, and caught an afternoon flight back to Wilmington.

20

CLARE HAD A MESSAGE on the answering machine from Lee Lyons at the advertising agency. He said a reporter from a local newspaper had noticed the change in the Sterling Homes TV ads and was doing a story for the business page. "His name is Hal Phillips and he wants to interview you," he said, and gave her the reporter's number.

She called him the next morning and the first thing she did was to ask him if he had spoken with Phil Sterling.

"I tried," he said. "I was told he was away on a business trip, so I left a message, as I did with you."

"You'll need to clear it with him," Clare said. "And you'll want to get some quotes from him anyway."

Later in the day Phillips called back. Phil had given the go ahead. After she answered the reporter's questions about taking over the role of Sterling spokesperson he opened a new line of inquiry.

"In preparation for this interview I did some online research and learned about your California background," he said. "That was a big decision you made to run for governor."

"Yes, and it wasn't an easy one. But I felt strongly that it was long past time California had a woman governor. I felt qualified to serve, I was able to assemble a highly qualified campaign team, formed a statewide organization of volunteers, raised the necessary finances and gave it my best shot," Clare said. "It wasn't good enough, but we women won't make any progress if we don't try."

"Why did you decide to relocate on the East Coast, and specifically Wilmington?"

"My family is in Georgia, and I wanted to be closer to them – but not too close. Wilmington offered some career opportunities, and it is a very interesting and livable city."

"Are you getting involved in North Carolina politics?"

"No, I had some special reasons for what I did in California, but I'm not interested in any more political undertakings."

"Mr. Sterling mentioned that you and his wife are involved in a project to establish a new theater."

"Why, yes, we are – along with some other friends. We have formed a company called the Tri-County Playhouse and we're getting started on our first production, *Good Wives*, a play adapted from Part Two of Louisa May Alcott's *Little Women*."

"Are you going to be in it?"

"I hope so. I have had some stage experience and I really enjoyed it."

"So are you thinking of making that your next career?"

Laughing, Clare said "That's a little ambitious, considering I haven't landed a role in the upcoming production yet. But tryouts are coming up soon, so we'll see."

"Well, thank you very much, Ms. de Lune…"

"Please, call me Clare …"

"I appreciate your taking the time to talk to me. This will be a good story for our Sunday edition. We'll need a photo or two to run with it. Would you want to come to the newspaper office or we can send a photographer to your home."

"I've got a better idea, Hal. Why don't you and the photographer meet me at the new theater, say tomorrow morning, and you can check it out and get some shots there?"

Phillips agreed to her suggestion. She gave him directions and hung up the phone, smiling.

The photo shoot went well. By a fortunate circumstance Barbara was inside with Gloria Levine. They happily engaged in a discussion of the theater project with the reporter. The photographer left with several good poses of Clare, including one beside the stage curtain.

Gloria was excited. She grabbed Clare and said, "Great going, girl! This story in the local paper will give us the sendoff we need to get the public interested in our project."

"I hope so. And the TV stations probably will pounce on it and that will be even more good publicity."

The story turned out to be less than they had hoped for. The reporter focused more on Clare's life in California – being married to Gary de Lune, serving in the state senate, running for governor – and the years before that. He had obtained a copy of her campaign biography, *Clearly I See*, and he made reference to her experience as a member of a troupe of cruise ship entertainers.

But he did mention the new theater venture and before long the buzz was going about the Tri-County Playhouse.

21

SURE ENOUGH the news reached California and one of the many calls she received was from Hector Perido, her political consultant for the California campaign for governor.

"Clare, I'm so eager to talk to you. Hope things are going well."

"Yes, Hector. Henry and I are beginning a new life in a new part of the country, and that requires some adjustments."

"I dare say. But you're certainly capable of that. In your new life I hope you haven't lost interest in politics."

"As a matter of fact, I have. I'm involved in theater. More specifically, getting a new community playhouse started in the Wilmington area. Why do you ask?"

"Why? Because it's the perfect time for you to carry forth our efforts to get more women into office."

"Well, as you know the reporter asked me about getting into North Carolina politics and I said no."

"I have something bigger in mind. I'm sure you follow the political news and you're aware that Hillary Clinton's campaign for president is off to a rough start. Her unexplainable behavior in using a private email account when she was secretary of state, her allowing the Clinton foundation to be used as an avenue for access to governmental favors, the botched announcement and trip to Iowa – all of those errors have Democrats in key roles discussing the possibility of an alternate candidate. They desperately want somebody who can win, and I think you're the one to do it."

Clare had to stop and take a breath over the magnitude of Hector's proposal.

"Hector, what you're suggesting is preposterous. For one thing, this is so far ahead of the campaign it's foolish to write off a highly capable woman who is so qualified to hold this high office. Secondly, if I had any thought of such a challenge, there is no way I could raise enough money for a national campaign. It was hard enough doing that for the California governor's race. That was only possible with Henry's help, and he is deeply involved in a real estate development career here in Wilmington. So please get this idea out of your head, Hector."

"I hear you, Clare, and I understand your position. But you can't blame an old politico like me for thinking of the possibilities."

"And I appreciate that. You're a good friend and I know you had my best interests in mind. But I'm comfortable with the direction my life is taking. How is Houston doing?"

Hector reported that Luna's bedmate was pursuing a successful career as a faculty member at Millard Fillmore University's Western Campus where Hector was dean of the School of Political Science.

She thanked him for his call and turned her attention back to preparing for her debut on the community theater stage.

22

ON THE DAY OF THE TRYOUTS, a Saturday, Clare and Barbara got to the theater early. There was excitement in the air as hundreds of eager wannabe stars descended on the old church that had been converted to the new Tri-County Playhouse to seek roles in the production of *Good Wives*. Among them was Clare Sullivan (she had dropped de Lune), who had spent countless hours learning the lines for Margaret March (Marmee), the mother of Louisa May Alcott's *Little Women*.

The director, Gloria Levine, began with the young women vying for parts as the four daughters: ascending in age, Amy, 16; Beth, 17: Jo, 19; and Meg, 20. The first few rows of the theater were crowded with girls from both high school and college – four or five for each of the four March sisters. This portion of the tryout consumed a large part of the morning.

When that was done Gloria called for a short break before moving on to the next round, which began with Marmee. As Clare and Barbara stood to take a stretch, a queenly matron strode down the aisle. Barbara whispered, "Here comes your competition, Victoria Potts, the ex-speech teacher who fancies herself to be an actress."

The new arrival paused at their row, drew herself up into a haughty pose, and said to Clare: "Do you honestly think the role of Marmee can be played by a showgirl?"

Clare replied coolly, "If you're referring to me, I am confident that I can do the best job. But that's what tryouts are for."

"The only talent you have is getting your name in the paper," Potts sniped.

Barbara interjected, "And the name of our new theater."

"Well, you might as well go on home so you won't have to bear the disappointment of being rejected," Potts huffed and continued her regal entry.

Rather than feel insulted by the other woman's rude behavior, Clare restrained herself from laughing out loud, as did Barbara.

As Gloria had the rude lady read some of Marmee's lines, Clare and Barbara exchanged glances and whispered:

"She makes the girls' mother seem like a boring old woman," Barbara said.

"I was thinking the same thing," said Clare. "That's certainly not my impression of Marmee."

Soon the tryout for Madame Potts was finished and she came striding up the aisle, frowning. As she approached Clare's row she heard a deep Shakespearean voice say, "Why, if it isn't Vicky Potts! I wondered what had become of you after you lost your job at the junior college. That story about you and the young male student surely was blown all out of proportion."

Potts turned red in the face and in a hoarse whisper said, "Shut up, blabbermouth!" and marched quickly out of the theater.

Elated, Clare breezed through her tryout, injecting warmth and humor into Marmee's role and delivering her lines with flair. Gloria's broad smile signaled her choice for the part was Clare.

23

REHEARSALS BEGAN RIGHT AWAY. Gloria had given Vicky Potts the role of the sisters' aunt and her agitator (whose name was Jonathan Bartholomew) was to portray their father, Mr. March. Clare arranged her Sterling Homes TV commercial taping sessions to avoid conflicts.

Clare found Gloria a pleasure to work with. Years of experience in Broadway theater enabled her to get the best performance out of every actor in the play.

Play practices demanded a lot of Clare's time but she applied herself to learning the part of Marmee with the same kind of determination she had approached other challenges in her life. Henry was immersed in his job so the frequent rehearsals didn't put a serious strain on their relationship.

In preparation for the tryouts Clare had downloaded a digital version of *Little Women*. With the dog-eared script for *Good Wives* in hand, she re-read part two of the book to study how other characters in the play related to hers. She stood in front of a mirror and spoke her lines to practice facial expressions and body language.

As the date for opening night drew nearer she grew more confident and also more excited about making her debut in community theater. Gloria was a strong taskmaster but she knew just how far to push without wearing out the actors before they faced an audience.

Ticket sales were going well, especially for a new theater company, and Clare told Henry she was optimistic about a sellout. Her hopes soared when one of the local papers carried an advance story on the play opening. It was bylined by Alicia Swift, the paper's entertainment columnist, who just happened to be a close friend of Hal Phillips, the reporter who had written the article about Clare. Swift had interviewed Gloria, who provided a number of choice quotes.

"The Tri-County Playhouse, the area's new community theater, will present its inaugural production, *Good Wives*, on three weekends this month beginning next Friday evening," the story began. "The play, adapted from Part Two of Louisa May Alcott's classic novel *Little Women*, will be directed by

Gloria Levine, a veteran of the Broadway stage. I spoke with Ms. Levine following one of the final rehearsals at the playhouse in Gourleyville. The interview went like this:

"Q: Are you and the new theater company ready to introduce an additional form of entertainment for this three-county area?

"A: Our founders, our financial supporters and our volunteer actors and stage crew are very excited about the response to our opening, as indicated by the advance ticket sales. We hope that theatergoers and other citizens of New Hanover, Pender and Brunswick counties will join in seeing what we have to offer.

"Q: Considering what Wilmington already has to offer in the way of theatrical entertainment, the venture of a new theater must have been quite a challenge.

"A: Indeed it was. But the more we looked at the abundance of acting talent in the area and the high interest in quality theatrical productions the more we were motivated to give residents of suburban areas an additional choice of offerings of excellent theater at affordable prices. And we're pleased that we did not meet with opposition from established theaters that have dedicated supporters and fans.

"Q: So you're not concerned about saturating the greater Wilmington area with too much culture?

"A: In these worrisome times I don't think people can get an overabundance of culture.

"Q: Tell me about your choice of a first production. Why did you pick *Good Wives*?

"A: It's the second part of *Little Women*, which has a universal and enduring appeal. This story of a family with four daughters struggling through the stress of the Civil War has been portrayed both on stage and screen. Our play is a little different. Louisa May Alcott's novel, published in 1868, ended with the father's return from the war at Christmastime. It was such a success that readers demanded to know more about the March family so Alcott wrote a sequel which was set three years later, detailing the girls' growing into adulthood. The two volumes later were combined into one book. It so happened that a friend of mine had written a play based on the sequel. It had not been produced and I decided it was a story that theatergoers would enjoy.

"Q: You have involved some of the new theater's organizers in the production, I believe?

"A: That's true. Clare Sullivan, who is known locally as the spokesperson for Sterling Homes, is cast as Marmee, the mother of the 'little women', and Jim Galloway, the son of Stu and Nancy Galloway of our founders group, plays an important role as Laurie, the boy next door. My husband, Ben, as well as Phil Sterling and Henry Jackson, have been tremendously helpful in raising money for our new venture."

24

HER EXPECTATIONS WERE REALIZED and the curtain opened on a full house for the inaugural production of the Tri-County Playhouse. The stage was bathed in light but the theater was dark. Therefore Clare did not recognize a familiar face down front.

Clare makes her entrance as Marmee in the opening scene, as do all the principal characters because they are preparing for a wedding. Meg, the oldest of the four March daughters (she's 16), has been waiting for John Brooke, her intended, to return from fighting in the War Between the States and recover from his wounds. The theater company was saved the cost of an elaborate set because Meg wanted a simple ceremony in the family home. She made her own wedding dress so as not to buy an expensive gown. Her sisters are her bridesmaids and they are wearing their best gray dresses. Meg and John take their vows before her father, a preacher since returning from the front.

Marmee's dialogue is that of a protective mother, reassuring the young bride she has nothing to be nervous about. In this scene the most desirable role actually belongs to Vicky Potts, as Aunt March, because after the wedding the guests celebrate with food and dancing. The normally restrained aunt joins old Mr. Laurence, who lives in a mansion next door to the March family's small house, in dancing in a circle around the newlyweds. His grandson, Laurie, leads the merriment.

In successive scenes Marmee counsels Amy, her artistically inclined youngest daughter, as she experiments with sculpting, drawing, painting and other media while attempting to become a socialite. Marmee spends less time with Jo, who enjoys writing and is likewise ambitious about her goals. She hides away in the attic, working on a novel. Meanwhile she writes sensational stories about murder and romance and sells them to newspapers for as much as $100. There is a touching scene involving Jo and Marmee when the daughter uses the money to send her mother and her frail sister Beth to the seaside to help regain her health after a bout with scarlet fever.

Amy's frustrations are relieved when Aunt March decides to take her on a trip to Europe. Jo subsequently also leaves home, going to New York to pursue her writing career and to get away from Laurie, who is desperately in love with her and she's not interested in marriage. Both Amy and Jo write letters home and the director uses a split-stage set to show the daughters telling of their adventures to Marmee through their correspondence. Both meet men but form no serious attachments.

The playwright placed Beth's foreshadowed death in the first scene after intermission so the audience – along with her family – would have two scenes to recoup from the sadness of that event. There is a highly dramatic moment when Beth reads a special poem Jo has written about her. Then she dies in her mother's arms.

In the latter scenes Laurie goes to Europe and he discovers Amy is there, too. They fall in love and get married. As the family is welcoming the couple back from Europe a German professor, Fritz Bhaer, whom Jo has gotten to know in New York makes a surprise visit. Over a lengthy period their friendship matures into love and they decide to open a boys home in the residence of Aunt March, who had died and left it to Jo.

Good Wives ends with three of the March sisters and their husbands celebrating the sixtieth birthday of Marmee, singing and giving thanks for their strong family bond.

As the house lights went up and the actors took their bows, Clare spotted an old friend from California: the eccentric but successful Hollywood movie director, Zacharias Bacharach. They had a chance to get reacquainted when Clare brought him along to a cast party in the home of Gloria and Ben.

"Henry, you remember Zach, whom you saw at the fundraiser in Beverly Hills right after we met two years ago," Clare said. Or perhaps you've forgotten. You were a bit preoccupied with the host's wife, Mimi, at the time." Henry's face reddened as he shook Zach's hand and invited him to ride with them to the Handelman home at the Cape Fear golf course.

After patronizing the well-stocked bar and introducing Zach to Gloria and Barbara, Clare said, "It's great to see you, Zach. I hardly recognized you without your beret and knee pants. What brings you to this part of the world?"

"Actually I'm scouting out locations for a new TV series I'm going to direct," he said. "As you know, Wilmington has been the site of a number of these, including the Stephen King series, *Under the Dome*."

"I believe you mentioned that earlier, Barbara," Clare said as Barbara nodded.

"Our show will be quite a bit different. It's a light comedy set in a restaurant on the beach and will have a cast of young boys and girls working there who spend a large amount of time running around half naked."

"Well, that's a proven formula for attracting viewers," said Henry, who had been eavesdropping on the conversation.

"That's true, but the central figure is the restaurant owner, a youngish widow with a sly sense of humor," Zach said. "She's modeled slightly after the title character in the 1980's sitcom *Alice*."

"That role was played by Linda Lavin," Barbara said excitedly. "She's well known in Wilmington. She and her husband established the Red Barn Studio Theatre."

"Yes, so I've heard. Well, what do you think of this series idea?"

"I like it," said Clare. "What's the title of the show?"

"We have a working title: 'Busboys.' But it's not final."

"It sounds good to me," Gloria said. "It's short and simple, it projects the image of exuberant, reckless youth. But at the same time it's about kids with jobs instead of loafing on the streets. And young people romping in the surf near a beachside restaurant will provide countless filming opportunities."

"What's your timetable?" Clare asked.

"I've checked out both Carolina Beach and Kure and taken a look at Wrightsville. And, of course, I'm familiar with the excellent studio facilities and the availability of experienced technicians and other workers. But it's still too early to tell when we'll actually begin shooting."

"Your project certainly sounds interesting," said Gloria. "Please keep us – or I should say Clare – posted as your plans move forward."

"I'll do that," Zach said. "I was really impressed with the local talent you found for *Good Wives*, including Clare."

"Now, now, Zach," she said. But it was a mild protest.

Later Clare asked Bacharach privately how long he would be in Wilmington.

"I'm going to New York for the weekend but I'll be back here next week for a few days," he said.

"Good. I'm going to have the theater organizers to our house for a dinner party on Wednesday and I'd like for you to come."

"That's very nice of you, my friend. It would be my pleasure to be there."

The party was a spur of the moment idea, but it was nothing new for Clare, who had entertained frequently in California. She quickly passed the word to Gloria, Barbara, and Nancy to "hold the date." She asked Barbara for recommendations for a caterer and florist. She almost forgot to tell Henry.

25

"HAVE YOU SEEN the morning paper?" Henry called to Clare, who was pouring her first cup of coffee. "The play got a good review."

"Let me see," she said, quickly scanning the lead article on the first page of the entertainment section. Alicia Swift did indeed critique the new theater company's first effort favorably, tossing bouquets at Gloria Levine for her "well-honed directorial skills" in bringing Louisa May Alcott's age-old story to life, the "simple but realistic sets" that reflected the era as well as the location of the scenes, and the "highly commendable" job of casting the principal characters. The writer devoted special attention to the young actors who played the parts of the four March sisters and Laurie and she singled out Victoria Potts for her "admirable portrayal" of Aunt March as a grumpy and critical relative who also could "let her hair down and enjoy herself" (as in the wedding dance).

Clare lingered over the paragraph about Marmee. "The feature role of Marmee, mother of the 'little women', was played with a combination of sensitivity, warmth and subtle humor by local TV personality Clare Sullivan, who made her the model of reassuring constancy as her daughters began finding the way to adulthood," the review read. "Her local acting debut was rewarded with generous applause by a standing audience at the opening performance."

"See what I mean?" said Henry.

"Not bad," Clare agreed. "Articles like this will go far toward getting the Tri-County Playhouse accepted by theatergoers from Wilmington and the surrounding areas. I'll be interested in seeing what the theater founders have to say when they come Wednesday evening."

"Yes, you did mention something about a party. Is there any way I can be of help?"

"Well, you can be responsible for the bar. I know you can choose some very good wine, Mr. Washington Winery President."

"That was a former life," Henry said. "But knowing good wine is something one doesn't forget."

The house in Landfall was a showplace and overflowing with Southern hospitality. As guests arrived they were greeted by a hostess with a tray of French champagne followed shortly by a welcome from Clare, who directed them to the family room where a table laden with hors d'ouvres and a bar with premium labels awaited them, along with Henry.

The men naturally congregated near the food and drink and the ladies gravitated to other areas of the house, admiring the various decorating touches Clare had added.

When Zach Bacharach made his appearance Gloria and the other theater organizers gathered around him, eager to hear any professional observations about their first stage production. His comments were sparse but on the whole complimentary – sufficient to encourage the fledgling group to think about a positive future for the Tri-County Players.

At Clare's request he spoke briefly about his impressions of the production of *Good Wives* and the project the group had undertaken to expand theater offerings for the greater Wilmington area. He answered a few questions then took his leave to return to his hotel and get ready for a busy round of appointments the next day.

As he was leaving Clare's phone rang and she recognized the calling number as that of her family home in Georgia. Her sister Rebecca Jean was calling. "I've got sad news," she said. "Aunt Dora died. The funeral is next weekend, and you've got to come."

Quickly collecting her thoughts after hearing the surprising, if not shocking, news, Clare said, "I just don't see how I can do that, Becky. I'm in this play that our new theater company is presenting and it's an important part and …"

Her sister broke in abruptly, saying, "Momma expects you to be here and she'll really be hurt if you don't come. And besides that, I want you to come. I need to talk to my big sister."

That personal admission was totally unexpected and caught Clare completely off guard. "What's wrong, Becky?" she asked.

"I can't discuss it on the phone. But I really need your advice. Please tell me you'll be here."

Hesitatingly, Clare said, "Well, if it's that important to you, I'll try to work something out. I'll call you tomorrow."

Needless to say Clare's mind was on her family in Georgia the rest of the evening. She told Henry of her dilemma and spent a sleepless night wondering what she was going to do.

The next morning she called Gloria and told her of the pressure that had been put on her. Gloria was sympathetic. "Clare, you owe your family a great amount of consideration. You really ought to go to the funeral. We can go on with the play. This is why we have understudies."

26

CLARE WASN'T TOO PLEASED with Gloria's solution – she gave Marmee's role to Victoria Potts for the next weekend's performance – but the arrangement did allow her to make the trip to Georgia. She called Becky and told her of the decision.

"Good," she said. "I'll meet you at the airport."

"You don't have to come all the way to Atlanta to get me," Clare said. "I'll get a rental car."

"No. I'll drive you to the house and on the way we can talk." Becky's voice was shaky.

"Well, all right," Clare said and gave her the flight number. "I'll see you Thursday."

When she saw Becky in the baggage claim area she knew something was wrong. Her hair was tousled, her eyes were red and pain was written on her face. The sister who had been so cold when Clare reunited with the family opened her arms and hugged her warmly. "I am so glad to see you," she said, with great emotion.

All Becky said as they walked to the car was, "My life is such a mess." Clare decided to let her explain when she was ready.

Once they got on the road Becky opened up.

"Momma and Daddy don't know any of this. It's just between us."

"Okay."

"My marriage is on the rocks. Harry's been having an affair." Clare wasn't too surprised at that revelation, having observed how cozy he was with the flirty blonde who came to the family dinner with him.

"With that floozy who works at the drug store?" she asked.

"Honey Belle? No. He's been seeing a woman from the next town south of us."

"How long has this been going on?"

"It's probably been close to a year now. He kept coming home late from work, when he was actually going to see her. The sneaky bastard actually used Honey Belle to cover his lies, telling me they were doing inventory or some other excuse. I got wise when she called one evening looking for him when they were both supposed to be at the store."

"Have you told him you know he's been cheating on you?"

"I held off, hoping we could stay together for the sake of Elizabeth Ann."

"Your sweet little girl."

"I just don't know what I'm going to do," Becky said, with a sob.

"I am so, so sorry. A divorce can be so hard on a couple, but then when a young child also is involved …"

"You haven't heard the worst yet."

"What else could be troubling you?"

"I'm pregnant."

27

"PREGNANT? Well, that does complicate things. If you and Harry are having another baby maybe it's a sign you should patch up your marriage and stay together," Clare said.

"That's not the way it is," Becky said.

"What do you mean?"

"Harry's not the father."

If Clare had been driving she might have run off the road.

"What ... how?" she stammered. "I know how, but ... Well, if Harry's not the father, you're telling me you've been sleeping with somebody else, too?"

"It was only one time."

"Once is all it takes. Becky, I find it hard to believe you would do that. Who is the guy?"

"A local doctor." She paused before blurting, "He's Elizabeth Ann's pediatrician."

"For heaven's sake. Tell me the whole story."

"He's a wonderful doctor ... a wonderful man. He has been so good to me and my little girl. She loves him."

"And so do you, apparently."

"I don't know. I do like him a lot. I'm so confused. But one reason I like the doctor ... Jim ... so much is that he listened to me pour out my troubles."

"In front of Elizabeth Ann?"

"No. We were usually his last appointment of the day and she went to the waiting room and read books. He was very sympathetic. And it turned out he and his wife were also having problems."

"Oh, no. He's married?"

"Actually, they've separated."

"So the two of you went beyond the doctor-patient relationship."

"We became very close. And then one day it happened."

"The day you did it?"

"I needed to go to his office to pick up some test results ... tests he had done on Elizabeth Ann. I left her with Momma. It was the end of the day and the receptionist had gone off duty."

"So the two of you were there in the office alone?"

"Yes. We got to talking and I just fell to pieces. I broke into tears. Jim took me in his arms and held me close. It was so comforting. And the next thing I knew we were kissing."

"And so then the pediatrician decided to play gynecologist."

"No! It wasn't like that. It just happened ..."

"Right there on the examination table ..."

"Please let me tell you the whole story. It was as much my fault as his. I felt so safe and so calm with him. He gave me some water ..."

"Did he put anything in it?"

"Certainly not! He took my hand and asked me if I'd like to lie down."

"I'll just bet he did."

"He had a cot in a back room where he would take a nap sometimes when he didn't have a full schedule."

"You don't have to go on. I get the picture."

"I knew I was beginning to have feelings for this kind man. But I didn't intend to let it go this far." She paused. "But you know, I didn't feel any guilt, what with Harry being unfaithful for so long."

"But now you're facing the consequences of your unintended actions. Does Jim know you're pregnant?"

"No. I just found out myself, right before Aunt Dora died. You're the only one I've told. I had to tell somebody. And you're my big sister."

"The one who left you and Momma and Daddy for my own selfish reasons. I don't blame you for the cool reception you gave me when I returned."

"I'm sorry about that. I had just kept my resentment bottled up for so many years. But after I saw you and you were so nice to me and everybody I got over it."

"I'm glad of that. But now we've got to figure out what we're going to do about your situation," Clare said, squeezing Becky's hand.

They rode in silence for a short while. Clare needed time to digest all that Becky had told her and to collect her thoughts.

"Okay, let's think about some possible approaches to the challenge you're facing. First, we probably should rule out abortion."

"Oh, Lord, yes!" said Becky. "Momma would never stand for that."

"That's what I figured. Well, then, if you're going to be carrying the baby …"

"I'm going to be showing soon."

"That's right. So one option is for you to go away somewhere and have the baby and give it up for adoption."

"I don't think I could bring myself to give away my baby. Besides I'd have to give some reason for leaving my family … unless I could take Elizabeth Ann with me."

"That would be difficult to pull off. If mending your marriage is out of the question …"

"I'm afraid it is …"

"You could just let everyone think it's Harry's child."

"I'm not very good at deceit. And Harry probably would blab that we haven't shared a bed in a long time."

Clare groaned. "It's worse than I thought."

"I'm sorry."

"Hush. Hooking up with Jim is looking better all the time. You said he and his wife are separated?"

"Yes."

"They're not living together?"

"No. She moved out and went back to Columbus. That's where they were before he had the opportunity to buy a medical practice in our little town. His wife was dead set against it and she hated it here."

"Do you think he would follow her back to Columbus?"

"I don't think so. He enjoys his work and he really wasn't happy with her anyway."

"Oh, I forgot to ask. Do they have any children?"

"No."

"Well, that's one break. Let's think. Are there any other possibilities?"

"I'm sorry. I just can't think straight."

"Becky, the way I see it: if you and Harry get divorced and Jim and his wife get divorced and you and Jim get married and start a family right away (they both snickered)…"

"That's the only way Momma and Daddy would stand for me getting divorced … and even so, I'm not sure this is the thing to do."

"Well, little sister, do you have a better idea?"

"No," Becky said quietly.

"We're getting pretty close to the farm," Clare said. "So let's put this aside until the funeral's over. Then we can talk again. I guess everybody's going to be very busy the next few days."

"Yes. It's a pretty big thing putting on a Southern funeral."

28

DORA MAE TAYLOR wasn't a well-known figure in the county's social circles but that didn't mean she didn't rate a first-class sendoff to the Promised Land. She was a maiden lady and had lived by herself all her life except for the few years she shared a dormitory room while attending college and a fairly short time when she had a live-in caretaker before going into a nursing home in Shellville.

She spent the major part of her adult life working in an abstract office in Albany. When she retired she came back to a rural area because she wanted to be closer to her sister Betty. Although she had few acquaintances there was no doubt she would have a big funeral because all of Betty and Pat's friends would turn out to show their respect.

Clare had a few childhood memories of her aunt and they were all pleasant. She remembered her as a kind, caring woman with a warm smile. She was not unattractive, although she sometimes wore a little too much rouge. With her portly figure her hugs were almost smothering, but they were given with sincere love. Even so, Becky never did quite warm up to her, Clare recalled.

When the two sisters arrived at the farm they found the house empty. Just to make sure, Becky called out, "Anybody home?" Hearing no response, she said, "Maybe we can continue our talk."

"Better not," Clare said. "We can't let Momma and Daddy know about this until the funeral's over and we have our story straight. After I use the bathroom maybe I'd better see about finding a place to stay."

"Oh, I forgot to tell you. Momma said you can stay in my old room," Becky said.

"Are you sure?"

"Yes. It's now the guest bedroom. You want to take your bag up now and freshen up?"

"That would be nice."

They both went upstairs together. Becky showed her the bathroom door in the hall and went back down to wait for their parents.

When Clare opened her suitcase a clipping of the review of the play was on top. She had stuck it in at the last minute to show her mother. She took out the dress she had brought to wear to the funeral and looked around for a place to hang it. Then she saw the bedroom closet. Opening the door she pushed aside some of her mother's old garments and hung the dress on the rod. It was then she got the surprise of her life. Looking up she saw on the closet shelf one of her old dolls – her favorite, actually. It was Marmee, from the *Little Women* collection. The red haired doll, clad in a plaid dress with a lace shawl, evoked a memory of her mother, who gave it to her on her twelfth birthday. Apparently after Clare left she passed it on to Becky.

Clare was thrilled and delighted. But she had to pick the right time to report her discovery. Her mother, for the moment, had enough on her mind.

At the sound of activity below, Clare returned downstairs as the Sullivans were getting home. They had been to the funeral home to complete final arrangements. There was to be a "family night" this evening and the funeral at 3 p.m. Friday in the First Presbyterian Church of Shellville.

Clare was not accustomed to seeing her mother dressed all in black. Although Betty Sullivan was in mourning her sad face broke into a bright smile at first seeing her eldest child. She hurried up the steps and hugged Clare tightly. "Oh, baby. I'm so happy to see you. Thank you so much for coming."

"I know how much Aunt Dora meant to you so I had to be here," Clare said. She turned and gave a hug to her father and they all went inside.

"Everybody have a seat. What can I get you all to drink? Lemonade? Co-cola?"

Becky broke in. "I'll take care of that, Momma. You must be exhausted. Sit down and rest yourself."

"Thank you, Rebecca Jean. I believe I will."

Clare was telling her parents about Henry's job and living in Wilmington and how she had joined with some other women to establish a new theater when Becky returned with some glasses and a pitcher of lemonade.

"Anybody want Cokes?" she inquired. Nobody did so she set the tray on the coffee table and filled the glasses.

"I see there's already some food for tomorrow in the fridge," Becky said. "I saw some stuffed eggs and tomato aspic. And there are cheese straws and a pound cake on the dining table. Looks like folks are bringing in stuff to have after the funeral."

"Well, actually I fixed all of that myself," Betty said quietly. "I know there'll be more, but you can't have enough to eat to have a proper funeral."

"I noticed the liquor cabinet is unlocked," Becky said cautiously. The Sullivans normally didn't drink anything stronger than an occasional glass of sherry, but a funeral was an occasion that called for spirits of a higher octane level.

"You know we have to serve the hurricane punch, Becky," she scolded, defensively.

"And that does call for rum, and I don't know what else."

"That't right. And you don't need to know."

Clare, seeking to calm down the conversation, said, "What can I do to help get ready for tonight and tomorrow?"

"Not a thing, dear. I just want you to enjoy your visit." ("It's a funeral, mother!" Clare thought to herself.) "A lot of folks who knew you when you were growing up are looking forward to seeing how much you've changed. There'll probably be as many coming tonight to see you as there will be to see Aunt Dora."

"Oh, Momma!"

Almost to the point of biting her tongue, Becky spoke up. "Well, I've got to go home and pick up Elizabeth Ann – I left her with Mrs. Sanders – and get ready to go to the funeral home. I'll meet you all there a little before seven."

"All right. Don't be late," Betty said.

Clare walked to the door with her sister. "Thank you so much for coming to Atlanta to pick me up," she said. "It allowed us to do a lot of catching up."

"It certainly did," said Becky, stifling a snicker.

"Are we going to have supper before we go?" Pat asked.

"Bless me, my mind has been on other things," Betty said. "I got a spiral-sliced ham for tomorrow, but we could have some sandwiches off of that with a stuffed egg. And we had some slaw left over from the barbecue we had last night."

"And maybe some chips?" said Pat.

"Yes, of course. And pickles …"

"That ought to be plenty, Momma," Clare said.

"Well, I never want to run short. Oh, I made a big batch of pecan tassies. We can have that for dessert …"

29

IN THE SOUTH the pre-funeral event is identified in various ways. It's called a reception in the Delta states. In other places it's known as a "visitation" or "family night." Clare remembered from her youth folks just passed the word to "come out to the house" after the funeral. It was a highly important event, requiring as much or more preparation as the funeral itself.

A few cars were already in the parking lot when they arrived at the Wagoner Funeral Home. Frank Wagoner was the town's undertaker. His daughter, Honey Belle, was the manager of Harry's drugstore. "You met her the last time you were here," Betty reminded Clare. "Yes, I remember her," she said, thinking, "Who could forget that ditzy blonde?"

They saw Becky and her little girl with one of the early arriving couples visiting before entering the chapel wing. The Sullivans extended greetings and then proceeded to the private room reserved for the bereaved family. Clare remained with Becky.

She took Elizabeth Ann by the hand and said, "Sugar, say hello to your Aunt Clare."

"Hello."

Clare knelt down and gave her niece a hug and said, "Hi! My, you've really grown since I saw you." It was hard to think of something to say, not being around small children much during her life. "I like your dress."

"Thank you," the little girl said shyly.

"I guess we'd better go on in," Becky said.

Presently the family members accompanied Frank Wagoner into the chapel and reverently passed by the open casket. "She looks very natural, Frank," Betty said. "Thank you, Betty," he answered. Becky checked the cards on the floral arrangements, muttering about some of the senders. There weren't that many since Dora Mae Taylor wasn't that well known, but too often the volume of flowers is overwhelming.

Friends and neighbors were already lining up at the back of the room to pay their respects so Betty, Pat, Clare and Becky took their places, in that order, to receive fellow mourners. Elizabeth Ann sat on the front row with her coloring book.

First was Shellville's mayor, Frank Davis (he claimed to be a descendant of Jefferson Davis), who was up for re-election. He put an anguished look on his face as he told the family how much Dora would be missed in the town. Shaking hands with Pat, he reverted to his usual down-home manner. "Pat, I hardly recognized you in that dark blue suit. I'm used to seeing you in overalls or jeans."

"Those are my work clothes, Frank," Pat replied, coolly.

The mayor's wife followed and then one after another of the town's leading citizens: the banker, the insurance agent, the grocery store manager, the farm extension service agent, the police chief, the fire chief, the school superintendent. Each one extended sympathy, then went to sit and gossip. After about half an hour the crowd began to dwindle. Clare looked down past the casket and saw Becky's husband, Harry Bradley, approaching. Elizabeth Ann went running to greet her daddy and he picked her up and gave her a squeeze, turning away from the casket so the child wouldn't be looking down at cold, dead Aunt Dora.

He said goodbye to his daughter and returned to the line. Clare heard him say to Betty, "I might not be able to get away for the funeral tomorrow but I wanted y'all to know I was thinking about you."

"That's mighty kind of you, Harry."

When he got to Clare he was full of Southern charm. "It's so good to see you again, Clare. How've you been? Well, I hope."

"Just fine, Harry. Just fine," Clare responded, without feeling.

When he moved past she overheard him whisper something to Becky, who said, "Harry wants to talk to me. Keep an eye on Elizabeth Ann, please?"

Clare nodded and watched them go toward the family room.

Only one or two couples came after Harry and the Sullivans went to circulate among the visitors seated and standing in the chapel. Clare remained in place momentarily until she saw Becky returning. Her face had brightened up. She was close to grinning. Clare went to meet her.

"What was that all about? And wipe that smile off your face. This is supposed to be a sad occasion," she said.

"I can't help it. Harry just told me he wants a divorce!"

"Here? Now? What did he say?"

"He said he was very sorry but he had come to realize the love had gone out of our marriage and while he hated to leave Elizabeth Ann he thought it was better for him to move out."

"Did he confess to having an affair?"

"No, but he acted guilty. And he made it clear he wasn't talking about a trial separation. He said we need to get divorced."

"He didn't ask what you thought about that?"

"No. But that's not unusual. Harry's always had to have things his way."

"So what did you say?"

"I tried to conceal my relief. I think I said something like I hated to see us break up for our daughter's sake but if that's what he wanted I wouldn't fight him on it."

"And ...?"

"He looked relieved. And he said he would come by and get his things next week."

"Well, this certainly is a surprising development ..."

"But it might be the beginning of a solution to my problem."

"Maybe so. But try not to look so damn happy about it, Becky – at least for a couple of days."

"All right," she said, snickering into her Kleenex.

"Are you coming to the house after this?" Clare asked.

"I don't think so. I ought to take Elizabeth Ann home and spend some time with her before putting her to bed. We've been apart all day long."

"And this is bound to be a stressful time for her, wondering what is going on."

"I've tried to explain to her about people dying," Becky said, "but she's really too young to understand."

"I remember when I was her age it was a very scary situation. There was one time a relative died and they brought the casket into the house for a couple of days. I couldn't sleep. I was afraid a ghost was going to get me."

"It looks like Momma and Daddy are getting ready to go, so I'll see you tomorrow."

"All right. Get some rest," Clare said as they went over to where Elizabeth Ann was sitting. Clare said goodnight to her and kissed her on the cheek.

Back at the farm, Pat finished reading the newspaper, watched an old Mayberry sitcom and when it got to be around 10 p.m. excused himself to go to bed. He told Clare again how good it was to have her back at the farm.

Clare had spent the remainder of the evening helping Betty stir up and bake a carrot cake, which was loaded with chopped pecans and heavily laced with bourbon.

"It keeps it moist," she explained.

"I thought the oil did that," Clare said.

"But it also improves the taste."

"Goodnight, Momma," Clare said, giving her a hug.

"Goodnight. Sleep well – it's Becky's old room, you know. If you need anything, just holler."

30

THE PARADE OF PEOPLE bringing food to the Sullivan farm began not too long after sunup. Clare was coming down the stairs around 7:30 a.m. when she heard a knock at the door. Betty came quickly from the kitchen and admitted a large lady with regal bearing carrying a huge foil-covered platter which sent tempting aromas into the entrance hall.

"Good morning, Henrietta. You're out and about before the squirrels are up."

"I knew you'd be expecting my famous fried Chicken, as will all of your guests," said the early-morning caller.

"You guessed it. This wouldn't be a successful post-funeral gathering without it. Thank you so much for bringing it."

"My name's on the bottom of the platter. It's from my family china, you know."

"Oh, yes. We'll be very careful with it and be sure it is returned in good condition," said Betty, relieving her of this very important contribution to the feast in the making. "Won't you come in? My oldest daughter, Clare, has come down from North Carolina. Clare, this is Mrs. Pettigrew."

The visitor looked her up and down before speaking. "How-do-you-do," she said. She did not extend her hand.

"I'm pleased to meet you," Clare said, clasping her hands behind her.

Still eyeing her curiously, the Pettigrew woman said, "I didn't realize the Sullivans had more than one child."

"I've been away for several years," Clare explained, "living in California."

"California!" she shuddered. "How could anyone live in that awful state?"

"It's really quite livable," Clare retorted. "But I'm finding Wilmington much to my liking. Have you been there?"

The haughty visitor drew herself up to her full height and huffed, "My husband and I have traveled widely, not only in the South but throughout the world."

Resisting the temptation to respond, "So have I, sister," Clare excused herself as she saw Betty coming out from the kitchen.

101

After the initial caller made her welcome departure, others came in rapid succession, bringing such standards as potato salad, chicken salad, deviled ham sandwiches and pimiento cheese sandwiches – the latter both on white bread expertly trimmed of crusts. The dining table groaned under the weight of a variety of cooks' specialties, including a wide assortment of sweet treats – all tested and proven at various church socials.

The final dish to arrive before the Sullivans had to get dressed to go to town for the funeral was brought by a pale, slender and quite frustrated woman named Emily Musgrave. Her hands were quivering, as was the bowl she set down in the only vacant space left on the table.

Betty came to greet her. "Oh, Emily," she said. "I was beginning to despair. I was afraid you weren't bringing your wonderful congealed salad."

"Oh, Betty, I've had a horrible morning," she said. "My Cranberry Delight simply would not jell. I had to make it twice. Maybe I added too much brandy the first time. I'm just so glad I had all the ingredients in the house. I thought I was going to have to substitute a tangerine for the orange, but then I found one in the back of the hydrator."

"Well, you came through like a true Southern belle. And I'm so happy you did. Now you might want to go home and put on a dress that doesn't have homemade mayonnaise on the front. And we'll see you at the funeral."

No sooner was Emily out the door than Betty flew into the dining room and took stock. She made sure every major dish was on freshly polished family silver. Folks had brought casseroles containing asparagus, broccoli, corn, green beans, green peas and squash, made with eggs, eggs, eggs, and cheese, cheese, cheese. Pie makers proudly displayed their favorites: apple, blueberry, chess, chocolate, lemon meringue, peach and sweet potato – nobody dared take a pecan pie to the home of a pecan grower. Betty's version could not be beat.

The parking lot at the First Presbyterian Church was almost full and cars were still arriving. Pat Sullivan parked in the spot reserved for them. Frank Wagoner greeted them with his velvet-toned mortician's voice, gave them copies of the funeral notice and escorted them to the pastor's study. A few minutes later they were joined by the minister, Rev. Paul Peterson, a Floridian who had just finished seminary. Many longtime members of the congregation complained he was too young to fill the pulpit of the 100-year old church. Betty liked him, however, so nobody would say a word against him in her presence.

While the organist played some music Betty had picked out (Dora was not a churchgoer so she had no favorite hymns) Rev. Peterson checked to make sure he had the biographical facts straight. (They had been through this exercise before Dora's obituary was sent to the paper, but the minister didn't want to make any mistakes – like the time he eloquently blurted out that a local lawyer had served a term in the state penitentiary instead of the state legislature (although some listeners murmured, "he should have.")

Throughout all these preliminaries that Elizabeth Ann had no way of understanding, she was quiet and well behaved.

The casket had been closed, covered with a blanket of roses and placed in front of the pulpit. The flowers from last evening plus more that had arrived later had been carefully arranged on either side.

Finally the minister led the family to the back of the church and they followed him down the center aisle to their reserved seats. About midway, Becky touched Clare's elbow and whispered, "There he is." At the same time Elizabeth Ann said sprightly, "Hi, Doctor Jim." Clare got only a quick glimpse of Becky's paramour but enough to see a handsome face and sandy hair – she was struck by his resemblance to her late husband, renowned racing enthusiast Gary de Lune.

Clare thought Rev. Peterson did a creditable job of conducting a service for a woman he had not met and knew little about. He read the appropriate scriptures, led the singing of some standard funeral hymns (he had a nice tenor voice) and kept his message mercifully short. It was clear that one thing he did know about Dora Mae Taylor was that she had never married. If Clare had one criticism it was that the minister dwelled too strongly on that point.

Peterson, himself a bachelor, emphasized that although the Bible endorses and encourages marriage, "anyone can remain single and lead a good Christian life." He cited the Apostle Paul, who was single, to support the choice of a woman, such as Dora, not to take a husband. As he touched sparingly on issues of sexual morality, Clare wondered what thoughts he evoked in the mind of her errant sister, but guessed she probably was daydreaming about her sexy doctor. In fact, at one point Becky emitted a giggle, which she quickly tried to cover as an expression of sorrow.

Rev. Peterson summed up on a note of inclusiveness and unity as children of God. And whatever Dora had done in her life as a spinster we can only imagine. She took that secret to the grave.

The service closed with a stirring rendition of a Presbyterian favorite, "Oh, God, Our Help in Ages Past," and the funeral attendees followed the pall bearers and the family up the aisle in reverent silence. Once they got outdoors, however, they raced to their cars to see how fast they could get to the Sullivan farm and console themselves with food and drink. Only the family and a small circle of close friends went to the cemetery at the edge of town for the interment ceremony.

31

HENRIETTA PETTIGREW made it her business to be the first to arrive at the Sullivan place. She had sat in the back of the church and had slipped out with her husband during the second verse of the closing hymn. She told herself she was being helpful to Betty, who naturally was delayed. But the truth was, she simply wanted to sneak a peek at the table and make sure her fried chicken was properly displayed.

The Sullivan family was not far behind. Betty dashed to the kitchen, put on an apron and took out the tomato aspic and other things that required refrigeration and squeezed them into places on the table. Pat stripped off his suit jacket and tie, and began retrieving the liquor – a bottle of Kentucky bourbon and a large container of Coca-Cola for the den and two bottles of rum. As he began mixing the punch, Mrs. Pettigrew looked on disapprovingly at the placement of a drum table which held the oversized punch bowl and glass cups.

First into the bowl was an ice ring, followed by a can of frozen limeade, orange juice, pineapple juice, a generous amount of white rum and a lesser portion of potent Jamaican dark rum. Pat gave the mixture a hasty stir and added a small bottle of club soda. He ladled himself a cup for tasting and pronounced it perfect. He offered some punch to Mrs. Pettigrew but she turned up her nose, said, "No, thank you!" and waddled off to fill a plate.

Pat's farm foreman was outside directing traffic into a field as the guests began drifting in. Clare and Becky filled in for their busy mother in greeting the arrivals and directing them to the dining room. Most of them knew the way from previous parties at the Sullivans'. (And that's what this was, a party, Clare thought.) In the South it is entirely proper and acceptable to gather at the home of the bereaved and trade their glum faces for happy ones. Some of the guests were quickly transforming themselves.

Elizabeth Ann's eyes opened wide at all the activity. "Honey," said her mother, "why don't you go to the playroom Grandpa fixed up for you and change – take off your pretty dress and put on a playsuit. They're in the dresser, you know."

"Okay."

"You've been such a good girl, you can watch that Disney cartoon movie Dr. Jim gave you if you'd like. Do you need any help?"

"No, thank you, Mommy."

"She is such a sweetie, so polite, so well-behaved," Clare said. "You've done a good job of raising her."

"Thanks. I've done it practically all by myself. Harry's just not home very much."

"Do you think Dr. Jim will come to the house? I'd like to meet him."

"I doubt it. But who knows?"

A short while later, who should appear at the door but Dr. Jim and Rev. Paul Peterson. "I hadn't planned to come, but Paul asked me for a ride," the doctor said. "And since he's new in town he wants to get acquainted with folks and hoped I might help."

"I'm glad you came," Becky said. "I want both of you to meet my sister."

"We met before the funeral," said the minister.

The doctor extended his hand, smiling, and said, "I'm James Vinson and I'm so happy to meet you, Ms. ..."

"Just call me Clare. Please forgive me for staring, but you look like someone I used to know ... actually my late husband," she stammered, a bit stunned by his blinding smile.

"I'm sorry for your loss."

"He meant a lot to me, but that was three years ago," she said quickly. "I've moved on."

"Remarried?"

"No," then seeing that the minister had moved on down the entrance hall, "but I have a special friend."

"I see."

Becky broke in, "His name is Henry. We met him when they paid a visit earlier this year. He's quite a looker."

"Becky!"

Turning his soft blue eyes on Clare, Jim said, "Well, I have to say Becky didn't get all the good looks in the Sullivan family."

Blushing slightly, Clare said to Becky, "You didn't tell me he was such a flirt."

"I didn't know ... I haven't seen this side of Dr. Vinson," said her sister, a bit flustered.

"Why don't you serve the good doctor some of Daddy's wonderful punch, Becky? I'll take over here," Clare said.

"I'd like to talk to you some more," said Jim, as they left.

Just when it appeared the roomy Sullivan house could hold no more people, more couples showed up before the arrivals began to taper off. Betty came from the dining room carrying a plate with some samples from the table. She offered it to Clare.

"You need to eat something, dear. Anybody else who comes will know their way around," she said.

Clare's feet were telling her to find a place to sit. She peeked into the living room and saw her father and three or four other men imbibing, and they weren't drinking punch. Pat was pouring from the bottle of bourbon and they were adding Coke and laughing it up. She passed on to the parlor, where she found Becky and Jim sitting together on a love seat. ("How appropriate," she thought.)

Jim started to offer her a seat but Clare pulled up a rocker and sat, with the food on her knees.

"You don't have anything to drink," he observed. "Punch?"

"I suppose I should taste it," she said.

When he left Becky said, "I was just telling him about the news Harry delivered last night."

"How did he react?"

"He was surprised, as was I. But he was still taking it all in when you came up."

Jim was back without delay. "The early run on the punch has slacked off," he said. "Here. Try this."

Clare cautiously took a sip and felt that sizzling burn that rum does to the throat, followed by a buzz that sets in for the evening.

"Thank you, I think," she said.

"My pleasure."

Emboldened by the drink, Clare said, "I needed this. I've just learned my sister is about to become a single woman."

"That's what she tells me," said Jim. "Harry wants a quick divorce, I take it."

"He made that pretty clear," Becky said.

"I understand you and your wife are separated, Jim," Clare barged ahead.

Blinking, Jim said, "I guess Becky told you ... she's gone back to Columbus."

"Well, I'm not trying to be a matchmaker ..."

"Clare!" said an embarrassed Becky.

"I'm just sayin' …

At that most opportune moment Clare's phone began vibrating. Taking it out of her pocket, she said, "Excuse me, it's Henry."

Becky's sigh of relief could almost be heard above the din as Clare sought a quieter corner of the house.

"Hi, sweetheart. You can probably tell the party after the funeral is in full sway," she said.

"That's pretty obvious. I hope you're having a good time. I'm home by myself and missing you and I just wanted to call and tell you."

"How sweet of you. Wow, this punch is strong."

"Sounds like it's stronger than my martini. Well, how are things going?"

"Fine. My folks are fine. Momma will be a lot less stressed now that Aunt Dora's funeral is over."

"What about Becky? Is she still treating you like the ugly sister?"

"Far from it. I've got a lot to tell you. But for now, just know that I've become her BFF."

"Her what?"

"Best Friend Forever. Henry, you really do need to get up to speed on social media chatter."

"I think I'll leave that to you. Are you still coming home tomorrow?"

"No, I think I'd better stay till Sunday, if I can change my ticket. So much has been going on with the funeral and the reception I haven't been able to spend much time with my folks. And Becky needs me."

"Well, I'll really be happy to have you back with me. But you know what you have to do. Just know that I love you."

"I love you, too, darling. Thanks for the call."

Seeing her punch cup empty, Clare headed for a refill, but paused on the way to make the rounds of the dining table. Everything had been pretty well picked over. She decided to try some of the desserts, beginning with Betty's carrot cake. She poured herself half a cup of punch and returned to Becky and Jim, who were both looking serious.

"What happened to the party mood? Clare asked.

"We've been talking about my new situation," Becky said.

"I've been thinking about what you said, Clare," Jim added.

"What did I say?"

"About matchmaking …"

"Oh, I'm sorry about that. It was the rum talking."

"Don't be sorry. It put an idea in my head."

"An idea?"

"Becky probably has told you that through her visits to the office with Elizabeth Ann we have become pretty close friends. We have even had some long talks about our respective marriages."

"Yes."

"We have both been pretty miserable. But with both of our spouses deciding to leave us that just seems to be a sign that maybe Becky and I are meant to be together."

Clare was rapidly sobering up. "I see what you mean, Jim. Let me ask you this: do you two have feelings for each other?"

"Yes, we do," they said simultaneously.

"I have become increasingly fond of your sister," Jim said.

"And it's obvious Elizabeth Ann is crazy about you," Clare said.

"She is a doll," Jim said. "I see lots of children, of course. But she is so special. And she and I hit it off from our first meeting. If I ever became a father I would want the child to be just like her ... except maybe a boy."

Becky and Clare avoided looking at each other, knowing what they knew.

"No wonder you were looking serious when I came back," Clare said. "You've been doing some serious thinking. Well, as I so recklessly said a while ago, I'm not trying to play Cupid, but from what I've seen of you, Jim, and knowing Becky like I do, I think you two would be a perfect match ... if you're ready to go that far in your relationship."

"With the world in the shape it's in today, we don't know what's coming tomorrow," Jim said. "If something seems right, it might be the time to seize the moment before losing the opportunity."

Clare bent down and said quietly to Jim, "Only you can decide what's right. But I would be happy to be your sister-in-law." She kissed him on the cheek and went to circulate among the crowd, muttering, "What's in this carrot cake?"

Clare spent the rest of the evening helping her mother and mingling with the guests. She had a surprise when she ran across Ted Bailey, who was her high school senior prom date. She remembered him as a bright student with a body built for athletics. But he preferred to play clarinet in the band. He was there with his wife, a mousy, shy girl he married right after graduation. Bailey gave Clare a card reading Theodore Bailey, PhD, and identifying him as president of a junior college in the county.

She saw no more of Becky and Jim until the evening was winding down and wives were collecting their dishes and their husbands. Her sister and the doctor were coming in from outdoors. "There was such a pretty moon we were sitting in the swing," Becky explained. "I really need to get going," Jim said.

Clare looked over his shoulder and inquired, "Didn't the minister come with you?"

"He left earlier. The Pettigrews offered him a ride. He's a nice guy and we have some things in common – age for one. He's a little younger than I am. But we're both beginning our careers in a small town."

"We're going to stay a while and help clean up," Becky said.

"Let me find your parents and tell them goodnight," Jim said as he walked away.

"Well?" said Clare, expectantly.

"We talked some more," said Becky. "His enthusiasm might have waned a bit, but he still sounded like he wants to move ahead."

"But he didn't propose?"

"No. But he asked me out to dinner tomorrow night. We're going up to Albany."

"That's good. It's too soon for you to be seen together and give the gossips around here something to dish about."

As he left, Jim stopped by long enough to tell Clare he was happy to have met her and he thanked her for her "good advice."

Becky remained at the farm about 45 minutes while she and Clare cleared off the dining table, helped wash and put away dishes, dumped the fruit from the punch bowl (all the punch had been consumed), put furniture back in place and ran the vacuum cleaner. When all that was done Becky went to the play room where she found Elizabeth Ann sound asleep on the cot that had been put in it for her to take naps.

Becky was about ready to find a bed for herself. "Momma," she said, "I hate to wake Elizabeth Ann. Do you mind if she spends the night? I'll be back in the morning."

"Of course not, dear. We always like to have our granddaughter with us."

"Goodnight, then," Becky said to Betty and Clare. "This was one of the best gatherings you all have ever had. It will be one to remember. See you tomorrow."

"I think it's my bedtime, too, Momma," Clare said. "And you'd better get some rest yourself. I think Daddy's already retired."

"I will," said Betty. "I'm going to sit down, put my feet up and have a nightcap first."

32

WHEN A RAY OF BRIGHT MORNING SUN streaming through the window aroused her, Clare dragged her tired body out of bed and found the bathroom. She madly searched the crowded medicine cabinet for a bottle of aspirin and quickly swallowed two, hoping to ease the pain throbbing in her head. It had been a long time since she had suffered this kind of hangover.

A hot shower helped. She did a hasty makeup routine, threw on her travel slacks and started downstairs, then remembered something. She wanted to talk to Betty about the Marmee doll so she got it off the closet shelf. She felt her way down the carpeted steps and headed for the kitchen, where she had a good guess she would find her mother.

"G'morning, Momma," she said.

Betty turned, her bloodshot eyes showing, and said quietly, "Good morning, baby. What's that you've got?"

She held the doll up, saying, "I saw it on the shelf of Becky's old room."

"It's one of your old dolls," Betty said.

"Not just one – it's Marmee. She probably was my favorite."

"Well, it was pretty special. When you left I gave it to Rebecca Jean. She didn't play with it very much."

Pouring herself a cup of coffee, Clare said, "Marmee is still special to me."

"Why's that?"

"You remember I told you I was in a play up where I live now. Well, it's a play based on *Little Women* and I'm playing the part of 'Marmee.'"

"I didn't care much for *Little Women*. Those girls were a little too wild," Betty said. "But I thought this was a well-made doll and she had a pretty dress – it's from the Madame Alexander line – Aunt Dora found it in an antique shop and she gave it to you for your birthday."

"When I was twelve. I'll never forget it. What are you going to do with her?"

"I don't know why I kept it – a memory of you, I suppose. It's yours, of course, although I don't know what you'd do with it now."

Clare had a passing thought of taking Marmee back home and making her a part of the decorating scheme. Then she had another idea.

"Maybe I'll see if Elizabeth Ann would like to have it," Clare said.

"That would be nice," Betty said. "She's old enough to appreciate good things.

Her mother took off her apron and said, "If you don't mind, fix yourself some breakfast. I don't feel too well. I didn't sleep much last night."

"I'm sorry to hear that," Clare said. She sort of knew how she felt.

"I kept thinking back to times I had spent with Aunt Dora. I'm going to miss her."

"I know. But she's in a better place."

"I'll be going there sometime myself."

"But not anytime soon."

"You never know."

"You go get off your feet. I'll have a bowl of cereal."

"There's eggs .. and bacon, if you want them. Or, there's some ham left over …"

"Cereal will be fine. "Where's Daddy?"

"I reckon he's out checking on things, like he does every morning."

"He seems to be in pretty good health."

"Yes, as far as we know. Well, I'm going to go sit a spell."

Clare was just finishing her shredded wheat when Becky drove up. Elizabeth Ann was first to come in the door. She had been playing outside and had joined her mother.

"Hi, Aunt Clare," she said brightly.

"And hello to you, sweetheart. G'morning, Becky."

"Hi, sis."

"Guess who's also got a hangover," Clare whispered, pointing to Betty, sitting in a recliner with her eyes closed.

Becky grabbed her daughter's hand. "Grandma's resting now, honey. You can see her later."

"Okay, I'll go to the play room."

"Momma said she didn't sleep very well," Clare said.

"Neither did I," said Becky. "I was too excited. And then Jim called right after I went to bed."

"Really!"

"He was excited, too. Said he couldn't wait for our dinner date tonight."

"I hope this works out for you, Becky."

"So do I."

They were both heading for the coffee pot when they heard sounds of people outside. Clare looked through the window and reported, "We've got visitors."

Betty had been jarred awake and she was on her way to the door to greet Adelaide Sprayberry and Cora Lovelady.

"Y'all come on in. I guess you come to get the dishes you brought the food in," Betty said.

They followed her into the kitchen. "Here's yours, Addy. And I want to tell you, your barbecue was as good as it always is. Cora, your sweet potato pie was outstanding," Betty said. "Won't y'all have a cup of coffee?"

The ladies launched into a gossip session about some of their dearest friends from the previous evening.

"Let's go out to the patio," said Betty. "I think it'll be cool enough."

Clare and Becky resumed their conversation about Jim's late night phone call.

"Did he say why he was calling?" Clare asked.

"He just wanted to talk. He said he wasn't sleepy and was still thinking about sitting in the swing with me in the moonlight."

"Did you talk long?"

"Oh, yes. I finally had to tell him I had to get to sleep – after I started yawning."

"And he was okay with that?"

"Yes. He apologized for keeping me up so late."

"So what are your plans for today?"

"Well, I thought I might go shopping for a new dress to wear tonight."

"In Shellville?"

"Hardly. I want something better than what they sell here. I was thinking about going to Albany."

"Hmmm. Could I go with you?"

"Sure. That would be wonderful."

"I can get a rental car there and drive to Atlanta and catch my return flight."

"Oh-h," Becky said. "I should drive you back."

"No, you need to be getting ready for your important date. I'll be fine."

"But I thought I heard you say something about changing plans and waiting till tomorrow to go back."

"That's what I told Henry. But people are going to be dropping in all day to see Momma, so I won't have much, if any, time with her. I might as well go on back. Are you ready to get around and go?

113

"Well, sure, I'll ask Momma to keep Elizabeth Ann for a couple of hours."

"I'll go pack and be right back."

"Okay. Oh, here come some more of Momma's friends."

Clare made a quick call to Henry as she was putting her things in the bag. He was pleased to know she had changed her mind about staying longer.

She and Becky went out to the patio to tell Betty about their plans. She introduced Clare to Mrs. Sprayberry, Mrs. Lovelady, Joyce Merrifield and Lillian Browning.

"Do you have to leave so soon?" Betty asked. "I was hoping you'd stay a few days longer."

"I'm just glad I was able to get away for this long. I've got a lot going on in Wilmington."

"I don't know how you keep up with that fast living up there, dear," said Mrs. Browning.

She gave her mother a hug and a kiss and started to go. She met Pat coming back from his rounds. Seeing her suitcase he said, "Are you leaving?"

"Yes, Daddy," she said. "I'm sorry, but I really need to get back."

They exchanged a warm embrace. "Take care of yourself. I love you," Clare said.

"I love you too, baby," he said, almost tearing up.

There wasn't too much time for Becky and Clare to talk in the half-hour drive to Albany. Clare wished her sister good luck on finding a perfect dress for the evening and made her promise to keep her up to date on developments in her quickly changing life.

33

CLARE WAS HAPPY TO SEE Henry waiting for her in the terminal after she landed. She was eager to get back home so rather than eat out they picked up some carryout. At home they opened some wine and settled in for the evening. She gave him an abbreviated version of activities associated with the funeral of Aunt Dora but gave him full details of Becky's marital and extramarital misadventures. He marveled at the devious plot the two sisters had hatched in a desperate effort to conceal a family scandal.

Maybe it was the wine but the whole scenario began to seem unreal to Clare. Or maybe she just wanted to put the sorry mess out of her mind.

"You know, maybe I'm thinking in theatrical terms, but with the experience of the past week I have assumed a new role – as a big sister. So what's been happening in your life?" she asked Henry.

He refilled glasses and sat back down. With a heavy sigh he said, "I also had a secret revealed to me."

Clare suspected she knew what was coming and had a moment of regret for not telling him her suspicions. "What is it?" she said.

"It appears my business partner is in over his head with some heavy debts."

Clare quickly adjusted her reaction. "He doesn't know about the gambling," she thought.

"Business debts or personal?" she asked.

"Personal, I believe. I overheard him talking on the phone. He seemed to be pleading with someone, almost fearfully, to give him more time to settle what he owed. What really made my ears perk up was him saying, "Please. I can't let this get out. It would ruin my marriage and my reputation.""

Clare took a long sip of wine, looked Henry in the eye and confessed. "I've been meaning to tell you this for some time," she said. "I strongly suspect Phil Sterling has a serious addiction to gambling. It sounds like the mob is moving in on him."

"The mob?"

"You've said yourself that Phil had been acting strangely," she said.

"Yes, long absences from the office as well as that evening in Charlotte."

Clare decided to tell him all she had observed, beginning with the evening in Myrtle Beach when she saw him coming off a floating casino. She mentioned the times in Wilmington and again in New Orleans when the men in dark suits had met with him, leaving him obviously greatly upset.

"I wanted to share this with you," she said, "but there wasn't any conclusive proof and I didn't want to worry you or plant doubt in your mind about your partner."

"I appreciate that. Do you think Barbara knows?"

"She has not shown any indication and I haven't brought up the subject with her. They deliberately keep their personal financial dealings separate."

"I'm really sad about this. Phil is a hard-driving businessman and very competitive, so he has made some enemies through the years. But I haven't doubted his integrity, up to now."

"What do you mean by that?"

"His desperate situation makes me wonder if he has been dipping into the business profits to cover his gambling losses."

"That would really make me angry, considering all the money you've put into Sterling Homes – not to mention all your time and devotion."

"I've tried to keep an eye on the books and if he did anything like that I think I would know." Henry thought a minute, then said: "But there is that separate account that Phil set up to buy land for that Skyway scheme of his. He's the only one that has access to those records."

"He could be selling some of the land he bought and using those profits to keep the mobsters away from his door."

Henry leaned back, stared at the ceiling and said, "I feel like I can't let this go on, but what can I do about it?"

"First of all, you don't have to bear this burden alone. I'm already into it pretty deep so I'll do what I can to help. Let's just be alert for any new evidence and if you become convinced he's taking money from your partnership for his personal use, you'll need to confront him."

"All right. I feel better sharing this with you," Henry said.

"And me, you. Right now, I'd like to go up and get ready for bed," Clare said, heading for the stairs. Looking back over her shoulder she added, "and show you how much I missed being away from you."

34

SINCE THE WEEKEND STILL HAD a day to go, Clare and Henry decided to take a drive down to Carolina Beach. That was one of the places Zach Bacharach said he was checking out as a potential location for exterior filming of his TV series *Busboys*.

It was a day that was almost as perfect as a day could get: brilliant sunshine, pure blue skies and a pleasant, gentle breeze. Shorts and flip-flops were the order of the day for attire.

"On days like this it would be nice to have a convertible," Clare said, as they left Landfall and headed south.

"Yes, but I think that's going to have to wait until we can have a three-car garage. But I do have some plans in mind."

"Oh, really. Please tell me."

"I'm enjoying the real estate business and I think I've gotten to be pretty good at managing the Sterling properties – which I've had to do a lot. But what I'd really like is to build a new development and promote it as an ideal place to live in the Wilmington area. One of the first things I would do is to build a dream home for us."

"How exciting, Henry! I had no idea, but I love it. How soon can you see this happening?"

"Not right away, I'm afraid. But I have a file of things I've thought of that need to be done to get to that point, starting with finding the right location."

"That would be of utmost importance," Clare said.

When they got to U.S. 421 it was a scant half hour's drive to what the tourist bureaus call Pleasure Island, or sometimes Paradise Island, a strip of land less than three miles across at its widest point, narrowing to half a mile at its southern end. It features more than seven miles of Atlantic coastal beaches. It is separated from the mainland by the Cape Fear River.

Arriving in Carolina Beach, the largest of two towns that attract vacationers who enjoy boating, fishing and other beach activities, the touring couple headed for the boardwalk to find Britt's Donut Shop, a family-operated business for 39 years. It is so popular it has a fan club. Regular customers showed up to wait in line for the doors to open at 8:30 a.m. By the time Henry and Clare got to the small shop with the blue-and-white-striped awning it was a little less crowded – not that they were in a great hurry anyway.

"I love the aroma!" Clare said as she inhaled the delicious smell of fresh, hot doughnuts. Regulars know not to look for filled, sprinkled or other varieties. Britt's built its reputation on the simple glazed version. A sign on the wall read: "Voted America's #2 Favorite Independent Small-Town Donut Shop" and they could see why when they took their first bite. Henry had ordered a dozen and two cups of coffee, and after reading some newspaper and magazine clippings and other displays of the shop's fame on the wall they took their purchases out to enjoy while strolling the boardwalk.

The sound of the surf rolling in mixed with the squeals of youngsters playing on the sand aroused memories of a former life in California, but Clare had no regrets. She had made a new beginning and it was a good one.

As they walked leisurely down the boardwalk, popping into shops along the way, breathing in the invigorating sea air, they felt totally at ease. After about an hour they returned to the car and continued their drive south to a much smaller community, Kure Beach. Its three miles of beach were much less crowded than Carolina Beach. A center of activity was the fishing pier, which jutted more than 700 feet into the ocean. They walked out on the pier hoping to see a school of dolphin that a tour guide had mentioned. But this wasn't the day for that.

Driving further down toward the Fort Fisher State Historic Site, marked by twisted live oaks on that part of the beach, they saw a van and some cars with people walking around pointing and actively engaged in conversation. As they drew closer, Clare could make out the writing on the side of the van: ZeeBee Productions.

"That's Zach's company," she said, and then spotting a familiar figure wearing riding pants and a beret, shouted, "There's Zach! I'll bet he's scouting out locations for his new TV series."

They stopped and got his attention. He was delighted to see them.

"Clare! Henry! What a surprise," he said. "I think I might have discovered exactly what I've been looking for as a spot for the restaurant where the busboys work."

"Good," Clare said.

"This quiet little town has some marvelous views and gorgeous sunsets. There are about 2,000 fulltime residents. It will be easy to find extras when we need them. I can lease a small parcel of land and construct a shell building with the exterior appearance of an eating place. And guess what? There's an aquarium here that has sharks!"

Zach obviously was thrilled with that discovery.

"I have to ask," Clare said, "why is that so important?"

"Because we can film the fish in captivity rather than go out into the ocean, which would be more costly, not to mention dangerous," he said.

"Well, congratulations," Henry said. "I wish you well on your new production."

"I'm about ready to get going," Zach said. "All I need to do is finish casting. And that leads me to this question. Clare, could I persuade you to play the role of the restaurant owner?"

"Wow!" said Clare. "Are you serious?"

"I'm just as serious as diabetes," Zach said. "I don't know of anybody who could do a better job."

"But I'm already doing TV ads and performing at the Tri-County Playhouse. I'm not sure I could take that on."

"Look," Zach said. "It wouldn't take too much of your time. We'll shoot several episodes on the same day. The interior scenes will be done on a sound stage in Wilmington and the exteriors here at Kure beach. And you know it takes less than an hour to get here."

"So are you telling me that doing this role would take only one or two days a month?"

"Three or four at the most."

"Henry, what do you think?"

"I have no doubt you can play the role. And it sounds as if it wouldn't require an inordinate amount of time. I know you'd enjoy it, so I'd say do it."

"I guess that settles it, then," Clare said. "When do I start?"

"I think I can have all the preliminaries wrapped up in a couple of weeks. I'll go ahead and get the first scripts to you so you can begin learning your lines. Of course, there'll be cue cards."

"Well, thank you so much for giving me this opportunity, Zach."

"Not at all. You're really doing me a favor," he said.

"Henry, I think we need to celebrate. Let's go get some seafood."

Clare could hardly wait to get back to Wilmington and share her good news, but they stopped at Michael's long enough to have a bowl of this restaurant's prize winning seafood chowder.

Arriving back home in late afternoon, Clare started to call Barbara and Gloria but noticed she had a message from her sister.

119

"I'd better see what Becky has to report," she said. "I'll put it on speaker so you can keep up to date on this soap opera.

"Hi, Becky. Got your phone message. How was your date?"

"Absolutely wonderful. Jim took me to one of the finest restaurants in Albany. We had a marvelous meal. And we had a good talk about our future."

"Details. I want to know details," Clare said.

"I don't know how he did it so quickly, but he told me he had spoken to an attorney and he's going to begin divorce proceedings right away."

"Really! Your guy certainly doesn't waste any time."

"It's something he was going to do anyway, but knowing how we feel about each other he was eager to become a free man. And here's the really good news."

"What's that?"

"His attorney told him that in Georgia it's possible get an uncontested divorce in 31 days."

"Unbelievable! And since Jim's wife left him she would have no reason to slow things down."

"From what Jim said, all she would be interested in is a generous settlement."

"And being a doctor, he should be able to provide that."

"I'm sure."

"So it looks as if things are going your way."

"Right. But Harry and I still have to end our marriage."

"He should be agreeable to a quicky divorce. As I see it the main thing you two have to work out is a mutually satisfactory child support and custody arrangement for Elizabeth Ann."

"That's true. You and I know we can't let this drag out very long. How can I get Harry to start moving on a divorce?"

"Well, offhand I would say you could just ask him, based on what he told you, does he want to start divorce proceedings or would he rather you do it. You said he was coming to your house to start getting his things out. Maybe you could bring it up then."

"Yes. I could call and ask him when he's coming."

"You don't want him to think you're in a rush. It's just that you'd want to know when to expect him so you'd be sure to be at home."

"He has a key, of course."

"Of course, but I think he'd understand that you'd want to be there with Elizabeth Ann so she could see her father."

"Okay. That's what I'll do. I don't know how in the world I can ever tell Momma and Daddy."

"That will be tough, all right. We've got some time to think about that — but not much."

"And right now what I've got to think about is this baby I'm carrying."

35

CLARE AND BARBARA met Gloria for lunch at Elijah's, a highly-rated seafood restaurant on the Wilmington waterfront. They opted for a table on the deck, hoping the large green umbrella would adequately block the sun's rays. They kept their stylish hats on anyway. Their decision to dine al fresco afforded the women an excellent view of the Cape Fear River and the bridge Gloria had crossed coming from Brunswick Forest.

When the server took drink orders, Bloody Mary was the choice of all three. They immediately plunged into conversation, as if they had been apart for months instead of a few days.

Before she reported on her trip Clare asked about the play performance she missed.

"We had a larger audience," Gloria said. "The newspaper review helped and I would guess those who saw it the first weekend gave it a boost through word of mouth."

"How was Vicky Potts in my role?" Clare asked.

"She turned in an adequate performance," Gloria said tactfully.

"I thought she was surprisingly good," Barbara said, inviting a frown from her best friend, Clare.

"Marmee isn't that strong a role," Gloria said, speaking as the director. "The 'little women' really are the ones who carry the show. The young girls in the cast are doing quite well."

"And Nancy's son, who plays the part of Laurie, was outstanding," Barbara said.

"Let me ask you something, Clare. Do you want to continue with the Marmee role or had you rather switch with Vicky and play Aunt March."

Clare, somewhat taken aback, said, "why, I hadn't thought about making a change."

"The only reason I brought it up is that while Aunt March is a much smaller role it offers more opportunity for acting, especially in the opening scene, which would allow you to display a flair for comedy. We're still feeling our way and this would give you a chance to broaden your talents. Plus, you wouldn't have many lines to learn between now and Friday."

The drinks had arrived and Clare took a long sip of the spicy concoction in the tall frosty glass and thought about what Gloria had said.

"When tryouts were coming up I just knew I had to have the part of Marmee," she said. "Other than the fact that she is a principal figure in the story, I just had a nagging feeling there was something special about me playing that role, like some forgotten memory locked away in my mind. During my trip I unlocked that memory."

She related the story of finding the Marmee doll in the closet and how thrilled she was, but also that she was totally willing to leave it there for Elizabeth Ann to have.

"Now that I know what led to my fervor about getting the part, I have to say I don't feel any particular attachment to it. And since Vicky handled it well I'm fine with letting her have it and I'll take over Aunt March, Glo."

"That settles that," Gloria said. "Now, let's hear about your trip."

Clare avoided saying anything about her sister's dilemma. She quickly reviewed the 24 hours involving the evening at the funeral home, the funeral and the gathering at the family home afterwards. Then she plunged into what happened after she got home.

"I do have some exciting news," she said. "Henry and I drove down to Carolina Beach yesterday and who should we see farther down at Kure Beach but Zach Bacharach. He found a spot that he thinks will be perfect for exterior filming for his new TV mini-series …"

"The one about the oceanside restaurant and the young people who work there?" Barbara asked.

"Yes. And guess what? He wants me to be in the show!"

"That is exciting," said Gloria.

"Are you going to be the restaurant owner?" said Barbara.

"Yes! And shooting begins in two weeks."

Clare told her companions what she and Zach discussed about the limited time she would spend on the show, making it possible to continue her TV ads for Sterling Homes as well as be in future productions of Tri-County Players.

"That brings up a subject I wanted to talk to you two about: future productions," Gloria said. "For balance I originally thought it would be good to follow *Good Wives* with a musical, and I'm still thinking in that direction. But I can't decide on a show that would be good to do – one that we could find enough local talent, acting and singing, for a complete cast. Also do we have enough resources to build the right set, as well as find enough appropriate costumes."

"There is a lot involved, all right,"Barbara said.

"And we still don't have an abundance of money. So here's what I've decided – and I want to know what you (nodding to both Clare and Barbara) think about the idea. I'm about ready to abandon the idea of a musical in favor of a mixture of scenes from several popular Broadway shows down through the years ..."

"A musical revue," Clare said enthusiastically.

"Right," said Gloria. "It would be a fairly inexpensive production. I could provide the musical accompaniment on the piano. I doubt we could find enough local musicians to put together an orchestra in the short time we have. And I believe we can produce an entertaining program."

"And selecting the cast would draw in a different array of talent from the three counties," Clare offered.

"Yes, but I also want to try to make use of the talent we've already identified with our opening production. You, for instance, Clare. With your experience in doing cruise ship shows you ought to be a natural."

"I do enjoy singing and dancing," she said.

"The young actors portraying members of the March family certainly might be possibilities," Barbara said, "and they would know other students who are musically inclined."

"Well, then, I'll move ahead on plans. I welcome your suggestions for songs from Broadway shows," Gloria said.

With perfect timing, the server arrived with their food orders: crab cakes for Clare and Barbara and shrimp and sea scallops for Gloria. They turned their conversation to matters unrelated to the theater and Clare managed to work in an inquiry to Barbara about Phil.

"Henry's concerned that he's feeling a lot of stress," she said.

"Phil is just not himself, that's for sure," Barbara said. "I do worry about him. He has a latent heart condition that could be aggravated by overworking and dealing with stress. But there's not a lot you can do with a hard-driving businessman."

"One thing about Ben," Gloria said. "He does get quite a bit of exercise, playing golf and engaging in other outdoor activities."

"We do need to encourage our guys to take good care of themselves," Clare said, hoping that would hit home with Barbara.

36

GLORIA GOT MOVING on the new concept for a second production at the new theater. Later that week the local newspaper carried a story by Alicia Swift announcing tryouts:

"On the heels of a successful opening at its new theater, Tri-County Players is moving on to a second production. Director Gloria Levine said the company will follow the play, *Good Wives*, with a musical performance.

"'We will be presenting a musical revue, featuring scenes and numbers from some of the most popular Broadway shows that have entertained audiences down through the years,' she said.

"Tryouts are scheduled Saturday at the theater beginning at 9 a.m.

"'We're looking for a variety of ages – from early teens, through high school and college. We also need young adults as well as, shall we say, those who remember some of the shows we'll be reprising, like *Oklahoma!*, which opened in New York City on March 31, 1943,' Levine said.

"'We are very fortunate to have a wide array of talent to draw on in our schools, and UNCW is an excellent resource,' she added. 'We also will attempt to utilize the abilities of the actors who gave such outstanding performances in *Good Wives*.

"As with the last production, Levine said, volunteers will be needed for set construction and other non-acting jobs.

"Asked about music for the musical show, Levine, who was a concert pianist in New York City before turning to directing, said she would provide the accompaniment on a grand piano.

"Some of the shows under consideration include: *Music Man, Hello, Dolly, My Fair Lady, Oliver, Annie, Damn Yankees, Guys and Dolls, West Side Story, Les Miserables, Phantom of the Opera*, and a number of Rodgers and Hammerstein hits.

"For up-to-date news about Wilmington's theatrical scene, read my column."

Gloria decided to have condensed scenes from four or five shows for the first part of the performance and single selections from a number of shows for the second part.

As the program shaped up, Levine found a remarkable 11-year-old, coincidentally a redhead named Annie, to sing the title song from this popular musical; a sensational baritone, a voice coach at a local private music school, for solos from *Man of La Mancha* and other shows and to pair with Clare on songs from *Oklahoma!, Anything Goes* and *Promises Promises*; a barbershop quartet to do tunes from *Music Man* and *Damn Yankees*; a troupe of youngsters who doubled as the orphans in *Oliver* and the Trapp family singers in *The Sound of Music*; and very important, a local dance school owner who became the show's choreographer.

Besides Clare, Gloria involved the actors from *Good Wives*, including Vicky Potts, who turned out to have a robust voice similar to Ethel Merman, and Jonathan Bartholomew, whose resonant bass matched Ezio Pinza's in *South Pacific*. The two fit well for duets from *Annie Get Your Gun* and *Gigi*.

Rock musical *Hair* and *West Side Story* were natural choices because they gave a chance for high-schoolers to style their locks and they were certain to tap the memories of the rebellious '50s and '60s. Gloria hoped she could round up enough skilled tap dancers to form *A Chorus Line*.

Meanwhile, Clare and Barbara shopped the local antique stores and consignment shops for props and costumes fitting the various eras represented in the show. At one place Clare found and couldn't resist buying a red shoulder bag similar to the one she lost in the California mudslide that destroyed her fabulous villa.

Excitement was building about this show in the Tri-County Players inner circle that was not present for the first production and Gloria was thrilled.

37

REHEARSALS FOR *A Broadway Musical Revue* weren't as intensive as for *Good Wives*. The entire cast did not have to be present except for a couple of run-throughs for staging purposes just before opening. That was good for Clare, who was busy learning her lines for the first few episodes of *Busboys*.

Zach Bacharach had rented space in one of the studios in Wilmington where a set depicting the seaside restaurant was built. Fortunately most of Clare's shots were scheduled in the studio. Zach had a second crew shooting scenes of the young players – busboys and waitresses – surfing, swimming and otherwise having a good time at Kure beach during their off hours. Clare and the actor playing her cook did make one trip to the beach and were taped together and separately in random scenes outside the replica of the restaurant and watching the young actors enjoying the surf.

Clare enjoyed the experience very much, but as she told Henry, "I really have to get used to jumping around in the script. It's a lot different from a play where the story proceeds naturally, as in real life. With movies and this TV series the story is put together in the editing process."

"Just don't wear yourself too thin," he told her. "How's the stage production coming along?"

"Fine. And for me it's a welcome break from the TV role. By the way, I had a surprise on the first day of rehearsals. I saw Vicky Potts coming toward me and I braced myself for another load of sarcasm. But instead she was very pleasant. She shook my hand and actually apologized for her behavior on our first meeting."

"What came over her?"

"She wanted to thank me for allowing her to take over the role of Marmee in *Good Wives*. And she complimented me on my acting."

"Well, what do you know. And are you liking your parts in the new show?"

"Yes. Gloria has paired me with a local voice teacher who's a very talented baritone. He and I are doing duets from *Anything Goes*, *Oklahoma!* and *Promises, Promises*. I also have a few solos sprinkled in the latter part of the program."

"You also mentioned some dancing, I believe?"

"Yes, I had to brush off my tap dancing skills and get some appropriate shoes. Glo is having me do a slow tap in the opening number."

"I can hardly wait to see you in tights and those fishbowl stockings."

"Fishnet, Henry. Fishnet!"

"Whatever. Either way, everybody's going to be looking at you."

"But I only have eyes for you, dear. Say, how's Phil doing?"

"He has been a great mood. He must have hit a winning streak."

"Let's hope he pays off some of his debt instead of gambling away his winnings."

"That would be good – both for the business and for his health."

38

ALICIA SWIFT'S PRE-PRODUCTION ARTICLES generated high interest in the Tri-County Players' first musical endeavor and it was, as they say in the trade, a "smash hit."

The show began with the curtains opened only wide enough to see a gleaming white grand piano spotlighted in the background at center stage. Gloria Levine, clad in a black velvet gown and wearing a stunning diamond necklace, strode through the opening to generous applause and welcomed the audience.

"We are enormously grateful for the reception given to our new theater's inaugural production. Tonight you will see an entirely different kind of performance. You've witnessed our players' acting skills and now we want to entertain you with an evening of song and dance. We're featuring tunes from the Broadway stage – a variety of music going back to the early days and extending into the present.

"The first part of our show highlights the history of Broadway musicals, showing the distinctive changes that have taken place down through the years. We begin with the 1934 hit, *Anything Goes*, which has been described as 'a shining example of classic musical theater, complete with amazing tap numbers … and eminently hummable songs … courtesy of the unforgettable score by Cole Porter. We follow with three memorable productions by the team of Richard Rodgers and Oscar Hammerstein II. They revolutionized the American musical and their music and lyrics made a lasting impact. One of their alltime favorites from the '40s is *South Pacific*. Its charm is so enduring it has spawned countless revivals.

"Another classic from that decade is *Oklahoma!*. It opened on March 31, 1943 and ran for an unprecedented 2,212 performances. Furthering the development of the 'book musical', a play with music and dance integrated into a story with dramatic highlights, *Oklahoma!* also broke new ground with Agnes de Mille's choreography, including a marvelous 'dream sequence' ballet. We won't attempt to recreate that tonight because of time constraints, although we do have some very talented dancers in the cast. In the '50s, *The Sound of Music* captured the attention – and the love – of audiences everywhere. It was a multiple Tony Award-winning musical and after it was adapted for motion pictures won five Academy Awards.

"Our evolution of Broadway musicals takes us into the '60s and the controversial rock musical *Hair*, a bold expression of hippie counterculture and the sexual revolution of those times. The show's profanity, depiction of drug use, general irreverence and its nude scene generated much comment. We don't want any members of our cast catching cold so they will not be taking it all off in tonight's performance.

"The remainder of the show, following a 15-minute intermission, will be a fast-moving presentation of hit songs from a variety of musicals you've probably seen on stage or on screen. Now, please turn off your phones, put away your cameras and other recording devices, sit back and enjoy the Tri-County Players' production of *A Broadway Musical Revue*."

Gloria then went to the piano and astounded the audience with an overture comprising a medley of Broadway hit songs. As the applause subsided, with only a short run of the keys as an introduction, Clare stepped into the spotlight and began a slow, sultry version of the title song from *Anything Goes*, gradually speeding up to normal time. The curtain opened fully revealing a chorus line of young men and women in sailor costumes singing the lyrics while Clare did her tap dance. After that number baritone Brad Harlow joined Clare for the playful "You're the Top."

Jonathan Bartholomew, Mr. March of *Good Wives*, unveiled his mellow deep voice with "Some Enchanted Evening" from *South Pacific* and the male sailors from the opening number sang, "There Is Nothing Like a Dame."

A beautiful romantic ballad brought Clare and Brad back to the stage to sing "People Will Say We're in Love" followed by a full chorus doing a lusty rendition of "Oklahoma!" during which Clare made a quick costume change and returned as Maria, coaching the Von Trapp children in "Do, Re, Mi". Some adult singers joined in for the title song of *The Sound of Music*.

The younger members of the cast drew spontaneous applause appearing in costumes of the 50s and 60s to close out the first part of the show with "Age of Aquarius" from *Hair* featuring Jim Galloway, who had received good reviews as Laurie (Theodore Laurence) in *Good Wives*.

The theater buzzed with patrons excitedly talking about the display of talent they had enjoyed and when the lights dimmed they quickly went back to their seats to enjoy the rest of the show.

With Glo playing strains from "A Chorus Line" the curtain opened slowly on 10 men and women dancing with perfect precision while Brad sang the show's most well-known tune, "One." The scene shifts swiftly to two racetrack touts (right out of Damon Runyon) singing the title song from *Guys and Dolls* followed by a quartet harmonizing on "Heart" from *Damn Yankees*.

Clare as Eliza Doolittle and Jonathan as Prof. Henry Higgins performed a crowd-pleasing version of "The Rain in Spain" from *My Fair Lady* and took short bows to make way for the young boys in the cast, dressed in the ragged clothes of orphans, singing "Food, Glorious Food" from *Oliver*.

Jim Galloway drew an enthusiastic audience response as Harold Hill doing the scene-setting number "Ya Got Trouble" from *The Music Man*. A full chorus greeted an elegantly-gowned Vicky Potts with the title song from *Hello, Dolly*.

Then her duet partner, Jonathan, stirred the audience with a powerful solo, "The Impossible Dream" from *Man of La Mancha* and then it was time once again for Clare and Brad, doing "I'll Never Fall in Love Again" from *Promises Promises*.

No musical revue would be complete without some tunes from *West Side Story* — "America" and "Tonight." And Jonathan and Vicky entertained the audience with "I Remember It Well" from Lerner and Loewe's *Gigi*.

The child star of the show, 11-year-old Margaret Bryan, had the audience in the palm of her hand with her delivery of "Tomorrow" from the musical *Annie*. Shifting back to a less cheery setting, baritone Brad, in appropriate costume, charmed the crowd with "Music of the Night" from *Phantom of the Opera*.

A "Jersey Boys" quartet did an upbeat set of tunes from the Frankie Valli group of the 1960's, followed by a powerful rendition by the entire cast of "Do You Hear the People Sing?" from *Les Miserables*. They remained onstage while Vicky Potts gave life to Ethel Merman leading the group with a rousing performance of the Irving Berlin classic, "There's No Business Like Show Business" to end the show.

As the singers and dancers took their bows the audience gave them a long standing ovation. The loudest applause was saved for Gloria Levine.

39

THE REVIEWS WERE GOOD and the show got better with each performance with the cast playing to a full house and receiving enthusiastic receptions. On the second weekend Gloria added some introductions to her opening remarks. Among those she spotlighted were Zach and the four young actors playing the roles of the *Busboys* – Clare's starring TV vehicle.

As word spread, *A Broadway Musical Revue* had a better boxoffice appeal than *Good Wives* and that cheered the founders of Tri-County Players, as well as their financial backers. Envelopes inside the playbills began to come in with checks from individual patrons. Many enclosed notes of appreciation for the formation of a new theater company.

Clare sandwiched in tapings of the TV series and ads for Sterling Homes, which meant some long days. Henry grew concerned and advised her to cut back on her commitments. But she was enjoying all of her activities because she was building a new career.

"This is a year of new roles for me," she said one evening when both she and Henry were free. "I've revived myself as a daughter and a sister in real life and I've become an actor on stage and on TV. I've taken on new challenges and in contrast to my losses in California I'm actually becoming victorious. It's an exhilarating feeling.'

"I'm very happy for you, Clare," Henry said. "I just don't want you to overdo yourself."

"I do appreciate your concern, my love, and I promise to pace myself. What about Phil? Is he any less stressed?"

"It's up and down. Next week he's making a business trip to western North Carolina – some place called Murphy."

Clare had a thoughtful look on her face. "That sounds familiar. Oh, I know. I saw an item in the paper – or maybe it was on TV – there's a new casino opening there."

"I thought his business trip excuse sounded fishy," Henry said. "But it's hard to believe he would drive that far just to find a new place to gamble."

"One of the cruise ships where I worked had a casino. It drew a large number of passengers on the first two days of the trip but not so many after that. I asked the cruise director about that and he told me that casino operators make it easier at the beginning for people to win at the tables and slots to get them hooked. Seasoned gamblers like Phil know this so they see it as a way to make some heavy winnings. A new casino opening offers the same opportunity."

"Again, I hope he makes enough to pay down his debt."

"So do I. Excuse me, I need to make a quick check of my emails before we settle in," Clare said. She went to a spare bedroom they used as an office and Henry headed to the bar to mix a pitcher of martinis. They were ready to pour when she returned.

"Well, I heard from Becky. She says divorce proceedings for both couples are under way and that both she and Jim soon will be free to get married."

"Sounds like the plan of the co-conspirators is working," Henry said sarcastically.

"I've got my fingers crossed," Clare said. "But there's still the problem of explaining all this to our parents." Raising her glass she added, "Oh, well. Let's celebrate anyway."

40

AFTER THE THIRD AND FINAL successful weekend of *A Broadway Musical Revue* Barbara invited Clare, Nancy and Gloria to lunch at the Landfall Country Club. The Sterlings always received special treatment at the club and this day was no exception. The women were seated at a choice table with a sweeping view of the well-kept grounds. By prearrangement a waiter brought a tray with four frosty copper mugs and served the drinks to the four women.

"What a surprise," Clare said.

"How nice," said Gloria.

"What is this?" asked Nancy.

"I thought we should celebrate the success of Tri-County Players with a round of Moscow Mules," Barbara explained. "To us!" she added, raising her mug.

The first sip brought a chorus of approval.

"This is good. What's in it?" Nancy inquired.

Clare volunteered: "Vodka, lime juice and ginger beer. It's a drink that has become quite popular in the past few years."

"It's part of a revival of the classic cocktail," Gloria added. "That was very much in evidence when we left New York.

"You sound quite knowledgeable about this drink, Clare," said Barbara. "Educate us adventurous drinkers."

"Well, if you really want to know. But let's get our orders in for lunch."

After the waiter left the table, Clare began to recite the history of the Moscow Mule, which she had learned while living in the Los Angeles area.

"First of all, a mule is a drink made with ginger beer. The other part of the name – Moscow – comes from associating vodka with Russia. The truth is very little Russian vodka is sold in the U.S."

"That's interesting," said Nancy.

Holding up her mug, Clare said, "This is the product of an accidental but quite brilliant piece of marketing. And it happened years ago – in 1941. There are many stories about the moment of creation. The one I heard goes like this.

John Martin of Heublein had acquired the Smirnoff brand but the market wasn't ready for it. One day Martin stepped into the Cock 'n' Bull bar on Sunset Boulevard in L.A. to meet his friend Jack Morgan, the bar manager. Morgan was having a hard time selling his homemade ginger beer. They decided, perhaps with the aid of a bartender, to mix vodka and ginger beer together with a large dose of ice cubes and some lime juice."

"So that was the birth of the Moscow Mule?" Barbara said.

"That's what I heard one evening at the Cock 'n' Bull bar. John Martin not only was a co-inventor but he also applied his genius to marketing the new drink. He bought one of the first Polaroid cameras and traveled around to bars photographing bartenders holding a bottle of Smirnoff in one hand and a Moscow Mule in the other. His efforts sparked a craze."

"What about the mug?" Nancy asked.

"There are different versions of that story, too. The one I like is that a friend of Martin and Morgan had inherited a large collection of copper mugs and wanted to get rid of them — just as these two men wanted to market their products. Needless to say the novel drink helped vodka replace gin as the 'white' liquor of choice until the Cold War turned Americans against anything that suggested the Soviet Union. But the cocktail revolution of the early 2000s brought it back."

"And aren't we glad," Gloria said, summoning the waiter for refills.

Shyly, Nancy said, "I'm not much of a drinker. But I like this."

"We don't want to encourage you to drink if you don't want to," Clare said.

"No, it's not that. It's just that my father was a minister and we didn't have alcohol in the house. And as the preacher's daughter I didn't want to do anything publicly that would embarrass my family. When I went away to college I dared to experiment with beer but didn't really like it, so I abstained from drinking for the most part."

"So you never experienced a Rusty Nail?" asked Barbara.

"Actually I did," said Nancy. "I had to get a tetanus shot."

Her companions couldn't refrain from laughing. Clare explained. "We don't intend to make fun of you, Nancy. But to us drinkers, a Rusty Nail is a cocktail made with Scotch and Drambuie, a Scotch liqueur."

"You know, thinking back, I tried a lot of funny-sounding drinks in my younger years," Barbara said. "I used to love Grasshoppers."

"I've heard of chocolate-covered grasshoppers, but that's not a drink," a puzzled Nancy said.

"A Grasshopper is indeed a drink, made from green crème de menthe, white crème de cacao and cream," Clare said. "I went on a Stinger jag once. That's white crème de menthe and brandy. I wouldn't do that now."

"Phil and I spent a week in Puerto Rico after we got married and I couldn't get enough of Pina Coladas," Barbara said.

Clare told Nancy, "Rum, coconut cream and pineapple juice. I still enjoy a Margarita made with good quality tequila with a Mexican meal."

"And there's nothing like a Bloody Mary to start off a Sunday brunch – not too much vodka and the tomato juice has to be seasoned just right," Barbara said.

"If you prefer orange juice," said Gloria, "you can have a Screwdriver, a Tequila Sunrise, a Fuzzy Navel or a Harvey Wallbanger."

"Good grief," Nancy said. "How did that last one get such a name?"

"From a California surfer who had one too many and kept stumbling into walls," Clare said wisely.

Nancy sighed. "You ladies certainly have spent more time in cocktail lounges than I have. But I do remember one time that I had a drink called a Shirley Temple."

When the four theater founders finally got serious they reviewed the state of the enterprise and talked about future plans.

"Whatever we do, it's going to take money," Gloria said. "Now that we've got our feet on the ground and people in the Wilmington area are getting to know about us, I think we ought to put on a major fundraising event."

"That's a good idea, Glo," Barbara said. "But I'd like to see it be something different – not the standard cocktail party."

"Although the three of you have certainly demonstrated your expertise," Nancy said.

"I think it needs to be an event where everybody can have a good time and feel motivated to write big checks."

Clare had said nothing up to this point. She had been thinking.

"During my campaign for governor one of my more imaginative backers threw a casino party," she said.

"How did that work?" Gloria asked.

"He had it in his home. It was almost large enough to be a gambling palace. It was a fancy dress affair. He rented tables for poker, blackjack and craps …"

"Excuse me?" said Nancy.

"Shooting dice. Also roulette wheels and other equipment. He had a committee of volunteers who played the roles of dealers and operators."

Barbara inquired, "How was the money raised?"

"I believe volunteers sold tickets which entitled the partygoers to light food, drinks and a certain amount of play money," Clare said.

"That sounds like fun but it would be an awful lot of work," Nancy said.

"Wait a minute," said Barbara. "I think I heard Phil mention a place in Wilmington that does this kind of fundraiser for charities."

"Good," Clare said. "How about getting him to be chairman of the event?"

"I suppose I could ask him." The others at the table all thought that was a marvelous idea.

41

PHIL AGREED TO CONTACT the professional party arrangers and the theater fundraiser was put into motion. It was decided to hold the event in the Leland Room in the Brunswick Forest Fitness Center, which could accommodate a large number of people. The room was used for exercise classes but it also could be transformed into a party setting. An annual Valentine's Day dance was such an occasion.

Alicia Swift, who had become an enthusiastic supporter of Tri-County Players, wrote about the casino party in her newspaper column. Crystal Bailey from the ad agency spread the word through various social media outlets.

In addition to using various means to encourage Brunswick Forest homeowners to attend, steps also were taken to inform residents of two other large developments in the area, Waterford and Magnolia Greens, about the event. To generate a large turnout, the planners decided against a "fancy dress" affair, knowing that casual attire was the preferred style in the community.

Phil had enlisted the help of Henry, Ben and Stu Galloway to obtain sponsors for the gambling tables in an effort to pull in some major contributions. Volunteers were recruited to sell tickets in denominations of $100, $500 and $1,000.

On the evening of the event, Phil had assigned himself to be a blackjack dealer. Henry was in charge of the roulette wheel, Stu the craps table and Ben engaged in his favorite pastime, poker. Their wives made sure everyone was having a good time and buying extra tickets.

Several comments were overheard about Phil's skill with blackjack. Clare and Henry were not surprised but kept mum. Barbara did observe that Phil appeared to really be enjoying himself.

"I'm not sure this will have any effect on his gambling addiction, but tonight at least he's not losing any real money," Clare said to Henry.

"It was a brilliant idea for you to suggest him to chair this event," Henry said.

Gloria managed to find a piano – a mere upright, not a grand – and led a sing-a-long of tunes from *A Broadway Musical*. She got Clare, Vicky and others to recreate their numbers from the show. (Clare declined to do any dancing in her heels.) This spontaneous frivolity had an effect on increasing the drink sales, meaning more money for the theater.

Everyone left with a good feeling and a Tri-County Players brochure that included a coupon for making future contributions.

Ben, the theater company treasurer, reported the evening produced an estimated $50,000 to keep the operation going.

Clare and her fellow organizers were thrilled about the outcome. They were happy not only about the success of the fundraiser but also by the opportunity to have a different kind of fun.

42

THEY SLEPT LATE and spent a quiet Sunday morning catching up on a few things. Around noontime the phone rang. The caller id showed it was Becky. She told Henry and put the conversation on speaker.

"Hi, sis," Clare said. "What's up?"

"It's Momma," she said. "She's in the hospital."

"What! What happened?" Clare stammered. "Is she all right?"

"She fell at church and hit her head on a pew. Jim said she has a concussion."

"Were you there?"

"No, I've been avoiding Momma, you know."

"But Dr. Vinson was there. What did Jim tell you? How did she fall?"

"It was Old Lady Wagoner's fault."

"Who?"

"Honey Belle's grandmother. Momma tripped on her cane."

"Becky, maybe you ought to start at the beginning."

"Well, Momma was serving communion. She's an elder in the Shellville Presbyterian Church. That's where Aunt Dora's funeral was held."

"Yes, I know. But I want to know about Momma."

"She was about halfway through and just as she got to Old Lady Wagoner's row her cane fell into the aisle and Momma tripped over it and fell forward. Jim said the communion tray with the wine slipped out of her hands and the wine splashed all over everything."

"That must have been quite a mess."

"People were wiping it off their clothes … and licking their fingers."

"Oh, come on," said Henry.

"That young minister left the pulpit and came running, saying, 'Thank the Lord we changed to white wine.' The elders had approved a large expenditure for new carpet not long ago."

"Go ahead, please."

"Momma tried to catch herself but knocked off Old Lady Wagoner's hat and her head struck the end of the pew. She fell to the floor. There was a big gash in her head and blood was gushing out. The minister threw up his hands and seeing the blood on the carpet said, 'Oh, no!'"

"Jim certainly gave you a lot of detail."

"He's very observant. Anyway, he rushed to examine her. She was unconscious. He held his handkerchief on the wound and told someone to call 911. Daddy had stayed home from church. Jim called and told him what happened. He and the ambulance got to the church at about the same time."

"And then?"

"The paramedics slapped a bandage on her temple and put a cold pack on her head. They put her on a stretcher and took her to the hospital in Camilla. Jim and Daddy rode along."

"What's her condition? What does Dr. Jim say?"

"He says it's not a life-threatening situation. She did regain consciousness and they gave her some medicine. She is resting well. But she apparently has suffered a loss of memory. She didn't know who Jim was or even Daddy."

"She didn't recognize Daddy? That's incredible," Clare said, horrified.

"Jim says it might only be temporary, but they just don't know yet."

"You haven't seen her, I guess."

"No, but I'm going to. Just as soon as I can get ready I'm driving to the hospital."

"I thought you said you were avoiding her."

"But if she doesn't recognize me ..."

Both Clare and Becky loved their mother. But they couldn't help smiling. This might be the answer to their problem.

43

CLARE HUNG UP THE PHONE and turned to Henry. "I've got to go see Momma," she said.

"Of course you do. What are your immediate commitments?"

"Actually, my schedule is pretty clear. I just finished taping Sterling Home ads for this month. No shootings for *Busboys* involving me are on the immediate agenda. And Gloria says it will be at least six weeks before we get going on another theater performance. I hate to leave just when I would have more time to spend with you, but I need to be with my family right now."

"I understand, sweetheart," Henry said. "We'll keep in touch by phone. And maybe when you get back I'll have some plans to show you."

"Plans? For what?"

"Our new home. I've had an architect working on a design for a place that better suits our needs. Our lease on this house is going to run out before too long. And after all, I am in the homebuilding business. Why not build one for ourselves?"

"How exciting! You did mention this when you told me about the new housing development you were interested in doing. I can't wait to see what our new home will be like."

"Well, you'd better be making some plane reservations."

For this trip to Georgia Clare managed to get on an early flight to Atlanta the next day with a connection via a regional carrier to Albany. She also reserved a rental car for her transportation after she got there.

She called Becky from Atlanta and arranged to meet her at the hospital. When Clare arrived she found Becky and Jim waiting in the lobby.

"Where's Elizabeth Ann?"

"I left her with a neighbor. I'm afraid she might creep out if her grandma is acting strangely. And by the way, your niece decided she wanted to be called Betty Ann."

"Oh?"

"Yes. She said one day if her grandma could shorten her name from Elizabeth to Betty, she could, too."

"Have you learned any more about Momma's injury?"

Jim spoke up. "The hospital has assigned a special medical team to her. They've done all kinds of tests, including an MRI. They haven't finalized a diagnosis – they're waiting on an internationally known brain specialist from Atlanta to come and examine her and give his opinion. We do know this: she suffered a severe blow to her right temporal lobe. The preliminary analysis points to a traumatic brain injury that affected her long-term memory. I remember that being mentioned in medical school but I didn't retain much of what the instructor said because I wanted to learn as much as I could about childhood diseases. I guess I figure if one of my young patients had a brain injury I would call in a specialist."

"So are you saying she can't remember long-time friends or even members of her own family?"

"We saw evidences of that yesterday when she woke up and asked me and Mr. Sullivan who we were."

"That must have really been a blow to Daddy," Clare said.

"Yes, he's taking it pretty hard," Becky said.

"What about you? Did Momma recognize you?"

"Well, I didn't see her. They were going to run some more tests. When Daddy came out he was so shaken up and almost in tears I decided it would be best for me and Betty Ann to go home with him. I also wanted to wait until my big sister came so we could both be with her at the same time."

An authoritative-looking nurse came toward them and said, "Are you her daughters?" Clare and Becky nodded. "You may go in now, but don't stay too long."

Jim walked them down the hall. On the way he told them something interesting about the nurse. "Last night when I came I saw Harry come in. He was met by this nurse. He gave her a hug and a kiss. She said, 'I'm so glad to see you, lover boy. They just brought your former mother-in-law in with a head injury.'"

"So she's the one he's been having an affair with!" Becky exploded.

"Shh!" said Jim. "It doesn't make any difference now. Here we are. I've got to go to the office. I'll see you later."

Betty Sullivan was barely recognizable herself. She had a large bandage on her right temple and gauze wrapped all around her head like a turban. Her face had a gray pallor and showed the strain of her shocking experience.

"Hello, Momma," Becky said.

Betty slowly opened her eyes and looked first at one and then the other of her two daughters. She continued to stare at them with a pained expression.

Slowly she formed the words they could hardly believe they were hearing: "Who are you?"

"It's Judy Clare, Momma. And Rebecca Jean – your daughters."

Betty studied both of their faces but still looked puzzled. Finally she said, "I don't remember having any daughters. I don't know you."

The sisters both cried softly. They wanted to hug their mother, but decided it might upset her.

"It's all right, Momma," Clare said. "You'll remember when you get well."

Betty's gaze on them remained fixed. Just then the door opened and in came the young Presbyterian minister.

He saw the two sisters and said, "Hello." Betty roused and turned to see who was there.

"Pastor Peterson. How nice to see you," she said.

"How are you doing Mrs. Sullivan?"

"Not too well. I've got a terrible headache. I don't know who these people are or I would introduce you."

Clare said softly, with a wave of her hand, "It's okay."

"I'm sorry about your headache. I'm sure they can give you some aspirin."

"Oh, they've given me every kind of pill you can think of, and shots in the arm and all kinds of things. I don't know how I got in the hospital in the first place."

"Well, you took a nasty fall during church and hurt your head. But I'm sure you'll be out of here soon and back in church next Sunday."

"We certainly hope you're right," Becky said.

"I just wanted to check on you, Mrs. Sullivan, but I can't stay," the minister said. "I'm on my way to a meeting of the Presbytery. Take it easy and you'll feel better, I'm sure."

Betty's eyelids were heavy. "I'm so tired," she said. "I need to rest."

"Okay," Clare said. "We'll be back to see you."

As they walked down the hall, Becky said, "I'm really confused. She recognized you but not us."

"Is that right? But you're her daughters."

"Let's see if we can talk to one of the doctors treating her," Clare said.

They stopped at the nurses' station and made an inquiry. Soon a distinguished middle-aged man in a business suit appeared and introduced himself as Dr. Richard Langdon from Atlanta – the brain specialist Jim had mentioned. He motioned to a sofa in the waiting room and they all sat down.

"We understand our mother suffered a traumatic brain injury when she fell and hit her head on a pew at church yesterday," Clare said. "When we came to see her today she didn't know who we were. But then the minister came and she knew him right away."

Dr. Langdon began a long explanation. "Impaired memory is a common result of a brain injury, in your mother's case a TBI. There are three kinds of memory, but I won't go into that. Her symptoms indicate, and a battery of tests tend to substantiate the diagnosis of the hospital staff physicians, that this patient's injury resulted in amnesia. There are two types of amnesia: retrograde, which means loss of memories for events prior to the accident; and anterior grade, in which case events following the accident have been erased."

"Which type of amnesia does our mother have," Becky inquired.

"From what I've learned, and as you described her condition, she has retrograde amnesia. She is unable to recall stored memories – but sometimes only bits and pieces are missing."

"I guess that would explain why she recognized Rev. Peterson but not us," Clare said.

"I believe so. She was probably focused solely on him just moments before her fall and that stuck in her memory. But she would have to call on her memory of places, happenings and people from before her injury in order to recognize the two of you."

"What about Daddy and Dr. Jim Vinson? They reached her soon after she fell and they rode with her in the ambulance to the hospital."

"Two things," said Dr. Langdon. "First, the blow to Mrs. Sullivan's head rendered her unconscious so she had no visual contact. Secondly, we have found that TBI victims usually don't remember events occurring around the time of the head trauma."

"She will get better, won't she?" Becky said.

"For most amnesiacs memory loss is a temporary condition and lasts only a short time – maybe a few hours. But depending on the severity of the trauma the duration of amnesia can be a few weeks or even months."

"And when our mother recovers will she be back to normal?" Clare asked.

"She probably will recall older memories first, then more recent ones. But please understand – I have to be honest with you – her recovery might be slow coming and it's possible she might not ever remember everything – and everybody she knew."

"Thank you, doctor. You've explained her condition very well," Clare said.

"And you've given us a lot to think about," said Becky.

As they made their way to the hospital exit Clare said, "Poor Momma. It's as if all of a sudden she's in an advanced stage of Alzheimer's disease. And I feel so sorry for Daddy. He's going to be so lost."

"I feel awful saying this, but you know what this means," Becky said. "Now I don't have to tell Momma – I can't, really – that Harry and I are divorced and I'm going to marry Jim and we're going to have a baby."

"You'll still need to tell Daddy," Clare said.

"I know. But I'm Daddy's little girl. I always have been. And in his eyes I can do no wrong."

"I wouldn't be so sure about that."

"I'm sure. He might have a hard time understanding what I tell him, in his current confused state. So maybe I'll wait and give him time to adjust to what's happened with Momma."

"You can't wait too long, though. It won't be long before you'll have to start wearing maternity clothes. Does Jim know you're pregnant?"

"Yes, I had to tell him."

"How did he take the news?"

"Oh, Jim was thrilled to learn that he's going to be a father. And he was fully understanding."

"Well, that's good. We'd better go see Daddy, and you'll need to pick up Betty Ann."

"Right. And of course you can stay with me as long as you're here."

"I don't know how long that will be, but I do think it's good for us to face this unexpected situation together."

44

CLARE AND BECKY found Pat Sullivan sitting on the porch swing when they pulled into the driveway at the farm. He was blankly staring into space. His expression brightened only slightly at the sight of his older daughter.

"Hello, Daddy," she said.

"Hello, honey. I'm glad you came."

"We looked in on Momma," Becky said. "She didn't recognize us either."

"I feel so helpless," he said.

Clare put a hand on his arm and said, "You're not alone."

"We talked to that brain expert from Atlanta," Becky said.

"What did he say?"

"Well, he gave us some hope," Clare said. "He said most brain injury victims do recover, some faster than others."

"I hope and pray it will be soon. I can't stand seeing Betty like this – not knowing me or the two of you," Pat said.

"I know. Is there anything we can do for you?" Clare asked. "Maybe I ought to stay at the farm with you."

"No, I can take care of myself. That nice Dr. Jim has been very kind. He said he would come by in the morning and we can go see Betty again."

"Jim is a very nice man," Becky said. "Well, we just wanted to check on you. I need to go see about Betty Ann and get some supper for us. You've got plenty to eat, I hope?"

"Yes, I'll be all right."

"We might see you at the hospital tomorrow," Clare said. Looking at his bloodshot eyes she added, "Try to get some sleep."

Becky kissed him on the cheek and said, "We love you, Daddy."

"I love you, too," he said, nodding to both of them.

They stopped briefly at the home of the neighbor who was keeping Betty Ann. She was excited to see "Aunt Clare" but she was anxious about her grandmother. All Becky had told her was that she had hurt her head and had to go to the hospital to get it taken care of.

"Can I go see Grandma, please, please?" the little girl begged.

147

"Not tonight, honey."

"Tomorrow, then?"

"You've got school, you know."

"I know," she said sadly. "But I'm worried about Grandma Betty."

Clare tried to console her. "Don't worry, Betty Ann. The doctors are taking good care of her."

"Like Doctor Jim takes care of me?"

"Yes, dear," said her mother, as her cell phone rang. After a few words she hung up and said, "That was a coincidence. It was Jim calling to say he'd like to take us all out for an early dinner."

"Oh, goody!" said Betty Ann.

"How nice," Clare said.

Jim picked them up about 45 minutes later and took them to a small restaurant nearby that served homestyle food and was pet-friendly. Betty Ann took his hand as they got out of the car.

"I'm sure you haven't had much time to do anything about meal preparation," he said to Becky.

"That's right. I was planning to pull something out of the freezer, although I hated to do that on Clare's first evening here."

"We are all very glad you came down, Clare. I'm sure you're as shocked as all of us about your mother's injury."

"What's really shocking is her amnesia," she said.

They filled him in on their visit with Dr. Langdon after Betty Ann excused herself to go look at a puppy a couple had brought in.

"It sounds like he gave you a short course on the human brain," Jim said.

"He cleared up some questions for us," Clare said.

"One thing is very clear," said Becky. "She doesn't know who I am, so that removes the concern I had about telling her about my divorce and our plans for getting married."

"I'm sure you feel guilty about deceiving her …" Jim started.

"But what she doesn't know won't hurt her," Becky finished.

By that time Betty Ann was headed back to the table and they were ready to proceed with dinner.

"Mommy, can we have a puppy?" she pleaded.

"We'll have to talk about that," Becky said.

"I like puppies. Do you like dogs, Dr. Jim?"

"Everybody likes dogs, don't they?" he said.

"Daddy doesn't. He hates them. But since he's not living with us, he doesn't have a say, does he?"

"Let's talk about this later, Betty Ann. What would you like to eat?"

"A burger."

The three adults ordered the special: meat loaf with turnip greens and mashed potatoes and hot rolls.

Betty Ann kept glancing at the cute puppy. "I wish I had a puppy to play with," she said sadly.

Becky looked at Clare, then Jim, took a long, deep breath and said to her daughter: "How would you like to have a little brother or sister to play with?"

The child's face lit up (while Clare's turned pale) and she said excitedly, "Oh, Mommy! Are we having a baby?"

"Are you happy about that?"

"Oh, yes! When?"

"Not right away. And something else." Jim stiffened. "You're going to have another daddy. Dr. Jim and I are going to get married."

At that Betty Ann jumped up and threw her arms around Jim's neck and hugged him tightly. Then she did the same for her mother and Clare.

"And we can be a family?" said the girl, her eyes sparkling.

"We can be a family," Jim said to her. "And I think every family should have a dog, don't you?"

"Can we?" she looked quizzically at her mother.

Shrugging, Becky replied, "If Dr. Jim says so."

"Oh! I can't wait. I think I'll save him part of my burger."

"Maybe not this burger," said Clare, "but that will be a very nice thing to do – when you're a family."

45

THE NEXT MORNING Clare was reviewing with Becky her surprise announcement at dinner that she was going to have a baby and that she and Jim were going to be married – both agreed that it was good to have that done and that Betty Ann took it so well – when the phone rang. It was Jim calling to say that the hospital had notified him that Mrs. Sullivan was to be released as soon as someone could pick her up.

"Already?" said Becky. "I guess you're right. Hospitals don't keep patients very long these days, even those who had their memory knocked out of them."

Clare frowned at that blunt description of their mother's condition.

"Okay, darlin', we'll be ready."

She turned to Clare, who was waiting to hear what Jim had to say. "The report from the hospital is that her head injury is healing well – the outside wound that is – and there is nothing the medical staff can do about her amnesia. That will be up to her family," Becky said.

"I hope somebody at the hospital will at least give us some advice," Clare said.

"Me, too," said Becky. "I wouldn't know how to begin. I wonder if we should take Daddy with us."

"I don't know. He is so shaken up right now. It might be better for him to stay home. But we definitely need to prepare him," Clare said. "The woman who's coming home today is not the one who left."

Betty Ann had already gone to school, so after Clare had called to alert Pat that Betty was getting out of the hospital they went out on the porch to await Jim. When the three arrived at the hospital they found Betty sitting in a wheel chair in the lobby with a nurse attending her. Rev. Peterson was sitting in a chair next to her and they were talking.

"I was just telling Mrs. Sullivan she was going home and that once she saw some familiar surrounding she would begin to remember things better," the minister said.

Clare excused herself to go to the desk and take care of signing out the patient. She saw Dr. Langdon come into the lobby and spoke.

"I'm glad to see you, doctor. I hope you can give us some guidance."

"That's why I'm here," he said. Addressing the group, he instructed them to follow him into a conference room where he outlined what would be involved in her recovery. He directed his remarks first to the patient.

"Mrs. Sullivan, do you know who I am?"

"Why, yes, you're that nice Dr. Langdon who came to see me yesterday," she said.

"And I told you that you had received a serious head injury."

"I already knew that, but you explained it a little better."

"I said there was damage to your brain, which caused you to lose your long-term memory. Therefore, you have no recollection of who these people are," he said, indicating her daughters and Jim.

"Just Rev. Peterson, that's all," she said.

"They are going to help you get your memory back."

"But they're strangers," she said, looking blankly at Clare and Becky. Their faces dropped.

"Mrs. Sullivan, let me assure you that they can be trusted. Everything they do will be in your best interest."

Jim spoke up. "You'll be going with us to where you lived before your accident. There you will see a man you also don't remember. But he is a very important person in your life and he also wants you to regain your memory."

As Dr. Langdon continued Betty nodded off and they all moved across the room and lowered their voices.

"As a part of her recovery regimen," the specialist said, "an occupational therapist will work with her and her family in the rebuilding of her life, using techniques to resurrect lost memories and to learn new information to replace what has vanished."

"Dr. Langdon, can you give us some pointers on how we should proceed? Should we show her some photograph albums with our pictures in them?" Clare asked.

"Yes, and videos if you have them. "But first you will need to familiarize her with her surroundings – her bedroom, her clothing in the closet, the kitchen where she has spent a lot of time in her life. Her general health is good so she won't be restricted in her physical activities. Let her do what she feels like doing. She shouldn't be allowed to drive a car alone."

"She might get lost, right?" said Becky.

"Right. Do I understand that Mr. and Mrs. Sullivan had been living here alone – no other relatives or caretakers?"

151

Becky said sternly, "Of course. Our parents are not senile. They don't need a caretaker."

"I understand," said Dr. Langdon. "But those living conditions have changed drastically. This place and what goes on around her will be new to her. Mrs. Sullivan will need to be carefully observed as she gradually adjusts to a completely new environment. And Mr. Sullivan can't keep his eyes on her every bit of the time."

"What are you suggesting?" asked Clare.

"It would be highly desirable if another family member could stay with her, at least for a few months. Could either of you do that?"

"I'm sorry, but I'm just visiting from Wilmington, North Carolina," Clare said. "I'm not sure how long I can stay. And Becky has a young child and other responsibilities in her own home. I don't see how she could move in."

Rev. Peterson interjected: "I'm sure there are members of her church who would volunteer to stay with her for certain periods of time," he said.

"That would be a very charitable thing to do," Jim said. "But from what Dr. Langdon has told us she is going to need around-the-clock supervision."

"Well, the health and social assistance agencies can arrange to have home care services provided around the clock," Dr. Langdon said.

"That may be the only alternative," Jim said.

"How soon could we get that started?" Becky asked.

"They are pretty responsive," Jim said. "I can check on it."

"Any more questions?" Dr. Langdon asked.

"I'm sure we'll think of several later on," Clare said.

Handing each of them a card, the doctor said, "Call my office and either I or one of our specialists will respond as quickly as possible."

"Thank you," said Jim. "Mrs. Sullivan …" Betty roused and looked at him. "… are you ready to get out of the hospital?"

"Yes. Everybody here has been very nice, but it's not the same as being at home," she replied.

"I'll be visiting you regularly," said Rev. Peterson.

"That's very kind of you, Reverend," she said.

The nurse wheeled her out to Jim's car and helped her into the back seat with Clare. Becky took the front passenger seat.

On the way to the Sullivan farm, Betty looked with childish wonder at the scenery she saw out the windows. She was still wide-eyed when they turned into the drive leading to the home where she had lived for over 40 years but to her was unfamiliar.

"What's this place?" she asked.

"It's where you're going to be living, Mrs. Sullivan," Jim replied. "You'll like it."

"I'm not so sure," she said, as she got out of the car and took a good look at the house and its surroundings.

As they climbed the steps to the front porch, Pat Sullivan opened the door and came out. He opened his arms wide to embrace his wife but seeing that Betty was startled Clare rushed to his side. "Daddy, I'm sorry, but she doesn't know who you are. She doesn't know any of us and we're going to have to help her get her memory back."

Still confused, he dropped his arms to his side and the couple exchanged long stares.

Betty said to Becky in a low voice, "Who is this man?"

"His name is Pat. This is his pecan farm and he lives here," Becky said.

"And I'm going to be living here, too? I don't think so," Betty said.

"It's a large house," said Clare. "You'll have your own room. Let's go in and we'll show it to you."

Pat held the door open and as they passed through he said, "Welcome home, Betty."

As they went down the hall to the back bedroom, Betty was shaking her head and mumbling, "How did he know my name?"

"You're still wearing your church clothes," Becky said. "I'll bet you'd like to change into something less dressy."

Jim brought in the small bag they had taken to the hospital that contained changes of underwear and cosmetics. Then he left to go be with Pat.

Becky opened the closet and told her, "Pick out something you'd like to put on."

"Anything?"

"Yes. They are all your size."

Betty found a skirt and blouse and took off her dress. Clare handed her a robe and slippers, saying, "You'd probably like to use the bathroom. It's right here."

"All right," she said. "Thank you …"

"Judy Clare," her daughter prompted.

"Thank you, Judy Clare."

After Betty closed the bathroom door, Becky said, "This isn't going to be easy."

"No, it isn't. And it's going to be so hard on Daddy. Maybe I can work out some way to stay longer than I intended," Clare said.

"That really would help."

When Betty came out Becky took her cosmetics out of the case and laid them on the dresser.

"You'll want to freshen your makeup," she told her mother.

"Why, thank you. And what is your name?"

"I'm Rebecca Jean. But most folks call me Becky."

"Thank you, Rebecca Jean."

"I'm going to go make a pot of coffee," Clare said. "I'll wait for you in the kitchen."

The aroma of fresh coffee floated down the hall as Becky took her mother's arm and guided her to the kitchen, where Clare had cups waiting. Betty looked around the large airy room with sunlight streaming through the windows.

"This coffee tastes good," Betty said. "I hope I remember how to make it."

"I'm sure you will," Clare said. "Before long you'll get back to cooking meals for yourself and Pat."

"You mean I have to cook for him?" she asked, pointing out to the porch, where Pat and Jim were sitting.

"You'll be doing things for each other," Clare said. "It's such a nice day. Let's take our coffee and go outside."

Pat and Jim stood up as they emerged and motioned them to have seats. Betty chose the swing, where Pat had been sitting. He hesitated briefly, then sat down beside her.

"It's a little breezy. Are you warm enough?" he asked Betty. "I can get you a light sweater."

"I'm fine, but thank you anyway ... Pat? Is that your name?"

"You know it ..." Pat caught himself and said, "Yes, Betty. I'm Pat ... Pat Sullivan."

"Sullivan? That's my name. We must be kin."

"You are," Clare said. "But we can discuss that later. Right now let's talk about lunch."

"I'm not very hungry," Betty said. "I had a good breakfast at the hospital."

"Let's see what's in the fridge," Becky said. She opened the door and found a package of smoked turkey and some potato salad. There also were makings for sandwiches. So that simplified the menu. The sisters prepared five sandwiches, took up the potato salad in a bowl and prepared some sweet tea. The refrigerator also held some lemon bars, which they had for dessert.

Pat again sat by Betty at the dining table. Maybe it was because of their similarities in age, but for whatever reason Pat and Betty carried on a conversation centering on getting acquainted with each other. The daughters were pleased to see their father's face light up in a smile a time or two.

After lunch Jim said he had to go to his office to see a patient. At Becky's request he took her into town to get her car. "I'll pick up Betty Ann and hurry back," she told Clare.

Betty and Clare cleared the table and put the plates and flatware in the dishwasher. Pat obviously had cheered up some. He let his Irish charm shine through as he invited Betty to accompany him on a stroll through the pecan orchard closest to the house. Clare opted to stay at the house and make some phone calls.

First she called Henry and got voice mail. She left a brief message, condensing as best she could the events of the past 24 hours. Before she could check in with Barbara, Henry called back. There was urgency in his voice.

"Zach Bacharach called looking for you. He needs to talk to you right away. Something about a shoot for the TV series. Do you have his cell phone number?"

"Yes. I guess he must have misplaced mine because I haven't had any calls. I'll get in touch with him right away. I miss you and I love you. Bye."

Wondering what might be so urgent Clare punched in the number. He answered on the third ring.

"Henry told me you were in Georgia with your family. You need to get back here as soon as you can."

"Why? What's going on?"

"We're going to have to move up the shoot at Kure Beach we had scheduled for next week," Zach said. "I guess you hadn't heard. There's a hurricane forming in the Bahamas. The weather people say their models show it making landfall in Florida and moving up the coastline sometime next weekend. We need to do our exterior shots at the restaurant before the storm."

"It's not a good time for me to leave my mother but I guess I'll have to. I'll check flights and let you know what I've worked out."

Fortunately Becky made a quick return trip. By the time she arrived Clare had made arrangements to make connections in Albany and get an early evening flight out of Atlanta. She was finishing her conversation with Zach when she looked out the window and saw Becky and Betty Ann. They had met Pat and Betty coming back from their walk.

Clare opened the door just as the little girl ran up to Betty, shouting, "Grandma, Grandma! Mommy and Dr. Jim are getting married and I'm going to have a little brother or sister!"

"Well, isn't that exciting," Betty said, obviously not making any sense of what she was so excited about. Clare did observe there was an immediate natural connection between the older woman and the child – a positive force for Betty's recovery. Betty Ann's outpouring of affection was reinforced when she turned to Pat and he lifted her up into his arms and gave her a tender hug and a kiss on the cheek. As he did so he looked straight at Becky and she knew right away she had some explaining to do.

It was so nice outdoors everyone was reluctant to go inside the house. Pat sat in the swing, Betty Ann jumped up and sat in his lap and Betty joined them.

Clare said, "Becky, I need to talk to you." They sat on a bench under one of the large trees on the lawn. She filled her in on the conversation with Zach and the urgent need for her to get back home. Becky didn't welcome the development because it meant she wouldn't have her big sister to lean on. But she could see that Clare's hasty departure was necessary. That would require her to take Clare back to her house in town to pick up her bag and her rental car so she could drive to Albany.

Without going into any detail, Clare apologized for having to leave. She gave her father a hug and said, "I love you", smiled at Betty and said, "You're in very good hands" and scooped up Betty Ann for hugs and kisses.

"Will you come back soon, Aunt Clare?" the little girl said.

"Not right away, sweetheart, but as soon as I can. How about if I call and talk to you on the phone?"

"Oh, will you, please? I really would like that."

Becky told the group she would be back shortly and off they went.

46

CLARE'S FLIGHTS WERE ON TIME and she was home by 10 p.m. She emailed Zach that she would make the shoot and filled in Henry on the momentous events of the past few days. She turned in early and was headed to Kure Beach early the next morning.

It was a beautiful late summer day and when Clare arrived the skies were clear and the temperatures ideal for sunbathing. She quickly checked in and changed into a swimsuit.

The beach was only a short walk. She relied on her flip flops to take her to a prime location where she could spread a blanket and learn her lines. Unfortunately she only got a few pages into the script before an emergency arose.

She had met a group of the actors portraying the busboys and waitresses returning to their quarters after a period of swimming, surfing, beach ball tossing and other leisure time activities before the cameras to provide some stock footage for scenes that would require it. One lone swimmer was still in the water, not too far from shore. She recognized him as Chip Lindley, a kid from the Midwest who loved the ocean and couldn't seem to get enough time enjoying the surf. Only his head and shoulders were visible as he moved slowly toward the water's edge.

Clare suddenly had a feeling of dread as she saw a fearsome sight: a dark shadow just below the surface and a fast-moving fin.

She couldn't believe her eyes. But a report she heard on the radio on the way down flashed through her mind. Swimmers had lost limbs and had nearly been killed by sharks on some nearby beaches recently.

Clare jumped up and ran toward the young man screaming, "Chip! Shark!" He turned to face the impending attack and began furiously swimming for his life.

Running as fast as her flip-flops would allow, she turned cold with fear, realizing she couldn't reach Chip in time to pull him to shore.

As the shark drew nearer Clare grabbed up a canoe oar lying on the sand and waded into the water just as the shark opened its jaws and bared its razor-sharp teeth. In a mindless act of bravery, she plunged the oar into the gaping mouth of the fish, which easily snapped it in two between clenched teeth.

She and Chip were both in waist-deep water, which slowed their escape, but luckily the shark, choking on the jagged edge of the oar, swiftly made a u-turn and headed back out to sea. They collapsed, out of breath, on the wet sand, thankful to be unharmed. Little did they know their close call had been captured on film by the departing camera crew.

"Wow, that was scary," Chip said. "You saved my life, Ms. Sullivan. Thank you."

"I'm just glad I got there in time, and please call me Clare."

Zach, dressed in his director's attire (riding pants, loose fitting shirt and beret) came to meet them and anxiously asked if they were all right. "That was quite a daring rescue," he said.

"I'm just glad that oar was there," she said.

"We had used the canoe for shooting some scenes on the lake. Incidentally, you may not have noticed but we got some great footage of the shark encounter which we're going to work into the script."

"No, Zach, I didn't notice," she replied sarcastically. "I was otherwise occupied."

The main reason for Clare's premature return from Georgia was to film a segment outside the restaurant involving her and the cook. Zach had said it was important to get that done before stormy weather set in.

"The light is good right now if you're willing to go ahead, Clare," he said.

"Sure, if it's okay with Fred," she said, nodding to Fred Fields, playing the role of the cook, also named Fred. He gave a thumbs up.

Fred was already dressed but Clare had to step into a temporary dressing room to change out of her swimsuit and put on the restaurant owner's costume.

With cameras in place, they did a quick run-through of their lines and went inside the structure that had been constructed to represent the restaurant where the "busboys" worked. The scene began with the two of them coming out the door with cups of coffee. Clare had the first line.

"We're going to be in for a busy weekend with the music festival going on."

"Good for business," said the cook.

"But rough on the help. Just hope everybody shows up."

They sat on a bench outside the fake restaurant and sipped their coffee and continued the conversation.

158

When they had covered four or five pages of the script Zach called, "Cut. Take Five" and dismissed the actors while he reviewed the results of the taping. He called Clare and Fred back from their break.

"Let's do a retake beginning from the point where you get up from the bench," Zach said. He shouted, "Places! Action!"

Clare rose from the bench and tossed the remaining coffee in her cup on the ground. "You've got to do something about this coffee, Fred. It tastes awful."

"What do you mean? It tasted just fine last night."

At the end of the scene Zach commanded, "Cut. Print" and they knew their work was done. And it was just in time. Dark clouds were gathering and the wind was beginning to upturn beach umbrellas and send them rolling. Zach's set crew went into action to save the properties.

"We had all better get ready to vacate," Zach said. "It looks like the storm is about to hit."

Clare didn't take time to change again but grabbed up her beach bag and ran to her car which she had parked nearby. She headed for Fort Fisher Boulevard and sped away north. She was barely ahead of the stiff winds and faced a challenging drive to outrun the approaching hurricane.

She passed highway crews putting up barriers closing U.S. 421 to southbound traffic. Before she got off Carolina Beach she encountered mile-long backups. Clare wasn't the only one trying to escape the fury of the storm. While waiting in traffic she tried to call Henry but cell phone reception was no good. She hoped he was tuned in to weather reports.

Once the bottleneck was cleared by drivers exiting to other routes, Clare was able to resume normal speed and conditions improved the farther north she traveled. She made it home in almost regular time and found Henry anxiously awaiting her return. Hugs were exchanged and she filled him in on her experience – purposely omitting any reference to the shark incident. She was glad she didn't have to explain a missing body part.

The destructive force of the storm became more evident with successive TV news reports. Although it never reached the classification of hurricane, the tropical disturbance left widespread damage in its wake after making landfall at a point south of Kure Beach. One of the victims of its powerful winds was the mockup of the restaurant that had been constructed for the TV series. All that remained was scattered lumber littering the beach. One TV station reached Zach Bacharach for an interview.

"Although there was no loss of life, it's a terrible tragedy," he said. Property damage was estimated to be in millions of dollars. "It adversely affected the TV series *Busboys* that is being produced here in the Wilmington area. We lost the set that was used for exterior scenes of the restaurant."

"Will production have to be suspended?" the interviewer asked.

"No," Zach said. "We still have the use of Wilmington's excellent studio facilities. Some revision of the script for forthcoming episodes will be required, but we have some skilled scriptwriters and some very adaptable actors who can make it possible to continue on course."

"Will you rebuild the set on the beach that was destroyed?"

"That decision hasn't been made yet," Zach said. "Fortunately we have enough episodes in the can to carry us for a couple of months."

Zach told Clare privately that her schedule would be lighter than originally planned and that her assignments for the immediate future would be confined to Wilmington.

47

EARLY THE FOLLOWING MORNING Clare received a call from Becky, who was aware of the news reports on the storm and was worried about her.

"I'm all right," she said. "I got out of the path of the storm in time to make it home safely. How are things going down there?"

"Momma is doing well," Becky said. "You wouldn't believe how she is adjusting to her situation. Thanks to Jim, we were able to arrange for some live-in health care aides and she is beginning to get some therapy. She is becoming familiar with the house, especially the kitchen. She is preparing most of the meals.

"Probably the best thing that's happened is because of Rev. Peterson. Some of the ladies of the church had told him they wanted to help Momma to get over the trauma of her fall. So he got them together with Jim so he could explain in medical terms why she didn't remember people and events because of the blow to her head. They explained to the ladies that Daddy and I were doing what we could but that Momma might benefit from having contact with others that she used to know.

"As a result of this meeting, a small group of the ladies visited Momma and asked if she would like to join their bridge club. (They hadn't yet formed one, but had talked about doing it.) Momma agreed and invited them to have their first meeting at the farm. They began to meet regularly twice a month — one of those times at the farm, the other time someone would pick her up and bring her home so she wouldn't be driving. The effect on Momma's health, mental and physical, has been quite noticeable."

"That's terrific. Now, what about Daddy?"

"He is a tremendous help. He has slowly accepted the fact that Momma just isn't the same person who used to live there and rather than try hard to get her to remember her former life he is helping her try to build a new one. In a way it's amusing. He has begun a brand new courtship and she is liking it."

"Well, what do you know! And how's Betty Ann?"

"Happy as ever."

"You've certainly given me some good news, Becky. I'm sorry I had to leave you with a heavy responsibility so hurriedly, but it sounds as if you're handling it very well. I really do appreciate that."

"I'm doing what I can. I just hope it's enough."

"I'll be checking in with you often. Thanks so much for calling. Bye."

The next call was from Gloria. She had some news of a different kind.

"Are you sitting down?" she asked.

"No, but I will," Clare said. "What do you have to tell me?"

"I have a producer friend in New York who is always on the lookout for fresh talent. I sent him a video recording of our *Broadway Musical Review* show. He was so impressed with your singing and dancing performances he wants you to try out for a musical he is producing."

"Are you serious? How exciting. Did he say anything about the show he's doing?"

"Yes, it's a revival of *Oklahoma!* and he's holding tryouts for the role of Laurey," Gloria said. There was a moment of silence. "Clare? Are you still there?"

"Yes," she said, after finding her voice. "I'm trying to absorb what you just said. Your friend thought I was that good just from watching the video?"

"That's right. And I didn't push him. Naturally I think you're that talented. But he made up his mind on his own."

"Wow! By the way, what's your friend's name?"

"Palmer Stone," Gloria said.

"Palmer Stone! I've heard of him," Clare said.

"I thought you might have. He's a bit eccentric but he has a long string of successes."

"When are the tryouts?"

"Sometime next week, I believe. Let me give you the name and number of his personal assistant. She can give you all the details."

"Oh, Glo! I don't know how to thank you. I owe you big. I'll start by buying you a Moscow Mule."

Clare began by calling Palmer Stone's assistant and learned the tryouts for Laurey were scheduled on a date only 10 days off. She got the name of a contact and started to make that call but thought better about it. She told herself not to be too impulsive. She really should talk to Henry first.

She decided to wait until evening and discuss the matter with Henry over a dinner she had prepared and a bottle of Mt. Jackson wine from the cellar.

Meanwhile, she felt she needed to check in with her best friend, Barbara, who was equally thrilled at the possibility of Clare playing a leading role in a Broadway musical.

"I know I'm getting way ahead of myself, but if this comes to pass I'll have to do something about my job as TV spokesperson for Sterling Homes," Clare said.

"Not a problem," said Barbara. "Phil mentioned last week that Darlene Shields had her baby – a girl – and she is available to go back to her old job if there's an opening."

"How interesting," Clare said. "New mothers seem to return to work rather quickly these days."

"I think Darlene really could use that income. And you certainly don't need it," Barbara said.

Clare had coq au vin warming on the range and Dom Perignon chilling in the bucket when Henry walked in the door and sniffed her perfume.

"That's something new, isn't it?" he commented

"Do you like it?" she asked. "If so, our special evening is off to a good start."

"What's special?"

"You'll see. Go change from businessman to beau and join me on the couch … sitting on the couch."

"OK … for starters."

Clare hadn't spent much time lately admiring the handsome hunk who stole her affection on first meeting him in that coffee shop in Seattle when she was exploring a campaign for governor of California. Those memories came rushing back and sent her blood pulsating when he returned wearing a maroon silk shirt and dark slacks. His French cologne floated seductively as he sat beside her, took her into his arms and in a throaty whisper asked, "What's for dinner?"

She pushed him away with a frown, ignoring his devilish grin, and poured two flutes of champagne. "Dinner can wait," she said. "We need to drink a toast; first, to your new housing development (they sipped) and second to an exciting career development that presented itself today (they sipped again) which I'm going to tell you about after you kiss me."

With that command Henry picked up where he left off, holding her tight and kissing her with a passion she hadn't felt in some time. He looked deeply into her enchanting blue eyes and whispered, "I'm so glad we met." She returned his kiss, then reached for her glass and asked, "Are you ready for my big news?"

"Eager, even," he said.

"OK, here it is. I have been invited to go to New York and try out for a part in a Broadway musical."

"Wow! That is really big news. Tell me more."

Clare relayed her conversation with Gloria, how it all came about and what it meant to her.

"*Oklahoma!* is one of my very favorite shows. I never dreamed I would have the opportunity to play the role of Laurey on Broadway."

"That's terrific," Henry said. "I am so happy for you. You'll be the toast of the town." He raised his glass and drank to her rising career as an actor.

"The auditions are a week from Friday. Will you go with me?"

"I'd love to. I should be able to get away," Henry said. "We'll have a weekend in New York together."

"That's really something to look forward to," she said, embracing him.

They proceeded to dine on her excellent chicken dish, accompanied by Mt. Jackson's finest blend, which Henry had arranged to be shipped for a special occasion.

This evening was very special, and it kept getting better.

48

HAVING TOLD HENRY about her golden opportunity, Clare was eager to share the news with others. She felt obligated to make Zach first on her list because if she did get the part it would almost certainly mean giving up her role on *Busboys*. In deference to their long friendship the easily excitable director managed to keep his temper in check but immediately began thinking about how to get the maximum number of performances from Clare before she left the show.

Her best friend Barbara was next on her list. She thought she needed a bit more encouragement before moving ahead. Barbara told Clare she was confident she would sail through the auditions and land the choice role. Then she called Gloria. She assured Clare she would do well but also passed along some professional advice that she could use to impress the casting director.

She returned a call on her answering machine from Hal Phillips, the reporter who had interviewed her earlier about being the TV spokesperson for Sterling Homes and had written stories about the new theater. He had seen Chip's postings on Twitter and Facebook about Clare's daring rescue of him from the shark attack. Phillips wanted to get the rescuer's side of the story and pumped her relentlessly for all the colorful details. Clare said she was sorry to disappoint him. "It happened so fast," she said. "I acted on impulse, seeing this fine young man in imminent danger. The canoe oar was the only potential weapon in sight and it probably saved both of us from harm." Clare decided not to mention the Broadway tryouts. That could be a separate story to come later.

After the interview she realized she should alert Henry so he wouldn't learn about the shark incident by reading it in the newspaper. She needed to see Phil anyway about stepping down as the Sterling Homes TV spokesperson so she hightailed it to the office. She managed to catch Phil in and there were no men in dark suits lurking. Phil said he was sorry to lose her but since Darlene Shields was available to take her place he graciously wished her good luck on the auditions.

Henry also was on the premises and as if she had planned it he invited her to go to lunch. Over oysters and wine she low-keyed the shark encounter and assured him she was never in any great danger. She made the story so convincing, even she believed it. "I'm sure the news reporter will make it seem much more sensational than it really was," she said.

After lunch Henry asked if she had any appointments and if not would she like to go see the site for his planned development. She happily accepted. They left the restaurant and headed out of the city to a rural location not far from a well-traveled highway.

"This is a beautiful area," Clare said. "So pastoral. I can see why you chose it. Anyone would want to live here."

"I'm glad to hear you say so. You and I will be the first residents.," he said.

Henry parked at a spot marked by a clump of trees on the horizon. He waved his arm and said, "This is it – the future site of 'Jackson Hills.' I thought about 'Jackson Heights' but it was taken."

"But I don't see any hills," Clare said.

"Well, how many hills did you see in Beverly Hills, California?"

Obviously enthused about his dream of an ideal real estate development, Henry began to reel off facts and figures, including the number of homes planned, recreational facilities and types of businesses in an upscale commercial area.

"A lot of site preparation will be required before building can begin," he said. Pointing to the trees he said, "Of course, that area will have to be cleared …"

Clare interrupted. "You mean those lovely trees have to go?" she exclaimed.

"I'm afraid so, to be able to do enough building to make the project profitable," Henry said.

"You can't do that, Henry," she said, agitated. "You can't cut down those glorious pines. Even if you have to sacrifice a few homes. Just look at the other developments in the Wilmington suburbs. They are all laid out with beautiful landscaping, including lots of trees. And isn't that a small creek I see?"

"Yes, we'll have to fill that in …"

"Oh, no! Leave it to wind through the development and with the trees and well-planned plantings it will be so inviting for families who don't want to live crowded up in the city where all they can see is other houses."

"Clare, please," Henry said. "You have to look at this through a builder's eyes. And the experts I hired to develop the preliminary plans didn't raise any objections to modifying the land.

"They really wouldn't with what you probably paid them, would they?" Clare argued.

Henry turned to her with a sad look of disappointment and said pleadingly, "I thought you'd be pleased. But you don't share my vision. You're asking me to go back to the drawing board."

"I'm so sorry," Clare said, seeing the hurt in his eyes. "I didn't mean to pour cold water on your great idea. I do think, for business reasons, you need to consider the importance of preserving the environment as much as possible. Won't you have to get a permit or something?"

"I've got lawyers looking into all the requirements. And between local, state and federal governments there are a mountain of rules and regulations that have to be met to do anything these days."

He put his hands in his pockets and turned to return to the car. "I might just have to say goodbye to 'Jackson Hills.'"

"But with a few changes, you could say hello to 'Jackson Grove'," Clare said.

49

HENRY HAD ARRANGED for a late-morning Thursday flight to New York from Wilmington International Airport. In about two hours they were on the ground at LaGuardia. They took their carryon luggage and got a cab into Manhattan and checked in at the Marriott Marquis hotel. Henry guessed that Clare would like being on Times Square.

The splendid lobby told them they had made the perfect choice for their weekend in the "Big Apple." Their view of the city from their upper story room in New York's second largest hotel convinced them they had made the right decision.

Drawing on pleasant experiences from previous trips, Henry suggested lunch at Sardi's, a popular gathering place for theatrical celebrities for 75 years known for its walls lined with caricatures of well-known Broadway figures. Crowded as always, the restaurant had enough space to accommodate the couple for their special New York visit.

They didn't recognize any of their fellow diners, but after all, it was lunch. Famous faces might be seen among the pre-theater or after theater crowds.

Clare opted for lunch from the appetizer menu, choosing Onion Soup au Gratin and Jumbo Lump Crabcake with accompaniments. Henry selected a Sardi's traditional special, Cannelloni au Gratin. He chose an appropriate bottle of wine from the wide-ranging menu.

After lunch they walked up Broadway to 47th Street and purchased tickets at the Ethel Barrymore Theater for that evening's production of *The Curious Incident of the Dog in the Night-time*, the 2015 Tony Award-winning play about a brilliant 15-year-old boy who has difficulty dealing with the stresses of everyday life faced with proving his innocence in the death of a neighbor's dog. From there they caught a cab to the Museum of Modern Art, which was featuring an exhibition of Picasso Sculpture in addition to its extraordinary collections of modern and contemporary art from around the world. They spent a major portion of the afternoon marveling at these treasures.

Walking on 54th Street toward 6th Avenue to hail a taxi, Clare paused to stare across the street at a building that aroused her curiosity. She was taken with its gold-lettered name accented by light bulbs like a mirror in an actor's dressing room.

"What is that?" she asked Henry.

"The Warwick Hotel," he said.

"It looks interesting," she said.

"It has quite a history. You want to take a look?"

She did and he gave her a brief introduction to the distinctive Manhattan landmark that had attracted her attention.

"The Warwick was built by newspaper publishing magnate William Randolph Hearst in 1926 for his mistress, actress Marion Davies, and their visiting Hollywood friends."

"I love this lobby," Clare said, admiring the soft lighting that offered a serene contrast to the city's busy streets and the exquisite chandeliers that exuded centuries-old class.

They peeked in the hotel restaurant, Murals on 54, which takes its name from original 1930s murals by Dean Cornwell.

"This looks lovely," Clare commented.

"You also have to see Randolph's Bar and Lounge," Henry said, pointing across the lobby. "Its martinis are some of the best – and largest – I've ever had." He pointed out the bar's rose-patterned carpeting, a subtle reference to "Rosebud", which was Hearst's nickname for Marion Davies. It also was a key word of the film *Citizen Kane*, which was modeled on Hearst's life.

Leaving the hotel, when they got to 6th Avenue Henry pointed to a marquis about two blocks away. "Hearst provided financial backing for Florenz Ziegfeld, Jr. to build a theater near the hotel, where Miss Davies often played," he said.

"Is that it?" Clare asked.

"No. The original Ziegfeld Theater was razed in 1966 and this one of the same name opened in 1969 and now is a large single screen movie theater. It contains a small Ziegfeld Museum that contains mementos of Will Rogers and other Ziegfeld Follies stars."

Because of their relatively late lunch and a rather early curtain at the theater, the touring couple decided to return to the hotel instead of dining out. They had cocktails and snacks from the mini-bar and became entranced with the magical beauty of New York as the skies darkened and glittering lights traced an outline of the world famous skyline.

Presently Clare broke the spell. "I'd better be getting dressed," she said. "Me, too," said Henry.

A short cab ride got them to the Barrymore Theater as the doors opened, admitting patrons who had been standing in line.

The play has such a powerful impact on audiences a New York Times reviewer warned, "be prepared to have all your emotional sensory buttons pushed." A highly talented young star carried the demanding main role backed by an excellent supporting cast. Also impressive was the set design. A basic box accented by graph lines on top, bottom and sides was equipped with a dazzling array of electronic equipment which produced spectacular visual and audio effects. Clare and Henry agreed that the play rightfully deserved the five Tony awards it received.

Back at the Marriott Marquis Henry suggested they check out the hotel's signature rooftop revolving restaurant and lounge. They found The View reminiscent of times they had enjoyed in San Francisco and Washington, D.C. when their romance was young. They opted for a table for two in the lounge, which offered both cocktail and buffet menus. Clare tried a variation of a Cosmopolitan, called Metropolitan. Henry was drawn to a vodka martini named Perfectly French. From the buffet Clare had a roasted beet salad and Henry chose the more hearty braised short ribs with red wine mustard sauce.

They saw no sign of dancing and by the time they finished their martinis and food the 360-degree rotation had been completed so they retired to their room.

Clare awoke early, filled with eager anticipation of the auditions, scheduled for 10 a.m. at the Whiteway Theater, recently reopened by producer Palmer Stone after years of inactivity. She practiced some tunes from Oklahoma! while she showered. She needed to be prepared for anything she was asked to do.

The contact she had talked to had been little help. She gave her the time and date of the auditions and the address of the theater. Clare had gone to the Internet to gain additional information on what to expect. She learned about the various types of auditions. Some specify hiring of only members of the Actors Equity Union. Clare was not and she had not been told that was required. For some auditions individual appointments may be made. This one was an open audition, also known as a "cattle call."

Glo had advised her to take copies of sheet music in her key for the songs she likely would be asked to sing. She also suggested Clare excerpt a section of dialogue from the script and memorize it, just to be prepared.

Guests were allowed so Henry accompanied her. When they entered the lobby of the theater it was almost fully dark. Clare spotted a sign on the auditorium door reading, "Auditions downstairs." She opened the door anyway to get a peek of the theater where she hoped to be performing. A dim light revealed a bare stage and seats for about 500 – the number given on the Whiteway website. "Oh, well. You have to start small," she said to herself.

They saw an exit and took the stairs down to the basement where they followed sounds of activity to a small meeting room where she saw a piano, a stool and scattered groups and individuals standing or sitting on folding chairs. She reported to a woman seated at a table and gave her the headshot and resume she had been asked to provide. The woman pointed to a sign-in sheet and handed her a form to fill out. She directed Clare to give her music to a man leaning on the piano.

After about 20 women had signed in a man who identified himself as a casting assistant addressed those gathered.

"On behalf of the casting director I want to thank all of you for coming. Today we are holding auditions for the role of Laurey in the forthcoming production of the Rodgers and Hammerstein musical *Oklahoma!*. If there is anyone here for another purpose, you may be excused at this time." Nobody left.

"Each one trying out is asked to sing two musical selections – a maximum of 32 bars each – and deliver a monologue, no longer than one minute in length. You may leave as soon as you have completed your audition. You will be notified within five days as to your status. We will take applicants in the order their names appear on the sign-in sheet. Audrey Harrison, will you please come up?"

A tall slender blonde rose, adjusted her short skirt, walked to the accompanist and gave him her music. The casting assistant said, "You may begin" and Ms. Harrison sang "Oh, What a Beautiful Morning" (hard "g") and "People Will Say We're in Love" (slightly off key). Then she recited a very short portion of dialogue with "Curly" after he bragged about the "Surrey With the Fringe On Top.":

"Only … only there ain't no such rig. You just said you made the whole thing up … Why did you come around here with your stories and lies, getting me all worked up that way? Talking about the sun swimming on the hill, and all – like it was so. Who would want to ride alongside of you anyway?"

Two out of the next eight applicants sang "I'm Just a Girl Who Cain't Say No" (Ado Annie's song) and almost everyone was hard pressed to do a decent monologue. Then it was Clare's turn. She presented a more challenging selection, "Many a New Day" and the stirring title song, "Oklahoma!" For her monologue, she chose a dramatic passage from a conversation between Laurey and her hired hand, the dark, moody Jud Fry. (When she first read the script

Clare could tell right away the rural Oklahoma dialect would require a lot of practice.)

"Air you making threats to me? Air you standing there tryin' to tell me 'f I don't allow you to slobber on me like a hog, why, you're gonna do sumpin 'bout it? Why you're nuthin' but a mangy dog and somebody orta shoot you. You think so much about being a hired hand. Well, I'll just tell you sumpin that'll rest yer brain, Mr. Jud. You ain't a hired hand fer me no more. You can jist pack up yer duds and scoot. You ain't to come on the place again, you hear me? I'll send yer stuff any place you say, but don't you as much as set foot inside the pasture gate or I'll sic the dogs onto you."

Henry couldn't help but notice that everyone in the room, including the casting assistance, was riveted to Clare's performance.

"Thank you, Ms. Sullivan," he said. "Next applicant."

Henry congratulated Clare on her audition. They decided to watch the remaining applicants, one by one, put their best foot forward. After they finished, the casting assistant huddled with a couple of women and the accompanist, then asked: "Is Ms. Sullivan still here?"

"Yes, I'm here," Clare said.

"Will you please come forward? We would like to ask if you could sing a few bars from two other songs in the show: 'People Will Say We're in Love' and 'Out of My Dreams.' We have the music and Pete can adapt to your key."

"I'll be happy to," she said as she walked to the front of the room. She sang the two songs with feeling, as if she were performing on the theater stage on opening night. The casting assistant thanked her and said, "We'll be back in touch with you."

As they settled into the back seat of the taxi Henry hugged her close and said, lovingly, "I have a hunch you've got the part."

"Thanks for your support," she said.

"Where to?" asked the cabbie.

"Chelsea Market," Henry said, and turning to Clare he added, "There's a great Italian restaurant there where I thought we'd have lunch."

"Sounds good," she said, still coming down from a high after the audition.

Macelleria, in the heart of the Meatpacking District, is an upscale Italian steakhouse offering prime cuts of meat and Northern Italian cuisine. They were seated at a table that afforded a pleasing view of the exposed brick walls of the former meat locker building. The authentic Italian lunch menu offered a wide selection of home-made pasta dishes and steaks fresh from the butcher. (The name of the restaurant is Italian for "butcher shop.")

Clare ordered Tuscan White Bean Soup and Straw and Hay Tagliolini and Henry succumbed to the prime, dry-aged T-bone. Both had to try the Tiramisu for dessert.

Halfway through his meal, Henry said, "I haven't had food like this since I was in Tuscany."

"I was just thinking the same thing," Clare said.

They walked off at least part of their lunch by strolling through the shops of the Chelsea Market and checking out the newly-re-opened Whitney Museum of American Art, which has a permanent collection of more than 21,000 examples of new media by more than 3,000 artists.

On the way back to the hotel Henry read a message on his phone from a wine industry colleague who somehow learned he was in New York. The friend was inviting him to a reception this very evening at the exclusive Union League Club. He called back to thank him for the invitation.

"We have tickets for a show at 8 p.m. so it will have to be a touch-and-go but I'd love to see you and I want you to meet my special friend Clare." They arranged to meet at the club at 6 p.m.

The Union League Club, founded in 1863, is situated in a clubhouse designed by architect Benjamin Wystar Morris and built on property once belonging to the family of J. P. Morgan. Its Georgian exterior, with its symmetrical red brick façade, reflects familiar motifs from Park Avenue brownstone mansions.

Clare was glad she had a last-minute impulse to pack a dress appropriate for the occasion which also would serve for the later theater event. Henry would have to make do with a dark suit.

As they entered the club they were struck with the beauty of the grand staircase. They opted for the elevator which took them up to the reception in the Grant Room, which held a collection of portraits of Ulysses S. Grant and other great generals who served under President Abraham Lincoln. The subdued lighting and the dark oak paneling made the room an elegant and cozy setting for the reception.

Henry spotted his friend right away and introduced him to Clare. He directed them to the open bar and while the two men engaged in conversation she took her wine and checked out the spread of appetizing finger food from the club's marvelous menu. She had to sample the club's famous foie gras. At the display of cold shrimp on ice, she was joined by another guest, a nice-looking well-tanned gentleman with a neatly-trimmed mustache.

"Excuse me," he said. "This is not a come-on line, honestly. But you look so familiar. I believe we've met before. I'm Ted Sargent, president of a winery in upstate New York."

"It's possible we met at a fundraising reception last year when I was running for governor of California. I'm Clare Sullivan deLune."

"That's it! In Washington, D.C.," he said.

"I was with Henry Jackson," she said, nodding in his direction, "of Mt. Jackson Vineyards in the state of Washington."

"Well, what a coincidence," he said, helping himself to a shrimp. "I'm so sorry you lost your race."

"Perhaps it was for the best," said Clare. "My life has taken a turn for the better."

"What brings you to New York City?"

Clare filled him in briefly on how she had begun a career in acting and that she might land a role in a Broadway show.

"I certainly wish you well," he said. At that point Henry began moving toward the table as Ted Sargent walked away. Henry was naturally curious and she filled him in. He didn't recall having met him.

After about an hour the two had had their fill of fellowship and food so they stole away for their theater date. When the elevator doors opened downstairs, they were startled to see a barrel-chested figure in a tux who looked vaguely familiar to Clare. He bore a faint resemblance to Orson Welles.

Staring at her with piercing dark eyes he exclaimed, "Aha! Here's my new star!"

For a moment Clare thought she was back in Hollywood. He broke the spell when he smiled and said in a loud voice, "Clare Sullivan, I believe."

Taken aback, she said, "Why, yes. And you are Mister ..."

"Stone. Palmer Stone."

"How delightful to meet you," she said, reflexively extending a hand. "But what you said – that's a little presumptuous, isn't it?"

"My casting director tells me you excelled in today's tryouts for the part of Laurey in *Oklahoma!*. He'll discuss the results with his staff again but we should have a decision by late next week."

"That soon? My, my."

"I have to tell you, Ms. Sullivan ..."

"Please call me Clare ..."

"... Clare, you are far more beautiful and vivacious in person than in your photo."

Feeling a bit annoyed, Henry intervened, "Please excuse us, Mr. Stone. We have an eight o'clock curtain."

"Oh, what are you seeing?"

When they told him, the Broadway veteran said, "*A Gentleman's Guide to Love and Murder* – you'll love it. I only wish I had produced it. Give my best to Gloria Levine. Enjoy your evening."

With a slight bow, he stepped into the elevator and ended the bizarre encounter.

Clare had a hard time concentrating on the farcical British musical, thinking about her meeting with Palmer Stone. "He knew who I was!" she thought to herself.

With crowds of theatergoers on the streets, they felt safe in walking to Rockefeller Center, where they went to SixtyFive, the sophisticated lounge at the Top of the Rock, to relax from their invigorating day. They tried some contemporary cocktails and had tuna tacos and wagyu beef sliders from the small plate menu.

The nighttime view was as intoxicating as the one from their hotel. They finished off the evening in high style with a few turns around the dance floor of the Rainbow Room.

Brunch the next morning at the Marquis Marriott added a memorable touch to their weekend in New York.

50

WHILE AWAITING FINAL WORD on the Broadway show tryouts, Clare was busy in Wilmington tying up loose ends in anticipation of an extended absence from home.

In line with her earlier conversations with Zach Bacharach, she did a number of soundstage shoots for *Busboys*. As much as she looked forward to a possible live theater experience, she realized she was going to miss working with the actors and the director who had made this TV series a success. After doing a wrap for the season her fellow performers made her the guest of honor at a cast party farewell on one of the interior sets.

Gloria hosted a dinner party in her home for the organizers of the Tri-County Players, Clare's springboard to a new career on the Broadway stage. She and Ben rewarded their guests with a memorable evening of food, drinks, sing-along around the piano and much fun in return for their hard work in getting the new theater enterprise off the ground.

Clare deliberately made time for some private lunches with best-friend Barbara, always managing to work in an inquiry about Phil, whose physical appearance made it clear he was stressed and not in the best of health. When she mentioned to Henry that his wife had said he was spending an extraordinary number of evenings away from home "on business", his partner had a theory about what he was doing.

"He's probably out playing poker," Henry said. "I've heard that poker games in people's homes is quite a popular activity around town."

"His gambling addiction hasn't shown any sign of weakening, has it?"

"I'm afraid not."

In the midst of her mad whirl, Clare received a call from Xavier Turner, casting director for Precious Stone Ventures, who said: "Ms. Sullivan, Mr. Palmer Stone asked me to tell you that you have been selected to play the role of Laurey in his forthcoming production of *Oklahoma!* at the Whiteway Theater in New York."

Clare managed to contain her exuberance at receiving the official word that she had won the part and politely thanked him for calling. She listened carefully as he again conveyed a message from Mr. Stone requesting her presence at a press conference unveiling the members of the cast for the Broadway classic, along with information about the schedule for rehearsals.

She quickly put her speed dial to work to share her exciting news with Henry, Barbara, Gloria and other local friends, and after a short pause she decided to phone Becky. When she answered Clare asked about their mother and father ("both doing well, adjusting nicely to the new living arrangement") and then told her about the life-changing adventure she was about to undertake.

"That's wonderful, Clare," Becky said. "And I also have some big news. Jim and I got married last week."

"You did?" said Clare. "And you didn't invite me to your wedding?"

"Nobody was invited. It was a quiet ceremony in Pastor Pete's office. For all Momma knows we were already married. And I had told Daddy ahead of time that was what we were planning to do."

"What about Betty Ann?"

"She was disappointed we didn't have a big church wedding, but she's very happy for us to be living with Jim because they have become so close."

"Well, this is a big development. I think our plan is going to work out very well."

51

PALMER STONE had developed a reputation for being a flamboyant theatrical impresario so it was no surprise to Broadway veterans that he promised some surprises in revealing his plans to stage a revival of the 1943 Rodgers and Hammerstein musical *Oklahoma!* Nothing seemed to faze him, including the fact that there have been nine revivals in New York, three of them closing after 15 performances.

Stone's confidence in his venture stemmed from the historical success of the show, which ushered in the modern era of Broadway musicals. The original production had a phenomenal run of 2,212 performances. The 1955 film version won two Academy Awards.

The news conference was scheduled for 10 a.m. at the Whiteway Theater. Clare and Henry had flown to New York the previous day and, by Clare's request, checked in at the Warwick Hotel, where they spent a quiet evening following a marvelous dinner in Murals on 54.

Henry had told her more of the hotel's history and she couldn't stop talking about the place where so many celebrities had stayed over the years. Elizabeth Taylor and Elvis Presley were frequent guests. The Beatles stayed there on their first visit to the U.S. Cary Grant was a resident for 12 years.

They ordered room service for breakfast in their room, which had a view of 6th Avenue looking past Radio City Music Hall and all the way to the One World Trade Center Freedom Tower. The simple yet elegant décor of the spacious Premier Plus bedroom conveyed a feeling of incomparable luxury. Both in the rooms and in the hotel corridors were black and white photos of Marion Davies and other famous figures of the Roaring Twenties.

"Marion Davies was long before my time, but she must have been pretty hot for a media magnate like Hearst to fall for her," Clare said.

"She did have a rather spectacular career, rising from the chorus of the Ziegfeld Follies to become a popular film comedienne, thanks in large part to Hearst's financial backing of her films as well as his promotional efforts. She acquired a small fortune and in her later years devoted herself to Hearst and charitable work."

"And they never married?"

"No. Hearst's wife refused to give him a divorce without a huge settlement that he was unwilling to pay."

"How romantic!"

"In some respects, perhaps. But their life together was actually quite scandalous."

"We can talk more about that another time," Clare said, "but right now we've got to get going to Palmer Stone's press conference."

This time when Clare entered the Whiteway Theater lots of lights were on. Signs were posted stating the press conference was in the theater. She and Henry found seats in the section reserved for the cast and settled in for a momentous development in their lives.

While members of the press and others were gathering, a giant projection screen was filled with promos of Precious Stone movies. The curtain was drawn to reveal the set for the opening scenes of *Oklahoma!*: a vast cornfield with a never-ending cloudless blue sky.

At precisely 10 a.m. the promos ceased, the screen retreated and Palmer Stone took the stage.

"Good morning, ladies and gentlemen. This is a momentous day in the theatrical history of Broadway musicals in New York."

The "ho-hums" among the veteran entertainment reporters present were almost audible.

Stone continued a Donald Trump-like recitation of his accomplishments for another five minutes before getting to the point of the press conference.

"Today we are announcing the members of the cast of the Precious Stones production of the fabulous Rodgers and Hammerstein musical *Oklahoma!*. Ladies and gentlemen, it is my privilege to present the casting director, Xavier Turner."

Turner introduced the members of the singing and dancing ensemble and the two dancers who would perform the dream sequence, as well as the actors portraying some lesser characters. He was followed by Anthony Milam, the show's director.

"I am pleased to present an outstanding group of actors who have been chosen for featured roles in this production," he said. "I will begin with Yousef Tehrani, who is The Peddler, Ali Hakim. Mr. Tehrani played the role in two London productions of *Oklahoma!* ..."

Milam continued with the portrayers of Jud Fry, the surly hired hand; Ado Annie, the boy-crazy farm girl; Will Parker, the cowboy who is in love with her;

and Aunt Eller, a bighearted but tough farm woman who looks after her niece, Laurey, and tries to keep peace between the farmers and cowboys.

Palmer Stone returned to the stage to reveal the identity of the two lead characters.

"*Oklahoma!* is a high-spirited portrayal of life on the American frontier, but it basically is a love story of two headstrong romantics: Laurey, a winsome farm girl, and Curly, a handsome cowboy, who find that love's journey is as bumpy as a ride down a country road.

"As most of you know, I am a 'new frontiers' type of entrepreneur. So I am presenting a slightly new interpretation of the characters in this Lynn Riggs play, *Green Grow the Lilacs*, adapted by the masters, composer Richard Rodgers and lyricist Oscar Hammerstein.

"That said, I want to welcome a pair of newcomers to the Broadway stage.

"It is an extreme pleasure to introduce you to Clare Sullivan. She has so many qualities of Laurey, I think she is perfect for the part. Clare brings to the stage of the Whiteway Theater experience in singing and dancing roles in Europe as well as a solid background in community theater. Clare was the star of two productions of the Three-County Players in Wilmington, North Carolina, where she was a local TV personality. And I'm sure you are familiar with her starring role in the TV series, *Busboys*, playing on your favorite cable TV channel. Ladies and gentlemen, I am proud to present Clare Sullivan."

As she had planned, Clare emerged from the wings, did a sprightly strut toward the microphone, and then a saucy spin to join the producer at center stage. She took a bow to the scattered applause.

"Thank you, Clare," said Stone. "And now I want to tell you something else you didn't know. Those of you in the press who have covered my exploits on Broadway are well aware that I enjoy surprising you. Clare Sullivan, a new face on the Great White Way, is one surprise. Prepare yourselves for another one.

"For the role of Curly, we have cast a nationally known figure from the world of entertainment, a man who built a wide public following as the star of a highly popular TV series and has continued to deliver winning performances in summer theater productions around the country. We are extremely fortunate that his schedule has allowed him to be available to adapt his acting and singing skills to become Curly in the Precious Stones production of *Oklahoma!*. Ladies and gentlemen, I present to you the star of the award-winning television series, *The Chief Executive*, Pat Brown."

52

FROM THE OPPOSITE SIDE of the stage, Brown strode to the center and took a deep bow to generous applause coming from a large group of his supporters who had unobtrusively entered the theater and taken some seats in the rear.

Clare was dumbstruck. In her wildest imagination she never could have predicted that her co-star in *Oklahoma!* would be the person who knocked her out of the open primary in the California governor's race. Her first thought was to tell Palmer Stone to "take this job and shove it" but Henry's strong arm around her shoulders and his encouraging, "Hang in there, girl", gave her the confidence that she could cope with this most unpredictable situation.

"Brown probably is just as shocked as you are," Henry said. "Palmer Stone is terribly wicked, but he's also a very smart businessman. You saw the reporters scattering to get their stories out. This will be front page news in *Variety* and the rest of the New York entertainment media. Sweetheart, prepare to become famous overnight."

"Well, since you put it that way …"

Clare was still trying to cope with this unexpected development when she saw a woman approaching whom she did not immediately recognize. It was Anne Malone, a veteran actress who had been cast as Aunt Eller.

After introducing herself she said, "My dear, I just want to tell you how much I look forward to working with you. I have enjoyed your performances in *Busboys* and I think you will bring just the right combination of spunkiness and tenderness to the role of Laurey. I know you're new to Broadway, so anything you need to get adjusted I stand willing and able to help."

Clare thanked her profusely. "I can't begin to express how grateful I am for your offer. This is a big step for me and I do welcome your support."

Turning to Henry, Clare said, "As much as I would dearly love to leave right now, I need to touch base with Mr. Stone and make myself known to the director. I'd like for you to come with me."

They made their way past the press section and onto the stage where she came face to face with Pat Brown.

"Well, Ms. de Lune, we meet again," he said with a smirk.

"It's Sullivan, but just call me Clare," she responded, coolly.

"I hope this experience won't be as combative as the last one," he said.

"There's no reason it should be. You play your part and I'll play mine and we'll give the audience the best we've got," she said, managing a smile.

As they parted she couldn't help but notice someone scampering to meet Brown, a dark-haired man short of height, brown of color, handing him his coat and hat.

She kept moving and encountered Anthony Milam, who extended his hand. Prolonging his handshake, the director said, "I am delighted to meet you, Ms. Sullivan …"

"Please call me Clare," she said.

"Clare. I look forward to getting to know you and working with you on this exciting production."

"Likewise, Mr. Milam. Or may I call you Anthony?"

"Of course. Or Tony, if you like."

"Thank you, Tony. As you know I've never done a Broadway show."

"And I've never run for governor of a big state or saved anyone from a shark. You're going to do just fine."

(He must have Googled me, she thought.) But if that didn't inspire her confidence nothing would.

She said a quick hello to Palmer Stone, thanked him again for the opportunity and shook hands with some of the other actors gathered around. Then she and Henry went on their way.

Since rehearsals weren't to begin until the following Monday they decided to catch an afternoon flight back to Wilmington. But first Henry negotiated a longterm agreement for Clare to make the Warwick Hotel her temporary home in New York.

53

OVER THE WEEKEND back home, Clare and Henry had dinner with the Sterlings and Phil betrayed no signs of his gambling addiction. He did mention he had been seeing a cardiologist. "Nothing to worry about," he assured his friends.

Clare's essential separation from Henry and her life in Wilmington was something the two of them talked about a lot. One thing they agreed upon was that Henry would fly to New York every two weeks while she was away.

They made sure their last weekend before her extended absence was totally private – cell phones off, no answering of doorbells, no monitoring of text or emails. It was a very special weekend.

Clare didn't know what Henry's negotiated contract with the Warwick included but it was readily apparent there was a champagne clause. Her first evening away was room service with bubbly.

She had brought enough clothing to last until she could go shopping. She really didn't need much more than jeans and turtlenecks for the routine that awaited her.

While rehearsals for Broadway musicals can last as long as six weeks, producer Palmer Stone was eager to open the show and director Tony Milam thought three weeks would be sufficient, considering he was working with an experienced cast (the exception being, ironically, the two leads: Clare and Pat Brown).

It would be a grueling three weeks, however. Rehearsals were scheduled eight hours a day six days a week, from 10 a.m. to 6 p.m., with possible evening sessions added as necessary. The final week would include a technical rehearsal for the benefit of sound and light crews and at least two dress rehearsals.

When Clare arrived at the theater at 9:45 Monday morning she was surprised to find a flurry of activity. Part of the cast was already there, some sitting, others standing, having coffee and studying their scripts. Clare had spent some time on the plane and in her room reading her copy, which had been sent to Wilmington by messenger. She was greeted with a cheery "hello" from Anne Malone (Aunt Eller).

"I'll refrain from warbling 'what a beautiful morning' but it is rather nice out, isn't it?" she said.

"I'm afraid I didn't get to enjoy the weather much, just hopping into and out of a cab," Clare said. "I do enjoy walking and I hope to find time to do that later on."

As the rest of the cast and crew assembled Tony Milam got their attention and began the first day of rehearsal with a little pep talk about the musical *Oklahoma!* and what a great opportunity it would be to appear in it.

"Anyone here from the state of Oklahoma?" he asked.

A slender young woman named Cheryl from the ensemble group raised her hand. "I am," she said. "I'm a graduate of Oklahoma City University."

"That's the school Kristin Chenoweth attended, isn't it?" Milam said.

"That's right. We're very proud of her."

"Perhaps someday they'll be saying that about you."

Milam opened the session by presenting the assistant director and key members of the production team: the stage manager and the musical director, who made brief remarks. As they were finishing Pat Brown came strolling down the center aisle, closely followed by the man Anne had identified as Brown's East Asian manservant.

Tony Milam, with a stern voice, said, "I'm glad you're here, Mr. Brown. Please be on time from now on. We'll now do a full read-through of the show from wherever you are on stage. Blocking will come later, as will the vocals."

"Excuse me, Tony."

"What is it, Mr. Brown?"

"The show begins with me – Curly – singing, and the dialogue is so intermingled with the lyrics I would prefer to do the vocal now as well as my lines."

"Very well," Milam said. Speaking to the pianist from the tryouts he said, "Pete, you've got the music?" Pete nodded. Continuing, Milam said, "Now, can we get started? Act One, Scene One. The scene is at Laurey's farmhouse. Aunt Eller is outside churning. Curly can be heard singing offstage." He cued Pete who gave a short intro.

"That's not a good key," Brown said, walking to the piano. While Milam and the cast waited impatiently, Brown found a key that was to his liking and he burst out with "Oh, What a Beautiful Mornin'."

After the first two verses, Brown spoke (shouted) his first line: "Hi, Aunt Eller!"

Anne Malone: "Skeer me to death! Whut're you doin' around here?"

Brown: "Why I come a-singin' to you."

He resumed the song, then more dialogue between the two.

When it came time for Laurey's appearance, she did as Brown had and began singing offstage.

The series of sharp exchanges between the cowboy and the farmer's daughter, with interjections by Laurey's aunt led into the second song, another solo by Curly, "Surrey With the Fringe on Top."

The read-through went much more smoothly after Curly's (Brown's) exit. Brown took a seat in the front row and his lackey brought him a cup of coffee.

Clare had to admit her co-star had a pleasant voice, but not a powerful one. He had relied too many years on a microphone in a quiet studio to make himself heard. Fortunately Clare brought with her experience both on the stage and in broadcasting. Additionally she had learned on the campaign trail how to project her voice to large crowds when a mike was not available.

With Brown temporarily silenced, Tony Milam wore a look of grateful relief on his face. The actor playing Will Parker skipped his solo since it wasn't interspersed with the dialogue (except for a couple of lines by Aunt Eller).

Clare was dreading the duet between Laurey and Curly later in the scene ("People Will Say We're in Love") so she was thrilled to hear Milam tell Brown to pass over that song.

By omitting, or at least abbreviating, the other songs and moving along without interruptions the cast was able to complete the read-through by early afternoon and they gathered for a lunch break in the room that was used for tryouts. Sandwiches and soft drinks had been provided for the cast and crew.

Several cast members whipped out their cell phones and spent the entire time reading messages and texting. Milam had banned them from the rehearsals. If a phone had not been turned off, the owner received a strong scolding.

The afternoon session of the first day's rehearsal was devoted primarily to blocking scenes involving the ensembles. Clare had learned that blocking was an age-old practice that began with Sir W. S. Gilbert, who used wooden blocks on a miniature stage to represent actors and dancers. This exercise facilitated the performance by determining positioning of players on the stage. It was especially important with large groups (ensembles) but also necessary with individuals or couples.

Brown was familiar with blocking from his television work and boasted about it. Clare also brought some experience from her appearances in cruise ship musical shows, but she kept that to herself.

The musical director met with all the actors doing solos or duets and alerted them to certain peculiarities of the Whiteway Theater and its stage. Then he passed out schedules listing times when one of the three meeting rooms in the theater would be available for them to practice their songs with recorded music. Those not doing so could use that time to study their lines.

To Clare's surprise the afternoon passed rather quickly and almost before she knew it the first day of rehearsals was over.

One item of business before being dismissed was assignment of dressing rooms. The assistant director explained that these spaces were limited and some sharing would be necessary. As leads Clare and Brown rated private rooms. Tiny as they were, the rooms provided an area for access to costumes, makeup and a table and chair with a reading lamp.

Dressing rooms would seldom be used during rehearsals because everyone took open breaks. But they were essential during the run of a show.

At five past six o'clock, Clare said goodbye to Anne Malone, waved at some of her other fellow actors and caught a taxi to the Warwick.

When she opened the door to her room she broke into a smile. On the bedside table was a vase with a dozen red roses and a note from Henry: "With love to the star of my life." She immediately called him and filled him in on her first day.

After changing clothes she went downstairs to the lounge and ordered a martini and a serving of calimari as she celebrated the beginning of a new adventure.

54

BOREDOM RESULTS from repeating an experience over and over – like watching political debates. While a Broadway musical is a much more exciting goal than an election, rehearsing can produce the same monotonous effect. After the first week Clare was finding it difficult to spend each day going to the theater, repeating the same lines, singing the same songs and occupying the same spaces on the stage for eight hours, and then return to the same lonely hotel room. She missed Henry terribly. Although with his job and her many activities they didn't normally spend a great deal of time together in Wilmington, being totally absent from one another 24 hours a day was painful. If it weren't for their nightly phone chats and his visits every two weeks she wondered how she could handle it for the long haul.

But she was committed to the show and it was something she definitely wanted to do so she forced herself to face each day with a positive outlook. One thing that helped was having breakfast in a popular diner about a block from the hotel. The Astro has been offering good food and service since 1980. It is a bright, cheery place, and that description extends to the wait staff. The first morning Clare tried the restaurant she slid into a green padded booth and was greeted by a waitress named Irma wearing a green "Astro" ball cap, carrying a menu and a pot of hot coffee. Clare learned later that a satisfied patron had posted Irma's photo on an Internet website, tagging her "the friendliest waitress in New York City." She ordered a scrambled egg with turkey sausage and was surprised to see that it came with grits. That was most pleasing to the homesick Southern woman's heart.

On subsequent mornings, Irma, a Russian immigrant who had been working in New York for many years, welcomed Clare and called her by name. She tried a variety of the diner's specialties, including delicious omelets; French toast, served with a variety of toppings; and blueberry muffins, which had a generous pocket of blueberry filling in the middle. The diner's Greek owners have a special menu featuring their own Greek yogurt creations.

Henry had arranged to have a small refrigerator in Clare's room, where she could keep bottled water, juices, milk, champagne and other life-sustaining substances. She could obtain these and other food products from a large market within easy walking distance from the Warwick.

Steady progress was being made in the rehearsals. Clare gradually got accustomed to working with Pat Brown, becoming more tolerant of his oversized ego. His valet was never out of his sight, catering to his every need. She and Anne discussed this strange relationship privately.

"Why do you think Brown feels it necessary to have a fulltime servant?" Clare asked.

"I'm not a shrink, but it may be to bolster his ego. He must have suffered quite a blow having his TV show cancelled. Losing the governor's race eroded his stature even more. When he had to resort to acting in summer stock he had to have something to prop up his public image. I guess he had enough money to hire Oo for that purpose."

"Oo?" said Clare quizzically.

"That's the guy's name."

"Oh."

"No, Oo. Win Ye Oo. I understand that stands for bright and brave."

"Oh. I see. Well, he certainly is protective of his employer."

Tony Milam stuck to a six-day rehearsal schedule so Clare had only one free day when Henry flew up for his bi-weekly check-in. He caught the tail end of Saturday's rehearsal and they spent a large part of the evening in Randolph's Bar and Lounge getting reacquainted.

Sunday was a nice day to get out and get the feel of the city so they took a walk. It was only a few blocks to Central Park, where they strolled at leisure for awhile. Then Henry spotted a horse and carriage rental and they headed that way. Awaiting them was a stylish coach drawn by a handsome brown horse with a liveried driver in a top hat holding the reins. Clare jokingly asked if there were any surreys available. The driver gave her a puzzled look and motioned for them to get in. The ride was about a mile and a half long and as they rolled along they admired the cherry and ginkgo trees. The route gave them views of Columbus Circle, the Wolfman Rink, the Carousel, the Plaza, the Essex House and the New York Athletic Club.

They resumed their walk and returned to the hotel by way of 5th Avenue, window-shopping along the way. There were many New Yorkers as well as wide-eyed tourists along the streets enjoying the good weather and the sights of the beautiful city.

Their time together had sped quickly and Henry reluctantly kissed his sweetheart goodbye and left to catch his plane. Clare sadly settled into a chair by a window in her room and after briefly looking out at the passing scene turned back to a novel she had started. It wasn't long before she nodded off. When she awoke she had a snack and a glass of wine from her refrigerator stock and read through the script one more time before retiring for the day.

At the beginning of the new week the cast began working "off book" – scripts were not allowed on the stage. By this point in the rehearsals everyone was expected to have their parts memorized. The stage manager or assistant director was on duty to "throw" the actors lines they might have trouble remembering. Day by day all the actors got better and by the end of the week they had the script down pat.

Clare had an easy time getting the lyrics to her songs right, but she did stumble a few times on the dialogue, some of which was very fast-moving. Pat Brown was bad about ad-libbing lines he missed, which drew sharp rebukes from the director.

Fittings for costumes were worked into the schedule. Clare was pleased with the dresses appropriate for the era that were designed for her to wear. Colorful and authentic costumes add so much to a Broadway show and Tony Milam was well aware of their importance.

The same is true for musical numbers involving dancing. The original production of *Oklahoma!* is remembered for the groundbreaking choreography of Agnes de Mille. While none could compare with this giant of the Broadway stage, Milam was fortunate to have a most skilled choreographer in Louise Carlotta. She put the dancers through their paces with precision and patience.

Leading up to the week of dress rehearsals, the full cast and crew did a technical rehearsal – a walk-through of the show in order of performance to make sure every light cue, sound effect and any other staging action worked as required. If adjustments were necessary this would be the time to make them. Brown muttered under his breath about having to endure this exercise. During breaks Oo was on the spot with hot coffee or a cold drink.

Over the weekend Clare caught a movie at the Ziegfeld Theater after taking a tour of the exhibits in the theater lobby, including a showcase featuring some stars of the Ziegfeld Follies: Will Rogers, W. C. Fields, Eddie Cantor and Fannie Brice. As she entered the theater Clare felt as if she had stepped into a bygone era, with its red carpet and chandeliers. The auditorium could accommodate 1,000 patrons in its red velvet seats. It was a magical moment in a grand movie palace. She only wished Henry could have shared it with her.

189

Tony Milam began the final week of rehearsals with an overall critique of the cast's performance, mostly complimentary. He stressed the importance of the dress rehearsals.

"This is the show," he said. "The only thing missing is the audience."

Luckily, no illness, accident or other misfortune had befallen anyone in the cast or crew. There would be no sneezing sopranos or barking baritones to detract from the beauty of Rodgers and Hammerstein's time-worn tunes. Seamstresses would be standing by at every performance in the event of a missing button or a stuck zipper. Wardrobe malfunctions could not be tolerated.

One big difference for the final week was the presence of a live orchestra. Up to now, the singers and dancers had practiced to recorded music. Dress rehearsals would be practices for both the performers and the musicians. Clare felt that singing with a band improved her delivery immensely.

She and Pat Brown had come through the early rehearsals without incident – Milam had stressed that regardless of any past conflict their behavior on stage had to be strictly professional. Truthfully, Clare enjoyed the sniping between Laurey and Curly in the opening scenes of the show much more than the romantic episodes later on. The hardest thing for her to do was in the second act when Curly proposed marriage, Laurey accepted and they had to kiss. But she pointed out the script did not call for a long kiss and Milam was all right with that.

One ironic thing was the friendship she developed with Lance Parrish, the actor who played the part of Jud Fry, the violent villain of the story. Laurey was deathly afraid of him, especially after she fired him as her ranch hand. In real life she and Parrish joked with each other and talked about their families. They were totally different when they played their scenes.

When the day came for the final dress rehearsal, it was time for the director and his various assistants to stand back and watch. The production had to flow without interruption. If anything went wrong the cast and crew had to handle it, That was the only way to be fully prepared to deliver the very best performance for the ticket buyers who came with that expectation.

Milam believed in giving everyone an afternoon and almost a full day off before the opening performance, which was Saturday night. Henry arrived Friday afternoon and met Clare at the Warwick. They decided to dine in – martinis in Randolph's Lounge and dinner in the Murals Restaurant, retire early and have an easy day Saturday. Clare introduced Henry to The Astro – unfortunately Irma had the day off and the only seating was at the front near the door, which subjected them to an icy blast every time a new customer arrived. She also wanted him to see the Ziegfeld Theater, so they took in an early matinee. Then she was off to the theater for her big evening.

One of the trade papers had an unflattering piece about the show, chiding producer Palmer Stone about trying to "milk profits from an old cow" by doing a revival of *Oklahoma!* and concluding that "the only aspect of the show that is somewhat promising is the casting of popular TV star Pat Brown as the handsome cowboy who sweeps a shy farm girl (an unknown named Clare Sullivan) off her feet with his charm." Stone blocked copies of the article from getting onto the set, so as not to upset the performers before the opening. He also ordered that performers could not use any electronic devices that evening as a further guard against disclosure of the article.

Show business historian John Kenrick gives an excellent description of the inaugural production of a show on the Broadway stage:

"Openings are still terribly exciting backstage. Flowers, gifts and congratulatory telegrams are received. Spirits run high, and good wishes of the traditional 'break a leg' variety are exchanged. Just before curtain time, directors give the cast a final pep talk, and the 'Gypsy Robe' ritual takes place. These robes are plain canvas material, and are passed on from one Broadway musical to the next. The most senior dancer in the chorus parades the current robe around the stage to bring good luck. Before passing it on to the next production, the cast embroiders a memento on the robe. When all the space on a robe is used up, it is retired and a new one starts from scratch."

Even without a glass of wine or other stimulant, Clare was feeling "up" for her debut in the big time. She felt confident about her ability to deliver her songs and her lines and to win the hearts of the audience with her smile. She did, of course, feel the thrill of anticipation as the hour for curtain time approached.

Finally the magic hour arrived and the lights went down, the orchestra broke into the overture, the curtain went up and Palmer Stone's production of *Oklahoma!* began. Peeking from backstage Clare could tell there was close to a full house and for her sake and the entire cast and crew she was most glad of that.

The first act went off without a hitch and the crowd was quite receptive. Clare felt good about her performance and she gushed at the compliment extended by Anne Malone, who had become her closest friend in the cast. During intermission members of the audience refreshed themselves at the bar in the lobby and returned with an enthusiastic response to "The Farmer and the Cowman", the rousing number that began the second act. The scenes involving Ado Annie, Will Parker and Ali Hakim drew generous applause and the stirring rendition of "Oklahoma!" brought the audience to its feet. Director Tony Milam had impressed on the cast the importance of the title song. In the original production, only after out-of-town tryouts had the director elevated that song from a duet to a choral piece and it replaced "Away We Go" as the show's title before the 1943 opening.

As the performers took their final bows, Clare experienced a special thrill when the audience rose and gave a standing ovation. She virtually floated to her dressing room after one of the happiest moments of her life. She quickly changed from her Laurey costume, expecting Henry to come and join her at the opening night party at Carnegie Hall. She had just finished applying fresh lipstick when she heard a knock on the door. She opened it to find Henry – but he was not alone. Standing there with him were her parents, Pat and Betty, and Henry's dad – Pop, and his wife, Jean.

Clare was so surprised she almost fainted. "Daddy! Momma!", she cried and embraced both of them. "Pop and Jean! I can't believe you are here!" She gave both of them warm hugs, then turned to Henry, hugged him tightly and gave him a big smack on the lips.

"We are all very proud of you, darling," Henry said.

Pop chimed in with, "You were great!" Jean followed with "We enjoyed your performance so much."

Pat stepped forward and took both of her hands in his. "This is one of the finest moments of my life. You have made me one proud pappy."

"Oh, Daddy. Thank you," she said. Turning to Betty, she knew she had to phrase what she said very carefully, considering her mother had not recovered her memory after her fall. She decided another hug was better than words. She was taken aback when Betty said softly, "I love you, Judy Clare."

"Enough of this," said Pop. "Let's go party."

On the cab ride over Henry admitted to arranging the surprise reunion. Pop had used the company's executive jet to pick up Pat and Betty and fly to New York. They had arrived that afternoon and checked into the Le Parker Meridien Hotel on West 56th, not far from the Warwick.

Clare was still trying to cope with the events of the evening – the successful opening of *Oklahoma!* and the surprise reception Henry had planned – when they arrived at the party room in Carnegie Hall where she had another surprise. As they walked in the door she saw some familiar faces across the room. Huddled together in conversation were her director, Tony Milam;

her TV series director, Zach Bacharach; her Tri-County Players director, Gloria Levine; and her best friend from Wilmington, Barbara Sterling.

As she walked toward the group their faces lit up and they broke into cheers. "You made quite a Broadway debut, my dear," said Tony. Zach chimed in, "I'm so glad to see you take your talents from the screen to the stage." Gloria and Barbara gave her hugs and added their praises. "It was a wonderful production, and you were truly the star," Gloria said. "I'm so proud I know you," Barbara giggled.

"Alicia Swift also came with us," Gloria said.

"The Wilmington entertainment columnist?"

"Yes. She went to the hotel to write her review for tomorrow's paper."

"I never dreamed all of you would be here," Clare said. "And I'm so glad you enjoyed the show. Oh, I see the producer. I've got to go give him a hug. Come on, y'all!" She motioned to her family group. "I want you to meet the greatest guy in New York."

Henry had taken the others to the bar. They returned with drinks and Henry had brought a glass of champagne for Clare. They all followed Clare toward the center of the room to one of the buffet tables.

Palmer Stone saw them coming. "Here comes my leading lady," he boomed, and greeted her with a bear hug and a kiss on the cheek.

"I have some dear friends I want you to meet," Clare said, introducing the producer. He greeted them with effusive praise for Clare and asked how they liked the show. Everyone raved about it.

Clare turned to look around the room to see who else was there. "I don't see Pat Brown," she said to Stone.

"He didn't come to the party," Stone said. "He said he thought he might have strained his vocal chords and went to his hotel to gargle and rest."

"I trust he'll be all right for tomorrow's matinee," Clare said.

"So do I," said Stone, "or we might have to get Henry to step in and play the part."

"You don't want to hear me try to sing," Henry said. "But I could do the kissing part."

Everybody laughed and began drifting toward the food. There were ample selections of good things to eat. If Clare had not known better she would have thought she was at a Southern pot luck dinner.

Tony and Zach had separated themselves from the group. The others took their plates and found a table where they sat and talked until the hour was approaching Pop's bedtime.

"I need to go but I'd like to invite all of you to brunch tomorrow morning at the Parker Meridien," he said.

"That's very nice of you, Pop," Clare said. Giving him and Jean another hug, she said, "Thank you again for coming all this way to share my big moment with me."

Shortly afterward everyone went their individual ways. Clare and Henry lingered until she could speak to every member of the cast and crew. Political campaigning habits die hard.

As they were heading for the door Stone's publicity director came running in with an armful of newspapers. She handed one to Clare before she was mobbed by others eager to read the reviews in the early editions.

"It's a theater tradition," she told Henry. They found a spot with some light and Clare blushed as she began to read:

"A new Broadway star was born Saturday evening as Clare Sullivan, making her debut on the New York stage, stole the show in the opening performance of the Rodgers and Hammerstein classic *Oklahoma!* at the Whiteway Theater. The vivacious redhead with the captivating voice breathed new life into an old standard which has endured countless revivals since its maiden entry in 1943. Radiating a personality as fresh as the open plains this Southern-born siren appeared to be having the time of her life as she was pursued by two sons of the frontier trying to win her favor. She was perfectly cast as Laurey, a spirited maid with homespun charm and a sharp wit.

"Sullivan is a delightful contrast to former TV cable show lead Pat Brown, billed as her co-star in this Palmer Stone production. Brown gave an able, but flat, performance as Curly, the dashing cowboy whom every girl in the Oklahoma territory wanted to marry. The collaborators of this pioneering musical play gave Curly some marvelous songs, including 'Oh, What a Beautiful Mornin'' and 'Surrey With the Fringe on Top', but although his singing was competent it didn't have enough sparkle to give these tunes the treatment they deserved.

"Besides Sullivan, also rating favorable mention is Anne Malone, who drew on her theatrical background to deliver a vivid portrayal of Aunt Eller, the wise-cracking sage of the countryside, who spent almost as much time on stage as the colorful sets.

"Credits also go to the show's dancers – a lively young chorus and two talented ballet artists performing the 'dream sequence' originated by choreographer Agnes de Mille. Also deserving of plaudits is the director, Tony Milam, who appears likely to add another award to his collection.

"Palmer Stone is a supremely confident producer and he believes strongly that his decision to revive an all-time favorite – *Oklahoma!* – will bring dedicated movie and television fans back to live theater. Only time will tell if he's right, but he has a good chance with this vehicle. The opening night audience obviously enjoyed the show, as seen by the standing ovation it received."

"Wow!" Henry exclaimed.

Clare, stunned, said, "I must be dreaming."

"No, darling," Henry said. "It's a dream come true."

55

POP ENTERTAINED EVERYONE at brunch with tales of life at Mt. Jackson Vineyards, proudly reporting that he and Jean were enjoying a happy marriage and that Andrew had matured in the job of president that he inherited from his older brother, Henry. He had not totally abandoned his interest in the vineyards and continued to develop new varieties of grapes that produced award-winning wines. Drew (as he preferred to be called) also had come near to ending his bachelorhood by his engagement to a pretty young schoolteacher named Wanda. Jean was quick to show photos of her and Drew on her smart phone. Her album also contained some recent shots of Luna and Houston, who both appeared happy in their respective jobs.

"I suppose they are still content to remain single?" Clare said.

"You mean, like you and Henry?" Pop shot back.

"Now, Pop, don't go getting judgmental," Henry said.

"Why, I wouldn't think of it," Pop replied. Betty, who had kept quiet throughout the meal, surprised Clare by saying, "Nothing would make me happier than to see the two of you get married."

Henry, embarrassed, cleared his throat. Clare, blushing, stammered, "Momma, you're sounding like your old self."

Pat relieved the tension by thanking Pop and Jean for flying him and Betty to New York. "We appreciate that very much," he said, "and also for including us in this delicious brunch."

"You'll have to come to Georgia and stay with us for a spell sometime," Betty said.

Pop finished his Bloody Mary and turned to Henry and Clare. "I guess you haven't given any thought to coming back to the West Coast," he said.

"No, we like living in North Carolina," Clare said. "But we really are far apart, and we do miss all of you."

"Hold on to that jet," Henry chimed in.

Noticing the time, Pop said, "Well, we hate to break up this gathering but we'd better get moving and put that bird in the air."

Clare again thanked them for coming all the way to New York for her opening night. "I hope we can get together again before too long a time has passed," she said.

Henry hugged Pop and Jean while Clare was doing the same with her parents. With a few tears but plenty of smiles the group broke up and went their separate ways.

Since it was only a five-minute walk to the Warwick, Henry and Clare took advantage of the sunny day and went strolling.

"Your mother appears to be making progress toward restoring some of her memory," Henry observed.

"Yes, she is. But somehow her personality isn't quite the same. She's more calm, or something," Clare said. "I'll have to check in with Becky."

"Whenever you can find time between shows," he said.

Their time together passed too quickly and Henry had to head for the airport. "Call me when you can," he said.

Clare took a short nap before going to the theater for the Sunday matinee. Most of the cast members were still giddy from opening night and the generally favorable reviews. That was with the exception of Pat Brown, who was glum and avoided contact with his fellow players, especially Clare. His valet, Oo, glared at her.

The performance went rather well and the audience was quite receptive. Brown made a hasty exit as soon as he changed and took off his makeup. The reviews had not been kind to him and he was not taking it well.

His manner remained the same throughout the following week and Oo was exceptionally attentive to his master, anticipating and meeting his every need.

Brown never joined the cast in the makeshift dining room for a light meal. Oo took food to him in his dressing room. This particular evening the servant carefully balanced two bowls of soup on a tray and in a surprising courteous act stopped by Clare's place at the table and served her one of the bowls. For the moment the scowl was missing from his face. "Why, thank you, Oo," she said. He nodded and went along.

The soup was steaming so Clare resumed a conversation she was having with Anne Malone and allowed it to cool. As she took a spoon to taste the soup a gray cat who frequented the theater came along, begging as usual. Clare wasn't especially hungry so she set the bowl on the floor for the cat, who quickly lapped up the contents. As she and Anne picked up where they left off they became aware of a choking sound from the cat, who was stretched out on the floor, wretching violently.

"Poor kitty," Clare said, reaching down to pat the miserable animal, just as he vomited a sizeable quantity of the soup. Then he jumped up and ran off as an attendant was on her way to clean up the mess.

"I feel sorry for that poor cat," Clare said.

"But aren't you glad you didn't eat that soup," Anne said. "It must have been from a can that was spoiled."

"I guess so," Clare said, somewhat skeptically.

Pat Brown began the performance showing no signs of discomfort. So the incident remained a mystery.

Monday was an off day and Clare wished that Henry could have stayed over. But he had a big business deal to close so he had to get back. This decision to live apart was looking more questionable all the time. But then she thought about the reviews and how much she enjoyed playing the part of Laurey and she felt better.

Nothing peps up a woman more than going shopping. And although Clare could afford to buy whatever she wanted, she couldn't resist a sale. She tried to limit her purchases, knowing everything would have to fit into her luggage for traveling, but she ended up returning to the Warwick with bags in both hands.

"Oh, well. If I have to I can always donate some of the things to Goodwill," she thought.

The evening performances for the rest of the week went well, drawing full houses and standing ovations. Director Tony Milam wore a smile all week.

Clare became a bit unnerved when on Saturday evening as she was about to go onstage a light came crashing down at the spot where she had been standing. Fortunately the music from the orchestra covered the sound and she put herself together and went on as planned.

She couldn't help thinking to herself about singing, "Don't throw bouquets at me, don't drop those heavy lights … "

But as Shakespeare said, "All's well that ends well," so the show went along with the audience not knowing about the backstage incident.

A similar close call came the next evening when Clare stepped on a slick oily spot on the stage as she made her entrance. A member of the chorus grabbed her and broke the fall.

Everyone from Palmer Stone on down was really upbeat about the way things were going, but then they received a shocker. Fred (The Sorehead) Fisher dropped a bombshell of a review pummeling the production from a surprising point of view: the age of the co-stars.

"Ever-hopeful producer Palmer Stone has been basking in some syrupy praise from sycophants he has rewarded with invitations to lavish parties in his penthouse suite. But anyone who takes a hard, cold look at his latest attempt at undeserved fame will have to say he has failed the theatergoing public again," he wrote.

"Stone dusted the cobwebs off of a timeworn musical play about illiterate hicks trying to eke out a bare living in a forlorn land by raising wheat and cattle while battling each other. Struggling playwrights Richard Rodgers and Oscar Hammerstein tried to inject a modicum of entertainment value into this setting by concocting a fanciful love triangle involving an egotistical cowboy and a bitter farm hand seeing who could be first to bed down with a comely maiden with a mind of her own.

"This tale of young love was hard enough to swallow in the original presentation back in the '40s but it's nigh impossible to accept the premise with the miscasting of the two leads in Stone's production. Both are far too mature to play the characters they are supposed to portray. I haven't checked birth records but anyone who has followed Pat Brown's career knows he had already been around for awhile before he landed the starring role in cable TV's *The Chief Executive* series. As for Clare Sullivan, making a virginal debut on Broadway, reading her biography makes it clear she is no spring chicken. She has a career that stretches back over years of traipsing around Europe before striking it rich in California by marrying a wealthy but self-destructive icon of racing and then using her inherited wealth to make a foolish attempt to win election as governor of California.

"The matinee idol handsome Brown could have redeemed himself if he had displayed any characteristics of the dashing cowboy Curly but his talents for acting and singing fell short on both counts. Sullivan's singing and dancing ability enabled her to fool the audience into picturing a youthful Laurey, whereas her age would fit her better for the Aunt Eller role.

"Rodgers and Hammerstein created a corny but classical Broadway musical that has pleased audiences throughout the world over the years with lovers that do not age. Why Palmer Stone thinks he can improve the work of the masters by altering their vision is beyond the understanding of this reviewer."

Stone was boiling mad but his pride kept a lid on his anger. Overnight he put together a positive public relations offensive that included joint appearances with Clare on two popular daytime TV programs, a radio interview and a sidewalk press conference in front of his theater – all on Monday.

The producer picked up Clare in his limousine at 7 a.m. for an early appearance on *New Day Dawning*, which was produced in a studio with a view overlooking Central Park. Stone swept in with Clare on his arm and wasted no time in decimating Fisher's damaging review.

After overtly charming the host, Stone zeroed in on the aging issue Fisher raised in his review.

"Look at her," he said, pointing to Clare. "A shining example of youth."

Clare did try hard to keep herself in good shape but that was not the only point Stone wanted to make.

"The audacity – the audacity of this upstart to presume he has any qualification whatsoever to dictate the characteristics of any actor on any stage in this great city … it is absolutely beyond belief," he said.

"The mark of an accomplished actor is to be able to play a part the way the playwright envisioned it. In Shakepearean times it was common for women to play men's roles – and play them honestly and straightforward, not as a caricature.

"In the final analysis, it is the producer of the show, the director, the musical director – all the other wizards of production – who make the script come to life, who transform imagination into reality – they do all this to inspire and entertain an audience that cares little about the actors other than their talent – their ability to act.

"In this production of *Oklahoma!* we have the finest cast, the most outstanding singers and dancers, the supreme among technical crews – in a word, the very best – and that is why crowds are flocking to the Whiteway Theater night after night to see this excellent production.

"And may I say to your viewers, this is a show you simply cannot miss."

Stone, as planned, had managed to consume all of the time allotted for this segment of the program – Clare had merely sat smiling and looking beautiful – and young. They thanked the host, waved to the TV audience and headed for their next stop, which was a radio station where Charlie McBain held forth every morning on his *Broadway Beat*.

This appearance had to be handled somewhat differently. In the first place, Charlie knew quite a bit about the theater business himself and his audience also was knowledgeable about the stars and their successes and failures.

But there was no way of getting around the fact that Fred Fisher's critical review was the hottest news on the beat.

"What about Fisher, does he have any case?" Charlie asked Stone pointedly.

"None whatsoever. You will recall, I'm sure, that when *Oklahoma!* was first produced in 1943 it broke new ground in many respects. It had been the tradition to fill the roles in musicals with actors who could sing. But Rodgers and Hammerstein preferred to cast singers who could act. There was pressure from the Theatre Guild to cast Shirley Temple as Laurey and Groucho Marx as Ali Hakim, but the collaborators and director Rouben Mammoulian prevailed and the leads were played by Broadway veteran Alfred Drake and Joan Roberts, a star of stage and radio."

"Ms. Sullivan, what's your reaction to Fisher's review?"

"One man's opinion," Clare said. "Actors can't get all hot and bothered by a review. It just comes with the territory."

"Spoken like a belle of the Oklahoma Territory," said Stone, seizing the opportunity to boost the show.

From *Broadway Beat* the pair went to the studio of *On the Avenue with Beverly Grayson*, located in a building with an excellent view of 5th Avenue. Ms. Grayson, a former writer for theatrical publications, was Clare's senior and tried to conceal her age with heavy makeup, which did her no favors, especially under the hot lights of the TV set.

"Hello, darling," she greeted Stone, and to Clare, "Good morning to you, dear. We'll be going live in ten minutes, but first I'd like to get your take on the Fred Fisher review. Is there any basis for his criticism?"

"He is way off base, Beverly," Stone said. "Just trying to get attention by finding fault with a production decision. He doesn't know what he's talking about."

"Mr. Fisher has a concept of Curly and Laurey as two young lovers showing no signs of the hard life on the prairie," Clare said. "We are trying to tell a more realistic story."

"And it's not the first time a producer has taken some artistic license with the original script," Stone said. "When a revival of *Oklahoma!* was produced at Arena Stage in Washington, D.C. in 2010, Curly was portrayed by a Hispanic actor and Laurey and Aunt Eller were played by black actresses. This production, performed in the round, broke all kinds of records."

"That is very interesting," the show's host said.

"Furthermore," Stone continued, "another contemporary production of *Oklahoma!* was presented by the New Jersey Youth Theater in 2014 with a diverse cast between ages 15 and 25."

They basically repeated these exchanges on the live show and Clare sang an abbreviated version of "People Will Say We're in Love."

Stone ordered his limo driver to go to the Whiteway Theater where he held a prearranged sidewalk press conference to address Fisher's review. He pronounced the morning's appearances a solid success in counteracting negative publicity that might have been generated by the review.

As the run continued, Clare found herself dreading the twin performances on Sunday – a matinee and an evening show. She mentioned this to Anne and she responded with some good advice.

"Have them put a cot in your dressing room so you can rest up for the evening performance," she said, adding: "Pat Brown has a cot. You deserve one, too."

Clare wasted no time requesting equal treatment with her co-star and a cot was placed in her dressing room. She was happy to see it when she finished the next Sunday afternoon matinee. She even found herself using it during the week to feel refreshed before going on.

With no more critical reviews coming forth, Pat Brown's mood improved, in spite of the overwhelming crowd response for Clare at each performance. Nevertheless, his manservant continued to coddle his boss as if he were the top star of the show.

On the fourth Sunday of the run, another round of reviews appeared in print and the majority of them favored Clare over Brown for their performances in the revival of *Oklahoma!* Clare found herself exhausted after the matinee and eagerly sought the comfort of her cot. As the rest of the cast drifted out of the theater, she quickly drifted off to sleep.

She was sleeping soundly when she became aware of an experience which she thought surely must be a dream. A cold wave of fear swept over her body as she felt the weight of someone on top of her with his hands on her throat intent on choking her.

She tried to scream but was unable to make a sound. She was gasping for breath and began to see her life flash by when she suddenly gained control and reached into her red shoulder bag that she kept on the floor beside her bed. Fortunately the bag contained what she needed to save her life.

She had not brought along her protective team, Smith and Wesson, because of New York City's restrictive gun laws but she had something just as effective.

She pulled out her weapon of choice and rendered her attacker helpless with a generous treatment of hair spray in the eyes, followed by a sharp whack on the head with the can. She pushed the limp body off and stood up to recognize her assailant was Pat Brown's manservant Oo.

Quickly calling 911, she described the attack in detail and shortly afterward two uniformed police officers knocked on her door. They came in followed by the stage manager, who looked in disbelief at the prone figure on the floor. Oo was still out cold. One of the officers called for an ambulance while the other texted the detective bureau. Meanwhile, the stage manager called the director, who showed up minutes later with his assistant.

"Are you all right?" asked Tony Milam. "I can't believe this happened."

"I find it hard to believe, too," Clare said. "Looks like Pat Brown wasn't too happy about the bad reviews."

"You think Pat is responsible for this?" Milam said.

"Well, who else would sic this madman on me?"

"I guess we'll see what the police investigation turns up."

"All right for you. But as for me, I want a lock on my dressing room door ASAP," Clare said, her eyes blazing.

"You got it," Milam said to his assistant and turned to leave.

"Tony, I think you'd better have the understudy do my role tonight. My nerves are shot," Clare said.

"All right. Get some rest."

As Milam and the other two were leaving they met two medical corpsmen with a stretcher and two grim-faced detectives. One of them photographed the inert body of Oo from several directions before allowing him to be taken to the hospital. The other officer had taken his fingerprints and examined him for injuries.

The two policemen followed the corpsmen out and posted themselves outside the dressing room door.

Clare was sitting on the cot collecting her wits when she saw one of the detectives begin to put her hair spray in a plastic bag. "What are you doing?" she demanded.

"Bagging it for evidence," he said.

"But that's a brand new can," she protested, to no avail.

The other detective began questioning her, first asking for her identification (she refrained from saying her name was on the theater marquis) and her current address. She added that her permanent residence was in North Carolina and that she had formerly lived in California He called up a website on his cell phone and punched in some commands before resuming the questioning. He took notes as she related her frightening experience. In answer to his inquiry she said she had escaped harm. He had to take a call and the other officer took over.

He wanted to know how long she had known Oo, what was their relationship and what they had been doing in her dressing room. She gave him snappy answers while eavesdropping on the other officer's phone conversation:

"Yeah, it's a typical male-female encounter. They work together in a show at the Whiteway Theater. This was between performances. They were in her dressing room, in bed together. There was some kind of tussle and she pushed him out of bed and onto the floor. She admitted striking him on the head with a steel can. She was unharmed but he was unconscious. So we couldn't get his side of the story and there were no other witnesses. She had one prior. While living in California she shot and wounded a war veteran. We need to follow up on that. We're about finished here. We'll go to the hospital and question the man she accused of attacking her. It looks like a 'he says, she says' situation."

Clare was livid but she decided not to say anything until she could talk to an attorney. The second officer thanked her for cooperating with them and they both left. After the room was vacated the policemen put up yellow crime scene tape.

Clare hurried back to her hotel room, got comfortable and poured herself a scotch on the rocks. Then she called Henry.

"I don't want you to worry, but I was involved in an incident a while ago that might be mentioned on the cable gossip channels."

"What happened? Are you all right?"

"Yes, but it was an unnerving experience so I'm not going onstage tonight."

She proceeded to relate to him the ugly details of Oo's attack on her. She could sense Henry's anger rising.

"I'm catching the next plane," he said. "I'll put Pat Brown in his place – maybe the hospital."

"Now calm down, Henry. We don't know the full circumstances. This creep might have done this entirely on his own. Pat Brown might not have had anything to do with it."

"Well, I feel as if I need to be there with you."

"That's sweet of you, but it really isn't necessary. The police hauled this guy off to jail and I'm getting a lock put on my door so I feel pretty safe. You're probably up to your neck in business dealings."

"I do have some contract signings tomorrow, but they could be postponed," Henry said.

"Don't do that. I'm sure I'll be all right. Let's wait and see what happens. For all we know, Pat may be leaving the show."

"I wouldn't mind that at all," Henry said. "If you're sure you'll be okay I'll hold off making a trip for now. But I'll drop everything and come to New York if you need me."

"I know you will. Thanks for understanding. I'll keep in touch."

56

ON MONDAY Clare had a call from Powell Stone, who told her he had assigned one of his attorneys to represent her in any kind of judicial proceeding that might grow out of the incident. The attorney called and she told him she wanted to press charges. Obviously he was representing Stone's interest, not hers. "Mr. Stone would like this matter to be handled as quietly as possible. That is in the best interest of the show and everyone in the cast," he said. "And above all, the producer and the investors," Clare shot back.

Later she had a visit by two different police detectives who questioned her intensely, pressing her for every detail. They were concerned that the embassy from Oo's country might try to protect him from prosecution. In the questioning, one of the officers asked: "Are you absolutely positive this man was trying to kill you?" Clare responded: "Allow me to show you what he did." With that she gripped his neck and placed her thumbs on his windpipe. Slowly she pressed until the passage was constricted and the man was gasping for air.

"You may have to prove your accusation in court, but I advise you not to try using that procedure on the judge."

"I would hope that I would have a fair judge who would not be that antagonistic toward the victim," she said.

Soon after she arrived at the theater for the evening performance, she had a knock on her door. She unlocked and found Pat Brown had come to apologize. He insisted he had no knowledge of Oo's plans, that he acted completely on his own.

"He has been a most loyal servant," Brown said. "I met him a few months ago on a shoot on location in his country. He was working as a porter in the hotel where I was staying. I got to know him and learned he had no living relatives. His entire family had been killed in an uprising. Partially because of his abnormal height he had no close friends. I guess I felt sorry for him and brought him back to the states to work for me. He was overly grateful."

"Well, that's all well and good. But in fact, you are his guardian, and that makes you responsible for his behavior. This man tried to kill me. He probably was behind the other incidents — the poisoned soup, the falling light, the oily spot on the floor. I was lucky to escape harm. But I almost choked to death. If you tell me all of this wasn't your idea, I'll accept that. But he committed a crime and he must be punished. I hope you'll agree."

"I understand your feelings," Brown said, "but under our system of laws a person is innocent until proven guilty. I hope you'll agree with that."

"He is unquestionably guilty. There is no doubt about it. Now, if you'll excuse me, I have to get ready for the show."

Brown slinked out with no further word.

To no great surprise Clare's attacker escaped legal punishment. Under pressure from his embassy he was released and authorities said there was insufficient evidence to file charges. The chief police detective pointed out there were no witnesses to the alleged assault. Stone's attorneys obtained a financial settlement based on potential damage to the theater's reputation and, incidentally, physical and emotional injury to a cast member. Clare was furious but after discussing it with Henry she decided it was best not to pursue the case any further. But she could not erase the thought of having to give up a brand new can of hair spray.

Soon afterward Pat Brown left the cast and Stone brought in a new actor with more stage experience to replace him. In the process, the inquisitive Anne Malone sleuthed out the information that both Brown and his successor were being paid salaries considerably higher than Clare. That was all she could take. She marched into Stone's office and told him off and demanded she be released from her contract. That cost her the pittance she had received from the settlement, plus an additional sum. But she concluded it was worth it. She had had her taste of Broadway and while much of it was sweet it had grown bitter. She was ready to go back to life in North Carolina.

Before she could tell Henry, he called her. There was urgency in his voice.

"What's wrong?" she said.

"It's Phil. He's had a heart attack."

57

AFTER THE STUNNING NEWS registered with her, Clare said, "How bad is it?"

"Don't know. The ambulance just left to take him to the hospital. I'm leaving now to meet Barbara there."

"I know you have to go. But I was just about to call to tell you I'm leaving New York."

"I don't understand."

"I'm coming home. I'll explain later. I'll call you when I land in Wilmington."

Clare packed quickly, reserved a seat on the next plane out and took one last look at the views of New York City from her hotel room. Then she went to the lobby to check out and get a cab to the airport.

She had a little time to think during the flight. An in-flight margarita helped to put things in focus.

She was well on her way to rebuilding her life on the ashes of California. She had re-connected with her family and made new friends in the South where she was born. She had reawakened an interest in acting and helped found a community theater.

All things considered, she felt good about the New York experience. She had realized a dream of a lifetime by appearing in a Broadway show.

But somehow there remained an emptiness to fill.

Maybe she had found it. She had met a wonderful guy and she had fallen in love with him and he with her.

Another margarita convinced her that the key to her future was Henry Jackson.

But before she could give any further thought to an action plan, Phil Sterling's condition demanded her attention.

Upon landing in Wilmington she got Henry on the phone and learned that Phil had suffered a mild heart attack. He said as soon as she got to the hospital a cardiologist would give them a full report.

Henry and Barbara were waiting in the lobby. After greetings and hugs, Henry signaled a nurse, who escorted them to a private room where they received a detailed report on Phil's condition. To put it in non-medical language, he was out of the woods but vulnerable to a future and more severe attack on his heart.

"Mr. Sterling has a condition known as atrial fibrillation, a common type of arrhythmia. Plainly speaking, this means the heart beats too fast, or too slow, or with an irregular rhythm.

"A-fib occurs when disorganized, rapid electrical signals cause the atria – the heart's two upper chambers – to contract very fast and irregularly."

As the doctor talked he pointed to a drawing of the heart.

"During fibrillation, blood pools in the atria and doesn't pump completely into the heart's two lower chambers, called the ventricles," he continued. "Simply put, the heart's upper and lower chambers don't work together as they're supposed to. And that increases the risk of a stroke.

"This patient also has hypertension, or high blood pressure, which also adds to the risk.

"I am prescribing some medications and I want to schedule him for regular checkups, beginning with one month, then three months.

"The most important advice I can give you is to do your best to eliminate stress from Phil's life," the cardiologist said.

Barbara, who had sat quietly through the session, spoke up.

"That means one thing," she said. "Phil has to retire and devote full attention to his health."

From the private room, the group went to see Phil. He was hooked up to all sorts of tubes and wires, but he was conscious and, thanks to who knows how many drugs, very alert and quite upbeat.

"All in all I'd rather be seeing you over dinner at the club," he said.

"We'll do that sometime soon, sweetheart," Barbara said. "Right now we need to get you out of the hospital and back on your feet."

"That's fine with me," he said "I can hardly wait to get back to work."

Henry saw his opportunity to become part of the supportive team.

"There's no hurry about that," he said. "You just need to rest and regain your strength. Meanwhile, the business is in good hands, so you don't need to worry about anything."

"With you as my partner, I know that's true," Phil said, weakly.

"You can depend on it," Clare said

"We're going to go now, so you can rest. But we'll be back to see you soon," Barbara said.

She held his hand and they both mouthed, "I love you." One by one, the group bade farewell and left.

"I need a drink," Barbara said. "Let's go to our place and open the bar."

And so they did. But Clare said she needed to stop by their home first.

"We'll meet you later – very soon," she said.

Clare wanted to change out of her traveling clothes and she also needed time to fill Henry in on her decision to leave the show.

As expected, Henry was quite understanding and supportive of her decision. He suppressed his anger about the experience she had suffered because of Pat Brown and the treatment she had received from the producer, Palmer Stone.

He took her in his arms and said, "I'm glad you showed Broadway what you can do, but I'm so glad to have you back."

"I'm glad to be back," she said.

On the way to the Sterlings' home, they had a brief discussion about Henry's future, in light of Phil's condition.

"I have a thought in mind and this might be the time to bring it up. I'd like to buy Phil out."

"That's a big step. Are you sure you're ready for this?"

"Right now the business is strong. But with Phil's gambling problem and his health condition, I'm not so sure he can be an asset. I think I can build on what he has accomplished and save his reputation while also saving the business."

Later at the Sterling home, over cocktails, he made the pitch and Barbara showed relief in supporting it.

"It's time for Phil and me to enjoy a life without stress," she said. "It will be tough convincing Phil, but I think he'll come around."

Later that week Phil was released from the hospital with a prescription to control his blood pressure and another for a blood thinner, along with strict orders to take it easy.

Clare and her circle of close friends got together for lunch in Wilmington because they were dying to hear her tell about her exciting time in New York. She focused on the fun and decided not to say anything about the way her adventure ended.

On the second round of drinks the conversation turned to the theater. Clare asked what Gloria had planned for the upcoming season.

"I'd like to lead off with *Promises, Promises* – I think the title would be very appropriate for this presidential election year." That drew hearty laughter and a toast to the director of the Tri-County Players.

Henry had a relatively light schedule, as did Clare, so he suggested a visit to his new development, tentatively called Jackson Grove, and the premier home sites. He was eager to show her how construction on their future home was coming along. She was thrilled and delighted at what she saw.

He had given the architect a description of Clare's villa on the California seaside, drawing on vivid memories of the large two-story dwelling overlooking the Pacific Ocean, with its spacious family room where campaign-planning sessions were held, the gourmet kitchen and the paneled dining room, and the balcony off the upstairs bedrooms where they enjoyed the moonlight and the call of the loon on his first visit. The building plans came close to recreating everything but the view.

Clare was amazed and quite impressed with Henry's thoughtfulness.

"I love it!" she said, as she looked up at the structure taking shape on a rise above a scenic lake which already had attracted some wild geese. He was somewhat startled when she added: "Is it too late to make changes?"

"I suppose not. What did you have in mind?"

"Oh, just some little things. Always before I've lived in houses somebody else designed. You always see something you would have done differently."

"Fine," he said. "But I do hope you're okay with the fireplaces."

"That would be a major correction, all right. But for one thing I'd like to enlarge the kitchen slightly. I'll be spending a lot of time there and I don't want to be bumping into anyone or anything."

"Tell you what. I'll get you together with the architect and you can go over the plans and tell him what you'd like to do and I'm sure he'll try to make it work."

"You're too good to me," she said, giving him a smack on the cheek.

"There is one more thing I want to show you," Henry said. They got back into the car and drove some distance to an area at the back of the property where a clubhouse would be built. As they drew nearer to a stopping place, a well cultivated slope came into view and Clare observed rows of plantings. Henry pulled to the side of the road and they got out.

"Do I see grape vines?" Clare asked. The plants were small but were easily recognizable for someone who had visited a number of vineyards in California and Washington State, where the Mt. Jackson Winery was located

"It might be a wild idea," Henry said, "but I wanted to try it. I did quite a bit of research, talked to state and university wine growing advisory sources, and consulted with my brother Drew."

"I'm sure there's a lot to consider – climate, soil ..."

"That's true. And since my experience in the wine industry has been chiefly marketing, I really had a lot to learn. One of the first things was that North Carolina has three major wine growing regions – Mountain, Piedmont and the Sandhill-Coastal Region. Wilmington is in the latter. While vinifera and hybrid grapes are grown throughout the Mountain and Piedmont regions, the coastal plain where moderate winter termpratures prevail is most adapted to muscadines."

"They make a sweeter wine, right?" Clare said.

"Generally speaking, yes. Muscadines, or scuppernongs, are the native grapes of North Carolina. Wines made from this grape are rich, full-flavored and very fruity. There aren't too many wineries in this region, but one of them, Duplin, is the largest winemaker in the South. It has been producing award winning wines since 1975."

"I'm surprised to see you've started growing vines already," Clare said.

"Well, I might be taking a gamble, but the more I thought about having my own winery, I just couldn't wait until spring. I ordered the vines and hired some day laborers that got the planting done in one day. I have a smaller crew that looks after them."

"What kinds of grapes did you plant?"

"Noble, which is the standard for muscadine red wine; and Magnolia, which is resistant to the cold and diseases and is popular for making white wine."

Clare put her arms around his neck and gave him a strong hug. "I'm so proud of you, Henry. And your father would be, too."

"I'm not too sure about that. But I mainly want to prove it to myself."

"And your housing development will be like no other in this area," she said. "Jackson Grove will be one of the finest in the South."

"By the way, what does Phil think about your project?"

"He hasn't been in the office much since I got into it. I haven't really had a chance to discuss it with him."

"What you're saying is that he doesn't know you're doing it?"

"All he knows is that I'm building a home for us."

"What about all the land you'll need for a housing development?"

"Well, let's just say Phil isn't the only one who has a holding company."

58

THE FOLLOWING WEEKEND they had been invited to the Sterlings' for dinner. Barbara thought it would be an ideal occasion for Henry to convince Phil to sell his share of the business.

On the way over, Henry showed Clare his proposal, which he had outlined in three pages. He had acquired a knowledge of the financial status of Sterling Homes so he could make a pretty fair estimate of what Phil's share was worth and he increased the figure slightly.

Clare smiled her approval. "You did a good job, which I expected."

"I'm afraid it's going to be a tough sell," Henry said.

"Why do you say that?"

"Phil came to the office one day this week. It seemed to cheer him up. He spent most of the day catching up on mail and returning phone calls. And shortly before he left I happened to overhear fragments of a conversation that I'd heard before. It sounded like he was talking to one of the men in the dark suits."

"A member of the mob, you mean?"

"I felt sorry for Phil. He was pleading for more time to get the money the man was demanding."

"That kind of stress certainly is bound to be harmful to his health. I think we can count on Barbara to lean on him to take your offer."

"I hope you're right."

The Sterlings' home was a picture-perfect setting for the special occasion – soft light, soothing music, the hostess pairing casual attire with elegance, which she did so well. Henry presented a bottle of Mt. Jackson's finest wine, which Barbara accepted graciously.

"Let's join Phil in the living room," she said. As they passed by the dining room, Clare offered a sincere compliment.

"Your table is beautiful, Barbara. I love the centerpiece."

"Why, thank you. I want this evening to be very special."

Phil rose from an overstuffed chair to greet them with a salesman's smile.

"Clare, it's so good to see you," he said, taking her hands. She noted they were cold. His face was drawn. He didn't look well. "We missed you a lot while you were up in New York performing on Broadway."

"It was the experience of a lifetime but I'm really glad to be back among friends," she said.

"I'm having Chivas on the rocks," Phil said. "What can I get you?"

"Let me do it, Phil," Henry said. "I think I know my way around your bar."

"Well, all right," Phil said, and sank back into his chair.

"I'd like to have some of your wine," Barbara said to Henry.

"That will be fine for me, too," said Clare.

Henry opened and poured the wine, then masterfully mixed a Manhattan for himself and the group reassembled as Barbara brought out a tray of hors d'oeuvres.

Over their drinks they engaged in small talk about the upcoming theater season, some new restaurant openings and the local real estate market. Henry had decided earlier to delay presenting he offer to buy Phil's interest until later when his partner was a little more mellow.

With everyone seated in the dining room, at Barbara's signal the caterers began to serve – first a seafood bisque, followed by an avocado citrus salad, and veal marsala, accompanied by French wines. Henry began to grow concerned about Phil when he began to show some drowsiness before the dessert course. Barbara aroused his attention by announcing: "Philip, we're having your favorite dessert: key lime pie. Will everyone have coffee? It's decaf.?

"Or an after dinner drink?" said Phil. The vote was for coffee.

Henry saw an opening and brought up Phil's health.

"We've all been concerned about your condition," he said.

Clare followed along. "I'm so sorry I wasn't here when you had your heart attack."

"Oh, it didn't amount to much," Phil said.

"Now you know better than that," Barbara corrected him. "The doctors said you were lucky we got you to the hospital quickly."

"Well, I'm fine now," Phil said.

"But your cardiologist did tell you to take it easy, right?" Henry said.

"I don't know how to do that."

"You're going to have to learn, dear," Barbara said, sternly. "You're got to reduce stress or the next attack could be much worse." She avoided saying "fatal."

"The big stress factor is the business, wouldn't you agree?" Henry said.

"I suppose so."

"I know you love your work and the company you founded. But let's face it. The pace you've set for yourself could kill you. You don't want that. You can have a long life enjoying the things you have missed by devoting all your time to your business. You and Barbara could leave these pressures behind, travel, see places you haven't been, do some of the things you've missed out on."

"You paint a very nice picture, Henry."

"And that picture can become a reality," Henry said, as he produced his three-page proposal. "Phil, I want to buy your share of the business. Here's what I'm offering."

Phil was stunned. He had a hard time taking in what Henry had just said. Hesitatingly he accepted the papers and reached for his reading glasses. He scanned the document quickly and hurried to the bottom line figure on the third page.

"I don't know what to say," he said. "You're asking me to give up my lifetime career, let go of a business I founded and built to become one of the most successful real estate development companies in this state."

"And I think you'll have to admit," Henry pressed, "I have helped you build a strong partnership."

"Yes, and I'm grateful. One of the smartest things I have done is to bring you on as a partner."

"You'll note that I plan to retain your name. The business will be called Jackson-Sterling Homes."

"It's a most generous offer," Phil said. "But I'll have to think about it, you know."

"Let's not take too long, darling," Barbara said. "I've been waiting for years to take that round-the-world trip we've talked about."

"I'll be more clear-eyed in the morning," Phil said. "It would be a big change and I can't make a snap decision."

Clare spoke up. "Just don't wait too long. The next heart attack could come anytime."

In order to spend more time with Clare catching up after her return from New York, Henry had cleared his calendar for the rest of the week, so he was at home when at mid-morning Phil called to follow up on the offer. It was a relatively short call. Henry filled in Clare on the conversation.

"Phil wanted a few alterations," he said. Clare frowned. "But he accepted the offer."

"Great!" Clare exclaimed. "You are such a good salesman." She threw her arms around him and gave him a congratulatory kiss, then asked, "What were his conditions?"

"Nothing I couldn't live with. Although it was implied, he wanted it spelled out that Sterling Properties, the holding company he formed in conjunction with his idea to capitalize on the new bridge project, was not included in the deal. He also asked for a larger payment up front and a shorter payout schedule."

"That sounds like an urgent need for a lot of cash," Clare said.

"And we both can guess why."

"Was that it?"

"Well, one more thing that kind of irked me, but I went along to stroke his ego. He wants the business to be called Sterling-Jackson Homes – putting his name first."

"That's nervy, considering you're doing him a really big favor," she said. "You're saving him from professional and physical ruin."

"Might as well help him save face, too."

"So where do things stand?"

"I told Phil I'd have the attorneys draw up a contract and meet at the law office at 2 p.m. It's convenient that the office is in the same building as a bank. So he can deposit the check I give him for the initial payment and not risk getting run over crossing the street."

Clare went to the phone. "I'm calling Barbara," she said. "I think we ought to be there to witness the occasion and celebrate."

The hour arrived and everyone gathered in the conference room. Before taking seats Barbara took some pictures of Phil and Henry holding the contract and shaking hands. She also got some shots of them signing the contract and Henry presenting the check. After all, it was a momentous event

After the official business was all done, a paralegal appeared with a bottle of champagne and glasses. Barbara digitally recorded the moment of a new beginning for posterity. The principals all wore looks of joy and relief, with handshakes and hugs all around.

Phil's eyes teared up as he grasped Henry's hand and told him how grateful he was for the buyout. He was a little unsteady on his feet so Henry accompanied him to the bank.

The wives hugged and Barbara whispered in Clare's ear, "This means so much to me. Now he'll be able to pay off his gambling debts."

59

CLARE DECIDED NOT TO pretend surprise at Barbara's admission. "How long have you known?" she asked.

"Not long. I knew something was wrong, terribly wrong. My first thought, you know, was wondering if he was seeing another woman. Although Phil has never given any indication he no longer loved me. And it was different. He didn't just act as if he were hiding something from me. He was scared. I could read it in his face and in his moods."

"Did he tell you anything?"

"Not intentionally. I found out what was bothering him when he started talking in his sleep."

"Really?"

"Yes. And then I knew when one night he began shaking and stammered, 'I'll pay you ... I promise ... I know I lost big at the casino ... but you'll get the money ... just don't hurt me or my wife.'"

"He probably wasn't the only one shook after you heard that."

"Right. I shook him awake and he broke into tears and told me over and over how sorry he was, that it started with small bets and grew into an obsession. I consoled him, told him how much I loved him and wanted to take care of him. But I also made it clear he was going to have to fight his addiction. And that I would help him."

Barbara paused and then looked straight at Clare and said, "You knew, didn't you?"

"I am so sorry, Barbara," she said. "Let's sit down." Clare proceeded to tell her everything, beginning with the night she saw Phil getting off the gambling ship at Myrtle Beach ..."

"That was before you came to Wilmington," Barbara said.

"We were on our way to meet you. I couldn't believe my eyes. I didn't say anything to Henry because I kept thinking I must have been mistaken. But then other things kept happening." She told Barbara about the day at the office when she heard the exchange between Phil and the men in dark suits.

"Later Henry shared some observations that concerned him, like numerous unexplained 'business trips' to places like Atlantic City and to the new casino in western North Carolina. But we told ourselves it was none of our business. Obviously we made the wrong decision.

"I know I should have told you about my suspicions much earlier, but I just kept hoping I was wrong and I didn't want to do anything to damage our friendship. But now I feel I have let you down as a friend and I am so sorry."

"It probably wouldn't have done any good. You were trying to spare my feelings. Or maybe you thought I already knew. But you're still my very good friend and I know I can count on your support and Henry's in getting past this. I can't tell you how thankful I am that Henry offered to take the business burden off of Phil's shoulders. I have thanked God the heart attack didn't kill my husband. It was a very solemn warning, though, and I want to do everything I can to restore Phil's health."

"We want to help in any way we can, Barbara," Clare said.

"What happened here today was a very big step and it's going to make a big difference. Phil will be able to settle up with the goons who have been threatening him. He will be debt-free and I've just got to keep him from getting to that point ever again."

"And we'll be behind you every step of the way."

The two women were hugging again when the men returned.

"Hey, isn't that the way we left you?" Henry said.

"We're just so happy," Clare said.

"We are, too – right, Phil?"

With that, Phil gave Henry a hearty hug, saying, "This is a very special day. I'll never forget it."

"I think we'll ride around a bit, maybe visit a winery," Henry said. "There's one right here in town, Noni Bacca, I believe it's called."

"Not going shopping for another business, are you," Phil said with a chuckle.

"Hardly," Henry replied. "We might be able to afford a couple of bottles."

"We're heading for the travel agency," right, Barbie?"

"Let's go."

When Henry looked at the directions to Noni Bacca Winery that he had copied from the website he discovered it was not far from Landfall, where they lived. In fact, it was on the same road. He and Clare had driven past the place many times but did not notice it because, as they discovered, it is in a strip mall. They parked and went into the unusual store front winery with a sizeable amount of curiosity.

They were greeted with a friendly smile by Toni, co-owner with her husband of the small but highly productive business, which has the motto "Globally Grown, Locally Produced." They learned that the boutique winery, established in 2007, offers more than 50 different varieties of hand-crafted wines using grapes from viticultural areas in various parts of the world including Italy and Chile as well as California.

The wines are displayed in long racks behind the tasting bar. A special section has bottles draped with some of the 111 international medals awarded since 2009 in the world's top three competitions.

Henry mentioned his connection with the Mt. Jackson Vineyards and said they would pass up the six-or-nine-wine tastings. The very personable Toni offered a selective tasting from the long list of premium whites and reds, plus fruit and dessert wines. They found most of them to their liking and greatly enjoyed learning about the couple who relocated to Wilmington from upstate New York, where their winemaking skills were shaped by their respective families.

They chose a varied half-case and while the sale was being rung up they peeked at the area behind the tasting room to see where the wines were produced. They thanked Toni for her courtesy and told her they would be back.

Clare and Henry, home with their purchases, didn't have an appetite for a large meal. Henry decanted a bottle of Amarone della Valpolicella, a rich Italian dry red wine, while Clare put together some flat bread with caramelized onion, sweet red pepper and goat cheese. They turned on the gas logs, kicked off their shoes and sat together on the couch and settled in to enjoy an evening of pure relaxation.

They reflected on the lives of four people taking a dramatic turn over the past 24 hours. Clare related her highly personal talk with Barbara and Henry reassured her that she had done the right thing over the long haul. Henry said he had a really good feeling about the business transaction.

"I like this wine," Clare said.

"'She's a Nice a, No?' as it says on the label," said Henry with his best attempt at an Italian accent.

"I want to make a toast," Clare said. "To Henry Jackson, North Carolina's newest homebuilding mogul."

"Now, let's not get carried away. By the way, this flat bread is delicious."

"Seriously, I salute you for the way you have learned all about the real estate business and applied the training you received at Harvard and your own real world experience to become a successful business leader," she said, raising her glass.

"We'll see about the leader part," Henry said. "But much as the winemaking business, I do enjoy seeing the fruits of our labors ....the satisfaction of watching couples and young families watch plans for their future homes become realities ... the development of new neighborhoods. It's all very rewarding."

"Coming to Wilmington has launched a new career for you and today has been a giant leap forward. Congratulations," Clare said, planting a big kiss.

"Thank you, my darling. Now let's talk about your career. You've certainly proven your ability for acting – both on the small stage and the world-famous Broadway stage, as well as the wide-ranging medium of television."

"Yes, I guess you're right. I've derived a great deal of satisfaction from what I've been able to achieve. Much of the success I've had since relocating on the East Coast has resulted from good connections I've made. Professionals like Zach Bacharach and Gloria Levine have been tremendously helpful to my career."

"Smart, ambitious people – like you – know how to use their connections wisely and well. But first you have to have the talent and the desire and the drive to go to the top. Do you think you want to stick with it?"

"I guess I'll always enjoy acting – and singing and dancing But after the way my experience in the 'big time' ended, I'm not sure the reward is worth what must be endured."

"That hatred and violence was terrible. I'm so sorry I wasn't there to protect you."

"I did a pretty good job of protecting myself, if I do say so. But Henry, sweetheart, I sure did miss you all those long lonely months. I had so much time to myself I was able to do a lot of thinking about the future. Reuniting with my family has put me on more of a solid track. And being your companion for the past couple of years has been one of the best things that could ever happen to me. And I don't want it to ever end.

"As I said, I've thought a lot and I have concluded that I want a new career."

"Oh, well please tell me."

"What I'd like to do for my next, and probably last, career is to be Mrs. Henry Jackson."

Henry's eyes opened wide and he broke into a broad smile.

"Or perhaps I should say, Clare Sullivan-Jackson."

Henry took her into his arms and said, "Call yourself anything you want — Cinderella, Fairy Princess — I'll be proud to be your Prince Charming …"

Clare put her fingers to his lips and said, "Let's not go there again," reminding him of the confession she extracted from him after the California campaign about the flirtation he had with a woman named Kate in England.

"Sorry, bad choice of words. There's nothing that could make me happier than for you to be my companion for life," he said, putting down his glass. He reached up and turned off the lamp. And the glow of their love rivaled the warmth of the glow from the logs in the fireplace.

60

AFTER THE LONG ROMANTIC NIGHT they had, the couple awoke feeling almost as if they were already married. They arose early. Clare went for a brisk walk. Henry checked news reports on TV and the web to see what kind of job the advertising-public relations agency had done with the announcement of the change of ownership of one of the area's leading real estate development firms. The agency's contract was up for renewal so to say he was disappointed in the poor showing would be a mild way of showing his reaction.

He sent a blistering email to the head of the agency, Lee Lyons, and ordered him to be in his office first thing Monday morning. By then he expected to be cooled off and they could talk dispassionately but firmly about whether the long relationship Phil had established with the agency would continue. He asked Clare for her thoughts.

"During the time I was the TV spokesperson I never had any problems," she said. "I always got along with Lyons. But that doesn't mean much. He certainly got off to a bad start with you."

"I want him to give me a full explanation of the mishandling of this important announcement," Henry said. "That's why I'm calling him in for a meeting."

"You're doing the right thing to withhold judgment until you know all the facts. Apparently Phil thought Lyons' agency had served him well over the years so you don't want to dump them without a very good reason."

"That's good advice. Thanks."

We made a big decision last evening, didn't we?"

"Yes. And I don't have any second thoughts about it."

"Neither do I. And I'm eager to move ahead if you are."

"You know me. I'm pretty action-oriented."

"I need to call Becky – check in with her and get a report on Momma. I'll have to decide how I'm going to tell her and Daddy about us."

"I ought to do the same thing with my family, too. I'll use the study."

Clare dialed Becky and was surprised when Betty Ann answered.

"Hi, honey. It's Aunt Clare. How are you?"

"I'm fine. How are you?" the little girl said in a very grown-up voice.

"Okay. It's been awhile since I talked to you or your mother, you know."

"Yes. You moved to New York.'

"That's right. But it was just temporary. And I'm back in North Carolina now."

"To stay?"

"Yes." She paused. Betty Ann said nothing. "Is there anything wrong?"

"No."

"Is your mother home?"

"Yes. I'll get her."

"Hi, sis," Becky said.

"Hi. What's wrong with Betty Ann? She didn't sound like herself."

"Oh, it's nothing. She got into a little mischief at school yesterday so I've grounded her for the weekend."

"She has no reason to be mad at me."

"Right now she has it in for all adults. But she'll get over it. Are you calling from New York?"

"No, I'm back in Wilmington. And that's one thing I wanted to tell you." She filled her in on her decision to leave the show and come home. Then she asked about Betty.

"She's coming along real well," Becky said. "She and Daddy are living together just fine. They weren't sharing a bedroom anyway because of his snoring so that part of the routine didn't change. And they enjoy each other's company very much."

"Has she regained any of her memory?"

"Not so's you'd notice. But she has adjusted pretty well. She has accepted the fact that I'm her daughter and Betty Ann's her grandbaby."

"Is she excited about you being pregnant?"

"Oh, yeah. More than I am."

"Have you had any problems?"

"No. It's just, you know ... well, you wouldn't know ... just being uncomfortable all the time and coping with the hormonal ups and downs."

"You and Jim are getting along okay, I hope."

"Yes. He's wonderful. He's my saving grace. How's Henry?"

"Couldn't be better. And we had a big event yesterday – two actually."

"What was that?"

"Henry bought out his partner, Phil Sterling. He was having health problems. So now Henry's the sole owner and he is very enthusiastic about some plans he has for the business."

"That sounds good. Tell him I wish him well."

"And there's something else."

"Oh? Tell me."

"Henry and I are going to get married."

"What! Well, my goodness. That is exciting news. Had y'all been talking about that?"

"No. We've been together ever since the campaign and I think both of us felt that we wanted to stay together. We just weren't in any hurry to make it a formal arrangement. But after being apart while I was working in New York – that made us think more about how lonely we were being separated. We were talking about new beginnings and careers last night over wine and, well, I told him I wanted my next career to be his wife."

"You proposed?"

"I guess you could say that. And that's not unusual these days. Women sometimes have to take the initiative."

"I agree. I just wasn't brought up that way. Well, have you set a date?"

"No. That doesn't matter much. We do want to move ahead. But we're not doing anything big, so we don't need a lot of time to get ready. I did want to tell you. And of course Momma and Daddy."

"You know Daddy will be very happy for you. And so will Momma. But you might as well get yourself prepared."

"What do you mean?"

"That bump on the head changed Momma a lot. But one thing did not change. And the ladies in the bridge club she sees so often have just reinforced it. She is a southerner. She is a southern mother. And southern traditions are ingrained in her. You saw that when you were here for Aunt Dora's funeral."

"What are you saying, Becky?"

"When you tell Momma you're getting married she is going to insist on a traditional Southern wedding."

"Oh, Lord! I hadn't thought about that."

"Where are you planning on getting married?"

"We really hadn't made any plans. I just thought we'd find a minister we liked and have a small, quiet ceremony up here."

"That won't happen," Becky said firmly. "Momma will demand to have the wedding down here, probably in our church, with a big reception to follow, with lots of flowers and food and everything. A daughter's wedding is a big event in a Southern mother's life."

"You didn't have a big wedding, did you? Either time?"

"Well, no. Harry and I eloped and Momma never forgave me for that. And of course she was still pretty blanked out when Jim and I went to a minister's home and said our vows."

"Maybe it won't happen like you said it would. After all, she says she doesn't know me."

"She knows what she has been told and she accepts you as her daughter the same as she accepts me. And besides ..."

"Besides what?"

"She will get caught up in the idea and it wouldn't matter if you were an actor hired from central casting, putting on a Southern wedding would be one of the biggest events in her life."

"Well, thanks a lot!"

"You know what I mean."

Clare sighed. "Yes, I'm afraid I do. Well, I guess I'd better get on with it. I'll call her tomorrow."

"Maybe you ought to hold off until I can get with her and explain what's happening. Then I can call and put her on the phone and stand by to help her absorb it. Okay?"

"Sure. Good idea. And Becky ... if I'm going to have to go through this traditional business to please Momma, can I ask you ... will you be my maid of honor?"

"It's matron of honor, since I'm a married woman. And, of course. I'll be happy to do that."

"One more thing. Tell Betty Ann I'd like for her to be the flower girl. That ought to cheer her up."

Becky called on Sunday afternoon after Betty and Pat had gotten home from church and finished lunch. She had filled them both in on Clare and Henry's decision to get married and as she predicted Betty quickly went into Southern mother mode and started getting excited about the idea.

When her mother came on the line she didn't bother with preliminaries — she just went straight to the point.

"I'm so happy about you and Henry," she gushed. "Tell me about your plans."

"Well, we really haven't made any. We'd like to move ahead but we haven't decided when and where," Clare said.

"Honey, there's no question about where. The wedding has to be here, of course. I'll want all of our friends to come. I don't remember anything about your sister getting married, but I want to make this wedding one that everybody will remember. Now, let's talk about a date."

"Well, let me look at my appointment book. Okay. I'll have to check with Henry, but it looks like our schedule should be pretty clear around the end of this month."

"Let me see. Oh, my dear, that's only two weeks off. It will have to be at least a month from now to allow enough time for the Burial of the Bourbon."

"For the WHAT?"

"Why it's an old Southern tradition. Exactly one month before the wedding a bottle of bourbon is buried upside down at the wedding site. That's to guarantee it won't rain on your wedding day."

Clare rolled her eyes. "But what if it does rain?"

"Oh, it always works," Betty said. "But regardless of the weather, the bourbon is dug up after the ceremony and it's served to the guests."

"Well, all right. But I'd rather have champagne."

"We'll have that, too, along with whatever else anybody might want. Oh, there's so much to do to get ready. We'll certainly need a month. I'm starting to make a list ... need to make sure Rev. Peterson is available ... reserve the church parking lot, and make sure nothing is happening in the gardens ... we can have a lovely ceremony there ..."

"An outdoor wedding? It darn sure better not rain," Clare said, with some exasperation.

"We can always have it indoors, if we have to. And the reception can be in the Legion Hall next door, if necessary. I'd better get that on my list. I know the ladies of the church will want to help with the food ..."

"Can't we just have the reception catered?" Clare asked.

"Oh, heavens, no!" Betty said. "I wouldn't hear of it. We don't do things that way in the South. Let's see ... oh, yes, flowers, and music and ... oh, the bridesmaids' dresses – we'll have to decide what color they should be ..."

"Bridesmaids? Momma, no. I don't want any bridesmaids. I can't. I don't know anybody down there."

"Well, it won't be much of a procession with just Rebecca Jean and Elizabeth Ann. Surely you have some old high school or college friends you could ask."

"I haven't kept in touch. What else is there?"

226

"I presume you can take care of the 'something old, something new' requirements …"

"Shhh!" said Becky, listening on another line.

"We've made a pretty good start. As I think of other things I'll call you."

"All right, Momma."

Clare hung up the phone and slumped in a recliner as Henry was returning from the study.

"What's wrong? You look exhausted."

"I just got off the phone with Becky and Momma. They're making a big thing out of our wedding. I'll fill you in later. How about you?"

"Talked to Pop first. He's pleased that I finally got my teeth into business. He actually said he was proud of me for taking over the real estate development company. He's also happy that we're going to get married."

"That all sounds good. Maybe he and Jean will want to come for the wedding."

"And bring my brother Drew. I asked him to be my best man."

"Great! Becky is going to be my matron of honor."

"Drew asked when the wedding would be."

"Yeah. We need to set a date." She told him about the "Bury the Bourbon" tradition that involved a month-long ritual. They consulted their appointment books and found a couple of dates about five weeks off to suggest to Betty.

"You know I'd rather just have a simple ceremony here sometime soon," Clare said.

"But traditions run strong, especially in the South. And this probably will be helpful in your mother's recovery."

"I suppose so."

She called Becky and gave her the dates. "I'm glad you warned me about Momma. She really is into Southern wedding traditions."

"She really is. And she's going to be so busy it will take her mind off of her amnesia problem. By the way, Betty Ann is thrilled about being flower girl. She's already talking about what kind of dress she'd like to wear."

"I guess I'd better be doing the same.."

"What are you thinking?" Becky asked.

"I've narrowed it down to something between a mini-skirt and long gown."

"Color?"

"Anything but white, I suppose."

"Go buy a bride's magazine."

"Good idea. Bye, sis."

61

WHEN HENRY CAME HOME from work on Monday he found Clare lounging on the couch thumbing through the pages of *Brides' Guide to an Awesome Wedding*. She looked a little embarrassed and quickly put it down on the coffee table.

"How was your day?" she asked.

"Not bad for the first day of a new life as a businessman."

"Mix us a drink and tell me all about it." She swung her feet to the floor and made room for him on the couch.

"I had my meeting with Lee Lyons."

"How did that go?"

"I underscored how unhappy I was about the screwup on the announcement. He apologized profusely and laid the blame on staff and a misunderstanding. They had prepared a news release based on what I had told them about the deal and the new name. But before it was distributed they got word from Phil to put a hold on it."

"And technically they were still working for him."

"Right. In retrospect I understand, because that was one of the changes Phil requested before signing off on the contract."

"But he didn't tell you and apparently didn't get back to the staff."

"They hadn't heard anything before the office closed on Friday so nothing went out. I told Lyons in no uncertain words that communications have to be improved to avoid something like that recurring and he agreed. He said a revised announcement would be released next weekend. He also pointed out that this will allow more time for business writers to prepare their stories and also improve the possibility of getting mentions in the weekly national news magazines."

"So in the end it works out for the better."

"In many respects, yes, it does. But I didn't let Lyons totally off the hook. We talked about renewing the arrangement with his agency. Instead of the customary two-year contract they had been operating under, I cut it to one year with option for extension."

"In other words, you put the agency on probation."

"Do you think that was a good move?"

"It's an ideal way to handle a sticky situation. You didn't kick them out the door but you made it clear they have a new boss and they've got to toe the line."

"I think he got the message." Henry took a sip of his martini. "The other thing I did today was to move into Phil's office. I also sat for a photographer to take shots of me for publicity and also for an official portrait to hang beside Phil's in the waiting room."

"As befits an important chief executive." Clare knew immediately she had used the wrong term.

Henry thanked her but added: "Wasn't that the name of Pat Brown's TV show?"

"He was just playing a role. You're the real thing."

Henry poured up the rest of the pitcher and mentioned something else he learned from Phil's executive secretary, who had quickly transferred her loyalties.

"She told me that Phil and Barbara met with a travel agent and they are leaving later this week for a long cruise in the South Pacific."

"I thought I had heard Barbara mention an around-the-world trip," Clare said.

"I guess they decided that would take too long. This one is about six weeks."

"I hope they can relax and enjoy it."

"The Sterlings will miss our wedding," Henry observed.

"I wasn't planning to invite anyone from here anyway," Clare said. "I think it would be an imposition to expect them to travel to Georgia for an event of only a few hours."

(As it turned out, Gloria hosted a bridal shower for Clare with a strict rule of no gifts other than wine or liquor.)

Henry slowly finished his drink and asked Clare, "Where would you like to go on our honeymoon?"

"I hadn't given any thought to it, but I guess I should. Do you think you'll be able to get away?"

"I think so. I'm reorganizing the staff structure so I can do more delegating. Phil was heavily into micro-management. My style is to hire qualified people, make sure they know what I expect of them and then leave them alone. That means I don't have to be in the office all the time."

"That's smart. I'll need to check with Gloria to see if I'm likely to be tied up in a Tri-County Players production. I'll do that right away."

Time seemed to fly by quickly and the wedding date drew nearer and nearer. In conversations with Becky and their mother Clare learned about other traditions that needed to be considered. Men's wear, for example. The bridal gown is not the only object of attention. Tradition dictates that because of the South's warmer climate men should wear lightweight, light-colored suits. But Clare told Henry he was not compelled to buy a pastel seersucker suit for the wedding.

Fortunately Henry found an Italian-made off-white linen suit on a shopping trip to Mayfaire. He was tempted by a wide-brim hat worn by the mannequin, but decided to skip it and instead had the salesperson include a gold striped tie and a tan silk pocket square. On that same outing he picked up another essential: the rings.

A Southern gentleman is obligated to spend whatever it takes to provide his bride with a ring that draws gasps from the wedding attendees. And he must choose a best man who will be infallible in having the rings ready to present at the proper time in the ceremony. (This applies to all ceremonies, of course.)

One of the bride's responsibilities is to provide a groom's cake. Liquor has been known to be used as a key ingredient, but a theme matching the groom's interests is traditional – and these may be one and the same.

The wedding was to be at 4 p.m. on a Friday afternoon. Henry made airline reservations for two days ahead and reserved rooms at a hotel in Albany. Pop had asked him to hold two doubles and two singles, without identifying the intended occupants. He had a wicked penchant for surprises.

Clare checked in with Becky frequently to see how Betty was holding up under the pressure she had put on herself as the de facto wedding arranger.

"Don't worry about Momma," her sister told her. "She's thriving on it."

"And how are you doing?"

"All right. But I'll sure be glad to have it over with."

"You're not the only one. Well, I'll talk to you again in a few days."

The next time they talked Becky was very frustrated. "I'm having a hell of a time getting something done about a dress," she said. "Maternity shops don't get that many calls for clothing for a matron of honor. I didn't have anything in my closet I could have resized."

"So what did you do?"

"I went to the biggest department store in Albany and picked out a nice light green dress two sizes too large and I'm having a local seamstress do a custom alteration. I'm not sure how it's going to turn out."

"I'll bet it will do just fine."

"I hope so."

Henry surprised his fiancee one evening when he brought home carryout from one of their favorite restaurants, along with a special bottle of wine.

"What's all this?" she asked.

"Getting married is a special occasion," he said confidently, "and I was about to overlook a very special part of it."

He got plates and silverware, set the table and opened the wine to let it breathe. He transferred the food to serving dishes and carried it to the table along with wine glasses. His old bachelor habits were coming in handy. He poured the wine and pulled Clare's chair out and invited her to sit. He then got down on one knee, took her hand and placed a jewelry box in it. Opening the box he said, "I know I have accepted your proposal. Now I want you to accept mine. Clare Sullivan, will you marry me?"

She found it hard to take her eyes off the sparkling engagement ring he had presented, but she did. Looking him in the eyes she said, "I will be very happy to marry you, Henry Jackson." He put the ring on her finger. They kissed, drank a silent toast to each other, and enjoyed their meal.

As they were loading the dishwasher, Henry said, "The next time you talk to your sister ask her something for me."

"Of course. What?"

"The groom's family, I understand, is supposed to host a rehearsal dinner. Pop's going to want a suggestion on where to have it. I would guess some place where the kitchen is pretty flexible. For all we know he might be flying in fresh Alaska salmon for the occasion."

"I'll see what I can find out," Clare said.

Becky was flabbergasted when Clare asked her if there was any restaurant in Shellville other than the diner where Jim took everyone out to eat.

"Gosh, I don't know. And that's a pretty small operation. Let me think. Well, there's a fairly new bed and breakfast just outside of town that's a pretty good size. How many people are we talking about?"

"Henry says probably about a dozen, if we confine it to immediate family members."

"They should be able to handle that," Becky said. "You want me to check with the owners?"

"Would you, please? You are doing so much for me and I really appreciate it."

"I read one of those bride's magazines and saw the matron of honor's duties covered about three-quarters of a page. I almost turned in my resignation."

"I'm glad you didn't," Clare chuckled.

"Don't count on me to help straighten your train. If I bend over I might not be able to stand back up."

"You don't need to worry. I don't think I'll have a train."

"And I know you're my sister and I love you ... but I draw the line at 'helping the bride pee in her dress.'"

They both broke up laughing over that one.

As the time grew shorter before one of the most important days in her life she became concerned about items remaining on her check list. At the top of things "to do" was "what to do" about a wedding dress. She had gone exploring at all the area department stores and boutique shops, finding nothing that seemed right. Although Clare had the figure to wear long gowns well, in her mind, brides of her age (almost 40) should not cloak themselves in yards of material to make that treacherous walk down the aisle. She would be perfectly content to wear a stylish business suit, but she knew that wouldn't be acceptable to her mother, who was all worked up about Southern traditions.

One day over pre-dinner cocktails, Clare expressed her exasperation to Henry. He thought a minute, took a sip, and said, "You know, Laurey looked really beautiful in that wedding dress she wore."

Clare put down her glass and ran to her future husband, hugged him warmly and kissed him not once, but twice. "You are wonderful!" she exclaimed, as Henry looked pleased and proud. "You're not only very good looking and terribly sexy, but you also have a brilliant mind."

"The dress I wore in *Oklahoma!* wouldn't do. It was fine for a pioneer days hitchin' but not quite classy enough for Shellville, Georgia. But you've given me a great idea."

"What's that?"

"I got to be very good friends with the wardrobe mistress. She's from South Carolina. I'll call her and get her advice."

She carefully picked a time when she knew that Mildred Childers would be available and not fitting or repairing costumes and gave her a call.

"Hi, Millie. It's me, Clare."

"Lord have mercy! I'm so glad to hear from you."

They spent a few minutes catching up and then Clare plunged right in and told her about the coming wedding and the dilemma she was facing."

"Don't you worry about a thing, Miz Clare. I can whip up something that'll make those rednecks' eyes bug out. Not meaning any disrespect for your folks …"

"Of course not. I don't know how to thank you. You've got all my measurements, and I've tried to describe the kind of dress I'm thinking about. I know you'll come through for me."

"I'll get back to you by the end of the week," Millie said.

Clare waited to check that item off the list, but drew a large star to signify a major accomplishment.

62

IN THE WEEK BEFORE the big event, "wedding countdown" had begun and Clare was feeling pretty good about her readiness to become a bride. The dress ("an original by New York fashion designer M. Childers") had arrived and it was fabulous. She rushed to try it on and it fit perfectly. She could hardly wait for Henry to see it, but that was an absolute no-no prior to the wedding. So she carefully packed it in one of the many pieces of luggage they were taking to Georgia. Henry had arranged for rental of an SUV at the Albany airport to have room for all their bags.

One large suitcase was dedicated for use on their honeymoon. Henry had made arrangements for a post-wedding trip but wanted to keep the destination a secret. When she asked him how she would know what to pack, he said, "All you need to take is your passport and two bikinis." This sounded familiar, like something he said before they went to the beautiful Greek island of Santorini after the California campaign ended for her.

Clare and Barbara had spoken only once since the deal-signing. She had called from Tahiti and sounded as if she really meant it when she said the Sterlings were having the time of their lives. "Incidentally," Barbara added, "I'm a little miffed that I had to hear from someone else that you and Henry are getting married. I thought best friends shared things like that."

"I'm so sorry," Clare said. "It's a decision we made after y'all left and life has been pretty hectic with all the demands my mother is putting on me to have a traditional wedding."

"So you're going to go to Georgia to get married?"

"Not my choice, but Momma insisted. She plunged right into plans, and the doctors say it will help with her recovery from the accident."

"Well, as you know we'll have to miss it because we won't be back yet."

"I'll have lots of pictures to show you."

"I look forward to hearing all about it."

"I hope Phil is looking better," Clare said. "He was so pale when we saw him last."

"Are you kidding? He has a marvelous manly tan," Barbara said. "This vacation is the first one we've had in many years and it has been good for both of us."

"It will be wonderful when we can all get together again."

Unexpected developments always seem to occur to fill the days leading up to a big event – days needed to finish last minute preparations. For Clare it was an urgent call from Zach Bacharach. He knew she was going to Georgia but had forgotten when. He insisted she had to drop everything and meet him downtown. When she protested, he turned on the pressure.

"Clare, I've got to see you – today!" he shouted.

"What is so important that it can't wait until after the wedding?"

"I'll tell you what's important: a decision is pending on whether the *Busboys* series will be renewed. We lost one of our major sponsors at the end of the first season. But I have another one – and even better one – interested. He's on the verge of signing, but he wants to meet the star – you. And he's in Wilmington and available for lunch. You've got to come, Clare. Do this for me."

Clare hadn't even made a final decision whether to continue in the role of the restaurant owner. She pictured married life as a more relaxed time when there weren't so many demands on her time. But shooting the episodes didn't require too much time and she enjoyed working with the other cast members. Plus, Bacharach had done a lot to advance her acting career.

"Oh, all right," she said. "I wouldn't do this for anyone else but you, Zach. And please do what you can to keep this from being an extended lunch. I really have an awful lot to get done before we leave."

"He's just down from New York for a few hours. I think he's almost ready to close the deal and you can make the difference," Zach said. "You're a darling! See you at 12:30."

Clare and the prospective sponsor, president of a national food products company, hit it off right away. She found him to be delightful, even before he told her that he and his wife had seen her in *Oklahoma!*. "We thoroughly enjoyed the show," he said.

When the time was getting close to two o'clock, Clare said, "I know you two have business to discuss so I'm going to scoot." To her new admirer she said, "It was very nice meeting you," and to Zach, "I look forward to hearing from you."

A text message from Zach later in the day told her that getting away for lunch was worth her time. A deal was made and the series renewal was assured.

No more emergencies arose for either Clare or Henry before the day of departure and they headed to the airport, elated and excited.

They made the regional airline connection without a problem and were on the ground at Albany slightly ahead of schedule. The rental car was just what Henry ordered. They loaded up and drove to the hotel where they found that not only was their room ready, they had been given an upgrade. Just as they had finished checking in, they heard a familiar voice.

"Welcome to the Southland, you all."

They turned to see Pop, with Jean on his arm.

"We saw you from the coffee shop," Jean said. "We're having lunch. Have you had anything to eat?"

"Just airline snacks," Clare said. "May we join you?"

"Certainly. Oh, what a gorgeous ring!"

Henry sent the luggage to the room with a bellman and the four headed around the corner. Pop pointed to a table in the back and four figures stood and waved.

"Luna!" Clare said loudly and ran to embrace her stepdaughter, whom she hadn't seen since leaving California. She hugged Houston while at the same time Henry was greeting his younger brother, Andrew, and meeting his fiancee, Wanda Lewis. Then they reversed roles and Pop grew impatient with their animated conversations, most of which contained references to Clare's stunning engagement ring.

"Sit down and let's get you some lunch," he said, motioning to a waitress.

"What have you done to your hair?" Luna demanded.

"Oh, just let it grow out some. And you've put on some weight," Clare said.

"I've stopped smoking. And maybe I'm eating healthier meals – not all junk food."

"I can take a little credit," Houston said. "I'm a health nut."

Jean observed, "I think life has been good for all of us."

They had a lot to catch up on and they spent the next 45 minutes filling each other in on how their lives had changed. Luna and Houston couldn't believe the irony of Clare being thrown together with Pat Brown again after their eventful campaign encounter. Both Henry and Clare were eager to talk to Drew, as he preferred to be called, and to get acquainted with the woman in his life.

They learned that Wanda was an art teacher at a school in the Seattle suburbs. She and Drew met through an Internet dating service and had been seeing each other since the beginning of the year. Shortly after she visited the Jackson Vineyards (occupying "Clare's cabin") they became engaged.

Their conversation was interrupted by a call on Clare's cell phone. It was Becky.

"Hi, it's me. I thought it was about time y'all got in and just wanted to check and see," she said.

"Yes. We're at the hotel and just finishing up lunch with Henry's folks, his brother – the best man – and his fiancee. Oh, and I'm so excited to see my stepdaughter, Luna, and her special friend Houston."

"So there's six of them?"

"Right," Clare said. "Why do you ask?"

"Well, you know Momma."

"What's she done now?"

"She wants to invite all of you for supper tonight."

"And she just thought of this today?"

"This morning. Like I said …"

"Well, we can go out, with all she's got to do …"

"No, she says we ought to show Henry's people some pure Southern hospitality."

"But it's too much trouble …"

"No use to argue. She says there's way too much food for the reception. Everybody she knows brought something. She's cooking a roast and she's just putting some pecan pies in the oven."

"Are you there with her?"

"Yeah. I told her I'd help."

"Are you sure you're up for it … in your condition?"

"Hell, if I can squeeze into my dress and stand up for you on Friday I can certainly set the table and pour some sweet tea."

"Of course you can, Becky, but …"

"No buts. Momma says come around five. See you then. Bye."

Clare filled the group in on the plans, omitting the fact that it was a last minute decision.

"That's very nice of your mother," Pop said. "It'll be good to see her and Pat again. We didn't get to visit very much in New York. Right now, I think Jean and I are going to go take a nap."

Drew and Wanda decided to go for a walk. Clare and Henry went to their room to unpack … partially.

Later, the visiting Jacksons got a good look at rural Georgia on the winding roads to the Sullivan pecan farm. As they pulled into the drive they saw activity on the porch; two women and a little girl were coming out to greet them.

Betty Ann came running, her arms outstretched for a hug. "Aunt Clare! I'm so glad you came back to see us," she cried.

"I'm happy to see you, too, precious."

"Thank you for letting me be your flower girl."

"I can hardly wait to see your pretty dress."

Henry introduced the others to Betty, Becky and Pat, who had followed them out. Betty Ann also collected some more hugs and a tickle from Pop's mustache.

As they entered the house there were several admiring murmurs about the delicious smells coming from the kitchen.

"Thank you so much for having us, Momma," Clare said.

"It's not anything fancy," Betty said. "But I don't think anybody will go hungry."

Nature's great dividing force sent the men to the den with Pat while the women followed Betty and Becky to the food preparation area. Luna and Wanda quickly realized they were just in the way and went looking at the interesting features of the old farmhouse.

Before the men got seated Becky waddled in and said, "Can I get y'all something to drink?"

Nobody answered. Finally Drew spoke up.

"I'll have a coke."

"Fine. What kind would you like? We've got Pepsi, Dr. Pepper, Sprite, Diet Coke and Co-cola," Becky said.

"Uh, Diet Coke, I guess," Drew said, shyly.

"The same for me," Henry said, and Pop echoed, "Me, too."

Pat pointed to a bottle on the lamp table. "You can spike your Cokes with a shot of bourbon if you like," Pat said.

Meanwhile, Betty was taking up a beautiful pot roast, which she transferred to a platter along with the vegetables and turned on a burner. Sitting on the range top to keep warm were a pot of collard greens, some mashed potatoes, a green bean casserole and stewed tomatoes.

"We'll be ready to serve up as soon as I fix the gravy," Betty said.

Clare noticed Wanda's eyes widen, apparently wondering what was wrong with the gravy that it needed to be "fixed".

"Rebecca Jean, you want to get the deviled eggs out of the refrigerator?" Betty said, as she stirred the gravy.

"All right, Momma," she said as she struggled to pull herself up from the chair where she had been resting.

"I'll get them," Clare interrupted.

"What can I do, Grandma?" Betty Ann asked.

"Why, you can set the butter on the table. Thank you, honey."

Betty poured up the simmering brown sauce (as Jean might call it) into a gravy boat and set it on the counter. Opening the oven door she took up some cornbread baked in a cast iron skillet and swiftly divided it into thick slices.

Hands on hips, she surveyed the array of food circling the group and ordered: "All right, everybody grab something." Betty took the platter of roast and the others fell into line and paraded behind her into the dining room. As they passed within earshot of the den, Becky called out, "Y'all c'mon. It's time to eat."

Jim had come to the farm directly from his office and joined the men having a bull session.

"I think Momma is getting some of her memory back," Clare said softly.

Becky answered: "She sure remembers how to be the kitchen boss."

Everyone sat. Pat said the blessing. Food was passed.

Clare skipped almost everything but her mother's pot roast, which she had loved since she was a little girl.

Compliments were offered appropriately by the visitors from Washington State, especially when they tasted the pecan pie.

"This is absolutely the best I've ever had," Jean said to Betty.

"Been making it all my life," Betty said.

After supper was finished and the dishes loaded for washing, Clare was antsy to leave, but Betty wanted to talk about the wedding.

"Now, everybody be on time for the rehearsal tomorrow," she said. "The church organist will be there around 3 p.m. and we shouldn't keep her waiting."

"Is the ceremony still going to be outside?" Clare asked. "I thought I heard a forecast of showers."

"Of course it is," Betty snapped. "It's not going to rain. Pat buried the bourbon to make sure of that."

Henry's family looked puzzled at that remark.

"The men of the church might still be working on the dance platform but we won't let that bother us," Betty said.

"You don't need to wear your wedding clothes," she added.

Clare spoke up. "I hope everybody got the word about the rehearsal dinner. Maybe we can make it in two cars."

"You ladies are going to be busy tying up loose ends tomorrow," Pop said, "so I guess the guys can just goof off."

Pat responded. "I've got another idea. There's a hunting preserve not far from here. Maybe we could go shoot some quail."

"I don't know," Henry said. "We didn't come prepared ..."

"None of us brought our guns," Pop said.

"No need to worry about any of that," Pat said. "This place has everything from camouflage clothing to shotguns and shells."

"Dogs?" Drew inquired with some interest.

"Finest bird dogs in south Georgia," Pat said. "For a half day's hunt, we get refreshments and lunch. They guarantee eight bobwhites per hunter. And they'll clean and pack them for us if you want them to."

"Will there be a lot of walking?" Pop asked.

"No," said Pat. "The guides will take us in a specially designed buggy that will carry all of us."

"What about licenses?" Henry asked.

"Yeah, you do have to have a Georgia hunting license," Pat said. "But you can get them online."

"We can use the hotel's business center to do that," Drew said, with some enthusiasm.

"All right," Pat said. "We can go from here."

Pop said: "What time?"

"It would be good if you could come around 8. And we ought to be back by one o'clock."

"Okay, we'll see you in the morning then," Pop said, signifying to Jean that he was ready to leave.

When the women heard about the plans Clare and Wanda couldn't believe the guys were going to go traipsing through the woods with such a big event to get ready for. Henry tried to calm them down.

"If we stayed here, we'd just be in the way," he said. "Pat is doing all of us a big favor. He's my idea of a good father-in-law." He paused to let those strange words soak in before driving back to the hotel.

"Better get a wakeup call," Pop said, before the group disbanded for the evening.

By the time Clare and the others gathered in the dining room for breakfast, the men had been gone for half an hour. The women tried not to show the anxiety they felt about these inexperienced sportsmen being turned loose with some big dangerous weapons to use against tiny little innocent birds. They were mostly concerned the shooters might do more harm to themselves than to their quarry.

But soon they turned their thoughts to the wedding. Clare filled them in on all she knew about the arrangements her mother had made. She was still skeptical about the weather, although the sun was shining brightly to begin the day before the outdoor ceremony.

"Becky told me Daddy had buried the bourbon on time," Clare said, then explained the odd custom to the visitors. She also had to educate them about grits.

Over breakfast they made plans for the day leading up to the rehearsal. Wanda said she had noticed the hem in a slip had begun to ravel and she needed to replace it. That reminded Clare of an emergency slip purchase she had to make in Seattle, where she and Henry had met.

Houston wasn't into hunting so he and Luna left after breakfast for a morning of sightseeing.

Pop had left their rental car with Jean so the women got around and headed out to a shopping center. They came across so many places of interest the trip extended into the lunch hour at a bistro featuring a half-price special on wine. Clare wanted to learn more about Wanda and she became increasingly forthcoming. She had not been married but had experienced two unhappy romances before meeting Drew.

"I think I've finally found the right man," she said.

"And he adores you," Jean said knowingly.

"I take it the two of you aren't inclined to rush into marriage," Clare observed.

"Drew is quite methodical in his approach to life and we both want to be very sure of ourselves because we want this marriage to last," Wanda said.

"We all want that," Jean said.

Clare excused herself to take a phone call. It was Becky.

"Momma wanted me to check on y'all," she said. "She wanted to make sure everybody is all right."

Clare wanted to say, "why wouldn't we be?" But her instinct told her that mothers just naturally worry about their offspring and that Betty wanted to make doubly sure nothing had happened to make her wedding plans go wrong.

"We're fine. Everyone is just fine," Clare told her sister.

"Well, you might want to head on down this way pretty soon."

"The guys ought to be back from their hunting escapade by the time we get back to the hotel. So we'll get changed and be along in a little while," Clare said, lapsing back into the vernacular of her Georgia childhood.

They found the men sitting around the pool in shorts and T-shirts relaxing after their adventure in the wild.

"Hi," Henry yelled. "Want a beer?"

"No, thank you," Clare said. "How was your hunting trip?"

"Great," Henry said and the others nodded. "Have a seat and we'll tell you all about it."

"Another time. We've got to get ready to go to the rehearsal," Clare said. "And that includes you," pointing to all three men.

"What? It's early!" Pop bellowed.

"I thought we didn't have to be there until 3 or 4 o'clock," Drew chimed in.

"Look at your watch," Clare said. "It will take some time to get there and Momma will have a hissy fit waiting for us."

"All right," Henry and the others grumbled.

When the group got to the church garden wedding site the first person they saw was Gladys Murphy, the church organist, setting up her portable keyboard and speakers. Gladys (students in her high school music class called her Glad-ass behind her back) was an accomplished musician and served the Presbyterian Church congregation well, notwithstanding the well-circulated rumor that she regularly had a nip of communion wine before the worship service.

Gladys greeted the arrivals as she continued connecting the cables and plugs that were essential to providing music for the wedding.

"Don't tell Betty, but this would be a lot simpler if we had the ceremony inside the church," she said.

Clare embraced her and said, "I agree, but you know Momma."

"Yes, everybody knows your momma."

The church garden was indeed a choice setting for a wedding. Small but expertly landscaped, the plot at the rear of the church property had an impressive iron arch at the entrance and winding walks that led past a fountain that sometimes worked to a clearing marked by another arch, covered with wisteria, which provided a backdrop for various kinds of ceremonies. The entire garden plot was enclosed by a tall boxwood hedge, decades old.

The garden was at its best in the spring, when it exploded with color from many sources. In the fall blooming plants were scarce.

Prominent among the variety of floral plantings were the roses – several types, many colors. For autumn there was always the reliable Knockout Rose and there were bushes scattered throughout the garden.

Chrysanthemums naturally occupied a place as queen of the fall flowers, quietly beaming in their yellow, orange and deep red splendor.

A few gardenias here and there accented the beds of Glory Lilies and Gerber Daisies. Confederate Jasmine growing on white lattices added both a pink-tinged flower and a magnificent aroma to the garden.

Rose campion (lychnis coronaria), a staple in a Southern garden, claimed inclusion, along with the low-growing ice plant, a succulent that blooms until frost.

To make up for the lack of blooms that the garden would afford in spring and summer, Betty had enlisted the help of the Shellville Flower Club. A week before the wedding club members dug and planted fresh annuals – Cockscomb, Impatiens, Marigolds, Pansies and Petunias. They also laid down fresh mulch to give the garden a special look for the wedding.

Large pots of bright flowering plants from the local nursery were placed near the spot where the wedding ceremony would be.

When Clare and the others had completed a tour of the garden they found Betty and Gladys deep in conversation. Clare waved but failed to get her mother's attention.

The men wandered around uncomfortably, wondering why they came so early. At least a couple of them were absorbed with their smart phones.

About that time, an unexpected visitor arrived upon the scene. She roared up in her Jeep and parked where she wasn't supposed to. Maybe she thought the large-lettered PRESS card in the front window would grant her special privileges.

She was a large woman and the vest with pockets bulging with photographic paraphernalia only added to her girth. The large camera with a telephoto lens larger than the main instrument dangling from a strap around her neck gave a clue to her identity.

Bessie Stringer was the editor of the local weekly newspaper. More accurately, she was the editor and publisher, reporter, columnist, photographer, advertising director and circulation manager. With all those titles she could have worn many hats, but folks around town knew her by the baseball cap that was always on her head, turned backwards to allow more freedom for taking pictures.

Clare was puzzled because Becky had told her that Betty had asked Jim to be the official wedding photographer.

They saw her march into the garden and overheard a loud exchange.

"What are you doing here, Bessie?" asked Betty.

"Just be glad I am," Bessie replied. "You didn't alert me to the wedding of the year."

"Anyone that was important knew about it. But couldn't you wait until tomorrow to crash the event?"

"A professional photographer has to be prepared, see the lay of the land, check out the angles, you know."

"Well, just don't get in the way," Betty ordered, then went to call in the group. They were impressed with the beauty of the garden but curious about the hammering noise they heard. Their curiosity was satisfied when they entered the clearing and saw the construction of a 15 by 15 foot dance floor in progress behind the arch.

Becky explained: "This was a last-minute idea that Momma had. She thought it would be good to have an appropriate place for the bride and groom to have their traditional dance. Plus, she didn't want her own high heels to sink down in the turf of the garden."

"Very thoughtful of her," Clare responded.

"I think everyone who needs to be here is here," Betty announced, "and some who don't need to be, so let's get started."

The group took seats in the white wooden folding chairs that had been set up for the occasion, the exception being Bessie, who was wandering around looking for good backgrounds for her candid shots.

Betty took a position in front and proceeded to dictate what was about to take place. She had to deal with some interference from two sources. She began:

"Gladys will play some appropriate music ... bam, bam, bam, bam, bam ...while guests are arriving. Everybody should be here and seated by 4 p.m. At that time, the processional music will begin (gesturing to Gladys) ... bam, bam, bam, bam, bam ... and then the minister, the groom and the best man will enter and stand on the right side – my left, your right."

Betty was interrupted by a squawking comment from Bessie. "Or they could come down the aisle with the rest of the procession."

Clare tensed up as the photographer came under the stony gaze of an irritated mother of the bride. "Please be quiet, Bessie. What would anybody from Oklahoma know about Southern customs, anyway?"

"My parents were from Arkansas," Bessie shot back, "and I've been to plenty of Southern weddings."

"This is the way this wedding is going to be done," Betty said firmly. The three men took their places and she was about to continue when she had another interruption. This time it was Gladys.

"Excuse me, Betty, but in the weddings I've done the minister, groom and best man wait until both sets of parents are seated before coming in," she said.

"That's what I meant to say. Thank you, Gladys," Betty said.

"You're welcome."

Betty went on. "So, now, the parents of the groom will be seated. And then, the mother of the bride will be seated. I will be escorted by my son-in-law, Dr. James Vinson, who then will return to the rear of the sanctuary.

"And at this point, the minister, the groom and the best man enter and stand to the right of the pulpit.

"Since Clare chose not to have any bridesmaids, next in the order of procession will be the matron of honor …"

"The flower girl comes next," blurted Bessie. Betty Ann jumped to her feet. "Me, Mommy? Is it time for me?"

"No, I don't think so," Becky said.

"Definitely not," declared Betty. "And for the last time, Bessie, don't interrupt."

Bessie responded with an impertinent blinding flash from her camera in Betty's face.

Becky started her unsteady walk to the front and about halfway down she stumbled on a rough spot. Jim, arriving at that very moment, rushed to her side but she had caught herself from falling. Nevertheless, the doctor declared his wife could not risk injuring herself or the baby and a substitute had to be found.

After a quick huddle, Betty, Becky and Clare decided that Luna was the only woman in the wedding party who was suitable to take Becky's place. Luna protested furiously. "I don't know anything about weddings," she said. "And I don't have a dress that's suitable. You'll have to get someone else."

"I'm afraid there isn't anyone else," Clare said. "You will do it well, just like you do everything. And I will be honored if you will be my maid of honor."

"All right. Luna, practice doing your walk now," Betty said.

Bam, bam, bam, bam, bam.

"Elizabeth Ann, now it's your turn. You come down the aisle tossing rose petals to the left and right. Today we'll just pretend, and save the real petals for the ceremony tomorrow."

The little girl proudly and perfectly did her role and took her place standing by Luna on the left.

"Now comes the Wedding March (nodding to Gladys) and the bride comes down the aisle on the arm of her father."

Clare and Pat did so and he took a seat where Betty would be sitting. Clare braced for another outburst from Bessie, knowing that another old tradition

245

would be for the father of the bride to remain standing with her until the minister asked, "Who gives this woman in marriage?" Betty had decided against doing that. Bessie kept her mouth shut.

Rev. Peterson, being familiar with wedding ceremonies, took it from there. The minister did not say all the words but simply told the audience about the charge, the pledge and the call to worship, leading up to the exchanging of rings. This did call for some practice, as did reciting the vows.

With the brief ceremony concluded the organist struck up the recessional and the unofficial married couple walked swiftly up the aisle followed by the rest of the procession.

Betty said, "That was very good, y'all. Now, let's have the real rehearsal without my giving directions."

Bessie had done what she came to do and left so there were no more interferences. The carpenters also had done their work for the day and said they would finish up "in the morning." Betty had artificial flower bouquets for Clare and Becky and an empty basket for Betty Ann.

The rehearsal went quite smoothly with no major slipups. Betty gave a silent prayer of thanks.

When the designated rehearsal dinner group arrived and got seated at the B&B just outside of town, Pop commanded: "All right, folks. This is an evening to relax and have a good time. We're going to have some good food, and some good wine, and I hope some good conversation. This is a coming together of two families. We're celebrating the forthcoming union of Clare and Henry, but I also want it to be a union of the Sullivans and the Jacksons.

"Let me begin by toasting the couple who brought us all together: my son, Henry, and his chosen lifetime companion, the lovely Clare. From the moment I met her I knew she was the one we all had been waiting for to make our lives complete." Pop raised his glass and the others followed suit.

"Secondly, I want to toast the woman who has done such a masterful job of planning and organizing this wedding. Because of Betty Sullivan, I know it will be an occasion all of us will remember for a long, long time." Betty glowed in her moment of glory, not showing the worry she must have had about something she might have forgotten.

"Now, my friends, let us enjoy this time of friendship and fellowship. Let's eat."

Pop got his wish. The woman who owned the B&B with her husband was a regionally well-known chef in her former life. She presented a five-star menu which rivaled outstanding meals that all the world travelers present had enjoyed in the past. The Mt. Jackson wines Pop had brought were a hit with everyone.

By way of pre-arranged seating plans, Pop renewed his friendship with Clare, Betty got acquainted with her forthcoming new son-in-law, Drew got a reading on his new sister-in-law from her sister, Pat and Jean swapped stories about their widely varying backgrounds , Luna and Jim managed to find some things in common, and Wanda and Houston exchanged views on their roles as teachers.

A delicious chocolate dessert prepared by the chef capped the very special evening.

63

WEDDING DAY for Clare and Henry dawned bright and early. The sun rose on a clear sky, making it a pleasant day for an excursion Henry had planned for him, Pop, Drew and Houston – a visit to a Georgia winery.

Henry had a special reason for going, other than occupying time before the late afternoon nuptials. Georgia is the national leader in the production of wine from the muscadine grape, which was the focus of his infant vineyard in North Carolina.

There aren't too many wineries in South Georgia. The one Henry had chosen was a little more than a half hour's drive from the hotel. He had read that it had a large acreage of muscadines, producing a variety of red, white and rose wines, several of which had won awards in both domestic and international competitions. Henry had called and arranged for a tour of the vineyards and the winery.

Each of the men had a particular interest in various phases of the winery operation: Drew, as the former overseer of winegrowing at Mt. Jackson Vineyards, naturally wanted to talk to someone about grape production. Pop's mind was more on the business side, and Henry looked forward to seeing an example of the kind of success he might realize from his modest start sometime in the future.

Clare had a hairdresser appointment but little else planned. She had deliberately tried to ensure a light schedule on this big day. Jean and Wanda were going shopping and Luna joined them to get a new dress.

Clare had asked Luna to join her for lunch in the hotel restaurant so they could have some private "catch-up" time.

During the course of the campaign in California and the calamitous events that followed, Clare and her stepdaughter had grown progressively close. They had actually established a relationship much like a mother-daughter bond, which had gradually slipped away as a result of being apart. She regretted this and felt a little ashamed that she had been negligent in keeping in touch with her by email or phone. But she told herself that communication is a two-way exercise and that eased her conscience a bit. She used this time together to reaffirm her gratitude to Luna for agreeing to be her maid of honor.

From the lunchtime visit Clare realized that Luna had matured somewhat and with her business success had acquired some polish. However, she was glad to know Luna had retained a generous portion of her basic brash personality, a trait she had inherited from her father.

Her time with Luna revived memories of her first marriage to Gary de Lunc. Luna's father was an adventuresome racing enthusiast who lived, and died, engaging in the fast life. The marriage, like their engagement, was relatively brief. It was full of thrills, notoriety and fabulous fun and good times. But she had found herself constantly searching for a deeper meaning for her life, which she had sought to achieve by running for high office. Failure to reach that goal had been difficult to overcome but with the help of the new love who had come into her life she felt she had come to terms with it and moved on.

Clare was to be at the church garden an hour-and-a-half before the ceremony. Since the men had not returned from their winery trip the four women crowded into the Jacksons' rented BMW and departed for Shellville shortly after lunch. Clare noted some clouds gathering in the sky and grabbed a light raincoat as a precaution as she left her room.

On arrival at the wedding site, she was met by Becky, who had a worried look on her face. Somehow this was different from the look of concern and anxiety she had worn throughout the final months of her pregnancy.

"What's wrong?" Clare asked. "You look upset."

"I'm more than upset. I'm damn mad. And you would be, too, if you had your picture on the front page of the local newspaper with your slip showing." She thrust the weekly edition of the *Shellville Beacon* into Clare's hands, at which point she saw the headline, "Local Nuptials for TV Star" by Bessie Stringer, Society Editor. The photo of Becky was taken from the rear during rehearsal before she tripped as she was walking down the aisle. Her face was not showing. The article also was accompanied by a head shot of Clare as the restaurant owner in *Busboys*. It read as follows:

"After achieving fame as a candidate in a high stakes political race and stardom on TV and the Broadway stage, Clare Sullivan came home to get married. The 1993 Shellville High School graduate was scheduled to take her wedding vows Friday afternoon in a garden ceremony at the Shellville Presbyterian Church. She is marrying Henry Jackson, owner of a real estate development company in Wilmington, N.C. He formerly was president of Mt. Jackson Vineyards in the state of Washington.

"Following graduation from the University of Georgia, Sullivan studied at Oxford and remained in Europe for some time afterward before returning to the U.S., where she settled in Southern California. Her marriage to businessman and state Sen. Gary de Lune ended with his death in an automobile accident. She succeeded him in the senate and in 2014 ran for governor. She came in third in an open primary.

"As a resident of Wilmington, N.C. she became involved with a group in establishing a community theater and appeared in some of its productions before being discovered by a Hollywood director who cast her as the restaurant owner in a cable TV series, *Busboys*. That led to a starring role in a revival production of the Rodgers and Hammerstein musical *Oklahoma!* in New York City.

"Sullivan said she would have a small, traditional wedding ceremony. Her stepdaughter, Luna de Lune, of Santa Barbara, Calif., will be her maid of honor. Her niece, Elizabeth Ann Bradley, will be the flower girl. Henry Jackson's best man will be his brother, Andrew.

"Parents of the bride are Pat and Betty Sullivan of the Sullivan Pecan Farm, Shellville. The groom is the son of Henry Jackson, Jr., chairman of Mt. Jackson Vineyards, and his wife, Jean.

"Other members of the wedding party are Wanda Lewis, Andrew Jackson's fiancee; and Houston Conover, of Santa Barbara, Calif."

Clare caught a glimpse of her father looking at a spot in the churchyard and went to see what he was doing and to compliment him on how nice he looked for the wedding.

"I'm just making sure I remember where I buried the bottle of bourbon," he said. "It's supposed to keep it from raining. But it's beginning to cloud up."

Casting a wary eye to the sky, Clare said, trying to sound reassuring, "Don't worry, Daddy. Everything's going to be all right."

"I sure hope so," he said, "after all the work your mother has done getting things set up to have the wedding in the garden. Anyway, we don't want the bourbon to go to waste. The tradition says you're supposed to dig it up after the ceremony and share it with the guests."

The minister had kept the church unlocked so the bride and the other women could change and all members of the wedding party could be outfitted with their floral accessories: corsages for the ladies, boutonnieres for the gentlemen. Clare and Luna took their dresses over to the back door of the church and went in search of a place to change in the basement. They ran into Betty, who was in a Sunday School room laying out the flowers. She directed them to another room where they could leave their dresses.

Clare, trying to ignore the distant rumble she was hearing, inquired brightly, "How's everything going, Momma?"

"Oh, all right, I hope. I'll feel better when Gladys is here," she said. "I know Jim can't get here too early, but he needs to get the posed pictures taken before the ceremony."

About that time Henry and Drew came in to get the flowers for their lapels. Clare admired the looks of her husband-to-be in his new linen suit. He smiled as he gave her a kiss on the cheek and whispered, "Have you seen what it's doing outside? We heard on the radio coming in that a thunderstorm is forecast for this area this afternoon."

"Hush!" she said.

As they went to the floral assembly line they heard a man's voice saying, "Betty, the garden looks better than I've ever seen it. You and the flower club members have done a marvelous job. I just hope and pray the rain holds off."

"It's not going to rain, Reverend Peterson. We've taken care of that," she said.

"Your faith in the Lord is your strength and shield, Betty. Well, you know you can always move the ceremony inside if you need to."

"Thank you, pastor. But I want the wedding to be in the garden and that's where it's going to be."

Clare suddenly came face to face with her mother. She felt moved to tell her how much she appreciated all the effort she had put forth on the wedding.

"What's a mother for?" Betty said with a shrug of her shoulders. "Oh, Clare – did you remember something old, something new ..."

"Most of it. I'd say something new would be my wedding dress ... or it could be my earrings (she pointed to her blue sapphire studs encircled by diamonds) ..."

"Or those could be your 'something blue' ... how about something old?"

"Oh, gosh," Clare said.

"Here," Betty said, handing her a small handkerchief edged in lace. "I have a set of these handed down through generations. I usually carry one for good luck, but you may use it if you like."

"I'd love to, Momma," Clare said. "Thank you. Now all I need is something borrowed ..."

Becky, standing nearby, handed her a perfume bottle with a sprayer. "You can borrow some of my perfume," she said.

"Will you spray me?" Clare said, quickly adding, "just a little."

"Hi, everybody." They looked and saw Dr. Jim Vinson standing at the door. "Clare, I think you and Luna had better get changed so we can take some pictures before the ceremony." As they headed to their changing room, Clare asked Becky about the whereabouts of Betty Ann.

"I told her to wait in the children's play room. Jim, can you go get her?"

Before leaving, he said to Betty, "I'd like to pose the pictures in front of the arch. Could you send them out as soon as possible? I'll go get set up."

A short time later Clare and Luna returned, dressed, to pick up their bouquets. Betty pinned a rose in the bride's hair. Clare pulled up the hood on the raincoat she was wearing to protect her from the weather and to conceal her dress until her grand entrance.

They moved quickly to the area where Jim was finishing up the group and single photos he was taking for the wedding album and quickly posed Clare and Henry separately, together, with Luna, with Becky and Betty Ann, with both sets of parents, and by accident, with Gladys, who was standing nearby.

"That's a wrap," Jim said, echoing a phrase he had picked up from some movie he'd seen.

As all members of the wedding party moved to the rear to allow the entrance of some wedding guests who had been waiting to claim seats, the first sprinkle was felt … and then the second and third.

Becky tried to calm a tearful Betty. "This couldn't be helped, Momma. And at least we'll have Jim's photos of your beautiful garden setting to remember."

"Everybody turn around and go to the church," Jim said to the guests. Pop and Drew went ahead of the group to head off late arrivals and point them toward the church.

Gladys scurried to scoop her music into a bag and drape a thick plastic cover over the portable keyboard before fleeing to safety.

A scene of sad but somehow comical frenzy ensued as people fought both wind and rain to get inside the church.

Ladies dressed in their finest clutched their hats with one hand while holding their skirts down with the other. Those who took time to put up an umbrella did so to no avail as they turned inside out and became collectors instead of shedders of raindrops.

Men and women ran pushing wheelchairs with spouses or other relatives, trying hard not to stumble and sprawl in the mud.

Old Lady Wagoner couldn't keep up with the crowd using her walker so she tossed it aside and grabbed the arm of the first man she saw to her right, who turned out to be a straitlaced widower who owned the town's largest bank.

More than one matron approached the church barefooted, carrying their new shoes close against their chest.

Mercifully, although the sprinkling rain grew in intensity it remained light and nobody got soaked.

The wedding party entered the back door of the church and managed to squeeze into the small space. Rev. Peterson was there to take over consoling Betty Sullivan, uttering comforting Bible passages while she sobbed uncontrollably. Finally she regained her composure and resumed command.

"All right, everybody. You all know what you need to do. You did it well at the rehearsal in the garden. You just need to do it now in the church sanctuary," she said.

Gladys spoke up. "One advantage is we'll have the church organ so the music will be of much better quality." That was followed by a chorus of approval.

Five young people were standing nearby with puzzled looks on their faces. Betty explained: "At the last minute I asked Gladys to see if she could get the high school boys quartet and Jennifer—a most talented – and beautiful – soloist – to add some vocal music for the occasion, and as you can see, she succeeded. Thank you. Thank you."

Turning to Rev. Peterson, she said, "Will you please say a blessing to remove the curse that has fallen on this service?" The minister obliged and Betty ordered everybody to "take your places."

Henry and Drew followed Rev. Peterson into the pastor's office. Gladys took her seat at the church organ and immediately began playing some instrumentals designed to soothe the wedding guests' rattled nerves. Everyone else went downstairs and walked through the basement to the opposite end and came up another stairway to an anteroom off the church's main entrance to wait their turn for the procession.

Betty detoured past the flower room to get a corsage for Jennifer and outfit the male singers with boutonnieres. They looked sharp in their blue blazers and white slacks. She had meant to press them into service as ushers, but because things got off schedule all the wedding guests had already seated themselves.

Houston and Wanda walked to the front and he sat on the second row, while Wanda took a seat on the groom's side of the sanctuary.

Jim hung his still camera around his neck and pulled his video camera out of a bag. He took time to inquire of Becky, "How are you holding up, darling?"

"I'm doing the best I can," she answered. "I just want this to be over."

"You're doing it for your sister and your mother," he said softly and, rubbing her "baby bump" "you're doing this for us."

"Us and Betty Ann," she said. She edged into the back row, grateful she didn't have to make that long walk.

At precisely 4 o'clock a jarring clap of thunder rocked the skies and unleashed a downpour of rain beating on the church's tin roof and almost drowned out the opening notes of the wedding ceremony. To get the audience's attention Gladys turned up the volume on the Hammond organ and played an abbreviated version of Jeremiah Clarke's "Trumpet Voluntary."

Without music, the minister, the groom and the best man – who had been waiting in the pastor's study – entered and stood on the right side of the pulpit.

Jim captured most of this on the video camera, then asked one of the singers – Kenny – to fill in for him as he prepared for the next step in the ceremony.

Gladys sent a thrill through the crowd with a lively rendition of "Ode to Joy" from Beethoven's Ninth Symphony as the parents of the groom – Pop and Jean – strode down the aisle to their seats in the first row on the right. Then the mother of the bride – Betty, escorted by Jim – was seated on the aisle in the front pew on the left side.

Jim returned to await the bride's entry. The group in the back of the church had begun to dwindle. Besides Clare, there remained Luna and Betty Ann. Jim had resumed operating the video camera. He was concerned the loud thunder and the pounding of the rain would spoil the audio quality of the recording. But there wasn't much that could be done about it.

Luna was obviously uncomfortable in her surprise role as maid of honor. She came to attention as she heard Gladys begin to play a Bach cantata that marked the beginning of the wedding processional. She picked up her bouquet, a colorful mix of blooms from the garden, and proceeded on her mission.

As she took her place to the left of the pulpit, she looked to see an expression of horror come over Becky's face and she shrieked, "Oh-h-h! It's time!."

The church erupted in a storm of panic.

Betty looked aghast at her daughter's predicament and frowned about the interruption in the perfect ceremony.

Becky pushed herself erect, shouting, "I've got to get to the hospital."

Jim handed the video camera back to Kenny and said to his wife, "I'll grab an umbrella. Let's go."

On the way to the door, Becky stooped to give her frightened daughter a hug and said, "Do good, baby. I'll see you later."

"Bye, Mommy," Betty Ann said through her tears. "I love you."

Throughout the ordeal Gladys had not missed a beat. Luna smiled at the little girl bravely starting down the aisle tossing her flower petals. She was the picture of innocence, wearing the crisp white frock with embroidered flowers around the hem that her mother made, carefully pacing herself as she had been instructed, making sure she took small handfuls of flowers from the basket so she wouldn't run out. When she reached the end she ran to Luna's side and felt the warmth of her hand on her shoulder.

Then came the moment everyone had been waiting for. The music stopped. The guests craned their necks and turned their eyes to the rear of the sanctuary. With the striking of the first notes of Wagner's "Bridal Chorus," the crowd rose as one and watched eagerly as Clare made her majestic entry on the arm of her father.

She was strikingly beautiful in her "New York designer" dress – a tea length semi-mermaid style fashioned from beige antique lace with a short-sleeved top of amber-beaded organza that allowed a modest amount of cleavage to show through. The form-fitting gown had fullness below the hips and the hem of the dress was uneven, curving lower in the back to suggest a train. She wore tan silk slippers with medium high heels, which supported what had been termed Clare's "sculpturesque" figure. She carried a large bouquet of red roses, which were complemented by an American Beauty rose nestled in her auburn hair, which she wore in an upswept style.

Clare felt as if everything was happening in slow motion. Her eyes were fixed on her groom as he stood waiting for her, indescribably handsome in his new suit with the gold-striped tie, his shoes polished to a bright shine, his hair perfectly in place and his smile unbroken. Her thoughts flashed back to the first time she looked into Henry's face, into his brown eyes filled with kindness, on that evening in the Seattle hotel café where they had their chance meeting. The events that followed zipped through her mind: meeting Pop at the winery, Luna's brash behavior when Henry came to the villa, how their budding love grew and he became an invaluable member of her campaign team, raising enormous amounts of money, always by her side in the stressful moments and holding her in his arms when the long days were done.

As she drew closer to the front her eyes shifted to Luna and she recalled how they had found what both of them needed – a true, loving mother-daughter relationship. Then before the final step in her seemingly long journey down the aisle, Clare faced her mother, who was looking backward to take in the full climactic moment of the wedding she had planned. Tears of happiness welled up in the eyes of both of them and all those years of being apart were forgotten. Clare used the "something old" handkerchief to hold the tears in check so her mascara wouldn't run and spoil the photographs that were being taken by what seemed like a hundred or more cameras.

Her father kissed her on the cheek and seated himself beside his wife as Clare finished her walk and turned to face the room full of teary-eyed but smiling faces and the music gave way to a reverential silence. The minister took his position and Henry joined the woman of his dreams in facing him as he began the service:

"Dearly Beloved, we are gathered here in the sight of God ..."

Reading from the Presbyterian Church liturgy, Rev. Peterson spoke of true love as "a love both freely given and freely accepted" and said according to the Bible, "nothing is of more importance than love."

He led the couple as they took their vows, pledging to "love, honor, cherish and protect ... in sickness and in health, for richer or for poorer ..."

At this point the male quartet, which had gone through the basement and come back upstairs, emerged into the sanctuary and sang in beautiful harmony, "I Love You Truly." They took seats on the front row of the groom's side and waited to escort members of the wedding party after the service.

Clare handed her bouquet to Luna and Drew came to Henry's side for the exchange of rings.

Following that ritual, Gladys switched to the piano keyboard to accompany Jennifer as she sang a solo taken from the musical *Oklahoma!* – "Out of My Dreams (and Into Your Arms)." This struck an emotional nerve with Clare because it was her favorite number from the show in which she was the female lead. She wondered if her mother had guessed that.

With a prayer to bless the bride and groom and the covenant of marriage, Rev. Peterson concluded the ceremony with the traditional pronouncement: "I now declare you to be husband and wife" and gave Henry unnecessary permission to "now kiss the bride."

"Ladies and gentlemen, I present to you Mr. and Mrs. Henry Jackson."

("Henry and Clare Sullivan Jackson," Luna muttered under her breath.)

"You are all invited to join the wedding party in a reception at the American Legion Hall across the street," the minister announced. Looking at the light streaming through the stained glass windows, he added, "And thank the Lord, the sun has come out!"

The church had no bell to ring, but Gladys and the organ rang the rafters with Mendelsohn's "Wedding March." The happy couple walked swiftly up the aisle, followed by the young men ushering the parents up and out the door ahead of the other wedding guests. Betty Ann came with Luna, tightly holding her hand.

As they headed across the churchyard to the reception, carefully avoiding puddles that had accumulated during the storm, Clare suddenly stopped and pointed to the sky.

"Look, Momma!" They both were thrilled to see a splendid rainbow stretching across a clear blue horizon. "What a perfect ending for the wonderful wedding you gave me."

Still clutching her bouquet, Clare gave her mother a strong one-armed hug and kissed away the tears flowing down her cheeks.

The volunteers who had sat in the back of the church went around the family group to get busy in the hall.

Pat excused himself to go to his truck and get a shovel. "I'm going to dig up the bourbon," he said. The others crossed the street.

"I'm anxious about Becky," Clare said. "I wonder if she's had the baby yet."

The wedding ceremony had taken only about 15 minutes. "It's probably too soon," Betty said. "Jim said he'd let us know."

Before the wedding volunteers from the Shellville Women's Club had set up tables and chairs, the bar and food tables in the large colorfully-decorated hall. Betty had arranged for a disc jockey to provide music for the evening. After the drama of the thunderstorm, everybody was ready to celebrate.

As they entered the hall one of Betty's closest friends – acting as hostess for the reception – met the group and showed them to their table, which seated 12. She brought vases for Clare and Luna's bouquets and another container of one dozen strawberries dipped in chocolate on skewers.

"These are from your husband," she said to Clare, who thought to herself, "Husband ... got to get used to that."

One of the bartenders (husbands of the volunteers) came to the table with an iced bucket of champagne and a tray of glasses. He obediently popped the cork and poured for the bride and others who took glasses from the tray.

As other wedding guests were entering the hall and staking out tables, Pat arrived and set a muddy bottle of bourbon on the reserved table. He was in a joking mood.

"I didn't have to dig it up," he said with a grin. "It floated to the top."

"Be serious, Pat," Betty said. "The 'Bourbon Burial' good luck charm didn't work, did it?"

"Who cares?" he said, deciding not to say that he had found the bottle had turned over and lay horizontally instead of upside down. "Everything turned out all right, and what a beautiful rainbow we had!"

If Clare didn't know better, she might have thought her daddy had already tasted the bottle's contents.

Pat suddenly got serious. "But you know something?" he said. "It's a good thing we didn't use the garden. I saw a deadly coral snake crawling out from under a bush."

Amid gasps from the crowd, Betty asked, "What did you do?"

"I chopped that sucker's head off with my shovel," he said proudly.

Betty Ann ran to give him a hug. "Grandpa, you're so brave!"

"I'd hate to think what might have happened," said Wanda, visibly shaken.

"If one of our guests had got bitten there would have been hell to pay, that's for sure," Luna candidly observed.

"You're a real hero, Pat," Betty said. "That snake could have totally spoiled all of my plans."

Others around the table lifted their glasses in gratitude.

One of the other bartenders, observing the arrival of the bourbon, brought to the table a tray of glasses, a bucket of ice and assorted Cokes and other mixers. He took orders around the table for other drinks.

"What'll you have, Mother?" Pat boldly inquired of the woman he was helping to restore to her role as his wife, following the fall that caused her memory loss.

"I'll just have some sweet tea to start, thank you," she said, reserving the option to have something stronger as the evening wore on.

When the drinks had arrived and the bourbon drinkers were ready, Drew came out of his shell and said, "I know my important toast comes later (in the traditional role of best man) but somebody has to do this. So I propose this private toast to the bride and groom, to their parents and to all the friends who have come to wish them well in their married life." He raised his glass and that was a cue for the DJ to begin playing some "gathering" music. He announced that the bar was open and called attention to the appetizers on the tables: benne wafers, seasoned pecans and baby-back ribs.

After a sip of the finest Mt. Jackson reserve wine he had shipped for the occasion, Pop saw fit to compliment Clare on her bridal gown.

"It is stunningly beautiful, my dear," he said. "But I have to ask one question. Why does it sag in the back?"

"Henry!" Jean scolded.

Shrugging in feigned innocence, Pop said, "I was just asking."

Clare obligingly replied, "It's supposed to suggest a train."

"Well," Pop said gruffly, "it looked to me like the train left the station without any cars."

"I just didn't want to deal with any extra baggage when I waltzed you around the dance floor, Pop," Clare replied.

Rather than have a receiving line, Betty led the newly married couple around the room, stopping at each table to thank the guests for coming to the wedding and to make them feel welcome. "Have what you'd like to drink and some nibbles and we'll have some real food in a little while," Clare said.

As they moved along, they passed a table laden with packages. "I discouraged wedding gifts," Betty said, "but some people just insist on bringing something."

"What's this?" Clare asked, pointing to a large container.

"It looks like … it is … a crate of fresh pineapples," Henry said. "It was shipped from Hawaii by the Sterlings." He quickly identified his business partner and his wife who were on a cruise in the Pacific.

"We won't be able to take them on our honeymoon and back to Wilmington," Clare said. "But you can divide them with Pop. They won't be a problem with his private jet."

About the time they arrived back at their table, the DJ formally presented the newlyweds, their parents and other members of the wedding party and announced that the new married couple would have their first dance. They had chosen the "Sweetheart" song from Sigmund Romberg's *Maytime* musical, reflecting the European experiences each of them had before they met. "It will be sung by Jennifer English, winner of the regional competition for soprano soloists," he said.

As they began to dance Henry told Clare again how much he loved her and how happy she had made him. Referring to the weather fiasco, he couldn't resist saying, "Considering what happened in California and again today, the rain gods must really have it in for you." She replied, "Well, today certainly wasn't any comparison. And it was mother that I felt sorry for. But she seems to have accepted it."

It turned out that a waltz was a good choice for the first dance because a number of couples followed Clare and Henry to the dance floor and the male dancers began to break in. Pop was first, stealing the new bride away from his son, who asked the bride's mother to take a turn. Henry told her sincerely how much it meant to have her daughter as his wife and he thanked her warmly for her thoughtfulness and hard work in giving them such a memorable wedding.

"Nobody will forget this day," she said ruefully.

For the second dance Clare and Henry had chosen "Love Is a Many Splendored Thing" and the quartet delivered a rendition of the Four Aces hit of the 1950's that stirred memories for many of the guests present. This time Pat broke in for a father-daughter dance. He told Clare what a high regard he had for Henry. "He's smart, he has high standards and … he's a good shot." Clare had to think before she realized Pat was talking about the quail hunting.

Betty sat this one out to have a chat with the hostess, who had pulled up a chair. Pop and Jean demonstrated their dancing skills, along with several of the wedding guests.

The DJ followed with some more upbeat music: Glen Campbell's "Southern Nights" and "I Got You Babe" by Sonny and Cher. The quartet transformed themselves into the Righteous Brothers for a romantic slow dance: "Unchained Melody." He closed out the set with another hit from the '50s, Bill Haley's "Rock Around the Clock", which brought Drew and Wanda onto the floor to show everyone some of their moves.

Clare excused herself to go over to the four young men and compliment them on their singing and tell them how much their talent added to the wedding. "I especially loved the harmony of 'I Love You Truly.'"

The bass singer said, "I was tempted to do a rap version, but I knew Mrs. Murphy would kill me."

She also posed for photographs with them and Jennifer, taken by Bessie Stringer, who had skipped the wedding but showed up to enjoy a free meal at the reception.

"We're a little nervous performing before the star of a Broadway musical," Kenny said.

"Maybe I'll see you in a production sometime," Clare said to all of them.

Before taking a break, the DJ had informed the guests that the buffet line was open and folks began lining up on both sides of the table, which was virtually covered with food – mainly dishes prepared and brought by friends of

Betty Sullivan (along with a generous portion of her own creations.) "It's just the way we do things in the South," she explained to the West Coast visitors.

The guests carried their plates back to their tables and refreshed their drinks. After they were seated the DJ returned to his turntables and played some softer music, much of it also nostalgic for the period that a majority of the crowd had lived through. Some diners went back for seconds but for the most part they saved room for samplings of the array of delicious desserts awaiting them.

Most had returned to their tables when a quiet murmur arose in the room. Dr. Jim Vinson had appeared at the door. Betty Ann spied him and ran to meet him. He picked her up, hugged her and whispered in her ear. She grabbed him around the neck and held him tightly as he walked to the DJ who interrupted the music, hit the fanfare button and said: "Ladies and gentlemen, our lovely flower girl, Betty Ann, has an announcement to make." He held her up to the mike and she shouted with glee, "I have a baby brother!"

A cheer went up and everybody stood and applauded. Jim took the mike and continued: "James Patrick Vinson was born at 5:33 p.m. He weighed seven pounds and eight ounces and measured approximately 20 inches. Mother and child are both doing well, and wish they could be here. Becky especially wants me to tell you all – but especially her mother and her sister – how much she regrets having to walk out, or I should say run out, of the beautiful wedding. To make up for that she wants to invite all of you to Betty Ann's wedding. Just don't expect that to be very soon. If Becky and I have anything to say about it, it will require someone very special to be good enough for her. We know Henry is already taken. Now that you have this news, let us return to celebrating the union of this wonderful loving couple. Thank you."

The room roared with applause and the quick-thinking DJ set an appropriate tone with the playing of "Baby Face." Jim couldn't resist placing Betty Ann on her feet and letting her have at least one dance before joining the family group. He gave her a nice twirl before sitting down. The table was abuzz with questions and good wishes for the birth of Betty Ann's little brother and their new son.

They turned their attention to the DJ who was making another announcement: "Now for a special treat. Jennifer and the quartet are going to salute the bride and her success in the entertainment business with a medley of songs from Broadway musicals, with piano accompaniment by Gladys Murphy. They begin with a song that Clare sang – and tap-danced to – to open a show for the Tri-County Players in Wilmington, North Carolina, "Anything Goes."

Gladys used the mike to introduce the next number. "Here with another selection from *Oklahoma!* are Jennifer and Kenny to sing 'People Will Say We're in Love.'"

As the two young voices blended perfectly Clare could not help reliving some moments of glory she had experienced on the stage of the Whiteway Theater in New York. Jennifer followed with a solo of the title song from *The Sound of Music* and then the quartet serenaded the bride with the words and music from "Mame" – substituting "Clare", naturally. In the same manner the five singers came to the family table and paid tribute to the wedding organizer with an adaptation of "Hello, Dolly" ("Hello, Betty").

Two members of the quartet, Kenny and Nate, did a duet, "The Girl That I Marry", from *Annie Get Your Gun*, and Jennifer showed her versatility with a bombastic Ethel Merman-style tribute to the church garden, "Everything's Coming Up Roses."

Clare jumped to her feet and led the audience in a standing ovation for the singers and Gladys for their rousing performance.

Betty excused herself from the table, saying, "I need to go see how the fried chicken is holding out." She returned shortly with a satisfied look on her face, just as the DJ brought Drew to the microphone for the best man's toast.

"I know a little bit about growing grapes and making wine, but I know very little about wedding toasts," he started. "I think I'm supposed to say something nice about both the bride and the groom. That could be a problem. You see, I can think of lots of nice things to say about Clare. She's beautiful. She's charming. She's smart and so talented.

"And then, there's Henry. He's not too shabby looking. So if he were a bottle of wine, I might pay a compliment to the label. He buys expensive cologne. So I guess I could give him a rather high mark on bouquet.

"As for body … I'm not going there. Clare will have to be the judge of that.

"She may think he's sweet. But if you've ever heard him make a speech … D R Y." A titter rippled through the room.

"I'm not doing very well using wine terms to describe my brother. I really would like to say something nice about him. Maybe the best thing I can say is that he had the good sense to bring Clare into the Jackson family.

"And one of the nicest things I can say about her is this: there aren't too many people who can get the best of my dad. I only know of two women. Jean certainly won his heart. And Clare played pickleball with him and won.

"It's just human nature, I suppose, for us to wonder what two people who get married can see in each other. Whatever it is that Clare sees in Henry is a mystery to me. But that's her choice. It could be that she just really wanted to be my sister-in-law.

"But what does it matter? They got married for better or for worse – I think that's still in the wedding vows. So let's raise our glasses and drink a toast to Henry and Clare. May they have a happy life together. And if I may use another wine term, may they have a l-o-n-g finish."

With that done, it was time to cut the cake, a three-tiered masterpiece in white frosting made by the town's leading baker. There also was a groom's cake, a smaller but even more appetizing chocolate creation. Clare knew she had to have a slice of that, too.

Bessie lined up her shot and the bride and groom held the knife together and made the ceremonial cut. They did forego the wasteful juvenile exercise of smearing each other's faces with the gooey, sticky icing. Clare made sure there was champagne left to enjoy with her cake.

Clare fortified herself for the final act of a traditional Southern wedding: the tossing of the bridal bouquet. The hostess took charge, leading Clare out to the center of the room and telling all the single women to gather in front of the family table. Clare turned her back on the eager group and on the count of three she pitched the flowers over her shoulder.

The suspenseful moment was over ... almost. It was a high toss, soaring above the heads of the standing women. The bouquet came down and landed smack dab in Luna's lap. She quickly tossed it to Wanda, also sitting, who happily caught and kept the beautiful roses.

Luna thoughtfully picked that time to give the maid of honor's mixed-bloom bouquet to Betty Ann. "Take these to your mother when you go to the hospital to see her."

"Thank you," the little girl said, and turning to Jim, asked, "Can we go now?"

"Perhaps we should, before it gets too much later," he said.

Clare dug her cell phone out of her evening bag and said, "Before you go I want to call Becky. She has her phone, doesn't she?" Jim nodded yes.

Becky answered on the third ring and the two sisters had a brief private conversation. Before hanging up Clare said, "I'm dying to see my new nephew. I'm not sure what our travel plans are, but I'll let you know."

As Jim and Betty Ann were leaving the DJ announced last call for food and drink and said, "folks, this will be the final set for the evening.

So guys, get with your favorite girl for the last dance of Henry and Clare's wedding."

The platter-spinner had chosen some appropriate numbers to wind up the evening: Donna Summer's "Last Dance"; "Unforgettable" by Nat King Cole and Natalie Cole; "The Dance" by Garth Brooks; Anne Murray's "Could I Have This Dance"; "(I'll Be Loving You) Always"; and "Goodnight, Sweetheart."

The dance floor was crowded with couples young and old, skilled dancers and those with two left feet. Some of those who remained seated were buzzing about Rev. Peterson and Gladys Murphy gliding smoothly around the room.

Henry and Clare timed it so they ended the evening dancing to "Always", pledging their love "till the end of time" – which wasn't on the DJ's list.

With members of the wedding party going their separate ways come morning, the Sullivans and the Jacksons exchanged a round of sad goodbyes underscored by warm hugs and a few tears. Betty offered to stay and help clean up, but the hostess said there were plenty of volunteers and she should go home and rest up. With Pat's encouragement she gave in.

"What about the wedding gifts?" Betty asked. "You said you can't take anything with you."

"I think Pop took some of the pineapple," Henry said. "The rest is yours to share."

"As for the other things, let's do this," Clare said. "Take whatever you can use. See what Becky might want. If that doesn't take care of it, give the rest to Goodwill – unless you're concerned some of your friends might recognize what they gave."

"That would be awful!" Betty said.

"But one big favor you could do for me is to send me a list of gifts and givers so I can write thank you notes as soon as we get back home."

"That's what a good southern wife would do," her mother said.

On the way to the car Clare asked Henry what time they were leaving to go on their honeymoon.

"We'll have time in the morning to go see your sister and the new baby," he said.

"I guess the party's over," she said, holding his hand

"And our new life begins."

64

"GOOD MORNING, HUSBAND."

"Are you talking to me?"

"Who else would I be talking to. You're my husband, aren't you?"

"What's this about?"

"I'm just trying to get used to this new husband and wife arrangement."

"How can I help?"

"You might bring me a cup of coffee."

"Wait on you, eh? Is that any way to begin a marriage?"

"And I'll have one of those chocolate-dipped strawberries, too."

"Are you sure you don't want a glass of champagne?"

"I'll forego that. I still have some packing to do. By the way, isn't it time you told me where we're going on our honeymoon?"

"Well, all right. Here's your breakfast," Henry said, handing Clare what she ordered. He got a brochure out of his briefcase and returned to bed. She saw right away it was from a cruise line. He opened a page with alluring pictures of palm trees and beaches and pointed to an itinerary. "We're flying from Albany to Tampa and departing at 4 p.m. for a 5-day cruise of the Western Caribbean."

"Oh, wow!" she said, and kissed him on the cheek.

"After a day at sea we'll stop at Cozumel on Monday, then on to Grand Cayman for a day and then return to Tampa. Does that sound like a good honeymoon?"

"You always plan well, Mr. Jackson."

"The travel agent tried to talk me out of it."

"Really? Why?"

"Well, it is the tail end of the hurricane season. So it could be stormy."

"But there are only two ports of call. And if the weather's not good we can just stay on the ship and enjoy all of its features."

"I do hope we get to go ashore on Cozumel," Henry said. "It offers some spectacular coral reefs, which are ideal for snorkeling And I'd like to explore the Mayan ruins."

"We'll just take what comes. We do enjoy adventuresome travel."

"We'll have time to go to the hospital and see Becky and meet the new arrival before catching our flight. But we'll need to have our luggage ready so we can check out and get to the airport in time to turn in our rental car."

"We'll want to touch base with the California-Washington delegation," Clare said.

"We should be able to catch them. I don't think Pop plans to fly out too early."

"I'd better get up and get showered. Thanks for pampering me," she said, holding up her coffee cup and the stem from the strawberry.

"Anything for my new bride," he said.

Over breakfast with Pop and Jean, Luna and Houston and Drew and Wanda, they recapped the hectic events of Henry and Clare's wedding day. In hindsight it wasn't so bad, even funny – as in when Luna accidentally caught the bridal bouquet. She wasn't very amused.

"It will be me who decides if and when I want to get married, not a batch of flowers," she huffed.

Pop expressed his appreciation for the fresh pineapple. "It's a little hard to come by in Seattle," he said.

He and Drew both made references to the Georgia winery visit Henry arranged. They said their talks with the winery owner and staff were most helpful. Clare and Henry hadn't had time to talk about that experience so she was interested.

Pop told Clare he really enjoyed meeting her parents, both in New York and in their home. "I knew you had had some good raising and now I know why," he said.

After saying their goodbyes and wishing each other safe travels, Clare and Henry returned to the room, brushed their teeth and called Becky. She was delighted they were coming and told them that Betty and Pat also were expected. That was a good working-out, because Clare hadn't expected to see them again.

Becky looked much better – quite happier after giving birth to a healthy son. Everyone admired his features: "He really looks good." "So much hair, my goodness." "He has his daddy's eyes." "Looks like he's going to be a sturdy Georgia boy."

Betty Ann was especially proud of her new baby brother. "I haven't got to hold him yet," she said to Clare. "He's so tiny."

"Yes, like a doll." Betty Ann giggled. "But he'll grow up before you know it. And you'll do a good job helping your mother raise him," Clare reassured her.

"You haven't told us where you're going on your honeymoon," Betty said, while Pat was admiring his new grandson.

"I just found out myself," Clare said. "Henry wanted to surprise me. He booked a cruise out of Tampa to the Western Caribbean."

"Oh, that sounds nice," Becky said.

"We're just going to two ports in five days – Grand Cayman and Cozumel. The rest of the time we'll just be sailing and enjoying the cruising."

"I hope you don't have any bad weather," Betty said.

"That goes for you, too," Henry said. "I think we've all had more than our share."

"Well, just keep our little girl safe," Pat said.

The travelers got to the ship in plenty of time for the 4 o'clock departure. In fact, they were able to go to one of the many eating places on the luxury liner for a late lunch. This allowed their luggage to be taken to their quarters so they could unpack and get settled well ahead of sailing time.

Henry had reserved a 330-square-foot Grand Suite on the upper deck, with a king-size bed, a roomy bath, a living room and a large private balcony. The suite was easily accessible to elevators which could take them quickly to dining rooms, bars and the main lounge – which featured nightly entertainment – as well as the spa and a resort-size pool.

The temperature was suitable for lightweight attire, which they wore to the main deck for a sailaway party with a band and specialty dancers. They returned to their suite and enjoyed a cocktail from the mini-bar lounging on their balcony and gazing at the vast blue ocean. After the obligatory lifeboat drill, in which they donned life preservers and assembled in designated areas, they stashed those and donned light jackets for dinner.

Their accommodations entitled them to flexible dining (no assigned tables or times) so they tried out one of the two large dining rooms. They found the menu to their liking and Henry was pleased with the wide variety of selections on the wine list. For a starter he chose smoked Hudson Valley duck breast and Clare had gazpacho andalouse. They each had escargots bourguignonne and for the main course Clare picked a heart-healthy seared fillet of redfish with yam and pumpkin hash and Henry selected chateaubriand with sauce bearnaise. The dessert menu was one of those "I'll have one of each" temptations. Clare opted for the black forest gateau and Henry had New York cheesecake.

On the other evenings of the cruise Henry and Clare engaged in variations of this routine, checking out the martinis at one of the many cocktail lounges, and trying something different from the dining room menus such as spicy alligator fritters and cappuccino pie.

After their gourmet dinner they took a leisurely stroll on the deck, pausing to lean on the rail and peer into the darkness and listen to the sounds of the sea. It had been a rather full day so they skipped the lounge show and relaxed in their suite. They decided to turn in early. After all, it was their honeymoon.

Day 2 was a day of cruising at sea, a perfect time to put on swim suits and go to the pool deck. A few hundred other passengers had the same idea so it was a challenge to find vacant deck loungers and there were none in the shade. So they spread on the sun lotion and prepared to get good tans. Young waiters were readily available to serve a variety of tropical drinks, although Henry and Clare preferred to stick to their list of longtime favorites, which included pina coladas and mai tais.

Henry spent more time in the pool than in the sun, primarily in the hot tubs feeling the pulsating jets loosen up his tight muscles. He had a few interesting conversations with other businessmen enjoying a holiday away from the office. There was one businesswoman whose advances he had to stall by flashing his new wedding ring.

Clare fell asleep reading the current tabloid magazine before she learned which movie star was cheating on whom. Alas! It could have been somebody she knew in Hollywood.

They enjoyed informal lunchtime dining in the Lido Deck restaurant and on an impulse made appointments for massages at the spa.

In the suite they stripped and laughed at their highly visible tan lines, then took turns in the shower and dressed, again casually, for the evening. While sipping pre-mixed daiquiris ("Let's go to the bar next time," Clare said) on the balcony, they scanned the travel material on Cozumel and gave some thought to how they would spend the next day.

This was the evening for the traditional Captain's Reception, an open bar event at which hors d'oeuvres were passed and unlimited glasses of champagne were poured. The captain had brief welcoming remarks and introduced the key members of the staff. After dinner they headed for the main lounge to stake out a seat in the theater for a stage show, featuring dancers, musicians and singers. Clare found the performance to be quite reminiscent of her experience on cruise ships in the Mediterranean years ago.

Day 3. Clare went along with Henry's strong desire to see the beauty of the coral reefs at Cozumel. Neither of them were scuba divers but both had tried snorkeling on one or two occasions. They easily found a vendor who would rent them equipment and guide them to a spot where they were "guaranteed" to see some wonderful underwater activity by fish and other sea dwellers among the colorful reefs. This took up most of the morning

They had lunch at a place in San Miguel with a great reputation for its margaritas and tasty Mexican specialties (after all, they were in Mexico). They could sit inside on the terrace and cool off beneath ceiling fans while listening to the soothing sounds of trickling fountains. It happened to adjoin one of the best shopping venues on the island.

Clare began by buying a large colorful shopping bag and proceeded to load it up with duty-free purchases. It turned out she didn't really need such a large bag because most of what she bought was jewelry, particularly black coral, and native handicrafts. Henry was interested in the history of the island, which derives its name from the Mayan civilization that settled there more than 2,000 years ago. He asked about seeing some ruins and learned that the best preserved sites were on the mainland. The best-known ruins, Chichen Itza and Tulum, required a day trip and they had not signed up for the ship's planned excursion.

They opted to take a seven-mile taxi ride to San Gervasio, which in its heyday had served as a ceremonial center dedicated to the fertility goddess Ixchel. Clare posed for a picture at a Mayan arch and they saw a few other small ruins.

Not wanting to run it close, to be back in ample time for the 4 p.m. departure, Clare and Henry did as much sightseeing and shopping as they were going to do and returned to the ship.

One of the ship's bars specialized in martinis, so after dressing for dinner they went to that deck and took a cultural journey, walking through a gallery of modern art until arriving at an oasis of chrome and glass with only a few customers sitting on barstools or enjoying table conversations. They found a spot near a window and just the right distance from the piano, where a singer sounding a bit like Harry Connick was charming his listeners.

The menu brought by the waitress reminded Clare of the 100-martini list at the Top of the Mark, the penthouse level bar at the Mark Hopkins hotel in San Francisco, one of the first stops on her 2014 campaign tour. She didn't see a "Double Dirty" – her choice on that occasion – so she ordered a "Chocolatini", figuring she couldn't go wrong on anything chocolate. Henry stuck to a dry gin martini with two olives.

For a variation on dinner they decided to try one of the specialty restaurants: the Mongolian Wok. This adventuresome meal involved choosing a type of noodle and selecting some vegetables. Then you tell the chef which sauce and meat, chicken or fish you prefer. The combo is up to the diner. Clare chose mussels and Szechuan. Henry went for beef and Thai barbecue. All of it served with rice. They finished off their dinner with refreshing sorbets.

Day 4. They got a panoramic view of the Cayman Islands from the ship's tender as they crossed the short distance to shore from where the cruise liner was anchored, along with three other large vessels. For their daylong visit to the second port on the itinerary they had opted to pass up tours to Stingray City and the Turtle Farm. Henry had made it clear he didn't want to go to Hell, and Clare knew what he meant because she had read about a group of short, black limestone formations bearing that name located in West Bay. And she nixed any thought he might have had of checking out a place on the North Sound called Booby Cay. They decided they would just spend the time relaxing in the Caribbean sun.

Grand Cayman's main attraction was the Seven-Mile Beach, a strip of coral white sand stretching along the island's western shore, contrasting with some of the purest blue waters to be found in any part of the world.

En route to the beach free-port shopping was plentiful on Cardinal Avenue in the capital city of Georgetown, where cameras, perfumes, watches, china and British woolens were for sale at reduced prices. Their route to the beach took them through a number of shops and Clare couldn't resist buying a small rum cake and a conch necklace, a cheap souvenir of the Caymans.

They took a cab the rest of the way. Henry instructed the driver to take them up the public beach far enough to find a less crowded spot.

Clare had brought a pair of beach towels in her large tote bag, along with suntan lotion and other necessities. They rented a couple of beach chairs and an umbrella with stand, knowing they would need a break from the tropical sun. Clare lotioned up and got back to the cheap romance novel she had brought along. Henry settled for peaceful napping uninterrupted by phone calls.

After a couple of hours of this idyllic life and with lunchtime hunger beginning to gnaw, they pulled up stakes and gave their choice location on the beach to another grateful couple.

Back on the ship the honeymooning couple quickly changed into shorts and almost sleeveless tops in the suite and sought out some place different for lunch. They did a little exploring and their noses led them to a pizzeria, where the aromas of hot, cheesy pizza served fresh out of the oven lured them to a vacant table. Open around the clock, this busy center of activity

270

was turning out hand-tossed specialties with multiple choices of toppings along with Caesar salad without keeping anyone waiting any longer than to finish their first beer.

Clare hadn't done any shopping since morning so they popped into the ship's gift shop and she bought a souvenir T-shirt and a cap for Henry.

"What would you like to do now?" he asked.

"I wouldn't mind walking around a bit more," she replied. "With all the wonderful food we've been having I know I'm putting on some pounds I don't need."

"I hadn't noticed that. But speaking of eating, I want to make a reservation for this evening for the Chef's Special Dinner." Sighting a guest services desk, Henry excused himself to make that arrangement. He left Clare admiring some unusual pieces of sculpture on exhibit.

"We got the last two seats," he told her upon his return. He explained that the multicourse dinner was prepared by one of the ship's master chefs and limited to a select group of 14. The exclusive experience featured appetizers, entrees and desserts not found on the regular dining room menus and included a tour to see the galley in operation.

To fill the time before the cocktail hour they found the ship's movie theater and saw *Casablanca* for the fourth or fifth time.

Day 5. They were still raving about the marvelous meal they had the previous evening. In addition to delicious gourmet dishes they also enjoyed the company of others who appreciated the finer things in life (and like Henry and Clare, could afford them).

This was another free day as they spent the entire time at sea sailing homeward after a short, fun-filled trip.

While lounging on a cushy leather chaise in a solarium overlooking the pool, Clare became wistful thinking not only about the recent time she had spent with her family and some highly personal moments with her best male friend who was now her mate for life, but she also found herself reliving the high and low points of her life. She reflected on the rebellious days of her youth, the thrills of seeing the world beyond rural Georgia, her adventure-filled path to wealth and fame with Gary de Lune, and the incomparable new romantic life she had begun by meeting Henry Jackson.

She reached into her bag for a Kleenex and her fingers touched an unfamiliar object. She quickly realized it was the magnolia leaf from the Sullivan farm that she had saved. It reminded her that she had indeed made a new beginning.

She turned her head to the lounge next to her where Henry lay dozing, his new cap covering his eyes, totally at peace with the world. Perhaps he was dreaming of building an exciting new career in Wilmington on his recent investment. She was eager, if a bit uncertain, about her new role as a successful businessman's wife.

A sudden signal on her cell phone rudely ended her reverie and jolted Henry awake.

"Hello. Oh, hi, Barbara. What a surprise to hear from you. Are you back from your wonderful South Pacific vacation? I thought you might be. How is Phil? What? What did you say?"

With a stunned look on her face, Clare sat upright and faced Henry, who waited expectantly for what she had to tell him.

"You're not going to believe this. Phil won the lottery … and he wants to know if you'll sell him back his share in the business."

— • —

Acknowledgments

This sequel to *Here's Clare* would not have been possible without the support and assistance of my wife. Mary Whiteside Haught, born and raised in Georgia and educated in North Carolina, went beyond her usual role as proofreader and editor and served as an expert consultant on Southern customs, traditions, food and other vital matters.

My appreciation also goes to Judy Smith, Ann King and other Ro-Rah Girls (graduates of Roanoke Rapids, N.C. High School) for being fans of Clare since I introduced them to her by outlining the first novel at a wedding reception.

I drew on some valuable references from Mary's library for various portions of the book. They include:

Having It Y'All: The Official Handbook for Citizens of the South and Those Who Wish They Were by Ann Barrett Batson

The Grits (Girls Raised in the South) Guide to Life by Deborah Ford with Edie Hand

Being Dead Is No Excuse: The Official Southern Ladies Guide to Hosting the Perfect Funeral by Gayden Metcalfe and Charlotte Hays

About the Author

ROBERT L. HAUGHT is a former Washington-based columnist who writes a daily commentary for his blog as well as articles for his online magazine at *haughtline.net*. His career includes service as a UPI correspondent, a top aide to two governors and two U.S. senators, editorial writer and newsletter editor. In addition to *Clare's New Leaf* and *Here's Clare* he is the author of two humor books: *The POTUS Chronicles: Bubba Between the Bushes* and *Now, I'm No Expert: On CATS and other mysteries of life*. He and his wife Mary live on a farm in the foothills of the Blue Ridge Mountains.

Made in the USA
Middletown, DE
20 July 2016